PORTSIDE SCREW
A Jack Cubera Novel

Author's Note: For you landlubbers out there, a PORTSIDE SCREW is the left propeller on a twin-engine vessel. It is also a devious swindle that takes place on or near a waterfront. Both interpretations are applicable in the following pages.

gregory s. dew

Thank you for purchasing *Portside Screw*. As a special thank you, I'd like to add you to my email list of loyal readers to alert you to upcoming events, including free and discounted book promotions on my future and other existing titles.

If you'd like to be added, please email me at gregdew@hotmail.com or go to my website at www.gregorysdew.com and fill out the short form on the Contact page. Ask about another one of my novels, *Subtropical High*, and I'll be happy to set you up with a free Kindle version.

Finally, if you enjoy *Portside Screw*, a positive review on Amazon would be greatly appreciated. It's quite easy and will only take a minute or two. Just go to https://amzn.to/2G73PNK, select a star rating, then write a 20+ word blurb on why you liked the book, who you might recommend read it, etc. Thanks in advance for taking the time!

To my wife, Cindy. Never stop dancing.

Copyright © 2018 Gregory S. Dew
ISBN 978-1-9806-5161-1
Dead Tree Editions
www.gregorysdew.com
Florida, The Lowest State

ALSO BY GREGORY S. DEW

Subtropical High
Nectar
The Barefoot Fisherman

Available on Amazon

CHAPTER 1

THE HUMAN HEAD bobbed to the surface of Florida Bay like a lobster pot marker, the bangs slicked down over the eyes and the ears so brightly backlit with sunset they glowed a fiery orange. Jack Cubera tried to blink it away, but the full body buoyed up and began rotating clockwise in a tidal swirl twenty feet off his kayak bow.

"Shit." Jack stowed his fishing rod then dragged a dry tongue over his walrus-like mustache.

His fishing partner, a neighbor's kid from the docks, cast his bait, plunking it along a mangrove shoreline off to Jack's left. "Shit what?"

"Nothing." In Jack's seven years of backcountry fishing, he'd happened across plenty of strange flotsam—bales of weed, Haitian rafts, an abandoned seaplane—but this was a first. Instinct said to just turn and paddle home to the Soggy Dollar Marina. Grill a spiny lobster, suck down a cold beer, then sleep deep in the air-conditioned darkness of his liveaboard Moppie V-berth. Hope it all just went away.

But could instinct be trusted? Surely, his was rusty, slow, dull after the many moons he'd been marinating in the Islamorada sunshine.

As he contemplated his next move, the corpse released a trumpeting fart, sank away, then resurfaced, the hair now slicked over the head revealing a face as pale and veiny as boiled haggis. Set over its hooked nose was a pair of mirrored sunglasses, each lens reflecting a sky bleeding those reds and oranges usually reserved for Mai Tais laced with grenadine.

1

The kid wrenched around and shielded his eyes against the glare. "That a manatee?"

"Not unless they've started wearing designer sunglasses."

"What?"

"It's a body, kid."

"Holy crap." The kid fumbled his fishing rod onto his lap then grabbed his paddle and pulled his kayak alongside Jack's. "Let's go check it out."

Jack glanced at the kid. His lean build and thatch of brown hair would've profiled him as a truant anywhere outside the Florida Keys. "What've you been smoking?"

"You're a private investigator, Jack. Let's investigate."

"Retired private investigator."

"Come on, old man."

There it was. Old man. Old man Cubera. It was true. Jack's forties had come and gone like a one-night stand. He was fifty-one now, just trying to coast through that forgotten decade when the scales slowly slide from wondering what you'll one day make of yourself to accepting what you've already become. He swatted at something gnawing at his left shoulder blade as a flock of ibises vectored off through the darkening sky. Little light remained before the wind died and no-see-ums swarmed. "Give me your cellphone."

The kid dug through his drybag and handed over the device. Jack dialed the sheriff's office, a number he knew too well, then glanced at the screen. No signal. He tossed the phone back to the kid then sank his paddle into the water and pivoted toward the distant shoreline of Plantation Key now blinking to life with street lamps and porch lights. "Let's get going."

"What are you talking about?"

"Not our body. Not our case."

"We can't just leave it here."

"Says who?"

The kid shrugged. "Doesn't seem right."

2

"So you're my moral compass now?" Jack exhausted a long sigh. What right did this little shit have dragging ethical behavior to the forefront? "Damnit." He pivoted his kayak and stroked toward the mangrove shoreline. "Bring your knife."

Jack lashed his kayak to a low-lying limb, slipped into the water, then bulled through the hip-deep tides toward the body. He'd never gotten used to corpses the way medical examiners and undertakers do. As a rule, he avoided death whenever possible, particularly his own.

He grabbed the body by the ankle, pulled it toward him, and gave it a quick once-over. Adult. Male. Caucasian. Overweight. Wearing only speed-swimmer briefs, navy with a pink hibiscus print. Judging by the intestinal bloating, the guy had been dead for a day or two.

As the kid waded in, a ripple rolled around the body causing its shoulders to shrug. "That's disgusting."

"The swimsuit? You aren't kidding."

Jack studied the victim. Whip-like blisters covered his face, in stark contrast to the pale, bloated flesh. With a thumb and forefinger, he pinched a stem of the Costa Del Mar sunglasses and pried them off the ears. The guy's wide-set eyes and acne-pocked cheeks were tough to forget. "You've got to be shitting me."

The kid splashed backward as though the dead man had grumbled to life. "What?"

"I know the guy."

The kid waded back in. "Who is he?"

"Ross Biggins. A real estate developer. And a major-league asshole."

Jack leaned closer and examined the fiery striations across the mug. A quick assessment suggested he hadn't died of natural causes. For starters, the welts went far beyond garden-variety jellyfish stings. The face was so blistered and swollen the eye sockets were nearly swallowed by the forehead and cheeks. Even the nastiest tangle with a man o' war wouldn't have caused that much damage, unless, of course, the guy had tried one on like a hat.

Jack pulled away. "This was no accident."

3

The kid drew his fingertips to his lips. "You saying someone killed him?"

Jack nodded. "Just my luck."

He twisted the sunglass by a stem then stopped, the grenadine reflections in the lenses now replaced with dark bruises of purple along the horizon. How had the sunglasses not fallen off the guy's face? Could they have been placed postmortem? Covering the eyes suggested killer's remorse. But, what idiot would squander a pricey pair of shades on a dead guy? Jack swished the sunglasses in the water, shook them dry, then slipped them onto his own forehead.

"Hey. That's stealing."

"Lecture me after you've read up on the maritime salvage laws." Jack raked his fingers through his shaggy mop. "Wonder why they didn't weight the body down?"

The kid's eyes popped wide.

"Not that I've got a ton of experience. But there's plenty of bottom feeders out here who would've taken care of the evidence. Why not use your natural resources?"

Jack leaned back in and slowly examined the rest of Ross in the failing light. A gold shark-tooth earring pierced his left lobe. A matching pendant hung on a golden rope necklace. He flipped the pendant over and read the inscription. *Chronic DH Fan # 672372.* Both items were signature wares peddled by famed gulf and western band Big Swinging Richard and the Twisted Jibs.

Jack started to unclasp the necklace.

"Jack!"

Jack eyed the kid, shook his head, then let go of the necklace and took Ross by the shoulders. "Grab his ankles and help me roll him."

The kid's arms fell to his sides. "But—"

"Sack up, kid. You're the one who wanted to investigate."

The kid stared blindly for a moment then eased forward and cinched his fingers around the mushy skin of the lower legs. Jack gave a three count, then they rolled the body, like a rotisserie, until the buttocks bobbed at the surface in the tight floral swimsuit.

4

The kid pointed toward a puncture in the Lycra about a quarter-inch in diameter. "That a bullet hole?"

Jack tugged the suit to the side exposing a pale, veiny cheek. "Don't think so. Look here." He tapped his finger on the edge of the wound. "The hole's a little oblong. Almost like it was stretched."

Jack let the suit snap back into place then glanced around the pocket of water, the way the body had been tucked into the mangroves. It hadn't drifted in on the currents. Somebody had parked it here. Or dumped it here. Or left it here when Jack and the kid came unexpectedly paddling into the scene. An unsettling notion crept in. Were they being watched? Or circled by things underwater? About fifty yards out, a shadow shifted behind a tangle of mangroves. Was it something crouching? Hiding? Sizing up the competition? Were those floating white orbs human eyes?

"Give me your knife."

Jack cinched his hand around the diving blade as words like *loose ends* and *eyewitnesses* looped through his mind. A branch rustled then something, or someone, waded off into the darkness.

So much for the easy-going life in the Florida Keys.

He sloshed over to a lobster pot marker, cut away a ten-foot section of line with a blue-and-white foam ball attached to one end, then handed the rig to the kid. "Tie one end around an ankle and the other to a mangrove root."

"We're leaving him out here?"

"Unless you feel like dragging the fat bastard back to shore."

"What about sharks?"

"Exactly. Now hustle up before they decide we're what's for dinner."

* * *

As Jack and the kid closed the gap toward shore, Islamorada appeared almost normal, its salt-riddled façade now shrouded in darkness and highlighted here and there by an incandescent glare, a strand of Tivoli lights, and the pulsing red light atop the newly erected cell tower.

Jack sank his paddle and dragged the blade through the water as they reached the cut into the Soggy Dollar Marina. When they cornered down canal #3, things grew brighter. A series of sodium lights illuminating the boardwalks cast reflections atop the water guiding them along a quay. A dozen catamarans, sport cruisers and motor yachts in various stages of disrepair lolled and listed in their slips. Halfway down the dilapidated stretch, Jack lifted his paddle then sidled up to the transom of his boat, *Subtropical Highlife*.

He climbed aboard and clicked on the shore power. A dozen strands of multicolored lights flicked on, etching the Bertram's profile clear to the tuna tower. The kid tethered his kayak alongside Jack's and followed him onto the boat.

"Pretty festive, Jack."

"Christmas in July."

"It's August."

"You sure?"

The 1963 Bertram Moppie had originally been owned by notorious Cuban sportfisherman Gregorio Fuentes then later sold off to a Little Havana cigar manufacturer soon imprisoned for cocaine trafficking. By the time Jack acquired her, she'd been moldering in a brackish canal around mile marker 42, untouched for the healthier part of two decades.

Her 120-square-foot cabin proved more than enough creature comforts for his modest existence, and a mattress wedged into the V-berth offered plenty of cushioned room for Jack, plus one.

In truth, what more did a guy really need?

Jack pulled a fresh case of Nice Day beers from a deck compartment and clunked the cans into a cooler filled with watery ice. "I hope you're a pilsner man."

The kid's eyes got wide. "That's a lot of beer for one guy."

"I like to say hello to all twelve apostles each night before I go to bed."

"Sounds like a problem."

"I'm deeply spiritual."

Jack sank into the fighting chair then propped his feet on the salt-bleached slats of a lobsterpot.

"What are you doing, Jack?"

"Relaxing."

"Shouldn't we call the cops?"

"Beer me, kid. And get one for yourself."

"But—"

"It'll help me game plan."

The kid shot over to the cooler then returned with two beers faster than a seasoned barback.

"Don't tell your mother."

The kid cracked open his beer then swigged long and deep enough to assure Jack it wasn't his first. "What now? What do we do about the body?"

Jack pressed his beer can to his lips then felt the cool dampness slither around the lump in his throat. While there was no pure shelter from the world, no absolute refuge, drinking had provided him the occasional shanty in which to duck and weather the most violent of storms. "What body?"

"We can't just leave him out there."

"Cold beer and tight lines, kid. What else do we really need?"

"What's that supposed to mean?"

"Keep things simple. Let somebody else deal with this nonsense."

"But what about—"

"Listen, kid. As you were nice enough to point out earlier, I'm an old man. By default, that means I've got better judgment than some dock rat who barely knows how to work a baitcaster. Trust me when I say we're better off just stepping away from this thing altogether. Pretend nothing ever happened. Maybe someone else will find the body. Maybe they won't. At this point, it's not really our problem, so let's not make it ours. The truth is the guy was an asshole. And a real estate developer. And, believe me, one less asshole real estate developer in the world is bound to tip the balance in the right direction."

"We have to do something."

"Hold that thought, kid." Jack pulled forward in the fighting chair as the drone of an inboard engine broke the quiet night. Near the mouth of the marina a vessel cornered into the canal then crawled slowly through the gridwork of docks with its green and red bow lights leading the way.

He stood and eased toward the gunwale.

Through the intermittent splashes of dock lights, a thirty-some-thing-foot Hinckley Picnic Boat came into focus. This was an unusual sighting at the Soggy Dollar. Most of these yachtie sorts slipped their vessels at glossier establishments up in Key Largo or down in Key West. This one had been sitting idle in a slip for the better part of two weeks, and, while Jack had admired its female owner from a distance, he'd yet to have the pleasure of making her acquaintance.

He adjusted to the stern for a better angle as the vessel swept by, the brunette vixen at the helm. "This is what I'm talking about, kid. Beautiful boats. Beautiful women. These are the sorts of things we should be focused on. Not obese men with mortality issues."

"We can't just do nothing."

Jack considered putting in a call to the authorities. Some desk jockey would want him down at the station to give a statement. Then he'd be forced into a site visit to the body after that. The nighttime no-see-um swarms alone made the decision easy, not to mention his last visit to the police station had not been voluntary. "How about I notify Sheriff Livingston? He's a buddy of mine. Will that make you happy?"

"Let's go."

"He's a day-shifter. Besides, that asshole Callahan with Fish and Game wheel locked my Volkswagen. I've got no way to get to the station."

"Maybe we can borrow my mom's car when she gets off work."

"Not a good idea, kid. My girl already thinks me and your mom have something going."

"But Jack!"

"Listen, kid. If you want to notify the cops tonight, be my guest. I'll be right here sipping the gospel until things start getting dim then finally fade to black."

CHAPTER 2

A HAND LASHED upward from the marina waters and cinched around a dock cleat. With a single overhand curl, the massive frame of a man emerged from the water and bellied onto the splintery surface.

As the specimen eased onto his feet, he drew a hand over his damp face and dripped onto the planks. He was shirtless, clad in burlap slacks rolled to the knees and strapped with a machete sheathed between his shoulder blades. A mesh dive bag dangled over one shoulder, the loaded end heavy, dripping, wriggling.

It was pre-dawn, his favorite time of day. The barflies were finally tucked in for the night leaving the road noise silenced for an hour or so before the wage earners awoke. There'd been a time, long before the island chain became fashionable, when the roadway catered to only the occasional wayward traveler or resident, the hum of radials on the blacktop an exciting break in the constant orchestra of earth. But nowadays the stream of road noise was as ceaseless as the crashing of waves against a barrier island. Was man part of the natural order or simply an invasive species?

He narrowed his eyes at the blinking cell tower, the martini bar, the air-conditioned vessels with their fancy indoor plumbing and electric lights. All the hustle and bustle of mainland living did not mesh with the wild man's ken.

He pawed the water from his eyes then gazed through the failing darkness along the boat transoms idly lining the quays. One eyelid held steadily open while the other winked up and down as though in synch with a metronome.

When the name *Subtropical Highlife* came into focus, he eased forward, trailing damp footprints large enough to be mistaken for a Kodiak.

9

He boarded the vessel, whisper-footed. Not even a pair of resident pelicans squatting on twin pilings lifted their bills from slumber. He stepped through the empty beer cans and other nautical paraphernalia and flipped open a cooler lid. A single pilsner beer, some off-label swill, drifted in melting ice.

He raked his fingers through the cool abyss then withdrew the can and popped the tab.

"Happy birthday to me."

He filtered the brew over his tongue then let a long pungent sigh slip between his pearly whites. The beer agreed with his dry throat. He savored each sip with those divine complexities akin to carnal lust. It was almost enough to arouse him.

Almost.

At his ripe old age of sixty-one, a taut tender female remained the preferable methodology for conjuring up some good subtropical wood. Maybe dressed up like a librarian. Or an elementary school teacher. He was a traditionalist.

Three swigs later, a slight engorging in his flaccid member caused him to stir unexpectedly.

You don't say?

He glanced around then slipped a hand into his trousers and jostled the plantain. After a few good tugs and some gingerly cupping, he shrugged off the anomaly as prostate inflammation and let his hopes bleed away.

Getting old sucks bananas.

* * *

Jack's eyes snapped open to the terminal darkness of his boat cabin, his mind muddled, struggling to escape an overlapping dream. He dragged his hands over his face, his fingers tingling with new blood flow, bringing him around to some obscure version of half-awake.

How long had he been asleep? Hours? Days? Weeks?

He'd drawn the opaque shades and cranked down the air conditioner to meat-locker level. Somehow he'd gotten undressed and wriggled under the covers.

As his pupils began to identify the vague shapes about the berth, pattering footfalls snapped him upright in the bed with the unsettling revelation that someone or something was aboard the Moppie.

His Ruger. Where was it?

He rifled through his mental inventory and saw it, tucked into the toe of an old sock then stashed in a tackle box and placed in a hold under the sofa cushion. The hiding place was poor and clumsy for a situation like this. Too many steps, too much time and noise to retrieve without drawing undue attention.

He eased from the mattress, slipped into a pair of shorts then tiptoed two steps into the galley. As his hand fumbled around a cabinet, another bumping sound reverberated through the fiberglass hull. He located a rum bottle then gripped the neck like a bowling pin and stepped toward the cabin door. Retired or not, a private investigator makes enemies with long memories, especially those who'd done time in state-level sodomy farms because of his efforts.

Maybe one of them had recently been released and decided to come calling.

He eased the door open to the dark deck. Other than the usual debris, the boat deck appeared empty—no feet or hooves to speak of.

Maybe it had been the wind or a pelican or the tailing edge of a dream.

He eased the door open then took three quick strides up the stair set, landing onto the deck with the weapon at the ready. As he turned to preview the foredeck, a series of footfalls thumped along the fiberglass, then the flash of a large shadowy mass rushed toward the bow.

Jack clamored toward the commotion as a deft splash broke the silence followed by a whumping sound as the water closed behind the mass. Jack reached the bow then glanced down as a hiss of foaming water tapered toward blackness.

Then nothing. Silence.

He set down the bottle and studied the waters for air bubbles, rips, ripples, anything that might signify life. But all remained still as the dead August air that shrouded his body.

After a few minutes of hopeless searching, he retired to the stern, ready to slough off the incident as some truant kid trying to boost beers or a petty thief scouring for pawn shop electronics. Plenty of those types were running around the Keys.

He settled back onto the mattress, but his mind wouldn't quit reeling. His adrenaline was piqued. Sleep, for the time being, was out of the question. He moved back to the deck and sank into the fighting chair as a warm whisper of wind blew across the film of sweat encapsulating his skin. He flipped open the cooler next to him then submerged his fingers into the icy bath to retrieve a beer.

But as his hand sank down and fished around in the coldness, something organic and noodle-like wrapped around his palm. For a brief second the cold of the ice water grew unbearable, then a fiery, pulsing sensation shot through his fingers as though he'd grabbed the business end of a livewire. His hand instinctively recoiled as a white-hot pain ripped across the tender skin of his palm.

He shot from the chair, a panic sweat already cropping up across his face as a series of welts began to emerge across the pink skin. As he studied the markings, the pain crept inward, his heart palpitating, his lungs filling with an odd prickly heat.

He dropped to a knee and braced an arm on the gunwale, keeping his head down and his breath in concentrated intervals. He brought a deep drag of air through grimaced lips then exhaled. Then again.

But his lungs wouldn't fill. They kept rejecting the influx, forcing themselves flat, leaving only room for shallow and desperate breaths.

He pushed up from the gunwale and stumbled toward the cabin. As he fumbled for a light, the pain metastasized through his wrist then crawled around his forearm, up his biceps and gripped his chest. He snagged a bath towel off the floor, doused it under the faucet then swaddled it around the burning skin.

What had stung him? Was he allergic? Was he in the grips of anaphylaxis?

He staggered onto the deck, flashing his eyes around the boat, the marina, the pilings, the pelicans. All still frames. Temporal. Moments in time without space. What were his options with no cell phone, no EpiPen, no pharmacy within miles?

Breathe.

His vision blurred, and his legs began to tingle.

Breathe.

He set a hand over his heart and told himself to be clam.

Now breathe.

Was this how it would all go down for old man Cubera? Alone on a boat without another soul in sight. A lifetime of hopes and wants and realties, of what he was and what he'd hoped he'd be, reduced to failing breaths, burning lungs and the utterly profound realization in the senselessness of it all . . . yet still fighting to continue.

He pressed two fingers against his carotid artery, registering a quick and erratic tempo. He knelt then shifted onto his butt, back against the stern.

Breathe.

He inhaled, this time through his nose, gulping his first substantial breath in minutes. Could it be? Was there hope? His lungs seemed to achieve full inflation, the oxygen-rich blood spreading into his organs and soothing the internal burn.

Breathe.

His vision stabilized, his eyes wide, seeing new things now. Fine details. The miniscule pitting in the fiberglass. The faint spider-webbing in the gelcoat. The veins running through his eyelids.

As the moments ticked by, his pulse eased into a slower, steadier cadence. His arms slumped to his sides. His breathing became involuntary, just one cool draft of wind after another, cyclical, circular.

A long sigh followed. He raked his fingers back through his hair. Yes, indeed. It appeared old man Cubera might see fifty-two after all.

But for what end?

His thoughts drifted to the lovely Summer Dahlia. Just eleven blocks away. A long three weeks prior, she'd been slumbering quietly down in the V-berth, warm legs twisted in cool sheets, available for rousing to soothe Jack's seething wounds.

But sometimes three weeks is a lifetime.

If he went knocking on her door now, would she even answer once she saw who'd come calling?

He waited until only the stringent hand burn remained then hauled himself onto his feet. Using his good hand, he fished his tuna gaff around the cooler, withdrawing a gooey biological lump from the icy bath. He hoisted the translucent intruder into a chevron of dock light. The thing's cube-shaped body was skirted with pinkish tentacles that dangled long and low enough to tickle the deck.

The species was completely foreign to him, a curious bit of information for an avid diver and angler of the local waters.

So much for truants and petty thieves.

He flung the gelatinous mass into a bait bucket, about to hunt around the cabin for some aloe, when he noticed his fillet knife wobbling, handle up, its tip stabbed into the baitwell lid at the stern. He stepped closer. A small coil of paper was crushed flat in the center, held steady by the tip of the blade.

He removed the knife then unrolled the miniature scroll. At first, deciphering the words in the dark proved difficult. He clicked on the Christmas lights, and, as his eyes narrowed into their conciliatory fifty-something squint, the message became all too clear.

Leave My Dead Bodies Be.

He glanced around, half-expecting to see the someone lurking in the shadows. But all was quiet at the Soggy Dollar except for a feral cat arching in a Halloween pose then slumping back to slumber.

He unwound the towel covering his hand. The series of welts now blistered across his palm with the distinct puffiness and irregular striations he'd seen on the dead man's face. What had happened to Islamorada? He'd fled here to duck out, become anonymous, stretch out in warm squares of sunshine and drink from the closest, most convenient watering holes.

Get as gridless as one could get.

But now that had vanished in an instant.

He examined the message again. The ink was peculiar, a yellowish goo, coagulated in a crusty brown along the edges, perhaps some type of animal fluid.

Dead Bodies. Plural. As in more than one.

So who'd come calling? And why? What contemptible soul had dared breach the sovereign square footage of the Moppie? Was his life now in danger?

He eyed the darkness like a man who's stared too long and often into a setting sun. There was only one option remaining. The time had come to shelve the affable drunk, the barstool philosopher, the hack guitarist, the backwater fisherman, the recreational star gazer and engage in something resembling real work.

At least it had been a solid run. A quiet seven years. A good stretch by anyone's standards and a remarkable stretch for a man with a history like Jack's. And what he'd lost in quickness through age he'd gained in wisdom.

Right?

Isn't that how it worked?

Older and wiser. Cubera the thinker. Cubera the sly and crafty fox.

Jack located a cigarette lighter and lit the coil of paper on fire. The biological ink popped and crackled against the flame until the paper burned so close to his fingers that he dropped it into the water. It floated still aglow for a moment then hissed to black and went out of sight.

Resigned but resolute, he cracked open a final ceremonial beer, suddenly regretting not having moved to a more remote island a little farther south.

Like Barbuda. Or Tierra del Fuego.

CHAPTER 3

AT 7:23 A.M., with eye whites like county roadmaps, Jack flung open the front door on the Monroe County Sheriff's Office and stumbled over to where Sheriff Raeford Livingston sat behind his desk. Raeford was one of those men who'd gotten sturdier with age. Leathery skin. Thick, hairy forearms. A look that could turn from charming to menacing in the bat of a lash. He wore a formal green uniform complete with a utility belt weighted down with a pistol, blackjack and handcuffs. As Jack approached, Ray's forehead wrinkled up like a boat wake reaching a shoreline then lapped at a tightly cropped hairline etched in gray.

"I hope you're here to either square up those fines or turn yourself in."

Jack shook his head. A single citation for illegally bagging bugs out of season had ballooned, with penalties and late fees, into an outstanding balance just under seven grand. "Not now, Ray."

"Don't give me that shit, Jack. Fish and Game's been climbing all over my ass."

Jack planted his hands on the desk. "I know. That weasel Ossie wheel locked the Volks and gave me until the end of the month to settle up or he's bringing me in and putting a lien on the Moppie."

"What do you expect?"

"Can that shit weasel really arrest me?"

"Of course. He's Fish and Game." The sheriff leaned back in his pleather chair and threaded his fingers behind his head. "Honestly, if he doesn't, I probably will."

Jack pushed up from the desk. "What's my current tab running, anyway?"

"It's an outstanding fine, Jack, not a damn tab." The sheriff slid open his desk drawer, bent back a notepad then mumbled for a moment under his breath. "Sixty-seven hundred and change."

"I'm retired, Ray. Living on a fixed income. Hand-to-mouth. How am I supposed to come up with that kind of scratch?"

"Ever think about getting a job?"

Jack eased onto the edge of the sheriff's desk accidentally knocking a stapler to the floor. "Working just seems so pedestrian at this stage in my life."

Ray rubbed the back of his head and exhaled a sigh that would've blown out grease fire. "All I know is I put my neck out for you, and you're making me look bad. Again."

"That haircut isn't helping."

"So now you've got jokes?"

Jack knelt, raked up the stapler as Ray came forward in his chair and laid his forearms across the desk.

"You hear about Coconut Key?"

Jack squared around. "What about it?"

"Breaking ground any day now."

"What? That got through permitting?"

"Appears so."

"How's that possible?"

Rays brows arched. "You know as well as I do how things get done here in Monroe County."

"What about funding?"

"Private money was all I heard."

Jack shook his head. "Sonofabitch."

The sheriff hooked a thumb in the general direction of the office bathroom then set an index finger over his lips suggesting Jack hush up. "Quite a development they're putting together, don't you think?"

Jack started to rebuff the comment, but the bathroom door swung open and County Commissioner Viktor Jimenez came sauntering out, pawing his hands on his silk shirttail and crop-dusting an unpleasant aroma in his wake. A darker-skinned man of indeterminate ethnicity, he wore one of those pointy-tipped mustaches fancied by men who'd done unmentionable things in their birth countries prior to migrating to the States. "Gentlemen."

Jack stood, moving into Jimenez's pathway. "Commissioner."

The man paused two steps out. "A supporter of mine, I hope."

"A quick question."

The commissioner eyed Ray then Jack. "Quickly."

"Coconut Key."

"What about it?"

"Did you really put your stamp of approval on that monstrosity?"

He nodded. "Hell of a thing for the local economy."

"You serious?"

"You'll be happy to know I helped get that eyesore of a marina under contract too."

"The Soggy Dollar?"

"That's the one. Damn thing's been a blight on this community for decades."

That explained why Jack had seen a team of surveyors with transit levels on the property earlier in the week. "Who put in the offer?"

"Sorry, pal." Jimenez swatted Jack on the shoulder with a firm, flat hand. "I've probably already said too much. I'm not supposed to talk about stuff in the pipeline. You know. Sunshine Laws and all that nonsense. Now if you'll excuse me."

Viktor stepped sideways about to sweep by Jack, but Jack eased his knee into the lane like a power forward. "What are they planning on doing with the marina?"

Viktor grinned and twisted one end of his mustache. "Like I said, can't speak on the matter. Now if you'll excuse me."

"Can't speak on it? Isn't that what my tax dollars pay you to do?"

The commissioner eyed Ray. "This one a friend of yours?"

Ray crossed his arms over his chest and kept quiet.

Jimenez grinned and twisted one end of his mustache. "This job of yours is an elected seat, Livingston. Man like me can play a hell of a role in swinging that vote one way or another."

"The people of this county seem pretty happy with my efforts so far."

Viktor grinned. "For the time being. But, with your particular history with the department, you should know better than to cross me."

Ray's lips drew thin.

"That's right, Raeford. Don't think I'm not aware of a certain indiscretion involving you about three years back."

Ray's face sagged.

"Don't feel bad, sheriff. A guy like me makes it his job to know these kinds of things. Now do me a favor. Keep your boy here in line. Guilt by association. Might sully your otherwise pristine reputation." Viktor turned back to Jack. "And you. I don't give a shit who you are, but you'd sure as hell better figure out who I am pretty quick." He tipped an imaginary hat brim then shouldered out the front door, the unseemly aroma still trailing behind.

As the door slammed, Jack turned to Ray. "What's he got on you? And why don't I know about it?"

"Not now." Ray snatched his coffee off his desk, sipped then grimaced into the mug. "That prick swings by here every morning so he doesn't stink up his own office."

"What?"

"Word is he's knocking boots with his secretary. Doesn't want to scare her off." Ray sipped again then rattled the cup back onto the desk. "So what are you doing here, Jack? I'm guessing it's not to watch me get lip jockeyed by my superiors."

"As entertaining as that was, it's actually not why I'm here. Unfortunately, after all this excitement, I'm not sure your old man heart can take the news I'm about to deliver."

"Kiss my old wrinkled ass, Cubera." The sheriff settled back into his chair and propped his boot heels on his desk. "Now what do you want?"

"Anybody report a missing person in the last twenty-four hours?"

"Not that I'm aware of." The sheriff dropped his feet back to the floor then sniffed at the air. "Are you drunk?"

"No, but I'm hoping it's only a temporary condition."

"Then why are your eyes so damn red?"

"Long night." Jack showed him the blistered hand.

"You fall into another campfire?"

"I wish."

"Wait a minute. You're sober. You're up early. What's going on with you? You coming down with something?"

Jack's grin vanished as he told Ray about the jellyfish attack.

"Kids at the dock playing a prank on you?"

"I might've thought that too if a dead body hadn't come into play."

The sheriff shot forward and boomed his hands onto the desk with such force Jack thought it might buckle. "What in the hell did you do this time?"

Jack eased off the desk. "Me and the kid came across a body on the backside of Whipray Basin."

"Kid? What kid?"

"That shaggy-headed shit from the marina who looks like he smokes a lot of weed."

"Hunter?"

Jack nodded. "That's the one. We were out fishing the flats around dusk last night when—"

The sheriff shot upright from his chair so hard it banged against the wall behind him. "*Last night?*"

Jack stepped a pace back. "Hold on now. I'm just being a good Samaritan."

The sheriff balled his fingers into fists then planted his knuckles into the desk top and leaned forward on stiff arms. "Any idea who it is?"

"You wouldn't believe me if I told you."

Ray moved from behind the desk then snatched his SHERIFF baseball cap from a nearby coat tree and tugged it over his head. "What the hell have you gotten yourself into this time?"

"Just get the boat ready, Ray. I'll run you out to the scene myself."

"Damn right you will." The sheriff shot around Jack toward the front door.

"Do you have your gun?"

The sheriff's brows wrinkled under the brim of his cap. "Why?"

"Whoever killed the guy might still be in the vicinity."

"So now you're saying it's a *murder*?"

Jack put a hand into the sheriff's shoulder, urging him out the door. "Deep breaths, Ray. Like you're pushing out a baby."

* * *

The sheriff cranked the twin Suzukis on the department's twenty-eight-foot Mako center console then idled from the marina. The morning air already hung thick and sluggish as they meandered down Snake Creek and crawled toward a dawning light diffusing in deep purples against the underbellies of distant thunderheads. Once beyond the Manatee Zone, Ray slalomed the vessel through a series of green and red channel markers delineating the narrow cut then hit the open backwaters and angled toward Whipray Basin.

The sheriff spun his cap backwards. "So where exactly am I headed?"

The wind roared around Jack's ears. "You know the cut that runs west of Pollock Key that'll carry you all the way up to Flamingo?"

The sheriff nodded as he feathered the trim tabs and leveled off the bow. "I'm familiar."

"Body's right there. Near Frangipani Flats. We tagged it with a lobsterpot marker. Blue with a white stripe."

"You just left him out there to get picked clean by sharks?"

"What was I supposed to do?"

"You could've called us out to help."

"No cell service."

The sheriff shook his head in obvious disappointment. "How about when you got back to the docks last night?"

"I was going to."

"But?"

"I got a little sidetracked."

21

"Right, Romeo. What was her name?"

Jack's mustache curled toward his ears. "Come on, Ray. You know I wouldn't sleep with any woman who'd lower her standards enough to sleep with me."

"Should I ask what's going on with Summer?"

"Not unless you've got a stomach for rollercoasters."

Jack nodded toward the water where it waned from blue to pale green. "Skirt just to the left of that shoal and run the tideline all the way out."

Ray adjusted their heading then settled back against the leaning post as they crossed the open waters in silence before reaching a grouping of islets a few miles offshore. Here the water drew slightly skinnier, the sandy patches lighter in contrast against the oyster clusters and turtle grass. The sheriff backed down on the throttles, dropping the boat off plane as they breached the shallower waters spreading between the mangroves.

The wind ceased, and the heat returned. The depth finder reading tumbled to three feet before a warning alarm began to sound.

Ray clicked off the device. "You think it's deep enough for me to get the boat back there?"

Jack glanced toward the area in question—a mangrove spread about thirty yards up. "Tide's out. Probably best just to anchor here and wade in the rest of the way."

"Wonderful." The sheriff clunked the engines into neutral as the sun broke through the clouds spreading a shimmering glare across the bay. "I love wading in waist-deep water when there's been a dead body chumming it up all night."

"Hammerheads are the only thing to really worry about."

"I'm not too fond of the bull sharks either."

"Just please don't make me listen to your shark attack story again."

The sheriff's eyes widened as he spun his hat back around. "I could've been killed by that man-eater."

"You got nipped in the leg surfing, Ray. It was hardly a Jaws moment."

"I had to beat the damn thing off with my fist."

Jack chuckled. "When you start talking about beating off sharks, you lose me."

"Juvenile."

The sheriff toggled a switch on the dashboard then a transom anchor telescoped a shaft into the sandy bottom securing the vessel. He killed the engines, unhooked his utility belt then clunked it onto the console. "Guess we should've brought swimsuits."

The sheriff unbuttoned his shirt, stripped off his uniform then refastened the utility belt around his waist.

Jack pointed at the gun. "Seriously?"

"In case of sharks."

Jack began peeling off garments until the two stood in their underwear about to ease into the warm waters. Jack wore boxers with a lobster pattern inked across them. The sheriff wore briefs a little too loose around the legs and a little too sheer everywhere else.

"Damn, Ray. The tighty's certainly gone from those whiteys."

The sheriff squatted on the gunwale then swung his legs toward the water. "Funny. I would've figured you for crabs not lobsters."

"You're lucky I'm wearing anything at all. I usually hang glide."

"Come on, Romeo."

Jack eased into the bay until his feet found purchase on the soft, silted bottom. The sheriff sank down next to him then slipped the Glock from its holster and began to wade forward with the gun in hand. The sheriff moved deliberately, lifting his knees high like a trotter and stirring a turbid wake in which Jack followed. When they reached the spread of mangroves and rounded to the blind side, a long torpedo-shaped creature shot toward a deeper pocket above a field of seagrass. Instinctively, the sheriff trained his weapon on the shadow and readied to squeeze off a couple shots.

Jack snatched Ray by the shoulder. "Easy now. It's just a tarpon. No need to turn this into a turf war."

The sheriff lowered the Glock but kept it at the ready.

Jack surveyed the waters. Other than the tarpon, the area appeared quiet and uninhabited by anything else dead or alive.

"You sure this is the spot?"

"Positive." Jack sloshed forward six paces then yanked on the blue-and-white striped Styrofoam ball. "This is the marker we used."

"Sharks get to him?"

Jack hoisted the line from the water revealing a cleanly severed tag end. "Afraid not. This line's been cut by a blade."

"You trying to tell me somebody stole the body?"

"I was pretty sure we were being watched last night."

"Jesus, Jack. What's going on here?"

"Good question."

"So who are we talking about, anyway?"

Jack's shoulders sagged. "Biggins."

"As in Ross Biggins?"

Jack nodded.

"Jesus." The sheriff holstered his pistol then placed his hands on his hips framing the foggy outline of his portly pecker head. "You really shit the bed on this one."

"Come on, Ray. I'm just the unlucky sonofabitch who found the guy."

"The history you two have. Or *had*, I should say. That's going to be a tough sell."

"He turned my bar into a martini joint. What would you have done?"

"Found another place to hang my head."

Jack grunted. "You know as well as I do that jackass swung on me first."

"Maybe so. But that still didn't give you the right to break three bones in his hand with a conch hammer."

"That third one was an accident."

"I'm on your side, Jack. But you may want to worry how all this is going to look to the average bear." Ray looked back toward the pot marker. "So, tell me, how is it that a hotshot developer goes missing and nobody even reports it?"

24

"My inner dick tells me it's all somehow tied to Coconut Key."

"Funny. It's usually your outer dick telling you what to do." Ray withdrew his cap and dragged a forearm over his damp forehead. "But you're right. That development's starting to look shadier than a gumbo limbo."

"You think Jimenez could somehow be tied to it?"

"That sonofabitch is crooked as the day is damp." Ray snugged the cap back over his head.

"What's he dangling over you anyway, Ray?"

Ray stared off toward the distant horizon. "Some other time."

"You know if we go after a heavy hitter like him, things might get a little squirrely."

"I know, Jack. That's why I'm over here thinking. Can't you hear the gerbils running around the wheel?"

"Well?"

"With your track record, I'm not so sure what we should do." The sheriff shot Jack a stern look.

"That was different, Ray. That was for your daughter."

"It's not that I don't appreciate what you did. But, with what I do for a living, I need to make sure I stay within the limits of the law. Or as close to them as possible."

"Are you and I good, Ray? That's all I care about."

"Let me tell you something, Jack. Most friendships have expiration dates. But the history we share, we'll be friends forever."

"Good to hear. Because I realize it's tough to be my friend sometimes."

"I figure that wisdom cuts both ways." Ray glanced off into the distance. "We'll figure out what to do about Jimenez later. For now, tell me what you know about Biggins. You said the death looked suspicious. How so?"

Jack glanced back toward the lobsterpot marker, slowly preening his mustache. "His face was lacerated with burns. Looked like the worst jellyfish attack I've ever seen."

"Man o' war?"

"Worse."

"Like what?"

Jack shrugged then shielded his eyes with an upturned hand. "There's another thing that doesn't make sense. He had a small puncture wound on his left butt cheek."

"A bullet?"

Jack shook his head. "Elongated on one side."

"Don't tell me you undressed the guy."

"He wasn't wearing anything but a wanger-hanger."

The sheriff's face wrinkled up like he'd just thrown up in his mouth. "You poor bastard."

"It's going to be with me for a while."

The two stood quietly for a moment as the shadow of a cloud swept over them dimming the light and darkening the waters.

"First suspicious death in Islamorada in how many years?" Jack asked.

"Make that days."

Jack brows went up. "What?"

"Another guy died a few days back diving out at Stingray City."

Jack thought back to the nighttime intruder. Bodies. Plural. "And?"

"This guy comes floating up to the surface with a live stingray pierced straight through his chest."

"What did the autopsy say was the cause of death?"

"Didn't get one."

"Suspicious death like that?"

Ray shook his head. "That body went missing too."

"Come on."

"The gal that saw him come floating up turned and started screaming for help. By the time anyone arrived, the body was nowhere to be seen."

"You're saying it just disappeared?"

Ray nodded. "You're going to love this. It was one of the guys behind Coconut Key. The Salucci family. Out of Jersey."

"You interview any of them after that incident?"

"I introduced myself. But I believe we're due for a more formal conversation now."

The sheriff surveyed the surrounding waters with squinted eyes. "You sure this is the right place? Lot of these little islands look the same. Especially at night."

Jack wiggled the cut line they'd used to secure the body. "Pretty sure."

"You're aware that company Summer works for was hired by the Saluccis to help secure the Coconut Key permits."

"Don't remind me."

"Maybe you should pay her a visit. See if she can help sort this out."

"We're not exactly on the best of terms but—"

"Why doesn't that surprise me?"

"What exactly are we even sorting out here, Ray?"

"Good question." Ray nibbled at his lip. "I can't exactly report this thing without a body or a stitch of evidence. I mean, this is about as official as unofficial gets."

"Would make for some splashy headlines for tourist season."

"Just what I need."

"How about we keep things on the down low until the body turns up or we figure out what's going on?"

"Agreed." The sheriff slipped his gun out of the holster. "Now let's get out of this water before something turns us into breakfast."

Jack pointed toward a duo of dark shadows moving along a neighboring shoal about a hundred feet from their position. "You mean like those hammerheads?"

Without warning, the sheriff discharged three quick shots in the general direction. Collateral spray rained down in the serene surroundings.

"Jesus, Ray. I was joking. It's just a couple tarpon."

Ray high-stepped toward the boat. "Kiss my ass, Cubera. Once you've been savagely attacked like I have, they're all hammerheads."

* * *

The bungalow was an adorable mess, just like its owner. It hid at the end of a sandy street behind a tangle of traveler palms eleven blocks from the Soggy Dollar.

Jack stepped under a pink and purple bougainvillea archway, wrapped his knuckles against the jamb and waited. Somewhere behind the door the adorable mess stirred and bumped around. A moment later, the front door sidelights began to glow with a faint aura from an interior room light.

The doorknob twisted, then the slab eased open revealing Summer Dahlia, her half-lidded eyes puffy and troubled, her lips plump with sleep, her thick broad tangles bleached pale gold and windblown falling over her shoulders.

"What do you want, Jack?"

"I just needed to—"

"You can't just show up here. Not anymore."

"It's not like that. I just need someone to talk about—"

"Go away, Jack. Go sleep it off under someone else's roof."

"You don't understand. I—"

Summer's face bent in confusion, her usual sarcasm-and-cocktail persona transfigured into those delicate, skittish features of an animal recently rescued from the pound. "Ten months, Jack. That's how much of my life I gave you."

Jack eased closer and dropped his voice an octave. "It was a misunderstanding, Summer. A mistake. It wasn't what you think."

"You were at dinner with another woman, Jack."

"It wasn't dinner. She was on a shift break. She works there."

"And that's supposed to make me feel better?"

"Her name's Sophia. She's a friend from the marina. She wanted to talk about her son. The kid from the dock. He doesn't have a father in his life. Or a man to look up to. So I'm keeping an eye on him. Taking him fishing. Sharing the occasional beer. You know. Kid stuff."

"Lovely." Summer's jawline flexed. "You're taking care of her kid now too?"

"What's this really about?"

Summer shook her head. "What happened to you, Jack? What happened that broke you so bad you can't be fixed?"

"Don't twist this around."

Her eyes narrowed. "Are you in love with her, Jack?"

"She's a friend. That's all."

"Maybe you should value your relationships more than your friendships." She shifted her stance. "So what are you doing here?"

"I was attacked last night." Jack glanced toward his blistered hand then back up. "Somebody tried to kill me."

Summer's eyes flickered down then seemed to register the bandage. "Jesus." The door eased open another foot bringing her into full view, a faint ambient glow backlighting wispy blond hairs around her head.

"I assume you know about Coconut Key getting approved."

Her eyes diverted toward the ground.

"Congratulations." Jack shifted his weight from one foot to the other. "Your hard work finally paid off."

She glanced back up. "I can't do this anymore."

"You need to tell me how you got this pushed through permitting."

"I didn't push anything through."

"Then your bosses. How did they do it?"

"That's above my paygrade, Jack."

"Like it or not, you had a hand in this deal going through."

"Screw you, Jack. Some of us have to work."

Jack shook his head. "How do you go from working at Fish and Game to working for the enemy?"

She bared her teeth. "What's the difference? One's corruption and the other's just government-sponsored corruption. What was I supposed to do? Start dancing the lunch shift down at Stiffy's?"

Jack started to lay into her about social responsibility and being a part of the collective conscience but bit his tongue. What right did he have to pass judgment? He'd been shin-deep in brown-bottle bass for years while the rest of the world unraveled. "I'm sorry for being so damned self-righteous. This isn't on you. And I understand we're going

29

through a bit of a rough patch, but I need you to put that aside. I need your help."

The door parted farther, and Summer pushed forward, one hand on the knob, the other shoulder-high on the jamb. She wore a thin white V-neck, long sleeve, cut just above the waistline with blue madras boxer shorts Jack did not recognize.

For a moment, Jack was lost in the faint impression of her breasts against the thin cotton.

"I won't jeopardize my job, Jack."

"I wouldn't ask you to do that. Not yet."

"How is it you think I can help?"

"Depends on how well you know your boss."

She let go of the knob, and the door drifted fully open. "He's a money-grubbing pig, if that's what you're asking."

"Not anymore."

"Why? Is he born again? Did he convert to Taoism?"

"Trust me. He's had a serious change in lifestyle." Jack eased closer. "Now, will you help me?"

Summer hooked a hand around the back of her neck and rubbed, drawing her shirttail upward revealing a glade of satiny stomach and a trail of faint blond hairs traveling southward toward a vacation spot Jack hoped to one day revisit.

She stopped the rubbing and canted her head. "I'll think about it, but I'm not making any promises."

* * *

The vixen brought the Hinckley in hot, swept by the Moppie then whipped the boat's tail around with the prowess of a charter captain. With a gentle tog of the wheel and a flick of the throttle, she backed the jet propulsion craft into slip 17 with a grumbling purr. A moment later, she curled her voluptuous red lips into a shrill, ear-bending whistle and motioned for assistance.

With no dockhand on the marina roster, Jack hustled down the dock and snagged a braided line that unfurled toward him through the hazy day. With a quick flick of his wrist, he snugged the boat to a cleat then repeated the act portside, securing the vessel solidly between the two splintered and rickety gangplanks that extended along each gunwale.

As the engine shut down, a relative silence returned to the marina, and the woman maneuvered onto the swim platform of *Exit Strategy*, registered in Cayman Brac. She wore a blue-and-white striped bikini top, short shorts snugged tightly around her pubic arch and rattan wedges far too tall and narrow to be considered appropriate footwear in regard to anything maritime.

"So I assume you're Jack, the private investigator."

Jack grinned and sagged back onto his heels. When you live the life of a loner on a quiet island in an out-of-the-way marina, it's best to know why someone's gone through the trouble of finding out who you are and where you live. "Actually, I'm a full-time boat bum."

"I heard about the mustache."

"That so?"

"Does it tickle?"

"That depends on the location."

"And that skin tone. Is that natural?"

"Some say it's dirty French."

"What do you say it is?"

He nodded at her then cleared his throat into his fist. "I tend to keep where I'm from and why I'm here to myself as much as possible."

"Interesting. I come from a similar locale." She shifted her weight from one slender heel to the other. "I'm Blanch. Blanch Theroux."

"Shouldn't you be yachting around the Vineyard or over in Captiva in a fancy boat like this?"

"It belongs to my sugar daddy." She glanced around the marina as though it were a squalid ghetto. "We're just keeping her here while we have the interior refit."

Jack eyed the Hinckley. A new interior? "She looks straight off the showroom floor."

"Don't be tacky. She's nearly two years old."

"How silly of me." Jack sank a hand into his pocket. "Mind if I ask how you happened to come by my name?"

"I'm looking for a good dick, and your name came up."

Jack grinned and let the comment wane. "Sorry to say, but somebody gave you some bad information. I retired from the PI business over seven years ago."

"How about a second of your time before you say no? I'll make it worth your while."

With the sweep of a hand, Blanch invited Jack onto her boat. He bumped aboard and glanced around at the plush and dimpled finishes before his natural line of vision settled onto her augmented chest.

He was impressed.

Quite.

The work reflected the highest standards. Clearly a surgeon with a love for shapes, like Picasso, had wielded the scalpel in the operating room.

"Like what you see?" Blanch jostled her chest up and down, the stiff orbs leaping in unison. "I invested in these puppies a little over three years ago."

"Certainly seems like money well-spent."

She fingered a glittery clutch off the helm, dug inside, then withdrew a pale white cigarette the length of a stove match. "You ever been married, Jack?"

Jack shook his head.

She set the cigarette between her teeth then spoke with the thing bouncing around her lips as she dug for a lighter. "All my life I've never been married. Not even once. Can you believe it? Most women my age have been married two or three times."

She withdrew a lighter then stepped from a shadow, the sunlight which had been falling at her feet now illuminating her face.

Jack blinked in rapid succession then steadied, his eyes registering on Blanch's facial attributes. The ears drew back a little too far. The brows arched in perpetual surprise. The lips protruded a touch too deftly against the philtrum. The beauty was evident, but through the medical

32

metamorphosis the facial structure appeared as though evolved through a different lineage, the ancestry traceable through something feline rather than a primate.

Blanch flicked the lighter then puffed the tip to life, her lipstick inking an apple-red imprint around the filter as she pulled it away. "My one indulgence. I don't even eat junk food since the lipectomy. It's all wheat grass and goji berries and green tea. Everything farm-raised and organic. Of course, there's the Bikram yoga and Pilates, but that goes without saying."

"Of course." Jack's thoughts began to sour. Each day, more cosmetically altered women drifted into the Keys causing the pool of natural lovelies to shrivel as fast as the River of Grass. To further exacerbate the issue, many of the more natural and saltier attributes that lent Islamorada its eccentricities and charm had also fallen prey to shinier, prettier things that catered to people like Blanch. Fish camps had given way to condos. Marinas had been reconfigured into dockominiums. Barstool drunks had been forced out by seasonal drinkers.

"So, Jack, how does a five-thousand-dollar retainer sound?"

Retainer? Jack's crossed eyes refocused. "Come again?"

She leaned closer, the acrid cigarette smoke corkscrewing toward his face. "Ross Biggins. You wouldn't happen to know the husky bastard, would you?"

Jack's pulse stuttered, and he wanted to turn and run but felt that would draw unnecessary attention. Could this be possible? Was she joking? What did she know? Had the kid ratted him out?

His eyes diverted toward the deck as he spoke. "Listen, Blanch. Before you go on I should tell you that this is probably something better for the local authorities to handle."

"What are you talking about?"

"The police."

"How are the police possibly going to help?"

"Help you find him, I guess."

"He's not lost, Jack. I just want him followed."

Jack's stomach stalled somewhere around his testicles then began to slowly ascend. What was going on here? Had nobody even reported the guy missing yet?

"What if I sweeten the pot a little?"

Jack blinked hard and when his eyes reopened two five-thousand-dollar stacks of hundred-dollar bills bound by rubber bands sat on a small cocktail table beside him.

"Well?" She blew a smoke ring into the air, her lips pursed in a manner to which she seemed accustomed. "You know him?"

Jack dropped the Costa Del Mars from his forehead over his eyes. No point showing her the confusion. "We've been known to swim in the same waters from time to time."

"So then you'll follow him for me?"

Jack handled the money stacks, set them edgewise in his hand then plucked at the rubber bands like banjo strings. As far as anyone from his former life knew, including the IRS, a man named Jack Cubera had sailed away from gainful, taxable employment many moons ago for a quiet life in Islamorada. Since then he'd occupied his free time, of which there was an abundance, in a leisurely capacity.

His sole financial commitment was the monthly $140 berthing fee he paid to the Soggy Dollar Marina to slip his boat (water and electric included), a fee he generally worked off in trade by scraping barnacles off neighboring boat hulls.

He maintained an existence uncluttered with things like consistent work and steady paychecks. When cash became an issue, he'd take tourists flats fishing, tinker on trawler inboards or ferry boats to and from the Bahamas in the dead of night.

Strictly off-the-books stuff. Cash only. No need for a 1099.

But ten grand. Ten easy grand. Without some sort of revenue influx in the not-so-distant future, austerity measures might start hampering his forecasted drinking schedule. So why not take on a case for a quick ten grand? That was just the sort of monetary influx that could stave off employment for a solid year under Jack's current annual per capita outlay. An offer with such a juicy presentation was rare. Packaged in a nice little blue box. Tied up with white ribbon and a silver bow. Still, the situation presented certain precarious components that demanded weighing, most perplexing of which was discerning whether there was anything unethical in taking on a case to follow a subject he knew was already deceased. Technically, he could fulfill his investigative obligation and follow Ross, assuming he could find the body again. The dude certainly had a knack for getting around despite his recent loss of motor skills. Also, the idea of prying into Ross's background for a client certainly seemed like better cover for investigating Coconut Key than just snooping around.

Worst scenario, if nothing became of the case, he could always justify the money as a gringo tax. Just a toll for yet another outsider heedlessly abusing the Islamorada infrastructure.

He plucked the rubber bands again then stalled and offered up his most sincere, brow-furrowing performance. "Looks like there's really no decision to make."

She smiled, lynx-like, then reached out and tugged at his mustache. "I like getting what I want."

"I sensed that about you." He slapped the money stacks against an open palm then tucked them into his shorts. First chance, he'd stash them in the tackle box with his Ruger. "Now, excuse me for being forward, but you're not Ross's wife, are you? I mean, in a traditional sense?"

"Not legally, if that's what you're asking."

Jack played along. "So is it safe to assume you think he's landed a new mistress?"

"I think he's fucking someone else, if that's what you mean."

"You mean someone other than his wife?"

Blanch stabbed her cigarette into an ashtray as her eyes turned glassy. "I missed my window, Jack. I was a fool when I was younger. I should've done what all the other girls at Tennessee were doing and gotten my M-R-S degree. But I had to be different. I had to be an independent woman. I wanted it all, and I ended up with nothing." She stumbled over to the helm, daubed a tissue under her lower lashes. "That's why I do all of this, Jack." She swirled the tissue about her face. "The tucking.

35

The plumping." She cupped her boobs, hoisted them, let them go. "The lifting."

"Women are always their own biggest critics."

"Who are you kidding? All you men want the flat stomach and the perfect little ass and the high boobs. Then there's the shiny hair and the lush lashes and the smooth skin. You expect us to have the whole pretty little package and dust it all in pretty little perfumes. Of course, most of you don't give a rip about yourselves. You get fat, go bald, have weird hairs growing out of your ears. And those of you that don't just got lucky with the genetics."

"Women age so much more beautifully than they ever give themselves credit for."

"Don't be a fool, Jack."

"I love the way women age naturally. The eye lines. The back of the hands. The way the—"

"Spin it however you like, Jack. Getting old is getting old. And all I know is that Ross is my best bet now." Blanch tossed the tissue onto the console then strode to the wet bar and unscrewed a bottle of Boodles. "Enough about me. Enough of my carrying on. How about a drink?"

Jack checked his wrist for a watch that wasn't there then looked back to her. "I generally don't drink gin before lunch."

"Suit yourself." She mixed up a two-cherry martini then sank into the regal pleats of a bench seat sighing as though she'd just finished a half-marathon. "Let me be honest, Jack. Ross and I have an interesting relationship. I keep him happy in certain ways, and he keeps me in the lifestyle I've grown accustomed to. You understand."

"I'm certainly in no position to judge anyone on lifestyle."

"We met at a Miami Dolphins party. He used to be an athlete, you know."

"Love at first sight?"

"Please. I'm much too pragmatic for that. Ross is the romantic. At least when it comes to Coconut Key, he is. That's why his wife left him."

"I didn't realize they were divorced."

"Just separated."

"Legally?"

"Geographically."

"I see."

"She took their two miniature schnauzers and moved back to Connecticut to be closer to her mother." She swilled the gin. "Anyway, he's not like most men. He gets giddy about things like permits and sand migration, regulations and ROGO points, FDEP restrictions and riparian rights. The sort of stuff that bores a party gal like me senseless."

"So maybe that's his real mistress?"

"I don't know, Jack. I'm not sure what he wants anymore. I mean I fuck, I suck, and I drive a boat. What's not to love?"

"I don't know." He shrugged. "Do you fish?"

"No, but I drink like one."

"Maybe he's just looking for someone to help with the dishes."

"Dear Lord. I hope not." She fanned a hand in front of her cheeks. "If my mascara runs, I'm going to be livid."

Jack didn't know whether to console her or pour himself a stiff cocktail, so he simply kept quiet as she gathered her composure.

"Anyway, Jack, I'm running out of patience with Ross. A woman my age should be married."

"So if he's fucking around, it'll make your decision to move on to a new suitor that much easier?"

"Precisely."

"So exactly what happened?"

"We had plans to go shopping in SoBe yesterday, and he never even showed. The fat bastard never even called to cancel."

Jack stroked his mustache. "There may be other explanations for why he stood you up."

She leaned forward. "Like what?"

"He's a developer, after all. In the Keys. There's no telling how many people have his name on their shit list."

Blanch nodded, as though impressed by this statistic. "Are you saying somebody might have done something to harm him?"

"I don't like to rule anything out from the onset." Jack settled his eyes on the kitten lips. "So when was the last time you saw him?"

"Yesterday morning. He was headed out to exercise. Then he said he had a meeting with the county."

"I believe you mentioned he might be of a larger build. What sort of exercise does he do?"

"I believe I said fat. But, yes, he'd started to shave off a few pounds with this Crisscross program of his."

"Crossfit?"

"That's the one."

Jack nodded. "Doesn't that regimen dictate a different exercise routine every day?"

"Sounds about right."

"What exactly was he doing yesterday morning?"

"Swimming, I think." She clicked her fingernails against her teeth. "Yes. I remember the suit. It was one of those tight things that isn't really flattering on his physique but sure accentuates his package." She grinned. "His last name is Biggins, you know."

"Well then." Jack pushed up from the cushion then clambered his way onto the dock. "Why don't you give me a few days? Let me see what I can come up with."

Blanch slurped at the martini. "In the meantime, you'll let me know if that mustache opens up for business."

"Sorry, you're my client now. It's a professional line I never cross."

"Well, I've got to admit, I'm a little disappointed."

"Don't feel bad, Blanch. I've been disappointing women for decades."

* * *

Jack clicked his VHF radio to channel 16, set it on the bench beside him then fell back against the gunwale. It was late at night, or early in the morning, depending on perspective. He guessed around two-thirty a.m. by now. Unable to sleep, he'd let the moon set then boated beyond the channel into the backwaters, killed the engine and laid back to revel at the celestial tapestry stippling the night ink. Of all the pollutions in the world noise was the worst, particularly that of political diatribe or personal watercraft. Light noise ran a very close second.

But not out here.

Out here in the backcountry one lived beyond pollution from both light and noise. Out here with the right eyes one could achieve snippets of a world that existed before the human onslaught.

He laced his fingers behind his head then hunted the sky until he'd found the northern tip of Orion's sword then Betelgeuse and down the constellation to Saiph. As his eyes adjusted and his brain worked to extract the full form of the starry hunter, the dome above began to shimmer with so many pinpricks of light he became overwhelmed. There are those rare immaculate moments when you feel like the only person on earth.

What often follows is the sense of absolute loneliness.

He dialed up the squelch on the VHF, thumbed the transmitter button then began to hail. "Saltwater Blond. Saltwater Blond. This is Subtropical Highlife. If you're out there, send me a sign."

It was a long shot. But he'd lived and died on long shots and so had the people who'd believed in him.

He released the button, waited for twenty seconds then repeated the hail. After another minute with no reply, he set the radio down and reclined onto his elbows, the silence returning as something almost tangible and brittle before the radio hissed with a female voice.

"Go to seven-three, Subtropical Highlife. Channel seven-three."

Jack rocked forward, rolled the dial to the private frequency then cleared his throat. "Are you out there?"

"Adrift as usual."

"Sorry to bother you so late again."

"It's nice to hear your voice."

"Do me a favor. Walk out into your backyard and find Orion."

"I'm already out here."

"You wanted to know what happened to me, right? You wanted to know why I'm so broken I can't be fixed."

"I only wanted to . . . only if you want to tell me."

"I don't want to tell you, but I want you to know. Does that make sense?" There was a long silence as Jack gazed into the darkness, his vision crossing at some waypoint in the distance so he saw nothing at all. "Seven years ago Raeford Livingston's daughter was assaulted then beaten beyond recognition. I was there for Ray. I was with him in the courtroom as the entire incident played out to a jury over a six-day stretch. I was there as all the evidence was presented. To see the sallow shell of my friend. To hear the grotesque details of the case. To watch the judge pound his gavel and dismiss the charges on a technicality and let the perpetrator walk."

"I kept tabs on the monster from that day forward. Thirteen months later, he was arrested on a similar charge and released on bail. I followed him one night as he left his country club bar. It was one of those humid nights where my truck windshield wouldn't quit fogging so I had to keep the wipers on. I had no idea what I was going to do. I just wanted to follow him. See what the monster did in the dark. When we hit that desolate stretch of A1A through Canaveral National Seashore, I got right on his bumper and began flashing my high beams. He pulled over, jumped from his car and came storming toward my truck with a nine iron in his hand. But it was dark, and my high beams were blinding so that by the time he reached my door, I'd crawled out the passenger-side and slipped around the front without him suspecting a thing. I hit him with a fist first. A solid belt. He slumped over but didn't go all the way down. Still, it was enough to knock him off balance. Long enough to pry the golf club from his hand. Once I had the club in my grip, it wasn't a contest. I started swinging. At some point, I dragged him across a series of dunes toward the rumbling surf then settled him down low against a high berm and made sure he'd never use his pretty face to seduce a woman again."

"I quit the PI business the next morning. Quit society. Quit life as I'd known for so many years. And I came south and settled here in the land of misfits and fools where a degenerate like me belongs."

"I'm not sorry for what I did. But I'm changed."

40

Jack released the transmission button and listened to the soft squelch before Summer's voice came over the line. "I'm sorry I forced you to drag that up."

"You didn't force it. I offered it."

The radio waves fell silent before Summer's voice returned. "You live your quiet life on your little boat in your little marina. Sometimes I wonder if there's room in your little world for me."

"I like to keep things simple."

"I have a sister somewhere in Idaho, but I don't have any family, Jack. And I can never have any family of my own. You're the closest thing I have, and I get afraid when I think about how far away you really are."

"I'm closer than you think, Summer."

"Then prove it to me, Jack. Give me something more than just words to hold on to."

CHAPTER 4

LESS THAN FORTY-EIGHT hours prior, the sixty-five-foot Viking Sportfish *FrigateAboutIt* motored into a protected diving sanctuary a hundred yards from the looming skeletal framework of the Alligator Reef Lighthouse. From inside the cabin, the stereo belched a riffy island jam into the ocean breeze as an anchor sank from the bowsprit and careened fifteen feet through a crystalline water column before smashing into a vibrant boulder of brain coral.

The flukes found purchase, then the stern swung down current drawing the scope taut as three men from South Jersey ambled from the salon onto the aft deck with freshly blended Mai Tais in hand. Mookie Salucci, the portly ringleader of the Italian trio, wore a silk guayabera unbuttoned to his navel and a golden cornicello the size and shape of a cayenne pepper swinging in his abundant chest shag. Chewy, the youngest and dumpiest of the bunch, was bound in a sleeveless T-shirt and silky gym shorts. The one built like a lumberjack, Johnny Bagels, sported a white tracksuit with twin black stripes running down the pant legs. All three puffed away on the damp brown tips of Cohiba Churchills.

Mookie slipped a white fedora with a black band over his dark frizzled hair then pointed his drink toward a Boston Whaler runabout hitched to a mooring ball two-hundred yards off their portside. "There he is. Mr. Fabulous himself."

The three men watched as the man known as Ross Biggins climbed onto the bow of his runabout then stripped off his gym shorts revealing a hibiscus print weenie bikini that arched over his veiny upper thighs like porticos over marble entryways.

Mookie plucked the cigar from his lips. "Would you get a load of that swimsuit? A guy could leave a little more to the imagination, if you know what I'm saying."

"You said it, boss."

The three watched as Ross cracked his neck, stretched his shoulders then nosed off the bow and into the drink with the grace of a walrus off an ice floe.

When his head finally resurfaced, he segued into a frantic doggy paddle as he refit his goggles. Then he clicked a few buttons on his wrist-watch, dunked forward and began the rather ambitious swim toward the *FrigateAboutIt*.

"What's with the exercising, anyway?" Johnny peeled off his track-suit top exposing two massive biceps and elbows branded with those puffy brown spider web tattoos commonly flaunted in the yard at Sing Sing. "Kind of out of character, ain't it?"

Chewy shook his head. "Says he trying to shed a few pounds for that goomah of his."

"Yeah, Bagels." Mookie waved his cigar in the air. "Some of us ain't like you. We gotta exercise and watch what we eat to stay in shape."

"Not me, boss. I ain't never lifted a weight or exercised a day in my life."

"Brawn you got, Bagels. But I'm not so sure you didn't get short-changed in the brains department."

Johnny hauled back and swatted Mookie so hard across the back Mookie nearly pitched over the rail. "That's funny boss. Brains depart-ment. I've certainly spilled enough over the years to make up for it though, ain't I?"

As Ross stroked overhand in their direction, Chewy held a finger up to his ear and listened to the music.

Life is a splendor with this gooey drink blender.

"Who is this band again, Mookie?"

"The man himself."

43

"Big Swinging Richard?"

"That's right. I finally got the contract ironed out for him to play at the inaugural event out at Coconut Key."

Chewy wriggled a pinky into his ear canal. "Sounds like two seagulls tapdancing inside a banjo, you ask me."

"Ain't no Springsteen, that's for sure."

Johnny tilted his head. "Reminds me of a bone saw going through a femur."

Mookie exhausted a breath. "Welcome to Florida."

Two minutes later, Ross arrived, latching onto the aft ladder on the Viking then hauled his overburdened frame onto the transom platform. There he slumped, gasping for breath and tapping at his watch face, seemingly confused by the time. After a few winded breaths, he stood upright dripping a pond of water onto the slip-resistant fiberglass. "How goes it, gentlemen?"

Mookie tossed a towel toward him. "Morning, sporto."

Ross palmed the towel then began mopping the thing, still folded, over his meaty face. A once-menacing fullback at the University of Florida, his mass had turned doughy from his cushy gig as CEO of SunState Entitlements, Inc. While not many considered him large in a traditional sense—certainly not in his hometown of Alachua where he scarcely tipped the scales of pleasantly plump—the U.S. Government's Body Mass Index established his six-foot one-inch 335-pound frame squarely in the category of fat ass.

"Nice tunes." Ross unfurled the towel then slapped it around his neck and grabbed onto each end. "Cocktails for breakfast?"

The three men nodded in unison as they crossed over to the portside, causing the big sportfisher to list. They gazed across the diving sanctuary puffing blue smoke into the fresh morning air.

"You ever see any sharks out there when you're swimming?" Mookie asked.

"Just nurse sharks and bonnet heads. An occasional blacktip. Nothing that'll bother you."

Johnny Bagels slurped his drink. "Maybe we should do ourselves some snorkeling."

Chewy pushed his drink at Johnny. "How about next time? When we haven't been hitting the sauce."

Mookie nodded. "Yeah. Them rip currents can be murder if you don't watch yourself." He moved from the gunwale then slumped into the fighting chair. "So thanks for meeting us out here on such short notice, Biggins."

Ross snapped the elastic on his briefs then sank into a series of deep leg lunges. "No sweat, boys."

Mookie tapped his cigar. "I wanted to let you know in person that me and the crew went ahead and signed on the outfits who are going to handle the dredge work for Coconut Key."

Ross paused the deep lunges then began bouncing up and down on his left foot trying to clear water from his ear. "You did *what*? I thought we were making these decisions together."

Mookie tipped his ash into the wind. "You know how it is. Things change. Ebb and flow."

Ross stopped bouncing and sank a pinky into his left ear. "That's not what we agreed on."

Mookie shrugged. "Ink's already dry. Work starts tomorrow. At least some preliminary sitework. I though you was ready to get this baby rolling."

Ross paused the ear cleaning and grinned. "*Tomorrow*? Well." He took a few deep breaths then suctioned his goggles over his eyes causing the rubbery tasseled ends to dance beside his cheeks. "I certainly like the sound of that."

Ross turned back toward the water as though about to disembark.

"Hey, Aquaman. Leaving so soon? We offend you or something?"

Ross tapped the watch face. "This is a Crossfit program. All about high reps and short breaks. It uses muscular confusion to hone your—"

"Enough already." Mookie waved his drink at Ross. "Talk like that's enough to make me break a sweat."

"Three more laps, then I'm all yours."

"Good. 'Cause you and us, we got some talking to do."

"Yeah," Chewy said. "Important things."

Ross nodded then clicked on his watch and arched his body into the sea.

* * *

The wild man drifted his canoe under the skeletal framework of the Alligator Reef Lighthouse and secured it to a metal crossbeam. The long, narrow vessel was hand-hewn from a single log of cedar, the prow fashionably whittled into the form of a Florida crocodile head.

There, in the shadowy refuge, he observed a portly specimen in a floral weenie bikini bulling back and forth through the water like a ferry boat.

After the swimmer's third pass, the wild man hauled a mesh bag from a water-filled five-gallon bucket then peeled back the lip. Inside, a transparent gooey life form appeared to ooze through the netting. The long whip-like tentacles of the specimen, when extended, stretched over twelve feet long and contained a poison powerful enough to cause a swift, yet painful, demise. Even a single tentacle gently abrading the skin could cause instant anaphylactic shock and, subsequently, full and resolute cardiac arrest.

But not to the wild man. A peculiar childhood made him immune to the creature's fatal toxins. What's more, through the years, his kinship with the watery world had evolved into something rivaled only by Kiribati spear fishermen.

Or great barracuda.

He sat patiently and waited until the swimmer readied for another pass. Then he peeled away his alligator skin vest and slid from his vessel into the briny waters with the mesh bag in hand.

Taking a deep, chest-filling breath, he bubbled downward through the water column then kicked toward a mooring cable rising from a concrete anchor compressed into the ocean floor. When he reached the cable, he wrapped a free leg around it, like a rhythmic gymnast on a rope, holding himself in position as he freed the jellyfish from the mesh bag.

The jellyfish was gelatinous in his fingers as he palmed it by the soft matter of the head, twelve-foot tentacles drifting off into the current like poisonous streamers.

A few bubbles trickled from his nostrils as, on the distant surface, the swimmer reentered the water just astern of the massive shadow of the sportfisher hull. A moment later, the swimmer splashed across the surface closing the distance with each labored kick and each arduous stroke.

The wild man unfurled his leg from the cable then positioned upstream. There he aligned the jellyfish with the swimmer's progressive path and let the thing go.

The exhausted swimmer stood no chance. By the time his stroking ceased and his head reared upward, he was already too far ensnared in the tentacles to be saved.

As the poisonous appendages continued to lick at his exposed skin and lacerate it with fleshy burns, the wild man drifted close enough to both see and hear the ugly ordeal unfold. Instinctively, the swimmer slapped off his goggles and eyed into the water to see what was attacking him. As he did so, the slimy invertebrate tentacles coiled around his ears and neck delivering a pain akin to one's nipples being removed with a hot razor blade.

The swimmer panicked, thrashing his arms and legs and further ensnaring himself into the labyrinth of stingers. When one particularly fat tentacle attached itself to the thin Lycra swimsuit just over the soft rumpled shaft of the swimmer's johnson, he howled so loudly underwater that the wild man began a hasty retreat toward his tethered canoe.

* * *

Johnny Bagels noticed the commotion in the water first. "What's that stupid bastard doing now? Water aerobics?"

The three laughed and puffed away at their cigars until the commotion abruptly ceased, and Ross's body began to heave and jerk like an epileptic.

Mookie dropped his cigar to the deck. "Get the donut!"

"What's a donut, boss?"

Mookie snatched a red and white life ring off the cabin bulkhead, hustled to the stern then launched the thing in Ross's general direction. Against a hefty headwind, it luffed like a poorly tossed Frisbee then splashed down thirty feet shy of the intended target.

With the three men already quite drunk, decisions arrived slowly. Actions took a few moments when they needed to be immediate. By the time they comprehended any real severity to the situation then scrambled onto the bridge, Ross, no doubt, was already drifting steadily toward the bright light, his life reduced to a handful of still-frames involving sunset-colored cocktails and chicks in coconut bikinis at Big Swinging Richard tailgates.

Mookie cranked the diesel engines then backed toward the victim. Fearing Ross would be chewed up in the propellers, he kept disengaging the thrusters prematurely then drifting further away only to circle back and attempt again. Finally, a mooring bridle wrapped around one of the propellers, anchoring the boat in a position close enough to see what remained of their business partner.

"Holy Jesus."

The three men gazed down from the bridge.

"Damn, boss. What the—?"

Ross's body was enveloped by some sort of slimy sea creature, his near lifeless mass twitching every now and again on some remnant electrical tic bleeding out of his nervous system.

The collective sentiment was that, at this juncture, the time for any type of in-water rescue had passed. Somebody suggested they search the boat for a defibrillator, but, before any hunt could be conducted, the freshly deceased nosed forward then his fatty arms and legs buoyed to his sides. All that remained, to the Jersey crew and a host of other boobies now circling overhead, was the numbing surreal visual of a full-sprawling drown victim who slowly rotated counterclockwise in an eddy caused by the portside screw that continued to turn.

Mookie plucked his cigar off the deck then blew the cherry back to life. "You think he's dead?"

Bagels shrugged. "I seen dead, boss. And trust me, messed up like that you'd wanna be."

"What now?' Chewy asked. "You want I should radio Fish and Game?"

Mookie ashed his cigar into the wind. "No can do. Two of us dead in three weeks. We'd probably better think this thing through before we get the authorities involved."

"But it was an accident," Chewy said.

"So was Jimmy B getting gigged by that stingray. Just a freak accident."

Chewy shook his head. "Makes a guy miss the quiet life up in Jersey."

Mookie tossed his cigar butt overboard. "Let's go check his pulse. Make sure he's dead then get the hell out of here."

The three men hurried down to the swim platform, and, using the razor tip of the fishing gaff, hooked Ross in the right buttock then dragged him to the transom like a prize dorado.

Mookie said, "Check the pulse."

Chewy shook his head and backed away. "I'm not touching the slimy bastard."

Bagels kneeled closer to the body. "I think it's safe to say he's moved on to greener pastures." He turned to Mookie. "You want me to drag him into the boat?"

Mookie panned the area. "You see anyone else out here who might want to involve us in this thing?"

Johnny and Chewy glanced around. "That something moving over there by the lighthouse?"

"Yeah," Mookie said. "Waves and wind. Now come on. It's just your eyes playing tricks on you from the Mai Tais."

"You're right, Mook. I think I'm starting to get the sea sickness."

"The way I see things a guy comes out for a swim, gets stung by a jellyfish and dies of a heart attack or some sort of angina. It's not like the guy's the poster child for health and fitness."

"How 'bout I dice him up into sizable chunks then run him through the macerator?" Johnny asked. "To be on the safe side."

Chewy shook his head. "Jesus, Bagels. You ain't right in the head."

"What?" Johnny shrugged. "So we just leave him?"

Mookie nodded. "Best we leave well enough alone."

"What about the Whaler?"

"Just leave it be. Tour boat's bound to discover it sooner or later and radio it in to the Coasties."

Chewy ducked into the salon then returned with a pair of high-end sunglasses and set them over the deceased's eyes. "Out of respect."

Mookie placed a hand on Chewy's shoulder. "That's a nice touch. Classy. Ross would've liked that."

Chewy gnawed at his cigar. "The man had a big heart."

"You said it. Heart like an elephant."

Johnny chuckled. "And a physique to match."

"Show some respect," Mookie said. "Death. It's a once-in-a-lifetime experience."

He whispered a small prayer then each man in turn made the sign of the cross as they unhooked the gaff and let the body drift away.

CHAPTER 5

JACK WAS UP at dawn, the air breathless and heavy with mosquitos. The early morning silence made the world feel hollow, a faint sense of ocean-in-a-seashell in his ears. He carved a cantaloupe for breakfast then waited until ten thirty and sank his bare toes into an inch of water sloshing around the bilge of his tender—a fourteen-foot Carolina skiff—tethered to the Moppie.

The flat-bottomed vessel was powered by a thirty-five horsepower Johnson commissioned the same year Dylan's Blood on the Tracks hit shelves.

Jack yanked the pull cord three times and sputtered the engine to life in a fit of smoke. After a bout of intermittent hacking, it settled into a rattling idle, then Jack began the three-mile jaunt across the gulf.

As he made his way, a steady wind built from the south so that each time the hull pattered over the half-foot seas warm brine misted his new Costa Del Mars. His skin-diving mask jostled about the bilge alongside a snorkel, fins, a pony air tank and a Gerber dive knife.

Fifteen minutes later, he nosed the skiff through Cowpens Cut and got his first glimpse at the Coconut Key construction site.

It was simultaneously spectacular and disturbing.

The construction area was segregated from the balance of the basin by a bright orange floating turbidity barrier installed in a spectacular two-mile by two-mile square. The massive bullpen of dredge boats, construction barges, tugs and other machinery was on par with a wartime flotilla. At its essence, Coconut Key was to be a giant manmade island constructed in the calm breakwaters of the Cotton Key Basin. From a bird's eye view, the sandy structure would assume the shape of a giant daiquiri glass, one of only a handful of engineering marvels visible from the stratosphere.

According to reports, Ross Biggins's grandiose vision of the key had originally arrived as an epiphany during his first Big Swinging Richard concert his freshman year at U of F. Ross, a simple man with a flair for the cheesy, had spent his entire adult life since that day caught up in the tinny riffs and whimsical ways of the musician. If a concert was scheduled within three-hundred miles, he bought front row seats. When a new album dropped, he downloaded it day one. When a biography, authorized or not, hit the shelves, he listened to it on tape cover to cover opening weekend. The music icon summoned from within Ross an insatiable adoration for flowery shirts, plastic leis and anything that promised tailgates overrun with bikini-clad women half-drunk on gooey blender drinks. He was, as commonly known amongst the most fevered followers of Big Swinging Richard, a serious Dickhead.

In its original conception, the island would be a completely sovereign nation—a land unto itself in both mentality and doctrine. It would have its own constitution, its own flag and a military force that only shot water balloons at the enemy. It would be, as Big Swinging Richard liked to croon:

> A place to live the life of a bum
> Of the beach variety, no sobriety
> Drinking up rum, soaking up sun
> A place to live the life of a bum

But this fatuous view of a utopian nation quickly yielded to dollar signs. The same capitalistic greed that had pervaded the Florida Peninsula since the Matanzas massacre superseded any notions of his communal nation. The unsettling idea that just any-one, wet feet or dry, could immigrate into his island without the proper documentation—a.k.a. proof of funds—ceased early on.

The island design ultimately pushed through permitting was a car-free 55-and-over retirement community, offering golf car pathways through a 480-unit condominium complex, 257 freestanding residences, two-dozen pickleball courts, two par-three golf courses, a marina, a dining district with live music 365 days a year, an amphitheater and a seventeen-story observation needle, complete with a rotating bar lending sweeping ocean vistas from any seat in the house—all Big Swinging Richard themed, of course.

Jack puttered closer then dropped the engine to an idle.

Unbelievable.

The fact that this catastrophic development achieved final permissions bordered on absurd. Not here. Not in Islamorada. Maybe in Orlando or Miami or Daytona Beach. But this miscarriage of justice was gross even by Monroe County standards.

Exactly how much cash and political capital had been thrown around to push this thing through government channels? More importantly, who had gotten pissed off in the process? In big gains, there's always someone at the bottom who gets burned.

Jack cut the engine a hundred yards out then set the hook into the sandy bottom.

The work zone bustled with activity. A mechanical hum billowed in the air as contractors buzzed about boat decks clamping hoses and cranking wrenches, readying vacuums and centrifugal pumps quietly hidden behind hundreds of tons of steel. Tenders shuttled workers from barge to barge while a series of security vessels patrolled the area with men armed with assault rifles and radios.

As Jack readied for his dive, a security boat nosed to the perimeter of the work zone, and an armed man stared him down for a ten count before idling on. Jack spit into his dive mask, rubbed it over the lenses to prevent fogging, then fitted his mask as tightly as he could over his bushy mustache and slipped into the fins. After clamping his dive knife to his waistline, he cranked open the valve on the handheld dive tank then bit down on the mouthpiece.

A cool hiss of dry air inflated his lungs as he toppled off the skiff, feet over head. Once underwater, he finned rapidly toward the worksite then glanced up through the water. Visibility was below average from the construction activity, but Jack could still see shapes of boat hulls moving atop the water.

Could the armed guards see him from above?

He unclipped his blade and sliced a three–foot slit in the mesh turbidity barrier. As he slipped through the opening, he sighted a large plain of turtle grasses that wavered in the shifting torrents.

He exhaled an air bubble from his lungs then kicked downward until his chest glided along the top of the blades. As the tiny bubbles aerated from his nostrils, the telltale whip antennae of spiny lobsters began to appear from the camouflaging grasses. A quick pass over a hundred-foot stretch revealed at least two dozen specimens, a handful of them in berry. A second pass reaffirmed the findings. A third sweep of the area hardened his resolve.

Enough observational investigation. It was time for confrontation.

Jack returned to the skiff, freed the anchor then sputtered toward the break in the turbidity barrier. As he neared the cut, the warning lights of a tender began to flicker yellow then the vessel shot toward him with the speed of a marine patrol boat. As the vessel neared, it came off plane then the bow settled low in the water, revealing a hired gun with an assault rifle set across his chest.

The hired gun squared his shoulders. "Hold your position."

Jack killed his engine then stood up in his unstable craft. An assault rifle? That certainly seemed like overkill. "I need to speak with whoever's in charge out here."

"State your business."

"This area is crawling with lobsters."

"Not for long, sir."

"I need to speak with a supervisor."

The armed man turned toward his cohort then back to Jack. "Nobody without the proper credentials is allowed beyond the barrier."

"Fuck credentials. I'm a Monroe County resident."

"Do you have a site pass?"

"Who's the project manager out here?"

"Turn your craft around, sir. This is a private enterprise."

"Private?" Jack's mustache curled over, tickling his lower lip like a whisk. "It's the middle of the goddamn bay."

"Turn your craft around, sir. This is my last request."

"Or what?"

The hired gun sighted his assault rifle then popped off two quick shots just off the skiff's bow. Instinctively, Jack slumped back into the seat. Had that really happened? Had the hothead just discharged two warning shots in broad daylight?

"Next one's in the engine."

"Are you out of your mind?"

"Last warning."

Jack nodded, understanding on some level this hired gun had been paid to protect his border and leave the heavy thinking for the higher-ups. He was doing his job, purely on instruction. No amount of reason would soften that resolve.

It was time to drop back and regroup, see what he could dig up on dry land. He set the choke, about to fire the engine, but the billowing of a maritime air horn stalled his action. He turned, and, as the horn sounded again, he clamped his fingers around the gunwales and held tight as a giant wake rolled through. The approaching vessel was the size of an iceberg with a high-set wheelhouse and a massive dispersing boom fitted on the foredeck like an oversized tank muzzle. The name *Bogart* was painted across the transom.

Once the boat breached the perimeter of the turbidity barrier, its bow thrusters began to whir and boil guiding the vessel into position.

An alarm suddenly screamed out with the intensity of an air-raid horn, and the massive dredger swung its boom across the bow. Below deck, some unseen mechanical grumblings belched from deep within the ship.

A man clad in a yellow jumpsuit materialized at the edge of a nearby stationary barge. He carried a bullhorn. After a few squawks and some indiscernible barking into the amplified mouthpiece, a sandy mist began to dispense from the boom. At first it coughed in fits and spurts, but soon the aperture achieved a full stream of sediment that rainbowed out and thundered into the bay with the intensity of trampling wildebeests.

Jack settled back against the warm outboard cowling.

So this was it: beach nourishment in action. From what he had read, the developers would use this technique to redistribute 17 million cubic yards of sand from an intertidal area of the Atlantic Ocean—the offshore borrow area—into the Cotton Key Basin. This ship merely marked the beginning of hundreds of deliveries continuing for months until the engineers, assisted by GPS triangulations and satellite imaging, achieved the perfect daiquiri-glass shape.

As the sand continued to rainbow down, Jack toweled off his mustache, the sun warm against his cheeks, his shorts dripping a steady cadence of droplets onto the aluminum hull below.

Perplexing. That was the consensus in his head.

Even to his untrained eye, the basin was clearly a lobster habitat. And, judging by the impregnated specimens, the tract was likely a breeding ground for the species. Any halfwit with a snorkel and mask would've reached that conclusion.

So how then had the development made it through permitting? Or rather, who had allowed it to be pushed through? Jack considered the two dead developers. Maybe somebody else out there had already begun to put up an offensive against the intrusive project.

He gave the outboard cord a half-dozen hard pulls before it sputtered to life. Then he glanced back at the construction zone one final time, at its esoteric and profound absurdity.

Welcome to the Sunshine State.

Utopia. Incorporated.

CHAPTER 6

JACK AND RAY stood dockside chatting as the kid puttered about the Moppie plucking empty beer cans and bottles to sell to the local recycle center.

"You got servants now, Jack?"

"Someone's got to keep the kid in weed." Jack stepped to the rail. "The gun. The uniform. The badge. Why are you here, Ray? Am I in trouble again?"

"I wanted to come clean about what Jimenez has on me."

The kid paused his operation, glanced their way then Jack motioned for him to mind his own business.

"Well?" Jack asked.

"BUI."

Jack chuckled. "Give me a break, Ray. Ninety percent of the boaters on these waters are well beyond the legal limit."

Ray shrugged. "It was after a dinner party over at McCarty's place. I'd had a bottle or two of wine when I left their dock in my dinghy. I'm idling home when Officer Callahan comes out of nowhere and lights me up."

"That ferret." Jack shook his head. "That's not even a half-mile to your house."

"I know." Ray glanced at the kid then back to Jack. "So Ossie gives me the field breathalyzer, the touch-your-nose test, the whole nine yards. Then he gets on the horn. My guess is with Jimenez. The next thing you know he's telling me he'll keep the whole thing hush-hush if I sign a plea of guilty affidavit."

"Who gives a rip about a BUI?"

"Civilian like you wouldn't. But me, it's a fireable offense if they decide to use it. No more pension. No more insurance. You get the picture."

Jack nodded. "Guy like you with such few skills and unpolished bedside manner might have a hard time landing a new gig in a place as quaint as Islamorada."

"You joke, but truth be told, it's always been a tough market for a below-average high school graduate with a background in smoking weed."

"So you think it was a setup?"

"I know it was. That's how Jimenez operates. Sneaky bastard was stockpiling for a rainy day."

"Things haven't exactly been sunny around here either."

"What's that supposed to mean?"

Jack informed Ray of his late-night intruder and his visit to the Coconut Key construction site.

"Sounds like you've been busy."

The kid rattled his half-full garbage bag and drew a hand across his forehead. "You want to pay me to scrub down the boat, Jack?"

Jack glanced around. "She looks fine to me."

"How about the brightwork?"

"You really want to earn a couple extra bucks?"

"Always." The kid flipped his hair out of his eyes.

"See those parking lot lights." Jack pointed in the general direction of his old local haunt, the Damp Tortuga, flanking one side of the property. Recently revamped into Tipsy's, the new proprietors had installed stadium bulbs throughout the parking lot, for safety measures, causing a light pollution around the marina that nearly evaporated the stars. "Figure out a way to dismantle those things. All seventeen of them."

Ray turned away. "Please don't include me in this conversation."

"Cover your ears for a second then, Ray."

The kid studied the lights for a moment. "How would I do that?"

"You're a truant. Be resourceful. They're worth ten bucks a pop."

"Seriously?"

Jack nodded. "That ought to score you a couple quarter bags."

"Let me see what I can do." The kid's gaze fell toward his shuffling feet then returned. "So, whatever happened to the—" His eyes widened. "You know."

"Good question." Jack tapped Ray on the shoulder and drew him back into the conversation. "I took the sheriff out there the next day, and the damn guy was gone."

The kid's jaw dropped.

Ray hooked his thumbs over his utility belt. "Don't worry, Hunter. You didn't do anything wrong."

"That's right. It's not our fault some asshole stepped in the wrong pile of shit." Jack tipped his head toward the parking lot. "You just figure out a way to take care of those, and let us handle the rest."

The kid nodded then slung the garbage bag over his shoulder and ducked into the cabin to continue cleaning.

Jack glanced around the dock for prying ears then turned back to Ray. "So anything new on Biggins?"

"Nothing. Not even a clue as to his whereabouts."

"And nobody's reported him missing yet?"

Ray shook his head.

"So what do we do now?"

"Let's dig for something on Jimenez. Find out his involvement in this development. Try to cut the snake off at the head."

Jack studied Ray for a moment, wondering if Ray's motivation was guided by self-preservation. "You've got better access to the commissioner than I do, Ray. How about you dig around for some dirt on him? If you get something to work with, I'll be more than happy to see how I can use it to apply some pressure."

"Good man." Ray's eyes turned serious. "Now, there's something serious I've been meaning to ask you for a long time now."

"What's going on, Ray? What do you need to know?"

"When in the hell are you going to shave that ridiculous mustache?"

CHAPTER 7

JACK STEPPED THROUGH the aromatic archway then rapped his knuckles against the wooden slab, a bait bucket swinging from his left grip. A lonely thud resonated through the home's interior. He waited a minute then, when footfalls failed to arise, slipped a key from the upper lip of a sconce, slid it into the lock then pushed inside.

The interior was cool and quiet, except for a VHF radio squawking in some unknown room. The place was quaint, eclectic, no alcove left ungarnished without a knickknack or craft. The motif was reminiscent of things left curbside at the end of garage sales.

Jack eased into the galley kitchen.

An army of prescription bottles stood at the ready in a counter corner. He glanced at them quickly, all set label-side out—Eskalith, Topamax, and Risperdal—then snuffed out a marijuana roach left smoldering in an ashtray. Is this where we'd arrived as a civilization? Existing amid the pharmaceutical smog. A white one to sleep. A pink one to wake. A blue one to subdue during the hours between.

Jack chuckled. Cubera the sot. Cubera the drunken hypocrite.

He stepped into a back-porch laundry room then glanced through a window. And there she was, sunning topless on a chaise longue in a rectangle of sunshine, the lovely Summer Dahlia one knee up, the other down, in the ways of movie stars and call girls.

She'd known he was coming over, hadn't she? Or had she forgotten? Was her being topless by carelessness or design?

Jack pushed into the thick outside air, and she spun around, instinctively folding an arm over her naked chest. A moment later she withdrew the shielding arm then smiled, the tan lines almost imperceptible from the swath of body usually left to the imagination.

"Jack. What luck. You're just in time to mix me a drink."

The words arrived languidly, rolling off her rum-wet tongue like the first hours of a long weekend. Jack paused. By all appearances, today was one of the good days. A true Summer day. Had his late-night hailing worked him back into her good graces? Had she let their little misunderstanding go? Or was she simply too numb from the pills and the booze and the weed to bother remembering?

He nodded toward her bikini top draped over the back of her chair. "What's the protocol here? Should I give you a minute?"

"Seriously." Summer rattled the ice cubes in her glass. "Why don't you join me?"

"Mojitos?"

"Fresh mint and limes from my garden."

"How are they?"

"Wet."

"I see." Jack nodded slowly, finding the errant bruise that always seemed to be apparent on Summer's body. Today it was on her left inner thigh, high up toward the Sacred Valley, in the shape of a fist.

"Well?" She rattled the ice in her glass again. "Are you going to make me drink alone?"

Jack stroked his mustache. "Yes. But it's against my better judgment."

She arched her back, pushing her chest upward and out, then relaxed against the obtuse angle of the chair. "Don't be such a drag."

"I'm actually working."

"I beg your pardon."

He set the bait bucket down then moved toward a potting table littered with an assortment of fresh herbs sprouting from pint-sized clay pots. Using a mortar and pestle, he muddled two pinches of fresh mint leaves then poured four fingers of Bambu rum into a clean glass and

61

filled it with ice. He added a lime wedge and a dribble of simple sugar then handed off the fresh mojito to Summer.

She sipped then showed her teeth like a lioness. "How refreshing."

Jack smiled, his eyes pausing on the dewy beads rolling over the bruise on her inner thigh. Dark was the word that came to mind. And damp. "So are you and I . . . good?"

Summer's tongue flicked at the drink then stalled. "I'm great. Maybe even fabulous." Her tongue swirled around the straw a few times then her lips clamped over the tip.

"You know what I'm asking."

She sipped, drawing the straw up with her teeth, causing a slurping sound. "It's tough to be mad at anything at the moment." She sat forward, settled the drink on the chair between her legs then brought her shoulders forward. "So what's this about you and work? I thought the two were mutually exclusive."

Jack stroked his chin. "Are you familiar with a woman named Blanch Theroux?"

Summer withdrew her sunglasses then bit down on a stem. "Don't you dare tell me that you and her are—" Her brows went up.

"Of course not. I've been chaste since we—" Jack offered a mournful glance. "Well, you know."

"Sure you have. And I've been sober." Summer slipped the sunglasses back over her eyes.

"She's hired me to find out if her lover's been cheating on her with another woman."

"Jesus, Jack. A case? What were you thinking?"

"It's a job. A revenue stream. I thought you'd be happy I took the initiative."

"I am happy you took the initiative. I just thought you were done with that line of work."

Jack eased toward her. "I wanted to be done. I really did. But this case came pounding on my door."

"You know that Blanch woman's sleeping with Ross."

Jack sucked air between his teeth. "Well, she was."

"Where are you going with this, Jack?"

"I need you to tell me how Coconut Key scored their permits."

"That's easy." She bit down on the tip of the straw and spoke through clenched teeth. "Shady politics."

"I'm talking about from your boys over at SunState. Who did they lean on to get what they needed?"

"They're not my boys." Summer rocked her head back against the lounger. She was employed by SunState Entitlements, Inc., an infamous gaggle of engineers, landscape architects, attorneys, ex-public officials and professional chin-waggers whose primary purpose was to secure land entitlements for large investment groups and master developers interested in quick land flips with huge upsides. "And they don't exactly give me those details."

"Who were they up against?"

"Bluewater was the main obstacle."

"The activist group?"

She nodded. "Bluewater not only filed a petition against the development, they also hired an independent firm from Rosenstiel to survey the basin."

Jack raked his fingers through his mustache. She was referring to the Rosenstiel School of Marine & Atmospheric Science out of Miami. "And?"

"Their findings were exactly as you'd expect. Moving forward with the Coconut Key development would seriously compromise the ecosystem. But it didn't matter. In fact, it wouldn't have mattered what anyone did. The report was quashed and the petition completely ignored."

"So Bluewater just folded?"

"Rumor around our office was that several over at their shop received threatening calls and anonymous letters suggesting they leave this one alone. They're a peaceful bunch, Jack. Kumbaya and all that shit."

"I just can't believe you're employed by these assholes."

"The last thing I need is you making me feel any lousier about this than I already do."

"Don't you care what happens to our waters?"

She bunched her long blond tresses atop her head. "Of course I care. I'm just a little high right now."

"And a little drunk?"

"More than a little drunk." She released a cascade of salty blond locks. "But don't worry, Jack. After you stopped by the other night, my wheels began to spin. I'm doing some digging on my own. Freelancing."

Jack's forehead wrinkled. He adored her mischievous and devilish bent, but the last thing he needed was something new to worry about. "That might not be such a good idea."

"Unfortunately for you, you lost the right to say those things to me about three weeks ago." Summer fished the lime wedge from her rum then squeezed the rind, dribbling the citrus into her glass. "So are you going to tell me what happened to your hand?"

Jack turned his wounded mitt over then curled open his fingers. The swelling had gone down considerably, but two whipping blisters now shown as a rudimentary X across his palm. "Drinking accident."

Her eyebrows arched beyond the radius of her sunglasses. "And here I thought you were a professional."

"I have a near-death experience, and you're poking fun?" Jack picked up the bait bucket then plunked it next to her chair. The mass had soured and shriveled.

"Smells horrible." Summer peeled off her sunglasses then glanced into the bucket. "Flowers would've been a much nicer touch."

"I just thought with your background, you might be able to identify it."

She glanced into the bucket again, her nose wrinkling. "It was dead when you touched it, right?"

Jack nodded. "Floating in a cooler."

She reached toward Jack. "Let me see your hand." She took his hand and rolled it palm-side up. "You said you almost died?"

As Jack nodded, Summer let his hand go then waved the bucket away. "I hate to spoil a good near-death experience, but you had about as much chance of dying from that sting as you do settling down with a nice woman." She grinned. "If it was alive, maybe. But dead. Not a chance."

He shoved his hand in her general direction. "Would you look at this?"

"Now, now. Don't pout. That's what those of us in the business refer to as a little booboo." She giggled and set her sunglasses back over her eyes.

Jack scratched his chin. If that were true, then somebody had left the jellyfish as a warning, not a murder attempt. Of course. It made perfect sense. A murderer wouldn't have left a follow-up note either. "Some guy left that thing in my beer cooler for a reason."

"With your history, I wouldn't be so sure it was a guy."

"I can't believe you're being so flippant."

She came forward in her chair. "Don't be so sensitive."

"Can't you take anything seriously right now?"

Jack gnawed at his lower lip as Summer pulled the sunglasses from her eyes. A soft sadness had washed over them. "Oh, Jack. I didn't mean to be . . . I thought you were . . . I didn't realize you were being serious." She pushed up from her chair and set a single hand on one of his shoulders. "Sit tight. Give me just a second."

She hustled across the yard and through the glass slider then returned with a large mixing bowl of vinegar and a sponge. She told Jack to sit, and he squatted on the end of the lounger. She sat next to him, set the bowl between her feet then dunked the sponge and began to work it over the blistery burns on his hand.

"This should help draw out any residual poison." She held his hand in one of her own and dragged the natural sponge across his palm, lightly squeezing as she went to release the juices onto his skin. "Does that feel good?"

Jack nodded, studying the back of Summer's hand as it worked. It was a beautiful thing built of slender fingers, ocean-polished nails and veins slightly too prominent for someone her age. He wondered where the hands had come from, about her childhood, about those things she refused to discuss.

"Tell me something about you that I don't know, Jack."

"What would you like to know?"

"Tell me about your parents."

"My mom died during childbirth, and my old man had a heart that knew how to love but did not know how to like."

She drew the sponge between his second and third fingers. "Was it a good childhood or a bad one?"

"It was colorful."

"How so?"

"Like a Ralf Steadman original."

Summer sank the sponge into the vinegar, wrung it out then began working over Jack's forearm. "Does it still hurt?"

Jack shrugged and rolled his arm. "Any idea what did this to me?"

She nodded toward the bucket. "That's a sea wasp. Commonly called a box jellyfish." She stroked the sponge down his arm.

"Impressive."

She smiled. "You learn a little something smoking weed with a bunch of marine biologists even if you don't have the degree."

"How common are they in the Keys?"

"Stoned marine biologists? Hundreds. Maybe thousands."

Jack offered a wry smile then stood and planted his hands on his hips. "I suppose you don't pick these things up at the local pet store."

"Afraid not. Whoever did this to you went through a lot of trouble to get their hands on it."

"How so?"

"The commercial shrimpers get them tangled in their trawls then sell them off to pharma companies for anti-venom research. They have to pass through the FWC before they go to market."

The Florida Fish and Wildlife Conservation Commission? Could Ossie have slipped the thing into Jack's cooler? More importantly, was Ossie somehow connected to Ross's death? "You ever run into Officer Callahan these days?"

She tossed the sponge into the vinegar bath. "That prick's the reason I left the commission."

Jack turned back to her. "I thought they let you go."

"Well, technically, I suppose."

"Would Ossie have access to those jellyfish?"

She nodded. "You might also be interested to know the FWC oversees marine sanctuary for the State of Florida."

"Meaning?"

"Meaning they have some serious input into what does and doesn't get built on and around these waters."

"You ever find anything weird tying Commissioner Jimenez to the project?"

"Plenty tying him to it. But just the usual governmental involvement. All legal. Nothing out of the ordinary."

Jack stepped through the small yard overrun with marigolds toward a brackish canal the color of Asian tea. A seawall, toppled into an unnatural riprap, spilling down the embankment and into the water. Down an intersecting canal, tucked just beyond the bow of a glossy motor yacht, a sketchy dude hand-lined from a canoe. "What exactly are you digging around for, Summer?"

She sauntered up to Jack's side and hooked a hand around one of his biceps. "Give me a little time to see if anything pans out."

Jack nodded toward the canoer. "You realize the guy is perving out on your tits right now."

"Jack, the protector." Summer stroked her fingers down his forearm then moved away and began strapping her bikini top over her breasts. "Seems like he might be the only one who really appreciates them anymore."

Jack turned toward her, his eyes sweeping over her entirety, over her freckled chest, over her tender skin glistening with perspiration. She was as young as the tight curves of her body but as old as her past. He only wished he'd met her before that past had aged her, before her curves had been cornered, back when her chicanes remained as pure as the unknown road ahead. He moved to her, pulled her close and traced his fingers along her nape.

She slipped out a quiet giggle before shrugging her shoulders. "That tickles."

"Maybe we should go inside and—"

"Do you really think I'm falling for this?"

"You're a complex woman, and you understand that life can be complex."

"Stop it, Jack."

"But you also know life has its simple moments. This could be one of those simple moments."

She hitched her arms around his waist and pulled close "There are no simple moments, Jack. Not for me."

Jack cradled a hand in each cheek, and her body rose onto tiptoes, her wet lips and sour-sweet scent as ripe and warm as the subtropical sunshine falling around. Their lips met for a moment then parted, a warm breath slipping between them.

"Maybe another day then?"

"Maybe another day."

CHAPTER 8

THE *FRIGATEABOUTIT* WAS anchored in the weedy bottom a quarter mile outside the Coconut Key turbidity barrier with Big Swinging Richard's *Island Time* blaring over the speakers.

"What is that thing, boss?" Chewy was lounging on the bulkhead bench, rolling a cigar nub in his lips. "Some kind of fruit juicer?"

Mookie perched behind a gas-powered blender mounted in a fishing rod holder. "Yeah. It's called a Daiquiri Whacker." Sprouting from each side of a pitcher was a small set of handlebars fitted with rubbery grips, each with an iridescent tuft of tinseled tassels, like garnishment on a young girl's tricycle.

Mookie poured eight ounces of dark rum into the ice-filled pitcher as Johnny Bagels came wandering out of the salon sporting a black polyester track suit with white stripes down the legs. He carried a small tweed briefcase.

Chewy snorted. "What's with the briefcase? You get a corporate gig or something?"

"Zip it, wiseass. Before I stitch your lips shut."

"Calm down, you two." Mookie looked to Johnny. "You got the thing in there?"

Johnny hefted the briefcase up and down. "Yeah, boss. I got the thing."

"Don't let that briefcase out of your sights." Mookie dumped a half can of liquid coconut mix into the blender, added two more handfuls of ice then yanked the pull cord. As the blender whinnied to life, he revved the throttle causing the pistons to scream like a flock of seagulls being inhaled through a 747 engine. After thirty seconds of the caterwauling combustion, he slacked the throttle, killed the engine and poured up three coconut daiquiris.

"Here." He handed one drink to Chewy, one to Bagels then swung his gaze toward the fleet of vessels diligently working to bring Coconut Key above the waterline.

"Thing of beauty knowing this is finally happening." He hoisted his glass in a toast. "To health and prosperity."

Chewy let out a long sigh. "Tough to toast with two of us dead in three weeks."

"Try to look at the bright side." Mookie stirred his frozen concoction with an index finger. "We each get a healthier split of the proceeds when they finally start rolling in."

"Come on, Mook. The bodies aren't even cold yet."

Johnny pressed the cool drink glass to his cheek. "Not in this sweltering heat."

Mookie licked his finger clean as Chewy pointed his frozen cocktail toward a speck emerging on the horizon. "There's your ride, Bagels."

Johnny slipped a handkerchief from his pocket then mopped it along his forehead as a sputtering engine noise reached the Viking, the plump physique of an Antilles Super Goose floatplane taking shape on the bright horizon. The peculiar aircraft sported twin turbine engines set high like bug eyes over a big-bellied fuselage that resembled a winged whale. The craft approached from the ocean-side, twenty feet off the deck then, a half-mile out, sank down onto the calm seas splashing a foamy wake out to each side before settling into a slow swim. Three minutes later, the aircraft idled up to the Viking and a side access door swung open.

The pilot poked his head out under the slowing portside tri-blade propeller. He looked like a war-torn Kurt Vonnegut, introducing himself as Chopper with a voice as raspy as work boots on gravel. Then he tossed a line toward Chewy who snatched it and held tight, keeping the two crafts from drifting apart.

Johnny shrugged. "A boat with wings. Whoever saw such a thing?"

"I hope you packed some clean jockeys," Chewy said.

"Why I should fly with a guy named after a motorcycle?"

"You're in good hands," Chopper said. "I've done this at least three or four times."

"You best be joking, chucklehead."

Mookie put a hand on Johnny's shoulder. "Calm down now, Bagels." Mookie turned to Chopper. "Johnny here ain't too keen on flying."

Chopper rung his hands. "You're Bagels? Johnny Bagels?"

Johnny eased onto the swim platform.

"Sorry, Mr. Bagels. Just trying to keep things light. I didn't mean to—"

Mookie gave them a big wave as they boarded the aircraft. "Do me a favor, Bagels. Don't crack any skulls while you're gone. Your own skull included."

CHAPTER 9

JACK AWOKE EARLY then puttered his Carolina Skiff through Snake Creek, hugging the shoreline. On the boat deck next to his feet sat a six pack of pilsners and a cast net in case anyone stopped to question his intentions.

No sir, officer. Not up to anything suspect. Just out netting goggle eye and ballyhoo for bait. Heard the dolphin bite turned red hot in the past couple days. Hoping to get in on the action . . .

For the better part of an hour, Jack combed a series of canals on the southwest end of Plantation Key, searching, hunting, slowly trolling up and down the stagnant waterways. Then he cornered down a secondary canal, his linen overshirt blowing open and revealing a leather holster plugged with his snub-nosed .38 Ruger. He tugged the shirt back into place then fastened two buttons to keep it from blowing open again. Today was one of those occasions where the piece might serve as more than a prop.

As he puttered down the canal, his eyes combed the shorelines. The neighborhood was a tactless development wrought with enough architectural variety to baffle any zoning board.

Baroque. Modern. Mediterranean. Victorian.

Here and there even an old, squat Florida joint of cinderblock and gravel roof remained upright, but they were few and far between. Most of these vintage classics had long since been tilled into the earth by a younger generation who'd not only inherited the real estate but also the financial means by which to raze them and erect something new.

Dock after dock, Jack pressed deeper down the canal until the house he'd been searching for finally came into view. The two-story affair was flamingo pink and etched along the hips and gables with enough icicle lights to illuminate a Caribbean runway.

Jack stalled the skiff just outside a boathouse sporting a matching paintjob. The boathouse was a tall and narrow structure with a metal roll-down door streaked with rust. The door was pulled down and latched shut, but the tide was low.

Jack surveyed the area for nosy neighbors, then, with only a single boat idling far down the canal, sank low into his skiff and glided it under the doorway into the musty boathouse interior.

As his eyes adjusted to the dim room, exposed studs and a crisscrossing of overhead rafters took shape. Dominating the space was a sling-style hoist large enough to cradle a thirty-foot vessel with a T-top.

At the moment, it was empty.

A wooden gangway ran along three sides of the perimeter providing easy on-off access from a boat deck. But now, at low tide, it was a two-foot step-up for Jack as he clamored from the skiff onto the dock.

Once on his feet, he hustled toward a workbench and began to scavenge. The thing was littered with scuba equipment, impellers, spare bilge pumps, fuses, a polished-off quart of cheap rum.

On the floor next to the bench was a mesh dive bag. He squeaked the metal lip open. A pair of waterproof gloves and a tickle stick nestled inside. Next to the bag was a Hawaiian sling. While all could be implements utilized in harvesting exotic jellyfish, they were also standard-issue equipment for anyone living in the Keys.

He moved on, prying open the lid on a crusty tackle box that didn't appear to have seen daylight for the better part of a decade. Inside, an inventory of swivels and snaps, lead sinkers and various bucktail jigs cuddled together in a crunchy white corrosion.

He clapped the lid shut then abandoned the workbench, about to head to the main house to jimmy a window, when something winking up through the water caught his attention. He knelt for a closer view then followed a length of cord that ran into the water toward a baitfish cage settled on the bottom. At a glimpse, the cage seemed to be brimming with a variety of gelatinous specimens the same color and consistency of jellyfish.

Jack slipped on a pair of fishing gloves to avoid further tentacle stings, then hauled on the rope, working the cage through the water until it broke the surface. As water poured out the mesh enclosure, he hauled it onto the deck. Green algae coated the wiry contraption. A salt-encrusted bungee cord held the trap shut.

He unbound the cord, flipped open the lid and peered inside.

At first, the cage appeared to teem with jellyfish, dozens of them, ranging in size from large tomatoes to small cantaloupes. But, as he continued to survey the contents, something struck him as odd. Were his eyes playing tricks? With a closer examination, each specimen appeared to bear its own individual manmade marking—a logo or trademark of some sort.

He tipped the cage onto its side and shook, dislodging three of the orbs, which rolled onto the deck at his feet. There were no tentacles to speak of.

Still cautious, he poked one with a gloved finger. It was taut, its thick membrane filled near-capacity with some translucent liquid. He rolled it over, and a faint holographic marking came into focus. It bore the name *Europrotex*. He checked another: *Sientra*. Then the third: *Allergan*.

That name he recognized as a medical device manufacturer. He handled the orb and gave it a supple squeeze. Despite a lack of reference to the physical sensation, years of passive research had honed a precise eye in regard to shape and size. No doubt these were all breast implant devices, each encased in its own specific elastomeric material and each bearing its manufacturer's logo.

He tossed the Allergan sample back onto the deck then glanced into the cage. There must've been fifteen or twenty different prostheses, each from differing manufactures, all varying slightly in consistency, color and shape.

Jack stood, scratching his head. What did this mean? What could possibly explain this? Had he just stumbled upon some bizarre sexual fetish? Oscar Callahan was a strange bird, but what possible joy could be satisfied from soaking breast implants in a bait cage? Surely, something more substantial was at play here than mere sexual perversion.

Jack returned the implants to the cage then splashed it back into the water. As it settled onto the mucky bottom, he moved to the workbench and dug a hammer and chisel from a rusty toolbox. With a solid whack of the hammer, he fractured a rusted lock securing the latch on a dock box. The lock split into three separate pieces then plunked into the canal.

He hauled open the lid.

Aside from a quart of boat soap and a marine battery charger, there was an assortment of reading material ranging from spiral-bound collections on outboard engine repair to stacks of legal notebooks of indeterminate subject. One professionally bound book on exotic fish species caught his attention.

He pulled it from the dock box then fluttered the pages. They were crisp, sharp-edged. Nothing dog-eared. It didn't appear to have ever been cracked open.

He set it back into place then hauled out the stack of legal notebooks. Bellying up to the workbench, he riffled through the stack then bent back a notebook cover labeled *Stillwater Dock*. The pages consisted of handwritten notes, various geometry equations and ultimately a dollar amount. He checked the next notebook: *Rosewood Bight*. The next: *Underhill Canal*. The next: *Smathers Beach Restoration*. Each notebook contained bidding notes, mathematical calculations and pricing for local dredging projects. Near the bottom of the stack was one labeled *CK Project*.

Coconut Key.

Did Ossie have a stake in the development?

Jack slipped the notebook from the pile then paused, held his breath, tilted an ear. A faint hum vibrated the air. Was a boat approaching? He listened for another minute, but the noise diminished so he returned his attention to the CK notebook.

The cover was swollen from getting wet then drying out. He fluttered open the now-crunchy pages, the majority of which contained complex notations and calculations for quantifying and pricing the redistribution of sand from a donor area to the recipient site in Cotton Key Basin. Toward the back of the notebook, two loose pages and a manila envelope were tucked inside. One was a schematic of a suction hopper dredger identified as a 327-foot Wuhan Pan-Asia. A few specifications, like *3D video monitoring*, *complex hydrographics* and *precision farming* were highlighted in yellow marker. The other loose page appeared to be the typed formal bid numbers for the Coconut Key project, spelling out the scope of work in a legal tenor then emphasizing the bid was good for a period of ninety days. Another line item stated that all environmental permitting and permissions was to be handled by others. A man named Gus Callahan had signed off on the document. Ossie's brother? Father? An uncle? Under that, a handwritten scribble etched the words *PAY THE BILLS*.

Jack canted his head as the noise of an approaching vessel revved higher then died out, the boat seeming to have paused at a dock several addresses down.

He turned back and slid a half-dozen documents from the manila envelope. They were official-looking, decorated with authoritative seals and stamps and chock full of governmental jargon and legalese. Words like *ROGO* and *Growth Management Act* and *Landward Limit of Jurisdiction* leaped from the script. He rifled through them, noting letterheads like the Bureau of Survey and Mapping and the FDEP. One section of pages appeared embossed with the letters *EPA* although deciphering them in the dim light proved difficult.

Jack shuffled into a dusty infusion of sunshine breaking through a louvered gable to get a better set of eyes on the documents. Across the header of one document the words Prostheses Testing caught his attention.

He previewed the page of data and started to make some sense of a cross-reference chart which fell below the header, but as he pressed the pages toward the brightness, the indistinguishable drone of a four-stroke engine reverberated through the clapboard siding and stalled his progress.

A boat closed in.

As he stuffed the Prostheses Testing document into his waistband, a vessel bumped along the seawall just outside. The boathouse shuddered. Next came a voice in the one-sided conversation of a cell phone call.

Jack flashed his eyes about the space. Short of submerging into the water, there was little in the way of a blind.

He tossed the remaining documents onto the workbench then scurried around the gangway to the skiff as the boathouse door eased open casting a narrow wedge of light into the musty space.

Quickly, he dropped onto his belly then, using his bare toes, pulled the skiff alongside the gangway. As the door inched farther open, he eased down into the skiff then scrunched into a supine position between the bench and the tiller.

He was low on the water now. Working hand-over-hand along the deck stringers, he slipped the skiff between two pilings and glided under the slimy dark shelter of the decking.

The boathouse door groaned fully open.

Verticals of light broke through the intermittent gaps in the planks as he eyed upward through one break, the back of his shirt saturating with a cocktail of saltwater and motor oil slopping around the bilge.

Above him, footfalls boomed into the space and resounded through the slimy undersides of the planks just inches from his nose. Mold spores and dust mites rained down and drifted into his nostrils.

He set a hand across his chest and found the rigid line of the pistol butt as the subject passed directly overhead. From his weird positioning in the boat, accessing the Ruger would be difficult. Quick access was out of the question.

As the footfalls softened, the subject's voice rang out again. Jack adjusted his angle of vision enough to glimpse the whiskered rodent-like profile of Oscar Callahan. Ossie remained engaged in the cell phone conversation, his nose twitching and his free hand fidgeting at his State-commissioned Glock, as he made his way around the room.

"Like I said, she's getting things ready right now."

There was a short silence before Ossie spoke again. "How about you? You ready to roll?"

Jack held his breath as Ossie came back into partial view with dark circles ringing the armpits of his ratty uniform. He paused at the dock box, his fingers tapping on the now-lockless latch.

"You sure nobody else knows?"

Ossie studied the opened lid then began to glance around the boathouse, his eyes chattering each corner of the space.

"Good to hear. I still don't know the exact day yet. Should be within the next few weeks. Just be ready when I give the word."

Ossie's eyes settled in the direction of the workbench then he scurried toward it, out of Jack's view.

"What the—? Sonofabitch. I've got to go. I'll call you later."

As the phone snapped shut, Jack wriggled his hand under his shirt and unsnapped the holster strap. A moment later Ossie reappeared with the misplaced notebooks tucked under his arm. He slammed the lid on the dock box then appeared to discover the hammer and chisel resting on the dock next to his feet.

He kicked at them, the chisel plunking into the water, then crossed the decking again, this time pausing directly over Jack, the black work boots a mere eight inches from Jack's nose. A beige etching of fresh dog shit compressed into the treads on the left sole.

Jack wriggled the pistol from his holster then aimed the barrel upward toward Ossie's feet.

Time passed like molasses through a colander.

One wrong move, one bump on the planks, and Ossie would surely find Jack's bulging eye-whites staring up through the slats.

Ossie set his hand on his Glock then unsnapped the strap. Grunting, sniffing the air, he worked the room like a K9 dog. From Jack's angle, the officer seemed to study each vertical stud, each run of corroding Romex, each nail head, until he'd conducted a visual sweep of the entire boathouse.

As Jack fought to control his breathing, Ossie's cell phone rang out again then he slapped it to his ear. "About goddamn time you called me back." There was some indiscernible quibbling, then the door flung wide open, crashing into the wall and further illuminating the space. Then just as quickly as the new light arrived, it vanished as the door slammed back into its jamb.

CHAPTER 10

THE ANTILLES SUPER Goose banked hard over the Gulf of Darién then nosed toward the shoreline where the ocean lapped at the ragged jungle along the remote *Córdoba region.*

Johnny Bagels slid open a window shade, discovering a runway, a mere strip of dirty earth cut in the dense foliage. He drew the handkerchief over his shiny cheeks as the plane sank toward the earth. He felt like some Third-World revolutionary being smuggled into Central America to assassinate rogue guerillas.

Moments later, the airplane wheels bounced along the dirt and rubble before the loud scream of reverse thrust slowed the craft to the end of the strip.

"Pura vida," Chopper barked over the radio.

Johnny, tweed briefcase in hand, followed Chopper out the door and onto terra firma where two paramilitants sporting dark skin and faces wrapped in scarves greeted them with matching Israeli submachine guns.

"Nice guns. Them's good for killing." Johnny offered a bone-crunching handshake to each man then handed them a roll of American hundred dollar bills.

The paramilitants nodded and pointed toward a hidden trailhead, then Johnny and Chopper ducked under a fruitbread limb and started down the secret path.

Johnny swatted at his neck the entire way. "You wasn't kidding about the mosquitoes."

After a couple hundred yards of muddy pathway, the four arrived at a soggy embankment on the periphery of a labyrinth of rivers and watery canals constituting a mangrove swamp. Chopper waved Johnny over as a flat-back canoe came gliding up under the rattle of two-stroke outboard.

"Rafael?" Chopper asked the captain.

The captain nodded.

Johnny curled his fingers around the briefcase handle. "Take us to Chupacabra."

Chopper set a hand on Johnny's shoulder. "Not us, just you."

"What?" Johnny narrowed his eyes. "You best not be setting me up for something."

"This is as far as they let me go."

Johnny tipped his head sideways at Rafael. "What about this guy?"

"Don't worry. Your reputation precedes you down here. Besides, they all know who you work for."

"These guys know Mookie?"

Chopper shook his head. "They all know the *big boss*."

Rafael motioned for Johnny to board the canoe then helped him onto the forward bench seat. Johnny settled in then set the tweed briefcase onto the deck between his Adidas sandals.

Chopper gave him a lazy salute. "See you in a few hours. Try not to dump the boat."

"Real funny, chucklehead." Johnny peeled off his tracksuit top and flopped it over his shoulder, his thick biceps and deltoids on full display through the armholes of the wife-beater tank top.

Moments later the canoe departed the mucky bank in a din of engine noise, and the vessel slipped along the black waters, cornering left then right into intertwining canals, each one growing narrower and less identifiable the deeper they pushed into the swamp.

Johnny clamped his fingers around the briefcase handle as he soaked in the scene. He was not a fan. Too much uncertainty. Too many things he couldn't identify and understand. Back home, in the concrete jungle of South Jersey, a man looked at him the wrong way, the schmuck got his fingernails removed with a pair of vice grips. Maybe a ballpeen hammer to the Adam's apple for good measure. But he'd never been in a real jungle before. Nothing rang familiar. Not by a long shot. South Jersey, for instance, did not cater to spiders the size of starfish and lizards the size of inner-city sewer rats. Nor was his hometown habitat common to the boa constrictors certainly slithering around every nearby branch. The size of the fruit sagging on the limbs alone proved that the creatures inhabiting the biome were large, aggressive and menacing.

Each caterwauling howl and screeching cry that erupted from the dense overhead canopy nearly sent him careening onto the boat deck. But he fought the urge and kept still as death. He had a reputation to protect. Besides, the only circumstance worse than being attacked by a rabid baboon or a Kamikaze toucan involved tipping the canoe and winding up in that black water. His brain could not fathom what sort of reptilian monsters and ravenous fish inhabited such a sinister place.

Johnny wiped his forehead with a tracksuit sleeve. "We getting close?"

"Right there." Rafael pointed toward a draping branch.

"Right where?"

Johnny looked around as the canoe slowed to a crawl then nudged up to a wall of vegetation dominated by a winding branch that grew just two feet off the water. A tribe of inch-long ants marched across the bough with severed leaf parts the size of sandwich lettuce clamped in their pinchers.

Rafael tapped Johnny on the shoulder. "Lift up that branch up so we can scoot underneath it."

Johnny's eyes widened.

"Go on. Before that coral snake drops into the boat."

Snake! Johnny hadn't noticed a snake. But surely he'd rather endure a nasty pimple bite from an oversized carpenter ant than anything that had evolved beyond the need for legs. He planted both hands on the underside of the branch then curled it upward. Surprisingly, it moved almost effortlessly, and the ants seemed oblivious to the action. As the canoe coasted under, Johnny passed the branch back to Rafael who in turn lifted it up and over then slid underneath.

Once free from the branch, Johnny turned back toward the bow. Instantly his mouth went agape, nearly inhaling a gnat swarm buzzing in front of his face.

Was he hallucinating?

An entire clandestine community rose up from a malaria-infested sanctuary amid a delta of sawgrass, palmettos and mosquitoes. No less than eighty workers and militants buzzed about.

As the canoe coasted up to the shoreline, the entire crowd hushed then began pointing and muttering amongst themselves.

"What are they whispering about?"

"You're somewhat of a celebrity around here."

"That right?"

"Particularly to Chucho."

"He the one in charge?"

Rafael nodded. "El Jefe."

Rafael secured the vessel, then the two dismounted onto the first in a series of wooden planks which formed a rudimentary infrastructure of stable walkways above the mushy swampland.

A short mocha-skinned man sporting a sleeveless camouflaged shirt and a scraggly salt and pepper beard hustled over and poked his hand toward Johnny. He couldn't have been more than four-foot six. "Bienvenido. Welcome to my camp."

Johnny nodded. "You the boss?"

"Si. Me llamo es Chucho." Chucho handed Johnny a steel box large enough to hold a coconut. "For the Mookie."

Johnny took the box. A small lock kept the hinged lid intact. "This is it?"

The host smiled, baring his golden grill of irregularly-placed teeth.

Johnny turned to Rafael. "That what I think it is?"

Rafael smiled. "They're all trophies from Chucho's enemies. He had them implanted like that just for your visit."

"Yeah? Well, ain't that something?"

"As a tribute."

"God love the sick bastard. Me, I don't even like a routine dental cleaning."

Chucho belched a hearty laugh then slapped Johnny on the back. "Jungle enferma! Comprende?"

As they started up the pathway, Johnny glanced around camp. A series of huts and tents flanked a larger compound of material goods which contained everything from giant rolls of fiberglass and Kevlar to water heaters to generators to marine batteries. Set along one open-air wall, a team of women wearing nurse scrubs and surgical masks conducted themselves like diligent factory workers processing some sort of packages. An adjacent shelter, this one with a tin roof and open sides, provided a dry area for a bank of personal computers and a number of nerdy men in white lab coats labeled *Ingeniero*.

Johnny set his tweed briefcase on the ground. He clicked open the latch then withdrew an envelope sporting a waxen seal logoed with the Salucci family crest. He passed it over to Chucho.

Chucho took the envelope between sweaty fingers. "Un momento."

Johnny stayed put as Chucho stepped over to the computer shelter and handed the envelope to one of the engineers. The engineer cracked the wax seal then slipped a piece of paper from the slit, unfolded it and nodded approvingly. He set the page down then appeared to transcribe what had been written onto the computer.

Chucho settled in behind the engineer, set his hands on the man's shoulders then began to massage his thumbs into the muscles and chortle in a low, under-the-breath way. A small bead of perspiration propagated along the engineer's upper lip as he continued to rap at the keyboard. A few keystrokes later, he flashed Chucho the thumbs-up sign.

"Muy bueno."

Chucho stepped toward a group of two dozen workers who'd congregated near the shoreline, then, in a show of festivity and flair, began a countdown from *dies*.

"Nueve."

"Ocho."

84

The remainder of the crew joined the countdown.

"Siete."

"Seis."

"Cinco."

"Cuatro."

As the men reached *cero*, the engineer stroked one more computer key then maneuvered a joystick. The dark mangrove water boiled and swirled in a manner that let Johnny know something large lurked just under the surface. Chucho yanked two submachine guns from the nearby paramilitants then, passing one off to Johnny, the two zippered off strings of ceremonial shots that peppered through the surrounding limbs until the clips ran dry.

Johnny set the machine gun against his shoulder, a twisted grin smeared across his cheeks. "Nothing but good words in my report back to the bossman. That much I can promise."

Chucho flashed his unconventional smile then turned toward camp. He raised his arms above his head and another cry rang out from the crowd. "Viva la Chupacabra!"

CHAPTER 11

JACK WALKED THE gangway, past a sea of pitted chrome and faded canvas, along a stable of chalky fiberglass and yellowing Eisenglass, by a gallery of guano-stained topsides and weathered teak, pausing at the glitter and sparkle of the *Exit Strategy.*

Blanch was not around, but a team of laborers were busy at work refitting the boat. One group, clad in hazmat suits, tended to a long translucent tube that ran from a dishwasher-sized pump staged in the parking lot, down the gangway then disappeared into the cabin. It appeared to be some sort of vacuuming system. A second group, in-water, paddled around the vessel checking the waterline with various measuring apparatuses.

Jack tapped a hazmat worker on the shoulder. "The owner around?"

Through the transparent lens of his head gear, the man muffled *no* so Jack continued. Fifty-feet down he shouldered into the Soggy Dollar Yacht Club, a windowless room with a faded sailfish mount, a microwave and a bookshelf skewed out of plumb by a healthy sampling of VHS tapes and paperback thrillers. A backroom provided two showers and three toilet stalls for transient boaters, but all was quiet now in the offseason, the snowbirds having flown their coops for cooler climes up north.

Jack tossed aside a tabloid paper and located the club phone. The hard wire job sported a pigtail cord that tethered the receiver to the base. He hoisted the thing to his ear.

Unbelievably, a dial tone beckoned.

He tapped out the ten-digit number then waited for the soft tenor of the lovely Summer Dahlia. She answered with a lissome voice.

"Hey," Jack said. "It's me."

"Who's me?"

"Cubera."

"Oh. Jack. I don't think I've ever heard your voice on a phone before. Are you in jail again?"

"Listen, I need a favor."

"I'm working."

"It's about Coconut Key."

"Jesus, Jack. You're calling me about this at work?"

"Duck into the bathroom or something. Whatever it is you office people do for privacy."

"Hang on a minute."

Jack waited through some shuffling background noise before Summer's voice returned as a hand-cupped whisper. "What's going on?"

"I took a fieldtrip out to the Coconut Key construction site. The place is crawling with spiny lobsters. The seagrasses are filled with them. I'm pretty sure it's a lobster breeding ground."

"That Rosenstiel study drew the exact same conclusions."

"Wouldn't the EPA have to sign off on a project to destroy that kind of habitat?"

She shook her head. "But the National Oceanic and Atmospheric Administration would."

"NOAA?"

She nodded.

"Did they review the Rosenstiel study?"

She was quiet for a moment then continued in a quieter whisper. "From what I understand, the study was presented to them, but they totally disregarded it. They decided to send in two of their own *experts* to survey the basin."

"And?"

"Word is the NOAA report is fabricated. A complete fraud. Either that or the two people who conducted it are completely incompetent."

"I need you to get me a copy of it."

"I don't mind helping, Jack. But there's only so much I can do. I can't afford to lose another job."

"With coworkers like you've got, it might be the healthiest thing for you."

"If I get caught, I could get in some serious trouble. These people don't play around."

"Time to atone for your past transgressions."

She huffed. "Hang on a second."

Jack kept his ear to the phone as Summer pattered her way down some hard-surfaced hallway. There was a brief verbal exchange with a coworker, a hiss of something carbonated being cracked opened then she returned. "Hang on a second." The clacking of computer keys came over the line. "What do you want to know? I can leave out the big words if you need me to."

"You're right. Attention span like mine. Best to just stick with the bullet points. The broad-stroke stuff."

Summer mumbled a few indiscernible remarks as she scanned the document, then she cleared her throat and began to speak. "It basically says that the NOAA surveyors conducted an underwater geolocation of the Cotton Key Basin surveying for native and invasive species, coral reef health qualities and a general inventory of the submerged aquatic resources. Next, there's some talk about measuring equipment. Blah, blah, blah. Then, after their comprehensive investigation, they concluded that the area in question was . . . and I quote . . . *a veritable dead zone* and an *inconsequential contributor in the overall wellness of the ecosystem.*"

"That's bogus."

"Listen to this. They recommended that a full impact analysis of the basin was not necessary. That Coconut Key would in no way adversely affect the basin or the surrounding biome."

"I need the name of the biologist who signed off on the report?"

"There's two. A Bill Shipes and a William Crooner."

Jack dug around the club desk for a pen. "Can you tell me those names again?"

Summer repeated them as Jack jotted onto a legal pad. Once down on paper, something in their appearance—Bill and William—struck him as familiar, although he wasn't sure why. "How about a contact number?"

Summer relayed the governmental extension which Jack transcribed next to the names.

"Now my turn," Summer said.

"For what?"

"You said Blanch hired you to follow Ross."

Where was Summer going with this? "That's right."

"You'll let me know what you find out?"

Jack considered his words. "There's something you should probably know about Ross, and it's not good."

"What did you do this time, Jack?"

"He's dead."

"He's what?"

"I found him floating out near Frangipani Flats."

The line silenced.

"Summer? You still there?"

"Barely." She cleared her throat. "But nobody here at the office even—"

"It's a long story, but me, Hunter and Livingston are the only ones who know anything about it. Well, and the killer."

"What happened to him, Jack?"

"Tough to say. He was dead when I found him. It was a complete coincidence."

Summer spoke in a rapid-fire whisper. "Are you sure it was a coincidence? I mean what are the odds that you'd be the one to find him?"

"What are you talking about?"

"Think about it, Jack. Maybe somebody wanted you to find the body. Maybe somebody wanted to set you up."

"Who could've known we'd be out there fishing?"

89

"It's certainly an angle to consider."

"What exactly do you know, Summer?"

"Nothing solid yet. But I'm working on a few things."

"How about you stop by the Moppie? Let's catch up and compare notes."

"I'll have to check my schedule."

"What if I promise to serenade you with my six string?"

"You forget that I've heard you play before. Now call me if you stumble onto anything new."

The line disconnected with a sharp click. Jack thumbed the hang-up button then brought the dial tone back to life. He called the Washington D.C. number then punched in the extension. A man introducing himself as Willy answered the phone.

"William Crooner?" Jack asked.

"This is Willy. Who's this?"

"Jack Crevalle from Subtropical Fishing Charters."

"Who?"

"You'll be delighted to know that you and a Mr. Bill Shipes have just won an all-expenses-paid fishing extravaganza in the beautiful Florida Keys."

* * *

Three miles offshore, Sheriff Livingston slipped into the *FrigateAboutIt*'s fizzling wake then lit up his patrol lights. After a few seconds, one of the two plump Italians occupying the flybridge backed off the gas.

As Ray closed in, the two shuffled down the ladder to the main deck, both with tufts of curly black hair cascading over their necklines. The younger, dumpier one's name Ray couldn't place at first. Then he noticed the damp, lumpy cigar and remembered: Chewy.

The other wore a black and white fedora. This one went by Mookie.

As the Mako sidled up to the Viking, Mookie waddled over to the gunwale with arms open wide, a half-spent cigar wedged between two fat fingers. "Sheriff Livingston. To what do we owe the honor?"

"Afternoon, gentlemen. Just a routine stop." Ray belayed his boat broadside to the sportfisher. "You mind turning off the music?"

Mookie snapped his fingers at Chewy. "Show the officer a little respect."

Chewy ducked into the cabin, the music silenced, then he ambled back out. "I gotta admit this Florida hillbilly music's catchier than a case of the mumps."

Mookie extended a can of beer toward Ray.

"Still on duty." Ray slipped a toothpick between his lips.

"Sorry. I just thought with the T-shirt and all . . . What do I know? Must be casual day at the Sheriff's Office."

"All my velour jump suits are at the cleaners."

"A small crisis that happens in my neck of the woods."

As Ray shut down his outboards, the duo turned away, seemingly mesmerized by an airplane coming into focus on the horizon. It flew low on the water like a pelican, then a half-mile out the big bird sank slowly. With a fanning splash, the floatplane landed on the ocean then idled toward the Viking.

Ray blasted the horn two good belts and brought the duo reeling back around.

"Expecting company?"

Once Mookie's eyes returned to their usual orbital size, he mumbled for a moment then seemed to find his line. "Our boy Bagels back from a retreat."

"Sounds interesting."

Ray withdrew a notepad from his pocket and scribbled down the plane's tail number as it crawled their direction under the chattering propeller wash.

Ray glanced at Mookie. "They've got a real nice airstrip back in Key Largo for rich guys like you."

"Ocean's a softer landing, officer." Mookie leaned on the gunwale. "Particularly if things don't go as planned on the final approach."

At twenty yards away, the twin engines shut down leaving the threshing of the props against the wind as they slowly stalled out. The side door on the aircraft flung open as Johnny's hulking physique filled the space. He was collared in a fluorescent orange life jacket. Clutched against his chest was a package of some kind, a cubical box fastened from diamond plate sheet metal just large enough to hold a human head.

Ray sighed. Wonderful.

Something about a middle-of-the-ocean rendezvous with these characters raised questions. And why was the plane stopping short? Why not pull all the way up to the Viking to offload? Was the pilot spooked by the presence of an officer?

Johnny stepped through the airplane access door, half-slipping, half-diving, and toppled headlong into the water. He disappeared for a moment then bobbed to the top with the metal box held over his head, the lifejacket snugged tightly under his ears and chin.

By the time Johnny clambered onto the swim platform, the float-plane's engines had whirred back to life, then the craft pivoted away and quickly began to accelerate. Seconds later blue sky broke between the ocean and the aircraft belly as it lifted then banked in a southwesterly direction.

Panting heavily, Johnny stripped off the life jacket and jumpsuit top and bottoms then draped a towel around his shoulders and stood drip-drying in black boxer briefs on the deck. Ray took note of the man's natural size, particularly the wrists. Johnny's were as thick as the business ends of wooden baseball bats. According to the police file on him, they'd fattened up over his twenty-seven years from ringing necks. And breaking quite a few. And who knew what else. Rumor was he'd earned the nickname *Bagels* after building a reputation chopping off debtors' digits with a bagel slicer.

Ray glanced down at his notepad. "Just getting back from vacation?"

Johnny worked the towel over his powerful shoulders. "Don't I wish."

"Caribbean?"

"Down that way."

Ray jotted a few notes onto the page. "How about clearing immigration?"

Mookie eased toward the sheriff. "Law says he's got forty-eight hours to check in before he's in violation."

Ray glanced at Mookie. "Who's the pilot?"

"Good question. Some guy says his name's Chopper or something like that."

Ray wrote down the name. "You think you could dig up his phone number for me?"

"Met him down at the docks. Never got any digits. Some fly-by-night outfit. He wanted cash up front."

Ray nodded toward the steel box which now rested precariously on the gunwale. "That some kind of souvenir?"

Johnny paused his toweling. "You talking about the box?" He slapped the towel over his shoulder. "It's kind of private."

"Go ahead," Mookie told Johnny. "Open the thing up for the officer."

"You sure, Mook?"

"Sure I'm sure."

Reluctantly, Johnny unlocked the box then folded back the metal lid. Cradled inside the interior of dense foam was a rubbery membrane the size of a coconut filled with a gelatinous substance. Johnny hoisted the thing with two hands, like a crystal ball, then held it up to the afternoon light.

Ray wiped a sleeve across his forehead. "That what I think it is?"

Mookie stroked his fingers over the rubbery skin. "Only if you're thinking it's a giant fake titty. It's a surprise gift for my gal. She's getting some new cans for her birthday whether she likes it or not."

Johnny poked at the membrane. "Like that Blanch needs a new set of cans."

Blanch? The sheriff shifted his stance.

Mookie pinched at the elastomeric skin. "This new technology is space age stuff. I wanted to see a sample in person. Some kind of rubbery silicone feels and squeezes just like the real thing. It's even got a little Teflon added to it for extra tinsel strength."

"Seems like overkill," Chewy said.

93

"Maybe to you. But with this stuff, it don't matter how rough you want to get in the sack, if you know what I'm saying."

Mookie settled the membrane back into the box then latched the lid as the sheriff removed his sunglasses, folded in the stems then hung them on his shirt collar. "So is the Coconut Key project still on schedule?"

Mookie nodded. "Broke ground, so to speak, a few days back. Why do you ask?"

"I thought things might've gotten postponed after your buddy went missing."

The three men looked at one another. "Jimmy B?"

"Weird way to go, don't you think?"

"Death don't wait for nobody. God rest the big lug's soul."

Ray glanced around the boat looking for anything out of the ordinary. Only a scab of maroon blood on the gaff tip created the slightest stir. "So how's the fishing been lately? The wahoo running yet?"

"Wish I could say." Mookie puffed at his Cohiba. "This boat don't know nothing about fishing. Not how to catch them. Not how to clean them. Damn sure not how to cook them."

Ray removed the toothpick from his mouth. That was certainly an interesting place for blood if they hadn't been fishing. He thought about Ross. Hadn't Jack mentioned a round, elongated wound on the victim's butt cheek, the sort of wound one might sustain from being dragged by a gaff? "Hell of a fishing boat not to wet a line."

"Truth be told, the only thing this boat seems to land these days is pussycats. You know, the kind that come gift-wrapped in bikinis." Mookie tapped his cigar ash over the rail. "So, officer, what is it you're doing out here today exactly? Checking for lifejackets and flares? That sort of thing?"

"On a boat like this, I assume you're all up to snuff on your Coastguard gear. I'm more interested in things like guns and contraband."

Mookie grinned. "Guns we got, officer." He tapped at an apparent concealed weapon tucked into the meaty folds of his armpit. "But we got the permits to match. Guy's got to protect his investments, after all. But contraband. Not my thing. There may be a little residue on a few C-notes in my wallet but nothing to raise a brow."

"How about your buddy Ross? You guys seen him around in the past couple days?"

"Biggins?" Johnny asked.

Chewy pointed a spit-riddled cigar butt at Ray. "Last we heard he was headed up to Hartford to see the wife for a few. Why? He in some kind of trouble?"

"Could be."

Mookie said, "Rumor is him and the Mrs. ain't doing too good."

The sheriff looked back. "Another woman, I'm guessing."

Johnny fished a beer out of the cooler and hissed the tab open. "Probably that tramp, Blanch."

"Hey." Mookie leered at Johnny.

Johnny shrugged. "I'm just saying that broad's been passed around like a pigskin on Super Bowl Sunday."

"Be respectful of a gal," Mookie said.

"Why you getting on me?" Johnny pointed at Chewy. "You tapped that too, didn't you, Chewy? Lord knows I clanked that dinner bell a few dozen times."

Mookie glared at Johnny. "Enough."

The sheriff cleared his throat. "So when was the last time any of you saw him?"

They all looked at one another and shrugged. "Three, maybe four days ago."

"Haven't seen or heard anything from him since?"

"Like we just told you. It's been a few days." Mookie puffed at his cigar. "So officer, we satisfy this little inquisition?"

"One more thing."

"What's that?"

"You mind if I board the vessel and take a quick look around?"

Mookie tossed his cigar butt into the ocean, watched it float for a moment then looked back. "Sorry, officer. It's an insurance thing. You slip and fall or something then we got ourselves a mess to clean up. You understand."

"I'll waive my rights to sue."

"Listen, sheriff. With all due respect, your boss's boss and I had dinner and stogies just last night. That is to say we're good people. The crew and I. You can rest your pretty little head at night knowing that."

"So then you won't mind if I take a quick look around."

"I don't think you're understanding what I'm saying here, so let me do a little clarifying. We've been given the blessing by your superiors to conduct ourselves around these islands the way we see fit."

"So you're refusing to let me board your vessel?"

"Not at all, officer. I'm merely suggesting that it's a bad idea for your particular career path toward full retirement. How much time you got left in your tour? Two years and thirty-something more days, right?" Mookie turned to Chewy. "Do me a favor, Chewy. Get Jimenez on the horn. See what his take is on Officer Livingston snooping around the *FrigateAboutIt* without any probable cause."

Ray slumped back onto his leaning post then slid his sunglasses over his eyes. If Jimenez was in their pocket, these guys had some serious juice. "No need to bother the commissioner on my account. I'm sure he's got more important matters to deal with than this right now."

"No sweat, officer. Maybe we can all hang out with the commissioner at the big party this weekend."

"The what?"

"The Dixen gala. Only the most spectacular bash of the year. Word is Tiger Woods might make an appearance. You didn't get the invite?"

Ray rolled the toothpick in his lips. "Must've been a clerical oversight."

"Tough break. I'd consider letting you tag along as my plus-one, but I'm not really into brunettes. You understand."

"Where are they having that event this year, anyway?"

"At the Little Palm Island Resort. Should be a real gas."

"Sorry I'm going to miss it."

"Chin up. There's always next year."

Ray cranked the twin engines then eyed the bloody gaff tip once again. "Never boated a single fish on this vessel, you say?"

"Like I said, not a one."

Sheriff Livingston nodded as he reeved the boat line then backed away. "I hope for your sake you've had a little better luck with the pussycats."

"Ain't that the godforsaken truth."

CHAPTER 12

THREE DAYS LATER two men, fresh off a commercial 737, ambled to the curb at the Key West International Airport sporting matching Tommy Bahama camp shirts, hemmed denim shorts and dime-store sunglasses.

Jack tapped his chauffeur on the shoulder. "That's them."

The driver wheeled the stretched Denali to the curb, and Jack jumped out. He'd forgone his usual shabby attire and, for the case, worn a linen top and the sharpest khaki shorts he could find on the floor of his boat. He'd even shaved for the occasion, his cheeks not mustache. He was as groomed and kempt as any charter fisherman south of Florida City.

He sauntered up to the men and snagged their suitcases like a porter. "Gentlemen. Welcome to the Keys. You must be thirsty from the flight."

The two men nodded like eager retrievers. "Parched."

Jack motioned toward the open limo door. "Great. Climb in."

Jack stowed their luggage then slid into the rear-facing seat. As the Denali lurched from the curb, heading east, Jack tugged a bottle from an ice bucket and presented the dewy label. "Mount Gay?"

The men nodded.

Jack handed each man an ice-filled tumbler then splashed a heavy snort of spiced rum into the glasses. "Your first time fishing the Keys?"

Willy nodded. "We were down on business earlier this year. Didn't have time to do anything fun like this."

"Business? What sort of business?"

"Government work."

"Secret Service?"

They snickered. "Nothing that exciting. We're with NOAA."

Jack crinkled his brows.

"The National Oceanic and Atmospheric Organization."

He stroked his chin. "Something funny about that acronym."

"We're biologists."

"Sounds important. I guess you guys have college degrees and all that."

Willy slogged back his rum as Bill pressed his nose to the tinted glass. "Look at that water. It's so blue."

Jack smiled. "Booked you guys in an oceanfront suite at the Cheeca Lodge. Five stars all the way. Wait until you see the view. Talk about blue water. Some might say cerulean."

Willy licked a rum bead off his upper lip. "How about the fishing?"

"We'll head out first thing in the morning. Today's all about unwinding. You know. Settle in. Relax."

They crossed the bridge onto Big Coppitt Key drawing Bill's nose to the window once again. "Where's all the beaches and bikinis?"

"Not many beaches down here in the Keys. That's a big misconception. But don't worry. We've got plenty of girls in a lot less than bikinis."

An hour later, the driver nosed into Stiffy's A Go-Go at mile marker 81. The clock only read noon, but the infamous joint served an all-u-can-eat lunch buffet to prod the lagging midday business. As they shouldered into the dark, music-bumping interior, Jack noted every lineman and ditch digger within a twenty-mile radius had made the trip for the famed shrimp cocktail and ass clapping. As Jack guided the biologists to three open bar stools, a gruff radio voice broke over the sound system.

"I'd like to direct everyone's attention to center stage for a preview of today's talent."

"Just in time for roll call."

A little A-frame sign rested on the bar in front of each open stool. RESERVED FOR PRIVATE PARTY. They sat as a stream of dancers emerged through a beaded curtain and began to strut their wares along the catwalk.

"They look like this up in D.C.?"

"Not since Clinton left office."

The two men fist-bumped as a topless waitress swept in, on cue, with a tray of three tequila shots. One thing Jack had learned over the years: No Washington D.C. lackey could resist tucking dollar bills into G-strings when shitfaced on some Two Fingers Gold.

"The lovely Ms. Daisy." Jack pointed to the only shot glass not garnished with salt and lime. "This one mine?"

Daisy winked. "No training wheels for you, sweetie."

Jack took the shot as Daisy tipped her head toward his companions. "And who are these two handsome gentlemen?"

"Bill and Willy. Big shot Secret Servicemen down from D.C."

"George Senior in town on another fishing trip?"

"Not sure." Jack leaned in. "They're not allowed to talk about it."

"Certainly sounds exciting." Daisy smiled then set the two shots in front of them. "You boys get the limes."

Jack hoisted his glass. "To help with the scurvy."

The three men clinked glasses then threw back the shots, Bill and William grimacing as they rattled the empty glasses onto the bar.

"How about a couple table dances for the big shots here? They've had a long day of travel and are looking to unwind."

"We can set that up." Daisy thrust her ample chest toward the two men. "You two see anything you like?"

Bill, whose speech had already started to garble, pawed at the heels of a sleek black stripper as she strutted past him down the stage. "I like that one. How about you, Willy? You like the brown sugar?"

Willy slipped a wad of money from his pocket and eyed around the room. "I'm more of a Latino man myself."

"Shouldn't be a hard thing to round up in South Florida." Jack turned to Daisy. "Orders up."

By the time she returned with another tequila round, Bill and William had relocated, at the request of their private table dancers, to a secluded booth tucked into a dark corner. Both men had slipped their wedding rings from their fingers and now utilized those same digits to grope gratuitously at the naked breasts of their respective dancers.

When the two began simultaneously motorboating into their strippers' cleavages, Jack knew he had them right where he needed them.

He cornered Daisy. "Are you getting this?"

"Frame by frame."

"Here." Jack slipped her a piece of paper with the two biologists' email addresses.

"I'll forward it to them tonight."

"I just need it there by first light."

After an hour of private dances and tequila shots totaling over eight hundred and fifty bucks, the two NOAA workers excused themselves for a moment. Jack followed them into the bathroom, ducking into a stall, as the duo lurched up to two of the six neighboring urinals and began jabbering in excited, drunken slurs.

"Can you believe the women in this place?" Willy asked.

"They're all porn-star hot."

Jack peeked over the stall divider, watched, and waited.

A moment passed, as they relieved themselves through half-engorged members, before the pair of dancers whom they'd just been openly fondling lumbered up to the two open urinals on each side. Then, hiking their skirts, the two dancers unbound their long sweaty johnsons and began whizzing into the porcelain.

William seemed the first to notice the new company. As his urine stream dribbled to a halt, his gag reflex fluttered, and he shot a stream of shrimp cocktail and tequila into the urinal. Bill, the poor recipient of William's seafood splatter, glanced down at his own dick then at the dancer's impressive shaft and appeared not to know whether to be sick or jealous.

In a quiet murmur, he zipped up and, helping his partner from the bathroom, retired back to the private booth where they both stared blankly at the reflection of a disco ball rotating in the wall mirrors.

By the time Jack wrangled the two men back into the Yukon, they were all but passed out, rambling incoherently and hiccupping small bubbles of bile. He left them with a dentally challenged desk clerk at the Key Low Motel and tipped him a hundred bucks. The clerk, glad to assist in any affair for a C-note, agreed to trundle the two men, one at a time, on matching luggage carts and park them inside the rented room.

"Make sure they get a wakeup call every ten minutes starting at five a.m."

The clerk folded the bill and slipped it into his front pocket. "You got it, buddy. I'll personally handle the calls myself."

* * *

The mechanical boot separated from the Volkswagen with less effort than Jack had anticipated. Just three solid whacks with a twelve-pound maul, and the thing cracked into two pieces then fell away.

He left the contraption in a heap in the marina parking lot then roared south in the Acapulco Thing with the ragtop down, arriving at the Key Low Motel shortly before dawn.

The two biologists were awake, leaning against the outside lobby wall with blood-ridden eye whites and disturbed faces. To Jack's amusement, they wore the same clothes they'd arrived in the day before and, in some lame attempt to look the part, floppy hats with a variety of crankbaits and spoons pinned in the bands.

"Morning, gentlemen. You two ready for a long day on the water?"

The two groaned then suggested maybe they should forgo the fishing until tomorrow.

"Nonsense. We're going for a grand slam today."

The two men glanced at one another then back to Jack. "What's up with the room? I thought you said something about a swanky lodge? This place is a dump."

"Yeah. We'd better not wind up with bedbugs. What would we tell our wives?"

"All apologies, gentlemen. A small scheduling snafu on my end. It'll be sorted out by tonight, assuming you decide to stay."

Willy scratched his head. "Why wouldn't we stay?"

"Come on." Jack combed his fingers through his mustache. "Climb in before we miss the morning bite."

The men eyed the rusted heap then eased through the door-less openings and settled inside. Jack sputtered two miles to the marina, parked and told the men to follow him down the quay. Judging by their bewildered looks, they were more than a little disconcerted by the condition of their guide boat as they settled into the skiff.

"Where's the fishing poles?" Bill asked, as the outboard engine rattled in a shroud of blue smoke.

"Right, right." Jack scurried onto the Moppie, returning with one rod, the tackle box containing several dozen corroded lures, his Ruger and a single lifejacket. He shoved the boat from the dock then goosed the gas, shooting them toward the bay.

"Just one pole?" Willy asked.

"This is grand slam fishing, gentlemen. Only one guy can fish at a time. The other two have to spot."

Bill, wrestling a wicked hangover, suddenly tensed up. "Forget the one pole. What's up with just one lifejacket?"

"You landlubbers kill me. We're backwater fishing. Water's hardly ever more than chin-deep."

Bill shifted on his seat. "What kind of outfit is this?"

Jack ignored the question, flipping open the tackle box and intentionally letting the two gentlemen see his Ruger nestled aside the large, but dwindling, knot of cash. He fished a jerkbait lure from the top tray then tossed it to Bill's lap.

Bill jumped as though it were a tarantula.

"You know how to tie a dead man's hitch?" Jack asked.

Bill seemed to nod more out of instinct than confirmation. With fidgety fingers, only partially from the hangover, he began pawing at the air for the tag end of the monofilament blowing about as the skiff rounded a point then cornered into a stiff wind.

As they separated farther from the shoreline, a series of questions arose regarding fishing licenses, safety flares, a VHF radio for emergencies and so on, but Jack fielded each one with a wide grin and some elaborate bullshit about his exemptions as a long-term Islamorada native. For the next ten minutes, the three splashed across the bay in relative silence, the two men seeming to grasp the disturbing realization this was not the garden-variety fishing expedition for which they'd signed up.

When Jack cracked open a beer then sucked half of it down in a single pull, Willy lost his cool, demanding Jack take them back to the dock.

"You want a cold one?" Jack asked.

Willy curled his fingers into his hands. "What I want is to go back to shore."

Not interested in bruising his knuckles in an altercation, Jack slipped his hand into the tackle box, withdrew the pistol then laid it across his lap. "Relax, gentlemen. We're almost there."

"Almost where?" Bill cried. "Where in God's name are you taking us?"

Jack nodded. "See that big dredger up there rainbowing sand into the drink?"

Bill and Willy glanced off in the general direction of the Coconut Key construction zone, the azure backdrop of a Chamber of Commerce day standing in stark contrast to the rather dark situation settling over their mugs.

"Holy shit." Willy cinched his fingers around Bill's knee. "Isn't this where we did the survey?"

Bill craned his neck around seeming to locate a few guidepeg landmarks from their previous visit to the Keys. He looked at Jack. "What is it you want from us?"

Jack eased back on the throttle, killed the engine then rattled his empty beer can onto the deck. "The truth."

"The truth about what?"

"I want to know why you falsified the NOAA documents to make way for this development."

Willy appeared insulted. "How dare you?"

Jack lashed his right hand out with an open palm and smacked Bill's left cheek so hard it immediately began to welt with finger marks. Bill cowered back into his seat, eyeing up through fanned fingers. Willy eased forward.

"I'm only going to ask you one more time."

"Then what?" Willy asked. "You going to shoot us?"

"Don't be stupid. I'll probably just pistol whip you then let you swim back to shore."

"This is absolute horseshit." Willy shifted his weight as though about to make a move. "Come on, Bill. There's two of us."

Jack laughed. "Before you do that you may want to check your phones?"

The two men glanced at one another then each slowly retrieved the devices from their pockets.

"You're going to want to pay particular attention to an email you received last night from a Daisy Lane."

Bill's face visibly sagged as Willy frantically sorted through his inbox then hit play. When the sound of Lou Reed's *Walk on the Wild Side* resonated up from the device, he immediately leaned over the gunwale and began puking up whatever shrimp cocktail residuals remained in his stomach from the night before. Willy kept his eyes focused on the video clip until it reached crescendo, turning it off just before a particularly lewd scene involving the strippers and an empty Boat Life Lager bottle. Once Bill finished then wiped his chin, the three swapped glances, all understanding on some basic level that even the skuzziest D.C. insiders would find it intolerable to see two married men with kids in kindergarten stepping out on their wives with the tranny dance duo named Nip and Tuck.

Willy, who appeared to have lost his wedding ring at some point during the previous night's transgression, asked Jack the obvious question first.

"You're not going to tell anyone, right?"

Jack shrugged. "A thing like this could go viral in a matter of days if it got in the wrong hands."

"Whatever you want," Bill said. "We'll do it. Just tell us what it is."

"I told you what I want. I want the truth."

Willy reached out, plucked one of the beers from the cooler then took a long swig. "We got paid off. Fifty grand each."

Bill gasped. "Willy!"

"Shut the hell up, Bill." Jack repositioned his hand on the pistol butt then turned back to Willy. "Who paid the money?"

According to Willy, a bundle of cash had been Fedexed directly to their office with explicit instructions on how to doctor the survey.

"Whoever it was, didn't ask us," Willy said. "His exact words were, *Do what I ask or pay the price.*"

Jack thought back to the handwritten note he'd seen at the boathouse. PAY THE TWO BILLS. Bill and Willy. Of course. Ossie. That shitweasel. Jack eyed the two men. "Don't you feel a certain obligation to protect the environment?"

"That's just it." Willy set the beer down. "The whole thing was harmless."

Jack pointed toward the construction zone. "You call that harmless?"

"That's what I don't understand. I have no idea how they could have done it. The only reason we agreed to doctor the survey was because there was no way in a thousand years the developers could ever accumulate enough ROGO points to get full approval on the project."

Jack leaned back against the outboard, relaxing his grip on the gun. ROGO points. He had a vague understanding you needed them to build in the Keys. "What exactly are ROGO points?"

"Rate of Growth Ordinance points. A system put into place to help prevent population explosion. You have to accumulate a set number of them to develop in the Keys."

"So how'd they get the ones they needed?"

"Hand to God, I've got no idea. Not for a development of that magnitude. It's impossible."

"Apparently not."

Jack turned to Bill who seemed to have drifted off to some distant land. The maroon finger marks were now clearly visible across his cheek. "That true, Bill?"

Bill jerked forward, sort of half-nodding, then bowed over the rail and blew another stream of yellow into the blue waters.

Willy leaned forward in earnest. "You've got to believe me."

"That's where you're wrong. I don't have to believe a thing you say."

"Seriously. I don't know how they could do it."

"Loopholes," Jack said.

"I don't think so."

"If there's enough money, there's always loopholes." Jack glanced at the construction chaos underway then looked back to the two men. "So exactly how would one go about accumulating these ROGO points?"

Bill snapped back into focus. "There's a few ways, but the easiest is either by aggregation of existing domiciles or land dedication."

"English, Bill."

Bill suddenly seemed eager to please. "Aggregation is when you buy up houses and knock them down, reducing the domicile density in an area. Land dedication is when you donate land to Monroe County."

Jack thought about Commissioner Jimenez. "County, huh?"

"That's correct."

"So the more houses you knock down and the more land you donate, the more points you get?"

Bill nodded. "With each domicile you raze you also get cesspit credits too."

Jack furrowed his brows. This whole rotten deal was starting to stink like a cesspit.

"It's all part of the ROGO system." Willy finished his beer then reached for another one, but Jack gave him a look that suggested otherwise.

Willy slumped back then cleared his throat. "So about this video. Are we good?"

Jack hauled back on the start cord and fired the engine. "I won't forward it to your wives, if that's what you're asking."

"We'd really appreciate that."

"But I can't promise I'm not going to use it for my own personal amusement."

The two dropped their chins to their chests.

"So what do you say, gentlemen. Appears the fishing's pretty shitty today. You think we should call it quits?"

The two men nodded solemnly as Jack came about then sputtered in the direction of the marina. "By the way, those were one-way plane tickets down here. You're going to need to fund your own way back to Washington."

CHAPTER 13

A QUICK FLIRTACIOUS visit with the clerk of courts revealed that approximately six weeks prior an outfit named Coconut Key Holdings had shelled out 7 million dollars for a forty-seven-acre mobile home community known as Shady Acres on the marshy fringes of Upper Matecumbe Key.

SunState handled the closing transaction.

As Jack eased the Acapulco through the trailer park entrance, his bumper parted a pack of feral dogs gnawing through a bag of raw garbage swarmed with bottle flies. While he'd never ventured into the neighborhood before, he'd driven by the entrance a multitude of times with a heavy foot on his gas and that *man I hope I don't break down here* mentality.

About a hundred yards down the rutted way, an overgrowth of kudzu and potato vine gave way to the squalid RV park. Apparently most of the structures which had occupied the acreage had already entered some phase of the deconstruction process. The shells of doublewides and campers were crumpled and shoved into heaping piles of steel and alloy. Those that had not yet been razed bore the word *DEMO* across their facades in orange fluorescent paint. An onsite recycle crusher had been erected in the middle of a now-barren tract. Sections of shorn-away chassis, quarter panels and drivetrains were fed onto a conveyer belt by a grapple loader that grumbled about in a shroud of dust. The conveyor belt then shuttled the dismantled vehicle pieces into a set of steel teeth that spun like gears against one another and blitzed the recyclables into manageable bits.

Jack parked, stepped out, glanced around.

The last remaining warren of standing structures constituted a bizarre collection of broken down fifth wheels and condemned mobile homes shoehorned in with a disconcerting closeness, row after row, like a shantytown in a hurricane-ravaged Haiti. Both their *recreational* and *vehicular* values had long-since expired and now trended toward things more closely associated with white trash and methamphetamine labs. Most, in fact, were too dilapidated to consider moving. They'd simply shear apart if tugged from their current positions. The others were either sunken down into the sandy foundations or anchored by stick-built staircases and shoddy screened porches that had neither been permitted nor constructed according to the Monroe County hurricane code.

Jack sighted a Rube's Realty sign. *Land Parcel for Sale 47+/- Acres. High-Density Residential. Unencumbered. Fee Simple.* The word *SOLD* shown in red block letters at a diagonal across the board, a status that frankly shocked Jack more than the park's physical appearance.

The sign rose up in front of what appeared to be an onsite office next to a community pool—an above ground bladder ringed with a splintery deck. The water was the color of pea soup.

Jack stepped through a sea of littered cigarette butts then rapped on the aluminum frame.

A hacking cough erupted then some grumbling arose before a crusty senior citizen appeared behind the veil of a screen door. His pants snugged up just under his floating ribs, and a parrot squatted atop his bald freckled scalp. "Who you?"

"Jack Cubera."

"That supposed to mean something to me?'

"Probably not. I'm a private investigator."

"One of them dicks, eh?"

Jack shrugged. "Never gets old, does it?"

The man tugged at his earlobe, seemingly confused, then squeaked the screen door open. "What you need, boy?"

Jack glanced inside. A collection of exotic birds—macaws, para-keets, bananaquits and toucans—balanced on a network of fake limbs reminiscent of an acacia tree from an African veld. The entire floor, wall-to-wall, was carpeted with yellowing newsprint and littered with hulled bird seed and black and white splatters of guano.

"Just a quick question for you. Maybe out here on the porch."

"You alone?"

Jack nodded.

"Make it quick. My bowels are starting to slide." The man eased out the door, glancing left then right, before shuffling onto the rickety planks with the parrot still balancing on his head. The talons latched so tightly to the thin skin it appeared they might flay open the scalp at any second. "Ain't got all day, boy."

"I was interested in talking to someone about buying the place."

"That train's already left the station."

Jack nodded. "I can see that. Any chance I might be able to get in touch with the new owners?"

"Not sure."

"You have their name?"

"Seems like I remember some finky looking dude wore a uniform. But Sly Clover. He's the one you want to talk to. He was pretty involved in the transaction."

The man pointed a curled index finger toward a trailer a hundred yards down a dirt pathway. "Lives right there. Runs a tattoo shop out of that thing without a license. Enter at your own risk."

"He in now?"

"Probably. He don't get out much."

Jack crinkled his brows again.

"Ain't got no legs."

Jack bumped down the wobbly steps then moved along a pathway littered with more cigarette butts toward an egg-shaped fifth wheel vin-tage 1950s. A spanking new Trans Am painted red, white and blue and sitting on twenty-six-inch chrome spinners was parked outside the camper. The vehicle had to be thirty or forty grand worth of machinery and added gadgetry, not the sort of luxury item you'd expect to see in a dump like Shady Acres.

Jack took a slow lap around the vehicle.

One window decal read: *Gun-toting God-fearing Redneck Onboard.* Another one stated: *Honk if You're On Lithium.*

Jack cupped his hands around his eyes and leaned into the driver-side window. The ride had been converted to hand-controlled gas and brake functions. He assumed it belonged to the legless Sly. He stepped around the flashy vehicle then started up a series of steps before a voice called out and stalled his progress.

"You eyeballing my ride, Leroy?"

Jack spun around. The voice seemed to have bled through the screen of an open window. He hustled onto the porch then rapped his knuckles on the door. After a few seconds of bumping and rustling from inside, the door swung open, and Jack found himself eye-to-eye with a grizzled old dude, bald on top with a long wispy horseshoe of hair around the perimeter. The man dangled, like a rearview mirror trinket, by a single arm from a ceiling-mounted handrail. He was pushing seventy and legless almost up to the crotch with camouflaged pants knotted below the nubs. He wore no shirt, a tan like an old baseball mitt and fingerless canvas gloves. A lit cigarette bounced between his lips as he spoke. "What you want with me, Leroy?"

"Mind if I ask you a few questions about the sale of Shady Acres?"

"What for?"

"Would you mind?"

Sly glanced over Jack's left shoulder then his right. "You come by yourself?"

"Just me."

Sly studied Jack's face for a long moment then swung to an adjacent handrail, one in a series that networked across the entire ceiling. "Come inside before the flies get in."

Jack eased inside then instantly regretted the decision. The hot and smoky confines were cluttered with a variety of assault rifles, hand grenades and olive drab ordnances in various shapes and sizes. Above a rolled out sleeping bag and pillow, an oversized poster with the words *These Colors Don't Run* was underscored by a Skull biting down on an Elite Forces knife blade set in front of a stars-and-bars background. In another corner, cans of baked beans, creamed corn and black-eyed peas stacked high next to nonperishable dried goods and copious gallon jugs of sterilized water. To accent the décor was a stack of Gideon Bibles, one heavily worn copy dissected by a couple dozen book markers, perhaps marking various passages of reverential scripture.

Rapturous or not, Sly was fully equipped for whichever End of Days came knocking at his metaphorical door.

Jack started to lean against a counter then wondered about booby traps. "So, do you mind telling me—"

"I didn't do nothing illegal, if that's what you was going to ask."

"I'm actually just curious who bought the place."

"Didn't nobody buy the place. Not from us, anyway."

"I'm not sure I'm following you, Sly. The sign outside says sold."

"We gave it away."

"I'm sorry?"

"We gifted it to the county. Then they sold it."

Sly swung across the room toward a chrome parlor chair cradled by shelves of tattoo needles and inks in a prism of colors. Behind the workspace, black and white tattoo facsimiles ranging from tribal bands to hibiscus flowers to naked gals wrapped in anacondas lined the wall.

"That's mighty philanthropic."

"What did you call me?"

"If you don't mind me asking, who's the *we* that gifted it?"

"Us shareholders."

"Shareholders?"

"Bunch of us traveling show folk got tired of all the politicking going on up in Gibtown so we dropped the tent and came down here to winter back in '62. We pooled our resources and bought this here piece of land free and clear. Most of us never left."

"A bunch of carnies?"

113

Sly bit his lip then nodded. "We formed a corporation then split up the shares so everyone got their own parcel."

"I see."

"Each of us was given our own little salty slice of paradise about twelve feet wide and forty feet long.

"That's truly a slice."

"Eight-hundred ninety-eight separate lots if I'm not mistaken. A lot of the original owners gambled theirs away or sold them off to pay debt."

"How many people had to sign off on the deal?"

"Don't know for exact, but I'd say around three hundred."

"So everyone just agreed to give up their land?"

"Ain't exactly the promise land anymore."

Jack stepped toward a window then bent down the blinds, and, through the yellow fog of the nicotine-stained glass, admired the Trans Am parked outside. That sounded like quite a few people agreeing to just give up their land for nothing. "Nice ride."

Sly's chest puffed. "First time I've been able to get behind the wheel in damn near forty years."

"That right?"

"She's even got a turbo-charged engine."

"Sounds pricey. You win big on a scratch ticket or something?"

"I came into a little cash is all."

Jack squared around to Sly. "Come on now, Sly. That sounds a bit shady even for a place like this."

Sly grinned like a cat digesting a canary.

"Sounds to me like somebody paid you for your signature." Jack eased closer. "Damn shame. I'd hate to see such a nice ride confiscated for evidence. Could tie it up for years to come."

"Evidence?"

"I'm working a murder case."

"Wait a minute. I didn't have nothing to do with no murder."

"Then what aren't you telling me?"

"Who are you? Who you with?"

114

"One quick call and the ATF will be crawling all over this place. I assume everything in this little cache of weapons is legal."

"Fine." Sly's chest deflated. "There was one hold out at first. One guy that wouldn't sign over his land. But I guess he finally came around."

"That holdout have a name?"

"Dude went by the name of Skeg."

"That a real name?"

"Most around here don't use real names."

"I'd like to look at his place if it hasn't already been knocked down."

"Wasn't nothing to knock down."

"What do you mean?"

"Follow me."

Sly swung outside, tumbled down the series of deck steps then planted his torso into a Radio Flyer. "You mind?" He held the pull handle up for Jack.

Jack took the handle then, at Sly's direction, pulled the load along a weedy pathway that resolved at a campsite situated alongside a narrow brackish canal. The camp consisted of a corrugated tin lean-to, freshwater rain barrels and a twenty-foot by thirty-foot vegetable garden.

"Looks like this Skeg guy was pretty self-sustaining."

"That's an understatement. Not only did he grow his own food, but he was one of them health nuts too. Grew what he called superfoods."

"Superfoods?'

"Kale, avocados, chia seeds, blueberries. All that organic shit you find at them fancy supermarkets. Even used our local manure for fertilizer."

Sly pointed toward a back corner where an array of cow patties speckled the yard, several of them providing foundations for white and purple fungi the size of hamburger buns. "Not to mention them mushrooms. They're the magic kind, if you know what I'm getting' at."

"I'm familiar." Jack took another glimpse at camp. Considering the surroundings, the place proved quite pleasant. "This parcel looks a lot bigger than the rest."

Sly nodded. "Skeg bought up six or seven over the years."

"No offense, but why would the county want this dump?"

"Apparently they didn't. About five weeks after we signed it over to them they flipped it to some investors."

"That must've pissed a few people off."

Sly shook his head. "Just Skeg."

"Any idea where this Skeg guy moved on to?"

"He's stopped back by a few times since. Always smells like a camp fire. My guess is he's sleeping under the stars somewhere."

"So how'd they manage to get his signature and close the deal?"

Sly shrugged again.

"Any idea what he drives?"

"He don't. He boats."

"Thanks for your time, Sly."

"You want me to call you if I see that dickweed again?"

"I don't have a phone."

"I guess a handsome sumbitch like you with legs and all probably don't really need one."

CHAPTER 14

RAY LIVINGSTON WHEELED into the Ocean Grove Nursery at mile marker 88, parked and ambled between two long, vibrant rows of perennials toward a slender woman ten years his senior. Her name was Clara, Clara Downs, a gal with the posture, poise and complexion of a snowy egret. She wore long white hair pulled back in a ponytail and soft gray eyes that peered out from under the brim of a floppy shade hat. As Ray approached, her pupils dilated against the pale irises. She been smitten with a schoolgirl crush since Ray started buying his garden supplies at her shop nearly a decade before.

"Sheriff Livingston. So good to see you. Where have you been hiding out?" She peeled a soiled cotton glove off one hand and took Ray by the wrist. Her fingernails were etched with a rich, dark soil at the distal ends.

"I know. I know. I've been trying to get by here, but work's had me busier than a one-legged man in an ass kicking competition."

Using a potting shovel, she pointed across an acre or so of bromeliads, jasmine and other plant material. "You'll be happy to know those cocoplum redtips finally came in late last week."

"How do they look?"

"Nicest I've seen in years."

"Could you pull one aside for me? I'll stop back by and pick it up when I'm not on the company dime."

"Of course." She sank the shovel into bag of peat and left it sitting upright then ungloved the other hand. "So what are you shopping for today?"

117

Ray pulled his baseball cap off and held it in both hands. "I'm actually here on business." Ray cleared his throat. "That brother of yours. He still calling the shots down at Islamorada Event Sourcing?"

"Lives and breathes that place. Why do you ask?"

"Word is he's the one staffing this Little Palm Island shindig coming up on Friday."

"The Dixen gala?"

Ray nodded.

"Poor thing. He's been stressing out about that event for months now." She drew the back of her hand over a cheek leaving a faint dirty smear. "I imagine he'll be a happy man once it's all behind him."

"He's using a pretty healthy stable of off-duty officers for security. Fourteen of them, from what I understand."

"I hear it tends to get pretty wild out there."

"That's the rumor."

"You think you could talk to him? See if he can get me on that detail?"

"For security, Ray? Isn't that a little—"

"I know, Clara. Not exactly my usual gig. But the truth is we've intercepted some pretty off-color threats directed at the commissioner recently, and I don't want to take any chances."

"I'm sure he'd be happy to help."

"Wonderful." Ray slipped the cap back on his head. "Now this is all on the down-low. Even from the commissioner. I don't want him worrying. I just want to keep an eye on him myself. And tell your brother not to worry. I'll bill the department for this so it won't screw up his budget. I just need him to get me in the door."

"I'll give him a call right now and set it up."

CHAPTER 15

RUBIO YIELDING, PRINCIPLE of Rube's Realty, clicked shut the driver door on a sea-foam green convertible Jaguar then stepped toward his office entrance. He was a lean gent dressed in shimmering slacks and a golden fleece polo. He sashayed with an effeminate swagger.

Jack crossed the side street and stepped toward him from his blindside. Along the highway at his heels, commuter traffic whizzed by. Construction workers. Housemaids. Sous-chefs. All part of the blue-collar world catering to a wealthier tier that came and went to and from the Keys like the thunderheads of a shitstorm.

Jack crunched up behind the man and poked out a hand. "Rubio Yielding, I presume?"

Rubio spun around, fanning the fingers of one hand across his chest while jangling his keys in the other. "Oh my. You startled me. Are you my three o'clock?"

On his left hand, a pinky ring with a floating diamond swiveled around its socket like a wandering eyeball. On the wrist, a slender diamond-encrusted timepiece twinkled in the sunlight.

"Call me a walk-in," Jack said. "Just flew in from Long Island."

Rubio's groomed eyebrows pinched inward.

Jack laughed. "Not New York. Long Island, Bahamas."

"That explains the accent. Or lack, thereof." Rubio extended a hand.

Jack took it up. It was the size and consistency of an adolescent rainbow trout. "I'm only in town for a couple of days, and I need to find a

119

place to slip my trawler. I hear you're the top dog around these parts when it comes to real estate."

"I've got my face on a few bus benches around town."

Jack nodded. This was an understatement. Every mass transit commuter from mile marker 73 to 91 had the distinct pleasure of passing gas into an oversized imprint of Rubio's corporate headshot while awaiting their diesel chariot.

"What exactly are you in the market for?"

"Nothing fancy. Just a little place to rest my head from time to time and service the occasional guest. About forty-five hundred square feet. Five beds and as many baths. Something around the three five range. Is that doable?"

Rubio checked his elegant timepiece then glanced around Jack and back to him. "Gulf or Atlantic?"

"Doesn't matter as long as it's on the water. It's the dockage that really concerns me. Something that can hold my Nordhavn with some generous dwell on each end."

Talk of a Nordhavn—a real boater's boat—seemed to gather Rubio's attention. "Of course."

Jack tipped an imaginary drink to his mouth. "I get over-served on occasion, and the extra lineal feet of dockage keeps me from looking like a bush-leaguer when I'm bringing her in. You understand."

"No need for explanations." Rubio jiggled the watch about his wrist. "How big is she, anyway?"

"A shade over seventy-five."

Rubio's brows wicked upward as he slipped Jack a business card. "How would Saturday morning work for you? I'll set up some showings. Say around ten?"

Jack studied the shiny gold card then slipped it into his pocket. "Make it ten sharp and that'll work just fine."

Rubio fingered through his key ring then slid a thick silver thing into the commercial front door lock. "Where would you like to meet?" He twisted his wrist, and the bolt snapped open.

"Are you familiar with the Soggy Dollar?"

Rubio grimaced like he'd just sucked juice from a lime, and his eyes lost a little light. "I hate to ask, but would you mind putting together a proof of funds letter for me? For liability purposes. Most of the sellers require them."

Jack shifted his weight. Being a real estate agent in the Keys required you to spend most of your waking hours around an ultra-wealthy tier or those pretending to be. "You familiar with Picaro Joe's?"

Rubio paused and turned back, propping open the door with the toe of his Manolo Blahnik. "The haberdashery?"

Using his hands, Jack framed his own face then bent his lips into a smug grin. "Yours truly."

Rube squinted. "Well then. Is that really your likeness on the logo?"

"In my much younger days, I'm afraid." Jack handled the door, relieving Rubio's designer shoe. "And not to worry. I'll have my man down in Cayman Brac fax you something over on bank letterhead."

"Perfect." Rube's spirits seemed to lift. "I suppose you'd like to go looking by boat."

"Is there any other way to preview waterfront property?"

Rubio grinned as an El Dorado wheeled into the parking lot in a fit of dust. "Must be my three o'clock."

As the dust cloud cleared, a British looking man in a black sequin jacket and silver boa stepped out onto a pair of platform leather boots then slunk toward them.

"Looks like you've got your hands full," Jack said.

"Another day in paradise."

"See you at ten sharp then, Rubio. Slip number seventeen. You can't miss her. She's the only Hinckley in the marina."

* * *

Jack settled back against the small mattress wedged in the Moppie V-berth, threaded his fingers behind his head and surveyed his old boat. Despite her neglected appearance, she performed better than any vessel her size even decades after being commissioned. The 170-gallon fuel tank and twin 330 HP Cummins diesels gave her a range from

Islamorada to the Out Islands at a cruising speed around twenty-six knots and a top end over thirty-five. From there, Jack could refuel and disappear anywhere in the Caribbean should the mood arrive. Just set her at a steady clip and drift on down into the Lesser Antilles where loners on liveaboards were as common and disregarded as cormorants.

There'd been times he'd plotted his departure. He'd shoot first for the Berry Islands then trickle down to the Exumas and onward to waypoints with names like Anegada and Bequia.

But so far that mood had not arrived with enough fervor to motivate him into weighing anchor.

So far.

"Jack, Jack. Are you in there? Jack!"

Jack shot from his bed, up the steps, and onto the deck, his peripheral vision warbling with dark haloes before returning to normal and discovering Summer at the rail, a sunglow aura behind her head.

He steadied a hand to the bulkhead. "Everything all right?"

She rushed in and sank her fingernails into his forearms. "Somebody broke into my house."

"What are you talking about? Who? Are you okay?"

"I'm okay. I think. I don't know. Maybe I'm still numb."

"What happened."

"I got home last night and could tell someone had been inside, had been rummaging around. All my papers were out of place, some on the floor. A bunch of Coconut Key stuff I've been stealing from the office."

Jack considered the threats. "Any chance Ossie would've been snooping around?"

Her eyes were sallow, and her head seemed to shake involuntary.

Jack stroked his mustache. "What about the Jersey crew? Or a coworker? Do you think somebody from work found out?"

"I don't know, Jack. I've been so careful."

"Jesus, Summer. Not careful enough." Jack tightened his grip on her biceps and braced her tightly. "It's not like you're the most responsible person when it comes to—"

She let out a small peep then looked up with haunted eyes and tugged her arms away from his grip. Her lower lids were puffed and strained. The gray-blue irises were ringed with a pale golden halo he had not noticed before. Her face drew long and confused as her fingertips tapped at dry lips. Her entire body began to tremble, and he tried to gather her into his chest. She resisted at first, like a stubborn child resists a mother's hug, pushing and wriggling and feigning punches. Then she gave in.

Jack set a big paw against her cheek then began to comb his fingers through the salty tangles of hair. "What about that canoer? You seen him around again?"

"Maybe. I don't know." Her face turned up toward him, her cheeks flushed and florid, then sank back down. "I feel so stupid. I feel like a little girl who can't take care of herself. I wanted to be strong, Jack. I didn't want to bother you with this, but . . ."

He stroked her head again then eased his hold, letting her body fall away from his, letting her take her weight back onto her own feet. With an index finger, he tilted her chin, her eyes no longer scared but washed with a healthy measure of anxious exhaustion. He wondered if she'd slept at all the previous night.

"I'm going to get Livingston over here to keep an eye on you while I make a quick run over to your place."

She began pulling at her shirt and wiping away tears that weren't there. "This is silly, Jack. I'm just being silly. Don't bother Ray."

She pushed away, reclaiming her own weight and space.

"Fine." Jack said. "You stay here. Sit in the sun. Relax. Make yourself a stiff drink. Whatever makes you feel better. I'm going to run the skiff over to your place and check things out. See if that creep is hanging around."

Her eyes softened, and she fell forward into Jack again, chin upward, mooning up. "My hero. My knight in shining armor."

"Rusty armor at best, I'm afraid. Now relax. I'll be back shortly."

Jack puttered away in the skiff, rounded a few bends, then nosed onto the embankment behind Summer's house. Once inside, a quick investigative lap revealed the intruder's access point—a jimmied window. With the turn of a few screws, he repaired the window lock then moved about stacking rummaged papers, straightening toppled books, then he locked up and returned to the boat.

With no canoer in sight, he idled up and down the neighboring canals, coming across a mobile boat mechanic who'd seen nothing odd in the three days he'd been working the area.

An hour later, Jack returned to the Moppie to find a remarkable transformation in Summer. Not only was the cabin spotless, but she'd mixed cocktails, even slicing an orange and grapefruit to accompany the spiced rum and soda over ice.

She handed one to Jack as he came aboard, which he took without protest. His first and second drinks went down like rainwater through a culvert. By the third, the soda found its way off the ingredient list, the previous night's B and E all but washed away on the amnesia of strong drink. At five, Summer cranked up Bob Dylan's *The Basement Tapes* and began dancing around as a distant squall blew across the late afternoon sky.

Around sunset, a warm and heavy headwind brought the leading edge of the downpour screaming across the bay. As it reached the marina, the world diminished into white striations, the waters a sea of ever-changing dimples, the hiss and thrum of droplets deafening and delightful to the ears. Life hushed for a pure and honest moment, and the two moved toward one another, fresh water washing over them, saturating them, until the downpour shut off like the turn of a church key on a meter main.

They stood face-to-face dripping as the clouds dispersed, daylight vanished, and a half moon climbed the sky, illuminating a world veiled in a gentle smoke that drifted like the remnants of a forest fire.

Jack took Summer's hand and led her into the cool darkness of the cabin.

At bed's edge, his eyes drifted down her wetness, her legs ascending and disappearing into inseams shy of a single inch. Above the low-slung waistline, a dewy shimmer of flat stomach slipped underneath a white cotton T-shirt, threadbare and saturated, offering the teardrop outlines of two unbound breasts, nipples fully excited.

As wet clothes peeled away, the two collapsed into a sea of linens and pillows, the sheets soon damp and twisted, their bodies mortising and releasing several times before coming to rest, each with a single leg entangled in the other's, staring skyward through the untidy and exhausted aftermath at the ceiling and things far beyond.

"Can we just stay down here forever, Jack? Can we just keep the door closed and never leave?"

Jack's breath was heavy, brows damp. "If only the world were that simple."

"I'm serious, Jack. I want you all to myself."

"Trust me. Nobody wants me all to themselves. Me included."

"I do, Jack. Really, I do."

* * *

The day before the Dixen gala, Ray ran the Mako down the Atlantic coastline past Marathon toward Little Palm Island Resort and Spa. Generally speaking, the private island resort was a secluded five-acre palm-riddled sandbar speckled with bungalows, a restaurant and a small marina that catered to the crispiest echelon. The night of the party, however, it would transform into a playground for unruly heathens and rowdy upper crusters getting piss drunk and yukking it up without fear of getting exposed to the public eye.

Ray cut the wheel, eased off the gas then inched toward the island. As he approached, the place bustled with hotel staff and event planners hustling about hanging white linens, draping lights through tree limbs and raking seaweed and storm debris from the sandy shoreline.

Fifteen feet out, he stalled the engines then hoisted a lobsterpot off his boat deck and steadied it on the rail. Inside the pot was a dry bag filled with electronics.

He glanced around and, reasonably sure nobody was watching, nudged the cage off the rail and splashed it into the water. The cage sank down six or so feet, the line trailing out behind it. A cloud of sandy sediment plumed out as it hit the bottom, then the marker, a blue and orange foam ball, slipped down current and drew taut, a small tidal wake parting around it.

"Sheriff," a voice called out.

Ray glanced up to find Clara's brother Ron standing at the shoreline, his pale-yellow topsiders getting damp in the lapping tides. Ray waved then shielded a hand against the midday sun reflecting off the water. "How things coming along out here, Ron?"

"Falling apart at the last minute as usual." Ron shielded his eyes. "Clara get those credentials to you?"

Ray nodded. "Thanks for that."

"Sure thing. Glad to have another set of eyes out here."

"What time should I clock in?"

"Eight would be good."

Ray made a mental note. "How you guys shuttling the guests to and from the island?"

"Some are going to dinghy themselves out here on their own. We've got two rented yacht tenders otherwise."

Ray located the dinghy dock. "They going to tie up there?"

Ron nodded. "What brings you out here today?"

"Just scouting things out in the light of day. I don't want any surprises."

"Speaking of. You know there's an absolute zero-tolerance policy on cameras, right?"

"I heard that."

"Cell phones too. We'll be checking them at the door like coats." Ron shook his head. "Last year somebody managed to sneak one in and get some footage of the governor in a conga line that didn't bode well for his political future. We were lucky they renewed the contract again this year after that little snafu."

"I'll be sure to be on the lookout."

"So what's with the lobsterpot?"

"It must've gotten dragged out here by the currents. Unless you want it moved before the party, I'll just leave it here for another week or so and see if somebody claims it."

"Won't bother me a bit." Ron waved then turned away. "Got to get back to it."

"See you tomorrow night around eight then."

CHAPTER 16

RUBIO YIELDING PUTTERED into the Soggy Dollar at six minutes before ten sporting a mock sailor's ensemble—a striped top, white Capri pants and baby blue topsiders with bone white laces—further accentuating his ectomorphic build.

He sat like a method actor behind the wheel of a Snug Harbor Duffy electric boat. His Dutch-boy blond hair had been styled with pomade then intentionally tussled.

Jack came around from the blind side of the Hinckley, as though its owner, then moved down to the end of the finger pier and waved Rubio over.

"Ahoy." Rubio stood, offering a Broadway wave.

As the boat bumped up to the dock, Jack gripped its scalloped canvas top with one hand while clutching a duffle bag in his other. Jack had expected a Zodiac luxury yacht tender or, at least, a posh dual console. But this electric novelty, this Snug Harbor, was a nautical travesty. Nothing more could be said about it.

"Morning, Mr. Positano."

Rubio had done his homework. Mr. Positano was the owner of the Picaro Joe's. "Morning, Rube."

Rubio studied the duffle bag. "Were you planning on an overnight trip?"

"It's a change of clothes in case it rains."

Rubio glanced around the sheer blue sky.

"You never know," Jack said. "Summer squalls crop up out of nowhere. That happens, you'll wish you had the foresight to bring along some dry clothes."

"About that proof of funds letter."

"My man faxed that over to you this morning." This was not true. Jack had used the marina fax machine to send an extremely faded, completely illegible document to the number on Rubio's card.

"It came through a bit on the light side."

"You know how these banana republics operate." Jack bumped aboard then tossed the duffle bag onto the bench behind the agent. It landed with a thud. "Now let's get to this. The Citation's scheduled to fly out tonight. What's on the agenda?"

"Well. Okay. I suppose—" With a flick of his dainty wrist, Rubio reversed the engine and backed away from the dock. Once clear, he started for the Gulf. "I've lined up four showings for us. Three I know you'll like, and one I know you're going to absolutely adore."

"Adore, you say?" Jack exhausted a throaty sigh.

"Absolutely. It has over a hundred feet of yacht dockage. Not to mention five bedrooms and six baths."

"Only four spots lined up?"

"Most of these owners live out of the country, and it takes a little time to schedule showings."

"In that case, what do you know about the Fuentes place?"

Rubio's plucked brows pinched into a V. "I'm not sure I'm familiar with that one."

"Gregorio Fuentes. A fishing buddy told me about it. Said it just hit the market. One of those listings no one knows about."

"A pocket listing?"

"That's right. That's exactly what he called it. A pocket listing. Anyway, it's Gulf-side. Down near mile marker 83. He said it's right next to the Pickled Porpoise."

"That establishment closed a few months back."

"Either way, he said to pull down the canal like you're heading straight to the fuel dock then it's off to the right."

"I wonder what property that could be?"

"Apparently the guy wants about two-and-a-half million for it, but my buddy thinks I can take it down for somewhere around two." Jack glared off toward the climbing sun. "Sounds like a good deal to me. I like a good deal."

Jack padded back and sat next to his duffle bag. "It's just around the bend in the next bight over. Let's go there first. Then we'll hit your stops. I'll show you the way."

A fine sheen had cropped up along Rubio's lip. "But we haven't even set up a showing."

"Don't worry. It's vacant. On a lockbox. And if it's the commission you're sweating about, then think nothing of it. I'll pay you the full three and a half percent on top of the asking price if they're not willing to take the cut. I just need someone to represent me. You know, make sure I don't sign anything stupid. Can you do that for three and a half percent?"

Rubio nodded as they eased along the shoreline. Up and down the stretch, shuttered houses braced against the potential elements, closed and locked, as they would remain all but about six days per year. Like most of these tax havens in the Keys, these served merely as lavish roosts upon which pelicans perched and shit and enjoyed the gentle breeze blowing through their feathers.

"Over there." Jack motioned toward a series of thin white poles rising from the water, denoting the deepwater channel toward shore. "That's our cut."

"You sure?"

"Positive. The Pickled Porpoise is just around the corner."

Rubio guided the vessel toward the shoreline under the soft electrical hum of the motor. Once they reached the break, he cut the wheel right then aligned the bow with an old Texaco sign marking the fuel dock.

"Which house is it again?"

Jack glanced around, playing dumb. "I'm not sure. Sonofabitch said we couldn't miss it. Big three-story thing with a metal roof and a mermaid fountain in the backyard."

They slipped into the network of docks and gangways, crawling closer toward the pumps. "Are you sure this is the right cut?"

Jack surveyed the destitute marina. Discarded power heads and blown lower units littered a service area. Most of the windows had been shattered. A gasoline spill, etched with a rainbow, slicked across the water. This was the right place, all right. "It's got to be. Tell you what. See that dock over there? The one back by the big game weigh station?"

Rubio craned his neck then pointed toward a gallows fitted with a hanging scale and block-and-tackle. "There?"

"That's the one. Pull up, and I'll check things out by land."

Rubio slid alongside the dock, then Jack secured the vessel with a line. The place was vacant aside from a feral cat slumbering on an old air conditioning unit and a mob of blowflies buzzing around a dead possum floating under the dock.

As Rubio cut the electric power, Jack squared around. "So I hear you're the lucky bastard that got the Shady Acres listing."

Rubio's posture straightened. "I beg your pardon?"

"Shady Acres. You were the selling agent on that deal, right?"

"Oh, right. That deal. What a marvelous turn of luck for the people of Islamorada flushing out the riffraff that lived in that ghetto."

"How long did that take to go under contract?"

"I'm sorry?"

"I'll tell you how long. Three hours. That place went pending in three hours and closed for cash in four days."

Rubio's glistening perspiration began to bead into rivulets that coagulated with a thick, powdery substance across his forehead. It appeared the man wore foundation makeup. "They say your first offer is usually the best."

"So how's your penmanship?"

"Excuse me?"

"How well are you at signing other people's names?"

Rubio started to stand from the captain chair, but Jack shoved him back into the seat.

"Answer the question."

"Who cares about that place? It was a bunch of meth heads and cripples."

"I suppose you're one of those just crippled inside." Jack cinched his fingers around one of Rubio's scant biceps. "Last chance."

Rubio jerked this arm away from Jack then reached over to crank the engine, but Jack slipped a leather blackjack from his duffle bag and brought the thing crisply across the small of Rubio's neck.

Upon impact, Rubio's body flexed stiff as a gurney then when limp and oozed slowly from the captain chair. With a firm hand, Jack slowed the descent and let the body sprawl out completely across the deck.

* * *

"One-hundred thirty-three pounds." Jack laughed as he hunkered over a fish-cleaning station carving a barracuda into bite-sized chunks while Rubio dangled upside down from the big game fishing gallows. "And that's dry as a bone, Rube. I wonder how much you'll weigh soaking wet."

Rubio's ankles had been bound with cord then the cord had been hooked onto the hanging scale. The block and tackle had brought the body up and off the ground, where it now dangled freely from the big game scales, registering the waifish total weight.

Rubio groaned then garbled something inaudible against his gag. His hands too were bound, lashed behind his back with duct tape. He was just beginning to regain consciousness.

Jack finished cubing the barracuda flank then stepped away from the bloody mess toward the swaying body. He reached out then pinched Rubio's cheeks, transferring a gelatinous lump of fish goo onto the agent's face.

"I'll take the gag off. But if you scream, you're going for a swim."

Jack snatched Rubio's head back by the hair, presenting the water below the gallows. An oily slick shimmered along the watery surface. Jack had been chumming the area for about fifteen minutes, and a host of great barracuda had moved in, quietly awaiting further food. At least a half-dozen fish the size of human legs drifted in the vicinity alongside several smaller specimens.

Jack tossed another hunk of freshly diced chum into the water. The water boiled in a furious fit of thrashing fish then went silent again.

Jack peeled the gag away.

"What are you doing to me? Do you know who I am?"

Jack released Rubio's jaw, the agent's head snapping back into the natural hanging position. "I'm trying to figure out the details of the Shady Acres transaction. Nothing more."

"I told you what I—"

"Before you get hysterical, let me assure you there's only two ways this thing can wind up. The first way is that I stuff your ears and nose full of barracuda then lower you into the water and let the fishes have their way."

"You're sick."

"I'm not saying that's the way I'd like to see things play out, but that's one option."

Jack stepped toward the block and tackle then clicked out some scope of the rope. Rubio's body sank down, head first, pausing about two feet above the dock and five feet above the water.

"The only other option is that you offer up enough information about the Shady Acres transaction that I can incriminate you at a later date if you ever speak of this incident."

"But all I did was sell the place."

Jack lobbed another hunk of meat into the drink. As it hit, the predators boiled the water so violently Rubio's face got splashed with saltwater.

"Tell me the truth, Rubio. Who forced the Shady Acre residents to sign over their land?"

"Nobody."

"You're trying to tell me they just signed it over out of the kindness of their hearts?"

Rubio's headed bobbed back and forth. "That's right. That's what I'm saying."

133

"Don't play stupid. It's too appropriate a part for you. Somebody forged at least one of the names. That I'm sure of. And it appears some money exchanged hands on the down-low."

"I had nothing to do with that."

"But what do you know about it?"

"I wasn't involved."

"Then who was?"

Rubio whimpered but said nothing.

Jack retrieved two more cubes of barracuda flesh then took a knee in front of Rubio's upside-down face. He spun the body a quarter turn then plugged one cube of bloody meat into the left ear then did the same in the other. Jack stood, the coppery smell from the blood wafting about his hands, then let the gallows scope out another foot and a half.

"Barracuda can jump, you know." Jack flung a handful of meaty chunks into the water then waited for things to quiet down.

"I swear it was a clean deal by the time it got to me."

"Again, that's not what I asked. You must be hard of hearing. Or maybe that's just the fish in your ears."

Jack eased his grip, the rope rasping through his hands until Rubio's head smacked the water then dunked under. A muffled voice bubbled up as Rubio's frail body whipped and thrashed and the water boiled. Jack let the head soak for a solid five seconds then hauled back on the line, drawing the body from the brine. As Rubio's lips broke the surface, a sharp howl waned toward a gargling rattle. Jack reset the block and tackle as Rubio coughed away saltwater and tears, a bleeding razor slice across Rubio's left earlobe, the trademark work of a barracuda's toothy smooch.

"Dear God. What are you doing to me?"

Jack knelt in front of Rubio. "Wow. Now that's got to sting a little bit."

As the gargling tapered into a gentle cooing-like whimper, Jack leaned closer to the agent. "You're losing a lot of blood into the water. That's bound to attract some larger predators."

"All right. All right." Rubio began to cry. "They were paid off. More money than any of those losers have probably ever seen at one time. So what?"

"Who anteed up the money?"

Rubio's lips tightened as tears rolled down his forehead.

"I'm not dicking around. Next time your head's going underwater for a ten count before I pull you back up."

"Jimenez was involved. That's all I know."

Jack reared into an upright position. "I knew that sonofabitch had something to do with this."

"They got their money, and everyone was happy. What's the big deal?"

"Not everyone was happy. Skeg wasn't happy."

Rubio sniffled. "The creepy dude?"

"You should know that Skeg's pretty pissed off about the whole thing. At least, that's the word on the street."

"What were we supposed to do? The entire deal was going to get killed over just the one guy. He didn't even have a house out there. Just a tent."

"A lean-to, actually." Jack stooped toward Rubio. "And regardless what it looked like, it was his home. His primary residence, in fact. It's not as though the guy's got a winter place up in Blue Ridge or out in Sedona. That was it for him, and you were a party in taking that away. So, tell me. Are you the one who forged his name?"

"No. I swear. There was another guy who got all the signatures before I was even involved. I only saw him once."

"I'm going to need a name."

"He wore a uniform. That's all I remember. I swear."

Hadn't Sly mentioned something about a guy in uniform too? "What kind of uniform?"

"I don't know. Just a uniform. Brown maybe."

Rubio began to snivel as a steady ribbon of blood dribbled from his ear into the water. "Don't you see? The deal was already done before I got the listing. I was just a front man to legitimize the thing. I really didn't even do anything."

"Three and half percent of seven mil?" Jack canted his head. "What's that? Just under two-hundred and fifty grand for a day's work. Not too shabby for not doing anything." Jack lowered the rope another six inches. "What about the Soggy Dollar? You have anything to do with that transaction?"

"I don't represent either side of that deal. I swear I don't."

"I'll take your word for it for now." Jack lowered the body onto the dock then rasped his blade across the wrist bindings. "But if I find out that you do, we're going house hunting together again."

* * *

Ray arrived at Little Palm Island at a quarter before eight, his rented tuxedo snugged nicely over his broad chest and shoulders, his silver cummerbund setting off the glint of gray in his hair.

Once the last of the sunlight evaporated beyond neighboring Big Pine Key, the resort island blinked alive with unnatural lights that strung from tree to bungalow to tree and swayed gently in a fortunate evening breeze. Somewhere wooden and shell wind chimes *tonked* and tinkled as event planners made last minute adjustments to chafing dishes and floral arrangements while Ray stood near the entrance, legs slightly parted, hands clasped behind his back.

The first two guests arrived about eight thirty, and, mortified to be the first to show, strode straight to the bar and ordered dirty martinis. Vivian, the host, who was already half in the bag, slunk in and drummed up some magnificent story that brought the three into a riotous laughter as the next guests arrived by personal dinghy.

Thirty minutes later, a steady stream of partygoers began to appear, the private yacht tenders commissioned for the event unloading them at the main dock twelve at a time.

An hour later, Ray watched the Jersey crew wobble in and huddle around the buffet table, noshing on shrimp cocktail and puff pastries while ogling women in evening gowns. Jimenez appeared about fifteen minutes after that and began methodically working the crowd with handshakes and hellos. As the minutes ticked by, the music and conversation climbed toward crescendo while cocktails began to take hold. Jimenez strolled through the gallery of people, offering toothy grins and head nods like any good politician. Only Ray with his eyes fixed on the subject was aware of the commissioner's constant head twisting. Every couple minutes, Jimenez snuck a glance toward a dark patch of shoreline on the maintenance side of the resort. Finally, the commissioner completed his lap and sauntered up to the Jersey crew with the look of a man greeting old friends at a reunion. But within seconds, something on that dark side of the resort seemed to catch his eye, and with a quick wink and nod, he excused himself from the trio and slunk away.

Ray tailed Jimenez into the maintenance area at a safe distance then slipped behind a latticework enclosure. Soon a small inflatable vessel nosed onto the clandestine shoreline and a man in black helped Jimenez aboard, then the boat zoomed away, the scene assuming the look and feel of a mercenary hostage extraction.

What was going on here? Was the commissioner using the gala as a front for something else?

Ray studied the boat's line, its angle of departure, then hustled back to the dinghy dock and located a tender with a four-stroke engine. He checked the party crowd for prying eyes then untied the bowline, sank into the boat and nudged it from the dock. Using his hands, he paddled across the dark water and retrieved the lobsterpot he'd set the day before.

He hauled the trap out, withdrew the dry bag of electronics then eased the pot back into the water. He tossed the bag to the boat deck then began hand paddling once again, this time moving away from the Little Palm shoreline.

About a hundred yards out, he knew the party crowd would not hear the faint rumble of the outboard. He cranked up then motored through the darkness with his running lights off in the general direction of the mercenary boat's angle of departure. About a mile and a half offshore he registered the vague outline of a large vessel anchored just beyond the reef line. The vessel was devoid of lights other than a faint glow from a forward salon. He dropped the 4-stroke into neutral then unrolled the dry bag and slipped a camera from the fold. Next, he withdrew a light-gathering lens and screwed it into place.

As he dialed in the aperture, a sleek two-tiered yacht began to take shape. Judging by the lines—the slanted aft, a nose that tapered down-ward toward the water—it was an Italian job, a Riva or a Baglietto, about two-hundred feet long. The hull was dark-colored, perhaps navy or gun-metal, the craft nearly imperceptible in the cloak of night.

Ray snapped a couple profile shots of the yacht, eased his tender closer then zoomed the camera lens in on four figures occupying the bow. They were Jimenez, a man dressed in all white with similar size and skin tone to Jimenez, the commissioner's secretary and a woman who, judging by her chest and heels, worked by the hour. The two women stood off to one side while the two men stood close to one an-other, utilizing the subtle pointing, nodding and hand gestures of a busi-ness meeting.

Ray clicked off a couple shots of the subjects then used the lens to scan the boat for crew and security.

Only one other person was visible from Ray's vantage: the man in all black who'd picked up Jimenez from Little Palm. He stood off to the side of the commissioner and the other unknown male subject, as though just out of earshot. Perhaps the remainder of the crew was asleep. Or inshore gathering provisions. Or had been dismissed so that these two men could hold a meeting in private.

Certainly something was going on here. Why else would the com-missioner have used the gala as a front?

Ray unscrewed the light-gathering lens, slipped on a high-resolution model then circled his tender and approached the yacht from the stern. He kept the engine at idle, the four stroke almost inaudible at such a low speed. As he neared, the name *Sueño Mojado* became visible across the transom. Maracaibo, Venezuela was the hailing port.

Twenty feet out, Ray killed his engine and drifted up to the hydraulic fold-down transom which provided easy access on and off the yacht. He lashed his tender to a cleat then clambered aboard, the camera dangling around his neck.

The yacht was dark and eerie, but it had not lost power. The lights had merely been tailored to achieve the sort of ambiance one equates with romantic interludes . . . or clandestine rendezvous. As he moved along the lower exterior walkway, faint orange floor lights offering the lumens of cigarette cherries lit the path while the soft tempo of Latin jazz drifted down from the upper deck. He eased up a flight of steps then moved along a second story walkway, keeping his back tight to the wall as he crept toward the bow.

As he neared, the sounds of footfalls on fiberglass halted his progress. He spun a half-turn, hustled back down the steps then ducked behind the risers. As he peered through the open staircase, three sets of legs descended the flight, two in heels, one in black patent leather. The three arrived at the main level then eased through a doorway leading into the boat interior.

Ray lagged back for a moment then eased the door open and followed them inside. The three were already out of eyeshot, their voices receding as they moved deeper into the boat. He started forward to tail them but abruptly stopped and reverted, the voices suddenly growing in volume as though coming back his way.

He hustled toward a door, yanked it open and ducked inside. The room was dark, save for a theatrical display of moonlight breaking through the vertical bands of a window blind. As he searched for a closet to hide in, listening to the voices grow louder, the door parted from its jamb once again and a hand began blindly pawing for a wall switch.

As a loud drunken voice rang out, a light clicked on bringing the room alive with gleaming white and chrome finishes. Ray swiveled on a heel and dove fast for the floor between the wall and the bed then rolled quickly, edging his body halfway under the frame.

One of the females chimed in. "Who needs lights?"

As the switch clicked off and darkness returned, Ray wriggled completely underneath the bed and kept his breathing quiet as the box spring above groaned once, then twice, then three times, the trio presumably sinking into the mattress.

A few moments later, some music, perhaps joropo, crackled to life, then the light clicked back on. There was some giggling then the sound of a bottle opening and liquid being poured. Then a pair of high heels bounced to the floor beside Ray's head, the long stiletto-style he'd seen on the hired girl. The next things to appear were two shapely calves, quickly shrouded by a bunched-up dress.

Ray set the shutter sound on his camera to silent then eased the lens out from under the bed just enough to click off a shot before the legs disappeared.

More giggling returned then some soft banter then the distinct sound of a bare hand across a fleshy bottom.

"You dirty boy, Viktor."

"Me next. Me next."

Ray tucked the camera back under the bed and checked the photo. It was Jimenez's secretary who, as captured by the shot angle, apparently had an affinity for panties bedazzled with rhinestones.

Ray zoomed in on the picture and discovered something fortunate in the background. Beyond the sparkly crotch-shot, on the ceiling above the bed, a mirror reflected the entire scene unfolding above him. As the spanking tapered away and the giggling turned to groans, the box spring began to squeak at more regular intervals. Ray slipped his hand from under the bed again, angled the camera upward and rattled off thirty or forty shots before something bounced off his hand.

He yanked the camera back under the bed and held his breath as a weird buzzing sound filled his ears. He glanced over as a single female hand, draped in diamond bracelets, began pawing about the ground, feeling along the carpeted floor. Finally, the hand latched onto the buzzing thing—a crafty little purple vibrator—then hauled it up and back into the fray.

"There you go, big boy. How does that make you feel?"

"Give it to me, honey. Give it to me good."

An hour later, the box spring finally settled back to a resting state, and the trio adjourned to the shower to clean themselves up. Ray waited until the water was running then slipped out to the tender and made his way back to shore.

CHAPTER 17

"YOU BRING OVER any of your own beer, Jack? Or are you just planning on drinking mine?"

"For some reason it tastes better when somebody else pays for it, Ray. Besides, two's my limit."

"I've noticed a few bars around town flying their flags half-mast since you started laying off."

"I'll make up for it soon enough."

The two sat in twin hunter green resin chairs on the upper deck of the sheriff's Gibson houseboat. The vessel was docked behind a private residence on a quiet canal at the southern end of Tavernier Creek. Ray slipped it there for free, as the absentee owners liked the idea of a gun-toting law enforcement officer keeping an eye on their interests. Aside from breaking free from its lines during Tropical Storm Irene, the vessel hadn't moved from the dock in over fifteen years. A series of potted plants—lime trees, various palm species and fiddle leaf figs—placed about the deck provided a smattering of shade and lent a domesticated aura to the bachelor's floating pad. The new cocoplum he'd picked up from Clara at the nursery occupied the sunniest corner in an otherwise shady environment.

Ray handed Jack a fresh beer. "So you and Summer on the mend?"

"Tough to say."

"Things a bit volatile?"

Jack shrugged. "You think it's the age difference?"

"Don't know. I prefer a solid age difference. But older, not younger. Easier to run away if the need arises."

"I don't know what it is, Ray. Summer does something to me. Makes me want to give up my complacent ways and dive into the unknown."

"Maybe you should give up beer instead."

"I'm likely to give up oxygen before that happens." Jack popped the top on the new can. "Any word on the whereabouts of our disappearing corpse?"

Ray shuffled toward a fig. "Still nothing. But I did have a little meet and greet with the Jersey crew."

"Anything of interest?"

"Some blood on the tip of their fishing gaff."

"Wow, Ray. That's some serious detective work. Blood on a gaff—"

"I didn't think too much of it either until Mookie told me the boat's never been fished."

Jack shrugged.

"Didn't you tell me there was an elongated wound in Ross's butt cheek?" The sheriff swung an imaginary gaff then hauled in on a heavy faux score.

"You could be on to something."

"Imagine that. From a government stooge nonetheless."

"But why would they want Ross dead?"

"I'm a little light on motive at the moment. But get this. Your new client. This Blanch gal. Her name came up while I was out there. Sounds like she's made her way around the entire crew."

"Bloom's certainly off that rose. But I don't know. The jilted lover thing seems like a bit of a stretch. Anything else?"

"Yeah. A floatplane stopped by their sportfisher about three miles offshore. I ran the tail numbers, and it turns out they were registered to a James Stephen Fossett."

"That name supposed to mean something?"

"Nope. But the numbers were retired back in '07."

"Any chance duplicate numbers could have been issued?"

Ray plucked a yellowing leaf from the fig and tossed it into the water. "Nope. They're one-and-done. Anyway, one of the Jersey boys, the Bagels character, was flying back from a business trip of some sort. He was intentionally vague about exactly where he'd been."

"What's that got to do with anything?"

"Not sure. But he came back with a peculiar package." Ray bent a fig branch down, studied a leaf then let it flip back into place. "He had this metal box with him. Inside was a rubber membrane filled with some kind of gel. Looked kind of like a jellyfish."

"Don't remind me." Jack examined the ligature marks on his palm. "So what was it?"

"Mookie said an implant device. You know—" Ray cupped his hands at his chest. "Said they were for Blanch."

What? This was getting a little ridiculous even by Florida standards. "You're not going to believe this, but I found an entire baitfish cage full of implants over at Ossie's place. Here. Check this out." Jack pulled out the piece of paper he'd taken from the boathouse and folded it open.

Ray took the page and studied it for a moment. "Impact rating. Underwater sustainability. Compression strength." He rustled the page then handed it back. "What the hell is that?"

Jack pointed toward the horizontal columns graphed across the page. "Some kind of test results. And look here." He traced his fingers down the vertical column in the left-hand margin. "These are all different implant manufacturers. Looks like Ossie was testing the products using these criteria."

"What for?"

"Not a clue. But it appears all of them failed at least one test or another to some degree."

"Now that I think about it, Mookie said something about this prosthetic being made from a new space-age material."

Ray stepped toward a Christmas palm and peeled off a dead frond as though shucking corn. "You think Ossie's somehow tied in with the Saluccis?"

"Tough to say."

Jack ran his fingers through his hair. "Is this some kind of plastic surgery racket?"

"Not exactly the mob's M.O. But it may be worth looking into."

Jack nodded. "I also found bid books in Ossie's boathouse. Looks like he's gotten into the dredging business."

"That would be his old man. Gus. Gus Callahan. And that would certainly link Ossie to the development."

"What kind of crazy shit is going on around here?"

"Good question."

Jack sipped his beer. "So why am I here, Ray? Why did you want me to come in person?"

"I got your message about Jimenez having a hand in the Shady Acres deal and didn't want to discuss things over a landline." Ray nodded toward an envelope sitting on a side table. "That's for you."

"What is it?"

"My retirement insurance." Ray handled a pair of pruning shears and stepped toward a Mexican palmetto. "I think you might be able to do something useful with them."

Jack bent back the envelope flap then slid a dozen pocket-sized photographs from the hold. He spun them right-side-up before his brain registered the subject matter. "Jesus, Ray. There's a little more skin showing here than I was expecting. A little warning would've been nice." Jack drew the top photo closer to his face. "So I'm assuming this is Jimenez." He flipped to the next photo.

"Pimple on his ass and all." With the shears, Ray began pruning the boots on the palmetto to a consistent length. "And that's his secretary. The one with the pigtails. I'm not sure who the other gal is."

"What's that he's doing to her?"

"Something called the flying wheelbarrow, if memory serves."

"Been a while?"

The sheriff sighed. "One long and empty stretch of open road for quite some time now."

Jack grinned, looked back to the photo. "Ambitious little maneuver." He riffled through the pictures, the last two showing the commissioner using a rolled up twenty-dollar bill to snort a white powdery line off the secretary's pelvic region. "So where did you get these?"

"The other night I followed Jimenez out to Valenciano's megayacht and did some snooping."

"Who?"

"Don't worry. I'd never heard of him either. But I did some digging after I shot those photos, and it turns out the commissioner's uncle is a guy named Valenciano Jimenez. And this guy's rich. Ultra-rich."

"What kind of yacht?"

"A Baglietto. One hundred seventy-three feet."

Jack exhausted a long, high-pitched whistle. "I'm surprised I haven't noticed that around here."

"I'm not. Apparently he's no longer a welcome guest in the United States. Some sort of hedge fund trading scandal. Fled the country before the Feds could get the cuffs on him. Spends his time now between Cuba and Venezuela according to the maritime logs I was able to dig up. It looks like he motored in just for this meeting with Viktor. Damn thing took place a couple miles offshore, completely under the radar. Boat was blacked out and everything."

"A guy like that could be the money behind the development and whatever else is going on around here."

"How about you, Jack? Anything breaking loose on your end?"

"Maybe." Jack scratched his two-day scruff. "Anyway you can run a name through criminal records?"

Ray pointed the pruning shears toward the stairs leading down to the main deck. "Grab the laptop off the kitchen counter."

Jack eased down and into the cabin then returned with the computer.

Ray bent open the laptop. "What's the guy's name?"

"Fella goes by Skeg."

"What the hell kind of name is that?" The sheriff clicked the computer to life. "Let's see if we've got anything in the system on a Skeg." He rapped at the keys then studied the screen for a moment. "Sure do. Says

146

here he was questioned in a vandalism incident during the cell tower construction."

"The one by the Soggy Dollar?"

Ray nodded. "But nothing ever came of it. Doesn't look like he had a driver's license or any form of legal ID." The sheriff grunted. "Not that unusual down here."

"Anything else?"

Ray shook his head. "Jacket's pretty skinny, Jack. Now what's this all about?"

"Just a guy who used to live out at Shady Acres who wasn't at all pleased about losing his home."

"What's that dump got to do with anything?"

Jack brought the sheriff up to speed on the ROGO points and zoning requirements necessary to get Coconut Key off the ground. "Jimenez certainly played a role in the land acquisition that made the development possible. Money was thrown around. Quite a bit from what it sounds like. There's nothing to tie Jimenez directly to it yet, but maybe Val is the source of that money. And maybe Jimenez pissed this resident off. Maybe if we can find this guy, we can see if Jimenez slipped up and did anything illegal to acquire that land."

Ray stopped pruning and stared at Jack. "I want you to take those photographs and use them."

"I appreciate the gesture, Ray. But I don't really have a soft spot for rightwing porn."

"I'm not dicking around. This Val guy's pretty much untouchable for a someone like me, but Jimenez isn't."

Jack slapped the envelope of photos against his free hand. "You're sure about this?"

"No. Actually, I'm not sure at all. I just know things need to change around here and that can't happen if everyone keeps doing the same old shit."

"You want me to ask Viktor to quit using your office as his private shitter?"

Ray waved Jack down the steps then disappeared into the Gibson, returning a moment later with a shotgun and a box of shells. "Here." He handed them to Jack. "Word is Viktor spends his free time at some swanky clay pigeon gun club up in Okeechobee. Outside Monroe County. In other words, outside my jurisdiction."

"I promise to keep it cool."

Ray stepped to a fig. "You forget how well I know you, Jack."

"Just a few simple questions should do the trick."

Ray plucked a caterpillar from a broad waxy leaf. "He's a bad seed, Jack. A bad seed who likes to shoot at moving targets in his playtime." Ray dropped the bug into the water then swigged his beer. "Just keep my name out of it. I don't need that sonofabitch causing any ripples this close to my retirement."

"Of course. I'm counting on that retirement as much as you are so we can finally start drinking together in public again."

CHAPTER 18

FOR THE FIRST time in seven years Jack crossed Jewfish Creek, heading north, parting from the Keys onto the mainland Florida peninsula. A twelve-gauge shotgun, a sleeve of #8 birdshot shells and the envelope of photographs occupied the passenger seat.

He ran State Road 27 up through South Bay then took the 441 through Port Mayaca. At 70, he turned west and motored toward Okeechobee. The Acapulco handled the open road like a Sunfish crossing the Stream. Every time an eighteen-wheeler blew by, the vehicle shuddered so violently he thought the wheels might sheer away from the axles and leave him grinding down the freeway in a fit of sparks.

Luckily, the Volks remained intact for the entire journey, aside from the left windshield wiper that went cartwheeling into a patch of bushy sawgrass as the tarmac gave way to dirt road. By the time he breached the entrance to Quail Creek Plantation his nerves were frazzled. As he bumped down the rutted entry the bottle-rocket pops of distant gunshots peppered the air.

He located the parking lot, shoehorned the Volks between two cattle trucks then shouldered into the lodge bar. As the door slapped shut behind him, he was greeted by a blast of icy air that ripped across a room finished in knotted pine and floor-to-ceiling fireplaces that glowed merely for effect. Jack ordered a sweet tea then sat and sipped, chewing the fat with an auburn-haired bartendress showcasing a country mouth and a robust physique, the sort of gal who picked up guys in bars more often than they picked her up. After some idle chitchat in the proper tenor he asked if she knew the man named Jimenez.

"Viktor?" The gal stopped drying the tumbler in her hand then flipped the damp bar rag over her shoulder. "Most of the girls around here do."

"He here today?"

She shrugged. "He usually doesn't stop into the bar until after shooting."

According to Jimenez's secretary—the one he was sleeping with—the commissioner spent every Tuesday here at the shooting club. Something in the concussive rhythm of gunshots made it easy for him to think. And, since he could only break away once a year to hunt mountain lions outside Jackson Hole, he felt entitled to a weekly jaunt to Quail Creek Plantation, funded, of course, on the taxpayer's dime.

"Do you know where I might find him now?"

"You new to the club?"

"Just a guest."

"Fresh meat." She bent over, resting her elbows on the bar and intentionally revealing her sun-freckled chest clear down to the upper arch of her pale areolas. "He's probably down at the shoot stand. Want me to have somebody show you the way?"

Jack tossed a ten-dollar bill onto the bar. "Thanks, but I should be all right by myself. What was your name again, anyway?"

"People call me Desie."

"The lovely Ms. Desie. It's certainly been a pleasure."

Jack pushed out into the stagnant inland air. He'd only been inside fifteen minutes, but the heat seemed to have increased by forty degrees. He meandered across a prairie of upland grasses, the concussive booms of shotgun reports growing louder as he approached. At the top of a slight upslope in the grade perched a three-tiered deck staged for the shooters. On the middle tier poised a man who, from a distance, matched the skin tone and build of Commissioner Jimenez.

Jack, with his own shotgun set against his shoulder, clunked up the steps to the second tier. He idled in the background as the commissioner traced his barrel across the horizon, cracking off three crisp shots and shattering three distant discs of clay.

The commissioner laughed as though impressed with his own prowess. He wore earmuffs and firing-range sunglasses with yellow lenses.

His mustache was waxed into sharp points, curled slightly upward at the ends.

As the commissioner turned around, he pushed his earmuffs beyond the cup of his ears then dead-eyed Jack. "So you're the guy?"

Jack let his shotgun barrel drop from his shoulder into his open hand. "What guy is that?"

"Rubio called. You really jangled that little fairy right down to his skivvies." The commissioner stuffed new shells into the pump-action shotgun. "You know he's my brother-in-law."

Jack's eyebrows went up.

"My sister swears he's into girls, but either way—" The commissioner pumped the stock on the shotgun clicking a shell into the barrel. "Anyway, I'm glad you stopped by. Saves me the trouble of tracking you down back in Islamorada."

This was not good news. "You wanted to see me?"

"What I wanted to do was knock your teeth out. But I'm guessing that would be political suicide, Mr.—?"

"Crevalle. Jack Crevalle."

"Hmm. Crevalle." Viktor turned back toward the field as though watching an English Pointer flush grouse from a meadow. "You look familiar. You one of Clayton's boys? He trying to get some dirt on me before the reelection?"

"I've already got plenty of dirt."

"That so?"

By the time Jimenez turned back, Jack had slipped the manila envelope from his shorts pocket and withdrawn a close-up pick of a naked leg and half an ass cheek.

The commissioner laughed but didn't touch it. "What's this?"

"Some racy pics of you, your secretary and a third nameless coed in some very compromising poses."

151

For a split second, the commissioner seemed surprised, but any look of confusion quickly evaporated as he snapped his earmuffs back into place then squared around. In the distance a series of sporting clays went whipping through the air. He traced his barrel across the sky then pumped the trigger four times, cartwheeling shrapnel into the elongated blades of wireweed and lovegrass thirty-five yards out.

As the ringing in Jack's ears ceased, Viktor swung his body back around then unsnapped the muffs from a single ear. He rapped the barrel against Jack's right clavicle hard enough to chip bone. The sulfur gunshot fumes accentuated the gesture.

"You trying to blackmail me, Crevalle?"

Jack handled the warm barrel then pushed it away from his chest, angling it slightly back toward the commissioner. "Are you threatening me, commissioner?"

"I'm doing what any cornered animal would do in this situation. Protecting myself by whatever means necessary. And believe me, you're not the largest animal that's ever had me cornered. Not by a long shot. Now what is it that you want?"

"I'm just looking for some answers."

"Then maybe you should try asking questions instead of threatening me with risqué photographs."

"Okay then. Tell me how you got all the signatures to push the Shady Acres through."

"I didn't." The commissioner rested the gun barrel against his shoulder. "A lackey of mine went door-to-door and got everybody out there to sign off on that deal. All legit."

"This lackey have a name?"

"Not that I can remember."

"Surely there were some holdouts that didn't want to sign their land over."

"Look here, Crevalle. I made the taxpayers of Monroe County a cool five million greenbacks on that transaction."

"Minus a couple hundred grand to your brother-in-law."

"All legitimate."

"Why not just have the residents sell it directly to the Coconut Key developers? Let them make the money?" Jack tucked the manila envelope back into his pocket. "Let me guess. It had something to do with ROGO points."

The commissioner nodded and coughed up a curt laugh. "Let's just say I had to make a small adjustment in zoning."

"Now we're getting somewhere."

"The land was zoned multifamily so I had to balkanize the parcel and give each of those RV lots its own deed."

"Sounds shady."

The commissioner's eyes dilated behind the yellow firing range lenses. "Perhaps. But it's not illegal. In 1985 the elected officials of this great state voted to initiate the Growth Management Act giving governing power over development to the counties." The commissioner grinned. "Hell, it's the reason I got out of private enterprise and into politics."

"So that's what gave the developers enough ROGO points to move forward with Coconut Key."

The commissioner kept quiet.

"Don't you know what Coconut Key will do to the aquatic ecosystem?"

"Now that's a glass half-empty attitude. Optimistic guy like myself sees jobs creation on a grand scale. Besides, I hunt. I don't give a flying fornication about fishing. You got a problem, take your beef to the State's Attorney."

"That doesn't explain who ponied up the cash for the bribes."

"Bribes? What bribes?" He snickered then twisted one end of his mustache into a sharper point.

"So who paid your fee to make the development a reality?"

"My perks tend to be less tangible. Tougher to trace that way."

What sort of perks was he talking about here? "Valenciano stroke that check?"

Viktor's mustache twitched three times. "If you'll excuse me, I believe I'm done with the Q&A."

Jack cleared his throat. "You know anything about these developers going missing?"

The commissioner blinked twice then offered up a warm smile that seemed so calm and content in the context of the question it made Jack's neck hairs stand on end. "What's your choice of weapon there, Crevalle?"

Jack glanced down at his shotgun then back up.

The commissioner slapped his own shotgun barrel against his hand. "This here's a Perrazi. Italian made, of course. A gun like this can set a guy back several hundred grand." He grinned. "What I'm saying is it's not for the faint of heart." He plucked a shotgun shell from a nearby box and held it to the light. "These little bastards are number eight Noblesports. Best ammo on the market. They travel over twelve-hundred feet per second." He stuffed one into the chamber then fingered another from the box. "So you've got to be pretty fast on your feet to dodge one if somebody's shooting your direction."

He slid the second shell into place then reached for a third. "Bear in mind that while I'm an avid hunter I'm also a gambler. And I'm willing to bet that those photos somehow get destroyed before you make it back to whatever rock it is you live under."

"Actually, I'm more of a water guy."

"I should've known. Jack Crevalle. That's a bottom-feeding species, isn't it?"

CHAPTER 19

JACK RATTLED THE Volkswagen south over the arching skyway known as the Jewfish Creek Bridge, his heartrate easing as he fled the racy pace of mainland America. His fingers loosened around the wheel as a warm sea breeze swirled through the cabin. There was something about crossing that bridge, about that high vantage, about glancing down at the sailboats and trawlers amid the vast expanse of Florida Bay that settled him, brought serenity to his otherwise restless spirit.

By the time he slipped onto Plantation Key, he'd almost forgotten about the dead body and the development and that he'd accepted payment to find a man whose spirit could no longer be found.

The flashing blue lights in his side-view mirror snapped him back from his dreamy state. He braced his hands against the wheel then adjusted the rearview. The pursuing vehicle bore the FWC logo, and the slippery sneer of Oscar Callahan showed through the broad pickup truck windshield.

What did that shit weasel want now?

Jack clicked on his blinker but kept the vehicle pointed down the main drag. He was only about a half-mile from the Soggy Dollar, a place he felt might offer a home-court advantage against whatever the hell Ossie was up to now.

A hundred yards up, the flickering lights were joined by a few belts of the horn and a warbling siren. Then the pickup truck nosed three inches from Jack's bumper, close enough for Jack to see Ossie hooking his thumb toward the road shoulder and mouthing the words *pull over*.

Jack slowed to fifteen miles an hour then eased onto the gravel but continued toward the Soggy Dollar entrance. Once Ossie attempted to pass him, perhaps to blockade the road ahead, but Jack had enough acceleration in the old gal to hold him off until he reached the turn.

As he bounced the VW into the parking lot, he jogged the wheel then careened toward a space near Tipsy's entryway, so there'd be witnesses if Ossie attempted anything unorthodox. He parked, jammed a hand into the horn a couple of times then climbed out of the car.

A few seconds later the kid came scrambling over from the dock, fishing rod in hand, a live shrimp flexing on the end of the hook. "Jack. Jack! Are you okay?"

"Pull out your phone and record this, kid."

The kid discarded his rod then slipped out his cell phone and began recording as Ossie stepped from his truck then came around the front bumper like a mongoose in heat. He wore his department-issued Stetson and a sweaty brown uniform. The blue patrol lights on the vehicle rotated slowly, however, he'd been kind enough to silence the siren. He crunched to a stop then eyed the kid. "You really want to get involved?"

The kid backed away a few paces, shaking his head but still filming.

"Come here, you little punk."

This caught the kid's attention. He tucked the phone back into his pocket then skittered down the gangway and out of sight. Ossie turned back, set a hand on his Taser then flashed Jack those beady eyes of a hungry wharf rat.

"You better have a damn good reason for not pulling over."

"What are you talking about?"

"I was behind you for damn near a mile with my lights flashing and my siren going."

Jack plugged a finger into an ear canal and wiggled it around. "You get to be my age and all kinds of shit starts breaking down on you."

"Turn around. Hands on your head."

"You've got to be kidding me."

Ossie unsnapped the strap on his Taser. "No more warnings." He withdrew the weapon and took aim.

Jack had been zinged by a Taser twice before. It wasn't pleasant. "Okay. Just calm down." He spun a half turn and laced his fingers on the back of his head. "What's going on? Was I speeding?"

"You get off tampering with federal property?"

Jack kept his head down. What was Ossie talking about? Did he somehow know he'd been snooping around his boathouse?

"You're going to jail this time. One way or another you've got to learn to respect the law. Sheriff should be here any minute."

"You're a grouper trooper. It's not like you're even a real cop."

As Ossie wrenched Jack's arms behind his back and clicked on the cuffs, Jack's thoughts began to align. A finky-looking dude in a brown uniform. One of the commissioner's lackeys. An old man with a dredge boat. The notes from the boathouse. Jack decided to dig.

"So you're the guy."

"The guy what, Cubera. I don't speak stupid."

"The guy who went around collecting signatures at Shady Acres. The one who conned them out of their land."

"You trying to slander my good name?"

Ossie kicked his boot treads into the soft meat of Jack's upper calves and dropped him kneecap-first onto the gravel. Jack bit down on his lip, waiting for the sharp sting to dissipate, then mustered up another jab.

"Is that how your old man managed a dredge contract with Coconut Key?"

"You back to being a dick?"

"It never really leaves you."

Ossie reached down and clicked the cuffs tighter as a crowd of Tipsy's patrons trickled out into the sunshine, cocktails in hand, to investigate the commotion. In the layman's world, happy hour was underway, and the parking lot now bustled with that sect of the Key's upper echelon who fancied themselves martini connoisseurs. Every couple minutes another exotic import roared up to a temporary valet then deposited a new couple in matching nautical garb before being parked in tidy rows across the lot. Jack kept glancing up at each arriving roadster and sedan until finally Sheriff Livingston slewed his truck into the lot then slid to a halt.

Ray stepped out shaking his head. "You're a real piece of work, Jack. What in the hell did you do this time?"

"Ossie's just pissed off because I'm onto him."

"Onto him about what?"

"Ask him about Shady Acres."

Ray crunched over, hauled Jack up from his kneeled position then looked at Ossie. "You really think the cuffs were necessary?"

Oscar tipped his Stetson. "The man's got at least one aggravated assault that I'm aware of."

"What's this all about, Jack?"

"Forgery."

Ossie hooked his thumbs over his gun belt. "You want to try and prove that?"

Jack turned to Ray. "And bribery."

Ray shook his head. "What kind of shit show is this?"

"This asshole went door-to-door at Shady Acres and conned them out of their land."

Ray looked at Jack then hooked his thumb at Ossie. "And why would he do that?"

"In exchange for a handsome dredging contract for the build-out on Coconut Key is my guess."

Ossie's eyes shifted sideways. "You're fishing without bait, Cubera."

"That's not what the commissioner told me."

Ray flashed Jack a sideways glance as Ossie puffed his chest, his gaunt physique almost comical in such a pose. "You think you know something?"

"That's enough." The sheriff stepped between them. "You two settle down. Now what's any of this got to do with you being in handcuffs?"

Jack nodded at Ossie. "This asshole's gone off on a power trip."

"Not true." Ossie nodded toward the two separated sections of the bright yellow wheel lock discarded in a back corner of the parking lot.

Jack had forgotten about breaking it off. Apparently Ossie had taken objection to his methodology for getting his car out of impound.

"Your boy tampered with government property. That's a federal offense."

"Is that what this is all about?" Jack asked.

"That rattletrap was off limits until those fines are settled."

"Not a problem," Jack said. "I've got the cash on my boat. How about I just settle my tab and be on my way?"

Ossie slipped off his Stetson, his greasy hair slicked back and ringed from the hat placement. He pointed it at Jack. "That ship has sailed, Cubera. Isn't that right, sheriff?"

Ray looked toward the crowd gathered in the parking lot. "You're coming with me, Jack. All this publicity, we've got to make this official."

Ossie snickered.

Ray took Jack by the forearm. "Don't worry, Jack. I promise you'll get your one phone call."

"Give me a break, Ray. You can't be serious."

* * *

Jack hung up the payphone mounted on the wall of the holding pen at the Sheriff's Office then turned and eyed through the bars. "Come on, Ray. How long you going to keep me in here?"

Ray chuckled then slipped a toothpick into his mouth. "Just be happy I didn't make you dress down in a jumpsuit. What's this? The third time I've brought you in?"

"Fourth."

Ray stepped over to the cell door, slipped his key into the lock then groaned the gate open. "Whining like that. It's conduct unbecoming a professional boat bum."

Jack was about to push out into the room, but the front door swung open and Commissioner Jimenez sauntered in. "Livingston. You got a minute?"

159

Jack eased the gate shut then lay down on the floor of the cell, cupping a hand around his face but leaving just enough room between his fingers to observe.

"You here to use the facilities?" Ray asked.

"Not this go around, Raeford." Jimenez glanced Jack's direction then shook his head. "Got a wino in the cage today, do you?"

"Just another lost ball in high weeds. One of those habitual offenders. Can't be rehabilitated."

Jimenez pulled a small wax canister from his pocket and pried off the lid. "You ask me, we should be running chain gangs with these vagrants. As many as we've got down here these streets ought to be squeaky clean." He grunted, seemed to drift away then came back. "Anyway, what are you doing the day after tomorrow? Mid-morning? Say, eleven?"

"Not sure, commissioner. I'll have to check my—"

"Clear your schedule." Jimenez swiped a thumb and forefinger over the mustache wax then began working it into the dark and pointy feature projecting from the left corner of his mouth. "You and me. We're going for a boat ride."

"I should be able to—" Ray shifted his utility belt. "What's this about?"

The commissioner turned back toward the exit then paused, checking his mustache in the reflection. "Just be ready at eleven." He slipped the canister back into his pocket. "I'll meet you down at the dock. We'll take the department boat."

"Okay then. Anything I need to know?"

"Just be ready."

The commissioner put a loafer into the door, swung it open then evaporated into the sunshine. A long pause followed—perhaps a full minute—before Jack pushed off the ground and stepped from the cell. "What was that all about?"

"That's what I should be asking you."

"Me?"

"What did you do with those photos, Jack? How in the hell did my name get dragged into this?"

160

"I promise you, Ray. Your name never even came up. But the meeting was a total bust. He couldn't have cared less about the pictures."

Ray checked the wall clock as a vein cropped up across his forehead. "Two years thirty-eight days and a few short hours, and I'm out of here, Jack. Please tell me you didn't figure out a way to mess that up."

"Certainly not intentionally."

Just then the front door to the office swung open again, and the lovely Summer Dahlia strolled in. She wore her hair pinned up and back, a white cotton top and denim jeans three generations faded.

Ray stepped over and embraced Summer, planting a kiss on her left cheek. "Damn is it good to see you, Summer. It's been way too long. You're certainly a finer sight than the last face that came through that door." Ray's hands paused at Summer's elbows then drifted away. "I suppose you're here to bail this juvenile out of jail?"

"Did you find the money on the boat?" Jack asked.

She fished the roll of hundred-dollar bills from her pocket and lobbed it over to Jack. Jack peeled sixty-eight bills from the stack and glanced at the shrinking roll. Maybe it was time for austerity measures.

Summer turned to Ray. "Ray, it sure is good to see you. You look great."

"Yeah, right. The Dick Clark of the PI world over there still looks thirty, and I've aged like a tomato left too long in the crisper."

"Ruggedly handsome."

"Well, I suppose I do look good for sixty." Ray puffed his chest and smoothed his thinning hair. "Crying shame I'm only fifty-three."

* * *

Summer stepped toward the driver-side door of a brown Peugeot cloaked in a heavy layer of pollen. "Neighbor let me borrow it."

"Then I owe you both."

Jack creaked open the passenger door then settled onto the chocolate vinyl seat, the back of his thighs singeing from the late afternoon sun. He shut the door, the heat heavy in the cabin, the black dashboard radiating the August rays in ways that made his face melt.

Summer began to hand-crank down her window. "A/C doesn't work."

"Then let's get some natural air conditioning blowing through this thing."

As Jack rolled down his window, Summer shifted into first gear then eased off the clutch and lurched toward the Overseas Highway.

"Much better."

Tipping her head, Summer motioned toward the seat behind her. "You may want to take a look at those."

Jack reached back and grabbed a binder of documents. "What's this?"

"Soggy Dollar's being sold off. It's set to close in fourteen days."

He flipped through the first four leaves of paper then slapped the binder against his free hand. "Nothing like going homeless." He tossed the binder over his shoulder and onto the backseat. "Maybe there's room for me at the local mission."

"I tipped off a friend over at Bluewater who's going to file an injunction to slow things down. Looks like some of the soil sampling might've been a bit sloppy. But, even if the injunction goes through, it'll only stall things out for a few weeks."

"What do the developers even want with the marina?"

"They're turning it into a ferry dock. A place to shuttle people to and from Coconut Key."

"This just keeps getting better."

They turned off the highway and slowed to a stop sign. A heat wave rolled through the cabin. Summer spun a quarter turn toward Jack, her hands firmly set at ten and two. "Where are we, Jack?"

He supposed she meant metaphorically. "Ten months in. It's fairly unfamiliar turf for me."

"That's what scares me."

Jack shrugged. "From what I remember, things start out simple and get more complicated as the days roll on."

"That's not very reassuring."

"I suppose it's time to give up or give in."

"And?"

"Like I said, this is unfamiliar turf."

Summer slid the shifter back into gear. "You're a real charmer, Jack Cubera."

CHAPTER 20

AS THE SUN broke over the backwaters of Florida Bay, the man called Skeg rolled from his hammock and strolled, buck naked, out into the knee-deep water. In the distant sky, the haze from the Coconut Key rainbowing operation hung in the air like a post-apocalyptic sandstorm.

He set his hands on his hips and, without bothering to aim, flexed his prostate, shooting an arch of golden urine into the drink. Rotating slowly side-to-side, he drew a proverbial line in the salty water.

Incorrigible shitbirds.

His mood was foul. The Coconut Key development was progressing far too quickly for his liking. The manmade island was rising. The concrete and glass were soon to come.

What then?

Water parks? Go-cart tracks? Shopping plazas?

What will remain when all the green is gone?

To make matters worse, news crews from across the Middle Forty-Seven had been flocking in by boat, helicopter and private plane to document the engineering marvel. For the past several days, his usual protocol of waking up slowly to the jostling of palm fronds and a morning boner had been replaced by the varying pitches of combustible engines and an irrefutable flaccidness in his overall demeanor.

Flexing his prostate again, he squeezed the last golden dribbles from his bladder then stood drip-drying in the sunshine and absorbing the cacophony of engine noises.

The whole goddamn planet had gone gas powered.

What ever happened to wind propulsion? Oars and paddles? Sails and spinnakers? How about some self-propulsion? Maybe a little exercise.

These people weren't getting any skinnier.

He lumbered back to camp, showered under a warm solar-heated system then polished his teeth with a miswak. After a judicious application of vetiver oil behind each ear, he dangled his tea kettle from a shepherd's hook set over a fire pit and stoked the embers until flames licked upward around the basin.

As the water warmed to a boil, he fed lumps of psychedelic mushrooms into the kettle. The fungi swelled like sponges in the broth then slowly bobbed up and down turning pale and soft as they steeped in the thermal currents.

After ten minutes, he steadied a hollow gourd into the sand at his feet then stretched a swatch of cheese cloth over the top. Tipping the kettle slowly, he filtered the mushroom juice into the gourd then tossed the spent fungi into the flames.

The wet lumps popped and hissed lending a soothing rhythm as he stirred a few triturated mint leaves into the concoction.

Once the water cooled, he took the gourd like a chalice, bringing the rim to his lips and swallowing long, his Adam's apple bobbing up and down seven times, before disengaging.

The liquid tasted hot and earthy. A hint of dirt. A flavorful note of earthworm.

Within minutes, the mushrooms began to effervesce within him, and the first hallucinatory wave of psilocybin arrived. The world around him began to undulate, the foreground receding and the background rushing in upon him.

He blinked his good eye and gazed around. The treetops bowed over like soggy broccoli stalks, and the understory clacked with oysters now exposed to the brightening day on the outgoing tide.

Aquatic castanets.

Perhaps a little acoustic accompaniment was in order.

He finished his tea then took up his ukulele and began to strum.

The first chord was vibrant and wicked, tickling his thumb tip as it rasped along the quartet of strings absorbing the vibrations up his finger bones and through his vertebrae. The second felt sublime. The third formed a Polynesian melody—all dark wood and damp sunsets.

It smelled of hibiscus blooms. It tasted like warm rain.

It was simple, just a G-C-D progression, but when played with the proper lilt and suspension it rang out like the first breath of air when you come up from a drowning.

He began to sing along, his raspy voice climbing to registers one would not expect from a backwater recluse. He closed his eyes, pitching higher yet, until something rattled him from his delicious high.

What was it? He paused and set the ukulele in the sand. It came again, this time by way of a pitchy scream he could hardly believe.

It belonged to a personal watercraft. No doubt. That caterwauling cried out as distinctly and discordantly as a hacksaw over banjo strings.

A rumor had surfaced about a new outfit moving into town. A foolish move on their part. These infestations had become a growing epidemic. Little huts renting Sea-Doos and WaveRunners for eighty bucks a half-hour had sprung up on every beach from Key Largo to the Dry Tortugas. Most disturbing, however, were the Florida laws and regulations regarding use of such crafts. There were, in fact, none.

No age limit.

No license required.

No training course necessary.

Skeg moved out to the edge of the island and tipped his ear toward the commotion. His skull ached as the tinny chatter carried over the water. His spine shivered each time some lame retread twisted the throttle and carved zigzags and figure eights through his pristine backwaters.

Back at camp, he jammed his feet through his burlap pant legs then holstered his machete. Slung over his shoulder was his wineskin bota filled with pure corn syrup. A personal watercraft operation simply would not be tolerated.

It was time to quell the infestation, one more time.

* * *

Skeg paddled to the mainland and located his source of distress. This time around a company called *Salty Johnson's Waterbike Rentals* had sprouted overnight in an abandoned *She Sells Sea Shells* building on Plantation Key.

The operation consisted of a metal warehouse serving as overnight storage and a shady place to crank wrenches. Fronting the bay, Salty utilized a cheap elephant grass palapa to hawk at passers-by like a carnival barker. Skeg paddled in close enough to witness the greasy little redneck in action for about fifteen minutes. Then he tracked a duo of renters as they went zinging across the gulf and disappeared into a desolate lagoon on a scrubby little islet called Crane Key.

Their waterbikes soon went silent.

Skeg paddled out to the islet then drifted around to the leeward side where a complex weave of mangrove roots climbed up from the knee-deep water. He secured his boat to a hearty trunk then shimmied into the branches.

Limb to limb, tree to tree, he monkeyed his way toward the lagoon, his feet never touching the sand below. As he neared the vegetation-fringed periphery of the lagoon, the WaveRunners came into focus, nudged onto the beach, their purple and red gelcoat finishes as out of place in the natural environment as Easter eggs in an osprey nest.

Their apparent renters were nowhere to be seen, probably hunkering down on a sandy patch for a little afternoon delight.

Skeg dropped from the mangrove branches on to the sand then slithered low across the beach like a salamander. As he approached, the water bikes ticked side-to-side in the ripples lapping the shoreline. He unscrewed one gas cap then the other then uncorked the bota. He aimed the nozzle into one opening, shot a hard stream of syrup into one tank then started on the next.

A fine smirk punctuated his cheeks.

He never even heard the young man approaching. All Skeg saw, as his head pivoted, were two sunburned feet that led upward to calves the

167

size of tree trunks. A voice from above was addressing him as *fuckwad* and threatening to beat him blind.

The dude meant it.

The young buff hothead possessed those wide set eyes attributed to excessive human growth hormone abuse. No doubt, he played line-backer.

Skeg moved quickly with the machete. Reaching over his shoulder, he brandished the tarnished blade from his sheath. The blade flashed in the sunshine as he swung the crude weapon at the tree trunks with the speed and prowess of a Honduran plantain harvester.

The blade stopped with a sharp pop as it connected with the football player's left fibula. A fine wedge-shaped divot of muscle and bone flung off into the neighboring tidal pool.

The act took maybe two seconds, but the effects would not be so quick to dismiss themselves.

The young man didn't even scream when he saw the blood gushing down his ankle and into the sand around his feet. Its brilliant color, not unlike that of the watercrafts, must've been surreal amidst the terror and shock of a machete strike.

Skeg scrambled onto his feet and took the football player by the throat. "Tell Salty it's time to shutter up the business and set sail for bluer skies."

The football player broke free of Skeg's grip then took seven bound-ing strides into the water before the leg refused to cooperate any longer. His body splashed forward, his face slamming into his petite female companion, who, upon seeing the maroon plume forming in the tide, instinctively screamed *shark*.

Skeg launched into the mangrove branches and out of sight then found a blind behind a thicket of leaves and watched with a satisfied pride.

It wasn't until the gal dragged her hulky boyfriend onto shore that he began to blubber like a small child. His hamstring dangled like two severed sections of surgical tubing that squirted blood with each rapid heartbeat. In a moment of compassion and weakness, his girlfriend gave up her Tory Burch bikini top for him to use as a tourniquet.

As Skeg admired her perky accessories from a safe distance, he couldn't help but snicker as the girl cried out to her beau he'd just been savagely attacked by a genuine Florida skunk ape.

She'd seen the thing with her own eyes. No doubt about it.

CHAPTER 21

THE DAMP TORTUGA had been an open-air dive catering to a bare-footed, over-served clientele, offering average service and heavy pours.

Her old deck planks had been ripped up and replaced with faux composite timber tinted pastel pink. The raw glassless openings now housed double-paned windows showcasing crisscrossing sash patterns. The beer taps made way for thirty-seven strains of vodka and gin, ranging from cupcake to salmon flavor. The once dangling incandescent bulbs were stripped away then transformed with indirect lighting—a splash here off the ceiling, a chevron here below the bar—and consisted of those energy-saving LED lights whose version of white cast an eerie bluish hue about the interior.

Tipsy's. A martini bar. The sort of place people went *cocktailing* not *drinking*.

Apparently, even the most southerly places could go south.

Thankfully, Jack's corner table lent him a peekaboo view of the bay where a dozen sloops moored in the yard and reflected the moonlight. In front of him sat the only beer kept behind the bar, Sagres, a Portuguese import. He worked on it slowly with a hard lump in his gullet as he awaited his scheduled meeting.

This wasn't going to be pleasant for Jack. He'd never informed a client that her significant other no longer moved amongst the upright. He wondered how to segue into it. *Well, Blanch the good news is your sugar daddy isn't sleeping with anyone else.* Or maybe he'd just come straight out with it. Rip the bandage off fast then let shock take care of the rest.

There seemed no sidestepping into such a heavy matter. No easing around the tough parts and passing it along one small bit at a time so that the whole did not seem so intense. The death of a loved one proved a harsh reality for the living but scarcely an inconvenience for the one who'd recently endured it.

The waitress swept back through the blue room, and Jack waved off a second beer as Blanch pushed through the front door with a set of diamond-studded sunglasses holding back her hair. She wore a dainty satin ensemble both the shade and sheen of a Petit Sirah. She appeared half-drunk or, at least, over-jovial and to Jack's surprise she was not alone. A portly man loitered in the hook of her arm, sporting dark pleated pants, a beige silk shirt and a white fedora with a black band.

Jack stroked his mustache. Interesting. Wasn't Blanch still dating Ross? Or, at least, didn't she think she still was?

Her eyes panned the room once then twice before stopping on Jack. "There he is." Her voice carried over the discordant murmurings of casual martini drinkers, before she started across the bar with the portly man in tow.

As they reached the table, Jack stood and hugged her neck, a garish perfume invading his nostrils with the flavors of maraschino cherries. He pulled back, hoping the smell hadn't transferred onto his clothes, then poked his hand toward the gentlemen for a shake.

The portly man declined, his musky cologne arriving like an uninvited guest to the already aromatic bouquet.

"I got this thing about shaking hands with strangers."

Jack bit his lower lip and eyed the guy. He was borderline comical—a head of frizzled dark hair poking out from under his fedora and accessorized by a matching fur which sprouted from his chest.

"Nice cornicello." Jack looked back to Blanch. "So, Ms. Theroux, how's the retrofit coming along on the Hinckley?"

"Retrofit?" The portly man narrowed his eyes at Blanch. "What's this about a retrofit?"

"I'm having some work done."

"You or the boat?"

Blanch waved him off. "I wanted to jazz up the interior for parties."

"More parties? As if half of Miami hasn't already made a pass through that yacht."

"In fact." She touched Jack's wrist. "The work is finally finished."

Finished? Jack hadn't noticed any additional commotion at the docks since the old interior was extracted. "That was quick. How did the new interior play out?"

"Why? You thinking about fixing yours up?"

The portly man squared toward Jack. "Enough about the Hinckley. Now tell me, pal, what is it exactly that you do?"

Blanch squeezed Jack's wrist. "He's the one who cleans boats and such here at the marina."

"That right?"

Jack set his Sagres on the table. It sounded like a probable enough job description. "That and I run a very unsuccessful snow removal business out of my Moppie."

The portly man eyed Jack up and down. "You lose your razor back in the seventies or something?"

Jack smiled, the furry garnishment tickling his nostrils. "I give a lot of mustache rides."

Blanch giggled.

"But, sorry, there's a weight limit."

The man swiveled toward Blanch. "This one's got a wiseass mouth on him, don't he?"

Jack cleared his throat. "I'm sorry. Do you know me or something?"

"Doubtful. Why do you ask?"

"Because usually only people who know me personally treat me with such tactless hostility."

"Yeah?"

"Yeah." Jack nodded. "And most of them have smaller, but much nicer boobs than you. Now if you don't mind, Ms. Theroux and I have some business to discuss. In private."

"Sure thing, Captain Mustache." The man pressed a hand into his rotund belly. "Lobster Louie I had for lunch ain't sitting so good. You two chat it up amongst yourselves while I go hit the can."

As the guy waddled off the waitress swooped over, and Blanch ordered a chocolate martini then sat at the table across from Jack.

"Well then." Jack dropped his eyes to the table then brought them back up. "Ms. Theroux. I've found out some information about Ross that I need to share."

"The prick still hasn't even called."

"There's a good reason for that. You see, I'm not sure if you're aware of this yet, but, uh, Ross, uh, Mr. Biggins, well, uh, he's no longer with us."

Jack reached across the table and covered Blanch's hands with his own, allowing her to absorb the news. The waitress, unaware, plinked the martini onto the table between them then, sensing the situation, quickly retreated.

Jack waited for tears or at least a quivering chin, but Blanch's botulinum-riddled facial muscles did not flinch. Instead, her right hand moved, drawing her martini off the table then she sipped the taupe liquid before cradling the glass close to her face.

"Are you trying to tell me Ross is dead?"

Jack nodded. "I'm sorry to be the one who—"

"Of course he is." She slumped back into her chair, exasperated, put out. "Well, fuck me. He and his wife had already separated. He was going to leave her so we could be together." Her eyes got misty. "Do you have any idea how much time I've invested in that fat bastard?"

Jack let the question wane. People tended to grieve on their own terms.

Blanch dug into a gold Louie Vuitton clutch and withdrew a long slender cigarette which she set between her teeth. "I should've known."

"How could you have known?"

"A woman should just know these things." She fumbled through her purse for a lighter. "So where is he now? Can I see him?"

"That's a bit complicated."

"What do you mean?"

"He's been misplaced."

"How do you lose that fat sonofabtich?"

"The truth is that due to the delicate nature of the situation, nobody's releasing any information about the death just yet."

She set a lighter on the table. "Are you saying my Ross was murdered?"

"I'm just saying there's some questions that need to be answered before that can be determined."

"Questions?" Blanch sifted through the napkin holder and pepper shakers for an ashtray then plucked the cigarette from her teeth. "Honestly, this no smoking thing is absolute shit. Do you mind if we step outside?"

Jack, mildly shocked by Blanch's demeanor, was delighted to flee the nouveau environment for a warm breath of nighttime humidity. They adjourned to an outside deck overlooking the moonlit bay peppered with sailboats, each with a single white anchor light tipping its mast and punctuating the night.

Blanch drew the lighter toward her lips, her face awash in wavering orange light as she puffed the cigarette to life. "So if he's dead, Jack, then what the hell am I paying you to do?"

"I'm still going to find him for you. If you like. The estate likes to have a body before they release any gifts and such left behind in the will."

"You think there might be something in there for me?"

Jack pulled back from the unfiltered drift off her cigarette smoke. "In my experience, there usually is."

"Then let's do what's right. Let's find him if we can."

"If you like, I could also look into potential suspects, assuming there was foul play."

Blanch's eyes drifted off then came back. "How much extra is that going to set me back?"

Between the NOAA guys and settling the FWC fines, Jack had pissed away all but about a thousand of the original ten grand. Still, while tempted, his moral compass could not direct him to ask for more. "It's all covered by the original retainer."

"Then let's look into it."

"Do you have any idea who might've been interested in hurting Ross?"

Her brows arched up. "With the development breaking ground, who wasn't?"

"Have you ever heard of some guy who goes by the name Skeg?"

"Skeg?" She exhausted a lungful of smoke. "That sounds familiar."

"How so?"

Blanch leaned toward Jack, the stale cigarette scent of her breath overwhelming. "The guy I'm with. I think I've heard him mention that name before."

"In what context?"

"I couldn't say."

"So what's your guy's name?"

"Mookie. Mookie Salucci."

Jack leaned back against his chair. "That's Mookie?"

"Stumpy little thing isn't he? But he's rich. And connected."

"Do you think he would have any reason to hurt Ross?"

"Wouldn't make any sense. They're business partners in this Coconut Key venture. Or were." She wrapped her lips around her cigarette then released. "Unless of course—"

"Unless what?"

"It's silly."

"Tell me anyway."

"Maybe it was a jealousy thing. Over me."

"Why don't I see what I can dig up." Jack took a long pause then shifted gears. "Do you mind if I ask you something personal? Off-topic."

Blanch grinned, the fingers of her free hand gently tickling down her chest. "They're triple Ds."

"Funny you should say that. I was curious if you're in the market for some new ones."

"Now, that's the most offensive thing anyone's ever said to me. Don't you see these puppies? Want to give them a little squeeze?"

So Mookie had been lying about the package brought in on the floatplane. "I apologize if I've insulted you. I agree. They're spectacular to look at. It's just that I thought I heard—"

"Heard what?"

"It's nothing. Truly. My mistake. They're perfect."

She thrust her chest forward. "Please don't offend me twice in one night."

Jack nibbled at his lower lip as his gaze fell toward the forbidden fruit. "Thanks, but I'm not sure my heart could handle it."

She licked an index finger then ran it around the rim of her martini glass.

"Mind if I ask where you got them done?"

"Coral Gables. Dr. Taratalinos. They call him Dr. Tatas."

"You wouldn't happen to know what brand of implant he used, would you?"

"Allergan. Same company that does my Botox."

Jack remembered that brand from the boathouse. "Is there a difference?"

"Absolutely. I did my research, and Allergan was the only way to go. They're made in the US. I know a few girls who went the cheap route and got PIP implants, and they're paying for it now."

"PIP?"

"They leak. You can't even get them done in the States anymore."

"So where does one go to get these PIP implants?"

"Venezuela's the hot spot for any cheap plastic surgery."

"That right?" Maybe that's where Johnny Bagel's junket *down that way* had been.

She nodded. "You thinking about getting some for your girl as a gift or something?"

Jack grinned and shook his head. "One last question."

She smiled, or attempted a smile. "It's a little landing strip."

Jack grinned. He admired the woman's tenacity. He leaned closer to her. "How is it that you're already with this new guy?"

She pulled away. "Please, Jack. He's not new. I'm a single woman. I like to keep a lot of horses in my stable in case one pulls up lame."

Jack took up his beer and sucked down the last sip. Stern, independent woman or not, something wasn't sitting right. Blanch was acting too blasé about Ross being dead. Now Mookie had entered the picture. Had Jack been hired on as a stooge to divert attention away from her? Could she have somehow been involved in Ross's disappearance? Maybe it was time to follow her and see how she bided her time when not dumping money into the Hinckley.

The patio door flung open and Mookie pushed outside with his hat in his hand. "You done with this goof yet?"

"Don't be so rude," Blanch said. "Give us another minute."

Jack stood and stepped toward Mookie. "One quick question for you."

"Fire away, ace."

"You seen Ross Biggins around in the last couple of days?"

Mookie narrowed his eyes at Jack then turned back to Blanch. "Snuff it out, cupcake. We got that thing to do, and I ain't showing up late on account of this clown."

CHAPTER 22

SUMMER AWOKE, DAZED and lazy, the sun blazing into her left eye through the gap between her sunglass frames and cheek. Her right eye was veiled in shadow by a tall figure, somewhat familiar, a wild head of hair and exaggerated arms, all silhouetted against the scorching blue sky.

"Sorry to wake you," a voice said.

She shook her head, her mind soft, her thoughts drifting on two milligrams of lorazepam she'd snorted an hour or so earlier, before bedding down in her sun chaise and dozing off into a warm wash of dreams.

"Who are—?" She pushed onto an elbow. "What are you doing here?"

"The better question is how can we help one another?"

The man slid sideways blocking the sun completely from her face, his features becoming more apparent and distinct without the trickery of blinding light. He was a towering specimen, nearly seven-feet tall. He flashed a grin of bone-white teeth, geometrical and properly set, playing in contrast to the rugged and natural landscape of his face. He flaunted those pale blue irises of a Siberian husky.

She leaned up and brought her feet down to either side of the lounger, her suit tied around her neck but untied in the back so that it hung loosely in front of her chest. She slipped the cups around her breasts then reached behind her back to tie the sash. As she knotted the fabric, she noticed the rustic canoe parked as still as an old mill log wedged against her riverbank. Her heart swiveled. She pushed up from the lounger then slipped a pair of denim shorts over her bikini bottoms, the muddled discordance from her nap beginning to dissipate.

"So have you been trying to entice me or incite me with those things?"

"I'm not sure I was trying to do either."

"Any way you slice it, it's doing the trick."

He winked, and Summer's face flushed with heat. Who was this man? She glanced left and gave a hearty wave to her geodesic neighbor, establishing a witness to her peculiar situation. As her balance tipped from fear to curiosity, something about the caller drew her in. The hair was wildly exotic, oddly sexy, and age wore on him like a fine patina. She watched him reach out, offering a friendly hand, his shirtless body shifting and rippling with cords of muscle like a young longliner. His hide was tanned the colors of a Brazilian hardwood.

"I'm Salvador Keane Gosling."

She reached forward, linking her hand in his massive paw. "Summer. Summer Dahlia."

"I know." The voice was a gravelly baritone. "Pleasure to formally put a name to the—" His eyes drifted down to her chest then back up "—face."

His grip softened, and she reclaimed her hand. "Give me just a second."

Summer retreated into her kitchen, poured a glass of vodka over ice then studied her reflection in the stainless-steel refrigerator. What was she doing? Was this guy even safe? Had he come with bad intentions?

She trickled the cool vodka down her warm throat then conferred again with her reflection. Of course the man was safe. If he'd come with bad intentions, he'd have already made his mark. Besides, her neighbor was in shouting distance. What could it hurt to hear Salvador out? She slid a lime wedge onto the glass rim then stirred the drink with an index finger as she stepped back outside.

"So, Salvador, how do you think we can help one another?"

"I was hoping we could work together." Salvador's left eyelid drifted down again into a gentle wink then eased upward. "You and I. We have the same motivations when it comes to putting the brakes on Coconut Key."

"How do you know that?" Summer watched the man's mahogany body shift as he moved about. "Who are you with?"

Skeg bent down and plucked a marigold from the sandy yard. "I'm more of an independent contractor. A steward of the sea, if you will."

"You know they've already broken ground."

"There's still options." Salvador plucked a petal from the flower.

"The guys at Bluewater didn't have much luck slowing them down."

"Maybe they didn't apply the right tactics."

"Seems impossible to get anything accomplished in this county unless you've got some political leverage."

"Not the way I do things." Skeg plucked another petal and let it pinwheel to the ground.

"Have you heard about the developers?"

Salvador narrowed his eyes. "What about them?"

"How they've become . . . how should I say it? . . . so accident-prone in recent weeks."

"Developing is dangerous business."

"Even deadly."

The man tossed the flower to the ground. "Are you implying foul play?"

"I believe I am."

"Well then, this all seems like more than just casual chitchat amongst newfound friends."

Summer nodded. "How do you think the developers gained approval in the first place?"

"Tough to say. But you're looking at this thing from the wrong angle."

Summer waited.

"The real question isn't why the development was approved. It's why anyone would want to build an island in the middle of an archipelago in the first place."

Summer set the cool vodka glass against her neck. "I hadn't thought about that."

"Seems not too many have."

"Do you have an answer?"

"I'm getting pretty close to one. Maybe with your help . . ." The man stepped over to his canoe, sank his hand into a bait bucket then withdrew a stringer of mutton snapper. "You like fresh fish?"

Summer nodded. "You catch those yourself?"

He flashed a crisp smile. "With my own two hands."

"Impressive."

"You should see what else they can do."

"A man of many talents."

"I'm like the Mozart of the watery world." The wink came again. "How about dinner? Get to know one another a little better before we start spilling all of our juiciest secrets?"

Summer felt her neck hairs bristle to attention. "I'm not sure I should—"

"Just dinner. Nothing more. Hear me out, and, if you don't like what you hear, I'll leave you be."

Summer's eyes dropped then came back up like an embarrassed adolescent. "Where would we—?"

"I know a quaint little place. Waterfront. Freshest seafood in the Keys."

"If I did decided to come, how would I dress?"

"If you must, then make it casual. Now grab a piece of paper and a pen. I'll jot down the directions before I paddle back to where I belong."

CHAPTER 23

JACK VEERED THE Acapulco off the roadway then parked in the shade of a gumbo limbo at the Disenchanted Clam. The clothing-optional raw bar was situated halfway out on Pier 66. Lining the remainder of the pier were a couple dozen sun loungers with taut vinyl strapping the colors of a rainbow. A pair of parade flags bearing the same vibrant color scheme flanked each side of the restaurant and snapped in the crosswinds.

Even from the parking lot, Jack could see most the chairs catered to middle-aged men, ninety percent of whom were buck naked. The clientele, however, was not a metrosexual homosexual strain. Things like man-scaping and overall body maintenance escaped their daily routines. As a result the men sauntered to and from the bar, ordering drinks, slurping raw oysters from the half-shell and bending over to adjust their seatbacks while their junk jostled about unkempt tufts of hair and layers of abdominal lard.

Oscar Callahan, whom Jack had been tailing for the better part of the morning, sauntered onto the pier and sat down at a table next to an older gentleman, fully clothed, whom Jack did not recognize.

The venue, not known for its beer temperature or its blackened mahi sandwiches, might well have been chosen as a clandestine destination in an otherwise small island chain.

Jack wanted to hear that conversation.

He considered his options. A nearby shanty advertised kayak rentals by the hour. He could paddle out and under the dock then eavesdrop from below the planks. One obvious flaw with that plan, however, was the unapologetic view of gazing up through dock planks as the naked clientele strolled about with all the modesty of Bearded Collies at the Westminster Kennel Club.

He had neither the stomach nor the appreciation for that.

Option two was only slightly less disconcerting. He rifled around the back seat of the Volkswagen, dug out a sandy beach towel then started for the pier.

When he reached the entrance, a posted sign suggested to disrobe at one's own risk. He wasn't sure what to make of that. Nonetheless, he slipped his shirt off first then his shorts then slapped his towel over his shoulder and started precariously down the pier clad in nothing more than flip-flops.

Oddly, it proved somewhat liberating, the wind dancing around and whistling through places not often exposed in the great outdoors. As he neared their position, an open lounger became available. Its previous occupant, a bald sixty-something—perhaps nicknamed grande huevos— gimped away from the seat, a sweaty imprint glistening up from the chair slats.

Jack stepped to it, keeping his back to Ossie and the other man, then loomed over the strapped lounger suddenly curious as to the antiseptic measures taken between loungees.

After a quick mental struggle, he spread his towel down over the smear of residual perspiration then scratched his head. How did one position oneself in a setting such as this? Bottom up or bottom down? The idea of getting his johnson flash-roasted in the subtropical sunshine held as much appeal as exposing his bare backside to the gaggle of cottaging old bastards intrigued by the fresh meat.

After a brief deliberation, Jack settled stomach-side down and canted his head. A break between a properly positioned waste bin and dish cart provided a partial blind as he watched and listened in on Ossie's conversation.

The older man bent open a laminated menu. "Interesting choice of venue, son."

Son? So this was Ossie's father.

"You like the place, pops?" Ossie asked. "Maybe we can find you a suitor."

Gus shook his head, his tightly woven nap of silver hair glinting in the sunshine. "I got no problem with the lifestyle. I just want our rainbows back."

Ossie laughed. "Wasn't my pick, pops."

"What time's the bitch-on-wheels supposed to be here, anyways?"

"Should've been here already."

"Figures she'd be late." Gus fished a hand into the breast pocket of a pearl-snap plaid shirt and withdrew an oblong pill the color of plumber's putty.

"Still dealing with the back pain?"

"Prolapsed is the medical term." He washed it down with a swig of beer. "You eating, son?"

A man walked by in a star-spangled G-string, the string portion of which dissolved between two ass cheeks mottled in brown and gray fur.

Ossie clapped his menu shut then slipped it back between the napkin holder and creamer canister. "My appetite's suddenly disappeared. I think I'll stick with a liquid lunch today."

Gus nodded. "I'll join you."

The waiter sauntered up, wearing only a utility apron and a pen behind his ear, and took their order. A few minutes later two canned beers arrived foaming at the mouths.

Ossie, still in his Fish and Game attire, wrapped his can in a brown napkin then gazed across the green waters of the bight. "You feeling good about everything?"

Gus sucked a long swig of beer then rumbled a hearty belch. "Warm as piss." He curled his lip at the can. "And, hell yes, I'm feeling good about everything. Thanks to you landing me this contract, I'm a regular pig in shit."

"Forget the dredging contract, pops. We'll make more in this one haul than those other chumps will make sucking sand in a lifetime."

Jack adjusted his angle. One haul?

"You just tell me when and where, son. I'm ready."

184

"You're still confident it'll work, right?"

"I've been running dredgers for over seventeen years. I can suck stuff better than an intern at the White House."

"That's what I like to hear." Ossie checked his wristwatch as a pink Cadillac careened over the nearby bridge with the ragtop rolled back.

Gus said, "There's the princess now."

"We need to play nice with her. We need her help pulling this thing off."

"Don't worry about me, son. I'll be sweet as Tupelo honey to the crazy broad."

* * *

Jack kept his head hidden behind his towel as Blanch Theroux clunked down the planks on three-inch wedges toward the two men.

Interesting. How was Blanch tied to these two?

One thing Jack had learned through his years as a private investigator: Too many coincidences weren't coincidences at all.

Blanch approached the table. "Jesus, Gus. You look tired. But you fit right in with the other patrons around here."

"Jeannie Joe. It's been a long time. You look different. Did you have a little work done?"

"It's Blanch now, Gus. Blanch Theroux."

"Still up to your same old tricks?"

Blanch slipped into an open chair then stabbed her cigarette out in the ashtray, leaving a broken cherry to smolder about the table.

Ossie turned to her. "So how are things coming along on your end?"

"The Hinckley's ready, if that's what you're asking."

Jack adjusted his angle. Ready for what? A gala?

"What about Mookie?"

"Clueless." Blanch fished a hand around her purse then withdrew a silver lipstick cylinder. "He has no idea that I know you two are working with him."

"Let's hope not," Gus said. "I've got no interest in going swimming in a pair of cement boots."

"Trust me. We'll be halfway to Block Island before he figures out what happened."

Blanch spun the lipstick cylinder then began caking on a gaudy orange makeup over her lips as she spoke. "How about you two? You ready to roll?"

Gus cleared his throat. "You know damn well this ain't my first rodeo."

"Well, in case you didn't know, Gus, this isn't goat roping either." Blanch completed the lipstick application then began swirling a facepowder pad around a makeup tin and daubing it down the ridge of her nose. "How about you, Oscar? Everything ready?"

Ossie nodded slowly, his lower lip pursing outward.

"What's with the face?" Gus asked.

"Nothing. At least I think it's nothing."

"Jesus. You're just like your father. Don't be such a pussy."

"Fine then." Ossie slicked his hair back with the palm of a hand. "Somebody's been snooping around the boathouse."

Gus crunched his beer can in his grip. "Mookie's crew?"

"No idea."

Blanch scoffed then snapped the compact shut. "You mean what's left of Mookie's crew."

Gus gave her a cross look. "Anything missing?"

Ossie shook his head. "Looks like whoever it was just rustled through some old bid books and went on his way."

"Anything out there that didn't need seeing?"

"Just those GPS coordinates."

Jack scratched his head. GPS coordinates?

"That could actually work to our advantage." Gus slipped a pen from his pearl button shirt then scratched something onto a cocktail napkin. "Here."

Ossie took it up. "This the new rendezvous spot?"

Gus nodded. "Best not take any chances. Now why don't we just memorize the numbers this go around? Keep prying eyes from catching on."

186

Ossie studied the napkin for a few seconds then slid it to Blanch.

Blanch glanced at the numbers then spun the napkin into a point and threaded it down the mouth of Gus's empty beer can.

"So when's the big day?" Ossie asked.

Blanch reopened the compact then studied her nose in the mirror. "Day of the concert."

"Concert?" Gus asked. "What concert?"

Ossie pulled the beer from his lips. "That Swinging Richard gig out at the new island."

Blanch nodded.

"All right then." Ossie settled his beer can atop the table then nodded for the tab. "Everything's set."

Blanch snapped shut the compact again then tucked it into her purse. "You look old, Gus. And tired. What in the heck happened to you?"

"A healthy lack of plastic surgery, Jeannie Joe. You might want to think about it before somebody mistakes you for a jungle cat and pumps you full of bird shot."

Blanch pushed back from the chair then sauntered away down the boardwalk.

Gus ordered another beer. "That godforsaken wench has always had an irritating knack for pissing me off."

"You're the dumbass that married the woman."

"Worse two weeks of my life. Only thing good ever came out of that cunt was you, son. Literally."

CHAPTER 24

THE NEXT MORNING as Jack stretched out on his bed, swim-exhausted, a grating high-pitched scream rattled through the marina. He pulled on some khaki shorts and his nicest oxford polo then stumbled onto the deck shielding his eyes from the glare with one hand while holding topsiders in the other.

"Morning, sunshine."

Jack blinked away the brightness until the vision of a bikini-clad Summer straddling a fiery red Yamaha WaveRunner came in focus. This he had not expected. Nor was he sure how to react. "I wasn't sure if we were on speaking terms?"

She nodded. "As long as we're talking business. Other than that, I'm just not sure where I am with this Sophia thing. Or anything else with us for that matter."

"There's no Sophia thing."

"Fine then. Just consider me damaged goods."

Jack slumped onto the lobsterpot then tugged the loafers over his feet. "I wish I knew how to make it simple again."

"Maybe it's too late." Summer drifted away for a moment then came back. "So what's up with the fancy threads? Last time I saw you in close-toed shoes you were on your way to a court appearance."

"Mandatory garb. No open-toed shoes allowed."

"Job interview?"

"Appointment." He stood then reached inside his shirt and withdrew a lanyard and badge. A hologram on the badge glinted in the

188

morning light. Summer bumped the gas on the watercraft and nudged close enough to study the document.

"NOAA?"

Jack eyed the federal seal. "Some new friends of mine hooked me up with the credentials."

"You almost look like you have a real job."

"Depressing, isn't it?" Jack let the badge swing into place. "So what sort of business are you here to discuss?"

Summer adjusted her bikini top. "I'm trying to figure out why these developers are building an island in the first place."

Jack began tucking the tail of the oxford into his shorts. "Same reason those guys did the Palm Islands in Dubai, I suppose. To sell them off and make a mint."

"One big difference."

Jack paused the tail tucking and eyed her.

"Those guys in Dubai didn't already have a bunch of islands they could choose to build on if they wanted to."

Jack let the loose portion of shirttail go then fumbled around his cooler before withdrawing a warm beer from the stale water. "Interesting point. What have you come up with?"

"Beach renourishment."

Jack furrowed his brows.

"Same rainbowing process they're using to build Coconut Key."

Jack shook the warm beer can. "I thought that was illegal."

"Only for natural coastlines. But manmade structures don't fall under the same regulations. Take Smathers Beach for instance. It's manmade. That's why they restore it every so often. You're allowed to actively maintain and restore any manmade coastline in the Keys."

"Sounds expensive."

"It is. But apparently Coconut Key budgeted for it. Turns out, there'll be one fulltime dredge boat on the payroll just to maintain the coastline once the island is fully developed."

"You think it's relevant?"

"I was hoping you'd see some connection I don't."

"It's a little early in the morning for deductive reasoning." Jack hunched over the shaken beer can, popped the top and spritzed his entire shirt and neck with the foamy mist.

"New cologne, Jack?"

"Getting into character."

"Dare I ask?"

Jack set the beer can down then stepped up onto the dock, half his shirttail still untucked. "I've got to get rolling."

"There's a few more things we should talk about."

"Such as?"

"I may have some insight into what's happening to these developers."

Jack's brows arched. "I've got an appointment in ten minutes that I can't miss. How about we meet tonight?"

"Can't tonight. Dinner. With a friend."

Jack planted his hands on his hips. "I know we're not in the best place at the moment, but I hope it's okay for me to tell you to be careful."

"How about we meet tomorrow? I'll have more details then anyways."

"Five o'clock?"

Summer nodded.

Jack rumpled his shirt collar. "So what's with the WaveRunner? I thought you detested those crotch rockets as much as I do."

"As much as it pains me, I rented it for the day. I need it to scope out the construction site firsthand then visit the scene of that tourist attack. See what I can put together."

Jack nodded. That seemed safe enough. "See you at five tomorrow."

"Sharp."

Summer goosed the throttle and ripped out of the marina at fifty-five miles per hour. Jack exhausted a long sigh then lumbered toward the parking lot and grumbled out into traffic like a regular working stiff.

* * *

At 10:00 a.m., the Chinese-built Wuhan Pan-Asia dredger known as *Bogart* steamed past the reef line and into the Atlantic Ocean proper. Jack Cubera stood on the bridge, in his Key's business-casual attire, next to Captain Gus Callahan, who manned the helm like a seasoned tar.

The captain sported a bristly nap of silver hair that squeezed out from under a Dilligaf trucker hat. "So you're some kind of compliance officer?"

"More of a special operations guy. NOAA flew me down to do a ride along. You know, observe the ins and outs of the operation."

"I hate to break it to you pal, but it ain't nuclear psychology."

"I know. Just another colossal waste of taxpayer dollars if you ask me."

Gus rolled up one sleeve on his plaid shirt then started on the next. "Funny. Most of you government sorts are too proud to admit that sort of thing."

"Please don't mistake my incompetence for lack of pride."

The titanic bow rose gently over a slow roller then dipped back down as Gus adjusted his course with a gentle jog of the wheel. "Mind if I ask you something?"

"Fire away."

"You go out big on the town last night?"

Jack crossed his arms in front of him. "Why do you ask?"

"Smells like you just clocked out of a brewery."

Jack laughed. "You got me. Truth is I just flew in yesterday evening. You know how it is. First night away from the wife and kids. We took it pretty deep last night."

"Duval crawl?"

Jack nodded. "Something like that."

"Hit any titty clubs?"

Jack wanted to garner trust. "Bare Assets. Wankers. Red Garter Saloon. I'm not sure there's any we didn't hit."

"It must've been a late one."

Jack groaned then rubbed his knuckles into his eyes. "All I know is that at some point it got too late to go home early."

"How's that head feeling about now?"

"I've certainly felt better on worse days than this."

"Maybe I can help." Gus ventured a hand into his breast pocket, withdrawing a menagerie of prescription pills which he rolled around his palm.

"That's quite the collection."

Gus pressed his fingers into his lower spine then arched backward. "Three herniated discs." He pushed the pills toward Jack. "Want one?"

"I'd better not."

"You sure? It'll knock that hangover clear into tomorrow."

"Random piss tests."

"Suit yourself." Gus crunched the medicine between his teeth then, sighting something on the GPS, feathered back on the throttles.

"We here?"

Gus nodded. "Yessir. This is what we call the Honey Hole." He stalled the big vessel to a crawl then began slowly trolling over a tract of ocean bottom. Rather than looking out the windshield, his eyes monitored an onboard computer screen displaying an image of the murky ocean floor.

"So what exactly are you looking for on the video monitor?"

"Right there." Gus rapped his fingertip on the screen. "See that lighter band of sand."

Jack leaned into the computer screen. "I guess."

"This here." Gus traced his finger in a diagonal line over a faint coloration change across the screen.

"I suppose I see it."

"Well, trust me. That's it. Pure continental sand's what they call it. It's a real solid composition of quartz. That's what the engineers want. Them granules are angular instead of round like some of the other sand out here. It's prime for island-building. That's why they chose this spot as the borrow pit."

"So I guess there's a little more to this than just snarfing up a bunch of sand?"

"Little bit." Gus shifted a lever, then the suction pump trailer arm came into view on the computer screen. With a few wiggles of a dashboard joystick, Gus swung the arm into place over the lighter band of continental sand. "Just a few feet in the wrong direction and the sand's no good." He eyeballed Jack. "And they don't pay for sand that ain't no good."

"Course they don't."

Gus flipped a series of dashboard switches, thumbed a button then the sound of an engine turning over arrived and died. "Pump's been giving me some trouble here lately." He gave the button another push, and this time a steady reverberation hummed through the hull. After one more toggle of the joystick, a plume formed around the mouth of the suction hopper then evaporated as sand began to disappear from the ocean bottom.

Gus tapped his finger on the screen. "See that there? That's a conch shell. And that there's a beer can."

Jack studied the screen as though viewing some archaic hieroglyphics. "Seriously?"

"Does a cat have climbing gear?"

"What happens if you accidentally suck that stuff up?"

"Macerator takes care of it on the way back out. Nothing larger than an eighth-inch minus gets rainbowed out. Watch this." Gus guided the suction hose toward the conch shell then sucked it away.

"Damn. I didn't realize you could get that kind of precision with one of these things."

"Surgical." Gus snickered, the paternal version of Ossie. "Back in the day I did contract work for Mel Fisher at the Atocha site. We were plucking gold coins and silver bars off the ocean bottom with a lot less technology than this."

"Impressive."

"I hate to polish my own apple, but when you been doing this as long as I have you can suck the buffalo off a nickel with only one eye on the monitor. Anyway, Mr. . . . . uh." Gus leaned in and read the NOAA badge. "Mr. Crevalle. Once these gauges say we've got a full fourteen thousand metric tons, we'll tuck in the trailer arm, steam back to the recipient site and blow this shit all over Shinola."

Gus settled into the captain chair then propped his heels on the helm.

"How long does it take to fill the hopper?"

"About two, two-and-a-half hours if all goes right."

Jack's brows arched. "So what now?"

Gus shook his head. "Give me a little advanced warning next time you're coming for a ride along, and I'll make sure to pack a cooler of cold beer."

CHAPTER 25

A 36 CAPELLA catamaran was moored in an iridescent cove a half-mile off the coast of Plantation Key. A bloody sunset had left the cumulous underbellies awash with pinks and purples while the lagoon shimmered with the rising moon.

Summer arrived to the dinner location by personal watercraft. Salvador greeted her as she nudged up to the rear of the left sponson. He wore burlap slacks and a linen shirt, unbuttoned and blown open revealing his chiseled features.

"Evening, Ms. Dahlia. Glad you decided to join me. Did you have any trouble finding the place?"

"Your directions were impeccable."

Salvador stretched his long fingers toward her. "Welcome aboard."

Summer swung a leg over her aquatic steed, her body almost levitating from the watercraft as Salvador lifted her up with a single arm. Her feet toed gently down onto the fiberglass decking, then Salvador swept an arm, ushering her to get comfortable.

"What a lovely boat."

"I found an old bottle of champagne in the galley. I hope you don't mind."

"I'd love a glass." Summer glanced around the desolate watery landscape now awash in a vintage dusky light. "Mind if I use the restroom?"

"We call it a head on a boat. But please, help yourself." Salvador motioned toward a small stair set descending into a hull.

Summer maneuvered down into the cabin then slipped into the head. She tidied up her windblown hair the best she could then preened the wrinkles from her shorts. They'd gotten slightly damp from the ride out, as had her white top, the lacy trim of her brassiere now visible through the thin fabric. At least it was getting dark outside.

She stepped back into the cabin. A series of photographs of an older couple with a Golden Retriever hung on a wall. A stack of unopened mail identified them as Patrick and Lisa Cunningham of Vestavia, Alabama.

She moved back onto the main deck. Night had arrived. Exactly how far away was she from home? And what about her meds? She'd failed to bring any extras along. "So I suppose you're friends with the Cunninghams."

"Don't worry. They won't be back down until winter."

"Do you look after the boat for them?"

"Sure. Something like that."

Summer's arm hairs prickled upward then a ticklish roller coaster sensation stirred in her belly. "Are you saying they don't know you're on their boat?"

"I'm saying they'd agree it's a waste for this beautiful vessel to sit idle for over half the year."

Salvador popped open the bottle of champagne, the sparkling wine spuming out the neck and onto the deck. A symphony of cicadas erupted into song from the nearby islet. Salvador filled two flutes then extended one toward Summer.

Summer took the glass and glanced across the backwaters. "Did you ask me out here to talk about Coconut Key or do you have other intentions?"

"Just two like souls getting together to solve the world's problems. And, if all goes well, maybe take a little dip in the drink." Salvador inched in behind Summer, and she spun around, gazing upward at his eyes. "Interesting mode of transportation you brought out here tonight."

"I didn't think it would be wise to paddle all the way out here."

"I see." Salvador stroked his chin. "Next time, let me know, and I'll pick you up in my tender." He nodded toward his crude canoe.

"Sorry. I just thought you'd want to—"

"No need for apologies. Let's just not let it happen again."

Summer's smile went flat, her eyes squinting for a moment until they snapped back open. The recent WaveRunner incident she read about in the papers. A silver-headed skunk ape responsible for the attack. Something about a football player who's hamstring had been sliced through and through with a machete. "Did you hear about that WaveRunner attack a few days back?"

He grinned. "Good news travels fast."

She shivered, her heart fluttering like a moth wing against a hot bulb. She set her fingertips to her lips. "I read that the wound was pretty serious."

"The human body is incredibly resilient."

"So it wasn't you?"

The man gathered his silver locks then pinned them behind his head using two long scythe-like shafts. "From what I heard, it was a buff football player not some handsome backwater beau."

"Not the victim. This so-called skunk ape."

"Ah, a skunk ape. Now that seems a little farfetched, don't you think?"

Summer nodded, letting her vivid imagination drain away as the two clinked champagne flutes and sipped their drinks. "Something smells delicious."

Salvador motioned toward a raw tuna steak on a prep table and a barbeque grill wafting plumes of garlic smoke into the night. "Baby clams in a red-wine reduction. I harvested them myself this morning." He flashed his pearly whites. "Also, I've taken the liberty of preparing a kale salad for starters. You do like superfoods, don't you?"

She nodded.

"I grow my own."

"Sounds tantalizing." She sipped her champagne again.

"There's tuna tataki for the main course. Pepper encrusted with a dribble of Key lime."

"I didn't realize this was a date. You should've told me. I would've worn something a bit more appropriate."

"Don't fret. You look splendid tonight." Salvador cast a leering grin. "Although I'm not used to seeing you in quite so many clothes."

She fidgeted with her sheer top then moved toward the rail. For a second she thought her eyes were playing tricks on her as electrical flashes of light effervesced through the water.

"Stunning, isn't it?' Salvador asked. "Bioluminescent plankton like to gather in this lagoon. Care for a swim?"

"I didn't bring a suit."

"Not to worry. Neither did I." Salvador slipped off his shirt and loosened the belt on his trousers. "You sure?"

Summer glanced down into her flute at the bubbles crawling up the glass. Maybe coming out here hadn't been the wisest idea. "You go ahead."

"Suit yourself."

The sound of Salvador's pants zipper clicked then the fabric slipped away with a whisper. He stepped out of the bunched-up legs, his muscular bum the same shade as the rest of his hide.

Summer turned away reflexively, then swiveled back around for a second glance. As Salvador arched off the stern toward the water she caught a fleeting glimpse of his endowment, something proportionate to a man of his stature. As he entered the water and speared into the depths, the water around pulsed with electrical colors then simmered back toward black as he surfaced with a gasp.

"It's absolutely amazing."

"It won't be for long thanks to Coconut Key."

After a few minutes of backstroking, Salvador swam toward the rear of the portside pontoon and started up the ladder. Summer looked away. The sound of Salvador's bare feet pattered across the hull, then a wet mahogany arm reached out and unfurled a towel with a quick popping snap. "Speaking of Coconut Key, did you hear another developer wound up dead?"

"I don't remember seeing that in the papers."

"I have my sources."

"What happened?"

Salvador, towel wrapped around his waist, moved directly in front of Summer, a single drop of seawater clinging to the tip of his nose and catching the moonlight. "I heard he got attacked by a jellyfish."

Salvador's left eyelid drifted slowly down then back up.

Summer's face flushed. The wink. What had looked like a come-hither gesture at her house now seemed more like a facial tic. She swallowed deep. "What was the developer's name?"

"Ross Biggins." Salvador laughed and scooped up his champagne glass. "I'm surprised you haven't heard, him being your boss and all."

Summer's mind stumbled back into a dark hole. Only four people knew about that death. Jack, Ray, Hunter and Summer . . . plus the killer. Her eyes suddenly darted about the boat deck, hunting for normalcy, familiarity, but found things obscure, abstract, disconnected.

"Crying shame. Don't you think?" Salvador reached out with a long, muscular hand and clasped her forearm. "Is everything all right?"

Summer shuddered, a numbness crawling down her face toward her chest. She slumped onto a cushion, her eyes reflexively looking up at Salvador, his charming qualities having evaporated in the context of the moment. Her lips parted, her voice as though not her own resounded from the hot and angry throat of a stranger. "What did you do to him?"

"Hmm." Salvador released her forearm and set down his champagne glass. "You're missing the point here."

"There's a point?"

"These shitbirds already took my home from me once. Am I supposed to let that happen again?"

"So you thought it was okay to do things your own way?"

"If this little project carries on, they'll be murdering hundreds of species in the Florida Bay. They may even put some into extinction. All for the sake of what? Greed?"

Summer glanced back toward the WaveRunner. From her vantage it appeared the key had vanished from the ignition. "What are you doing? Why am I out here? Where's the key? I need to get going."

"Now, now, Summer. There's no need to raise your voice."

Salvador stepped closer, hovering over as her champagne glass slipped from her fingers and bounced twice then rolled along the floor.

"What do you want with me?"

"I was hoping we could work together on this thing." He reached toward his prep table and withdrew a previously unseen machete. "My solo tactics don't quite seem to be doing the trick."

"You mean killing people?"

Salvador shrugged then scooped up the serving plate of tuna tataki. "What's another dead developer?"

"You can't just kill people over something like this."

"It was out of necessity not out of some kind of sick sport. What do you take me for?"

He slumped onto the cushion beside Summer and, using the machete, began carving up slabs of the raw tuna and popping them into his mouth. "Well, this has certainly turned into an awkward situation. Now what the hell am I supposed to do with you?"

CHAPTER 26

THAT EVENING AS Jack waited for a few straggler Soggy Dollar residents to turn in, a man with a stack of red flyers tucked under his arm arrived with a hammer in one hand and a fistful of roofing nails in the other. He wore nothing but construction overalls and hummed a Swinging Richard tune called *Three Sweet Leis in Three Sweet Days* as he barefooted onto the boardwalk.

When he reached the first slip on the dock, number nine, he paused and nailed one of the red flyers to a piling. Once finished, he shuffled to the opposite side of the quay, repeated the move then began to volley his way from piling to piling nailing up flyers as he went. Seconds later, Hunter sprinted down the dock with one of the flyers crumbled in his grip. He raced by the man, feet kicking high, then came to a sudden stop at the stern of the Moppie, his breath deep and his speech fast.

"Did you see this, Jack? Do you know what it means?"

Jack took the flyer then smoothed out the creases. The header read 30 DAY NOTICE TO VACATE followed by two paragraphs of legal jargon. Jack scanned the document then handed it back to Hunter. "The buyers want us out of here in the next thirty days."

"They can't do that, can they, Jack?"

Jack watched the man in overalls move to the next piling. "Tough to say, kid. These guys are heavy hitters."

The kid seemed to digest the information then leaned closer and whispered. "That dead dude ever turn up?"

Jack shook his head. "I promise to let you know if anything happens on that front." Jack glanced toward the Hinckley nestled quietly in slip 17. "You want to earn a couple extra bucks tonight?"

"I'm still working on those parking lot lights."

"Not those, kid. This is the easiest money you'll ever make."

They waited until the man in overalls tacked the last notice into place then eased down the dock to the Hinckley.

Jack glanced up then down the gangway. "Whistle if anyone comes around."

The kid nodded as Jack slipped onto the Hinckley then hustled toward the cabin and nudged the salon door. It was locked.

According to Blanch, the retrofit was complete, but he had to see this for himself. A retrofitted two-year-old Hinckley. Absurd. And when had they even completed the interior? He hadn't seen workmen at the docks since the guys sporting the hazmat suits. He stepped to the helm then dug through the glovebox, locating a round key with a circular shaft. He slipped it into the salon lock and twisted. With a gentle nudge, the door swung open.

As he negotiated the steps in the dark, a waft of some oil-based chemical lit across his taste buds. Feeling along the walls, he located a bank of marine switches. He flipped one then a second with no reaction. The third switch brought the interior into a stuttering vibration of yellow light.

He glanced around. To his bewilderment, the entire cabin remained gutted clear down to the hull. Even the sink and head had been removed. And nothing had been replaced.

Questions flooded in.

Why would Blanch lie about such a thing? Had she run out of financial resources since Ross disappeared? Was she embarrassed to tell the truth? And why had Mookie been so surprised when he'd overheard about the retrofit?

Jack swept his eyes through the cabin. In various points about the walls and floor, fiberglass patches had been installed over the original finish work. Using a pocket knife, he peeled back the corner of a patch then poked the blade inside. The tip sank into something soft and crunchy. He pried the blade tip up then withdrew the thing, a hunk of orange foam now pierced on the tip.

Jack raked his fingers through his mustache. Those workers in the hazmat suits. They'd run that large hose from a dishwasher-sized contraption down the dock and into the cabin. At the time, it had appeared to be some sort of large industrial vacuum. But had that device actually been pumping something into the cabin?

Jack crunched the orange matter between a thumb and forefinger. It was the dense foam used by boat builders to add buoyancy to a watercraft. So what about those divers in the water with their measuring devices? Were they calculating the changes in the waterline as the new foam was distributed into the hull?

Jack pounded a fist on an interior wall then moved along the hull like a doctor checking reflexes.

The damn thing was rock solid all the way around.

Next, he boomed his foot onto the deck like a plodding horse. No echoes or reverberations. There wasn't a hollow spot to be found.

He tucked the sample foam piece into his pocket then worked the blade back over the fiberglass patch, smoothing it into place.

Why would Blanch add buoyancy to a Hinckley? Did her galas get that crowded and out of control?

Perplexed, Jack returned topside and locked the cabin door. The kid gave him a nod so he shuffled to the helm, toggled a few switches and the GPS came alive with a preset image of the surrounding waterways. Before leaving the Disenchanted Clam, he'd confiscated the crumpled beer can containing the rolled napkin Blanch had stuffed into it.

Now he unrolled the paper, plugged the GPS coordinates into the computer, and waited for the device to acquire its satellite feeds.

Would the coordinates be familiar? Was it the Three Peaks fishing hole? The Riptides? The Islamorada Hump? After a series of blinking lights, the screen resolved into a map showing a dotted white line leading from his current position in the marina to a locale off the coast of Key Largo.

He zoomed in.

The location was obscure, set over a relatively deepwater trough about a mile and a half off the coastline. From what Jack could tell, there appeared to be no geographical significance. It was remote, abstract, desolate. The middle of nowhere in particular. So then what, if anything, was its significance?

He clicked off the electronics, hopped off the boat and slipped the kid a ten-dollar bill.

"Thanks, Jack."

"Keep your eyes peeled, kid. Something fishy's going on around here, and I'm not talking about the snapper bite."

CHAPTER 27

MOOKIE CRAWLED HIS Lincoln Navigator to a halt on the gravelly shoulder at mile marker 67, stepped out then angled down a trail through the slice of brush separating the road from the water. He wore a silk shirt, loafers and his fedora. It was almost midnight. The glow of his lit cigar led the way down the dark pathway.

He reached the water's edge then checked his Submariner a few times before a canoe came slipping across the bight toward shore.

When the vessel reached land, Mookie put a loafer onto the crocodile prow and steadied the boat as Skeg climbed out then balanced in the shin-deep water. Swamp mud covered his face, an apparent mosquito repellant, which alongside the silver dreadlocks lent the appearance of a Haitian witchdoctor. His towering height stood well beyond what Mookie had expected.

"Christ Almighty," Mookie said. "You're a big one in person, aren't you?"

Skeg grunted.

"How tall are you, anyway?"

"What is it with you people always asking that?" Skeg's lazy eyelid winked up and down.

"No need to get bent out of shape." Mookie extended an envelope of money. "The big boss just never mentioned you was a freakshow."

Skeg took the envelope then nodded approvingly.

"Went just as planned," Mookie said. "Nobody suspects a thing."

"Ross never saw it coming."

"We didn't know what to do with the body so we just left him for the sharks."

"I know. You guys ain't the brightest bunch. But don't worry. I took care of him for you."

"You did what?"

"I took care of him."

"How?"

"Don't worry about it. It's done."

Mookie shook his head. "I was wondering about something."

Skeg sucked air through his pearly whites. "What now?"

"Those spikes you got in your hair." Mookie hooked an index finger around his cigar then slid the damp shaft from his mouth. "Them is stingray barbs, ain't they?"

Skeg nodded. "Sun-bleached."

"Funny thing. Those are the same things they say killed Jimmy B."

Skeg reached behind his head then drew one barb from the loose ponytail. The thing was bleached white, seven-inches long and curved like a scythe. He presented it to Mookie. "I extracted them myself."

"You didn't have anything to do with that death, did you?"

Skeg laughed. "Your buddy Ross was my first."

"You sure?"

"Not the kind of thing a guy forgets."

"Good. 'Cause Jimmy B dying of that stingray barb, that's how I got the idea for this little assassination operation of mine."

"You're a clever one, Mookie."

Skeg slipped the barb back into his knotted hair as Mookie thumped his cigar butt into the water. It hissed. Skeg was out quick with the machete, a maroon streak of blood visible over the entire length of the blade. "You're going to want to fish that from the water and dispose of it in a proper receptacle."

"What gives? You one of them bunny-fucking hippies or something?"

Skeg grinned, flaunting his pearly whites clear back to the molars. "More of an eco-maniac. Now get it."

"You serious?"

"Deadly."

Mookie kicked off his loafers then gingerly waded across the root-riddled shallows and snagged the floating butt. As he turned back, a quiet wake rolled through and dampened his silk shorts up to the crotch. "Sonofabtich."

Skeg slapped the envelope of money against his palm. "I don't really give a shit about the money. I just figure I've got to charge you something for my services."

"Freakin' scallywag."

"Scallywag? Now that's got a nice ring to it." Skeg blinked deliberately, one lid drifting up and down while the other held steadfastly open. "You want me to go ahead with the next one?"

"Yeah. What do you have in mind this go around?"

"Don't worry. It'll look completely natural." Skeg grunted. "But let's make the next one twenty grand."

"What's this? You just said you don't care about the money."

"I don't. But I've got a feeling you do."

"Twice the price. It had better be special."

"Oh, it will be. That I can promise. Which one do you want me to take out next?"

"The short fat one."

"The short fat one?" Skeg laughed. "I figured I'd save you for last."

"Hey, hey wiseass. You don't watch that mouth you're gonna get clowned."

Mookie flipped a photograph from his pocket. The picture showcased him, Johnny Bagels, Chewy and Jimmy B posing at the Southernmost Point marker in Key West.

"That's some pedigree."

Mookie pointed to Chewy. "This one next. We call him Chewy 'cause he chews his cigars into these brown lumps look like wet dog turds. It's disgusting."

Skeg studied the picture. "How about we do this Johnny Bagels character next instead? He's more of a liability. Let's get him out of the way before he causes trouble."

Mookie canted his head. "Okay. Sure. Why not? Just watch yourself with that one. He's a few screws shy of a full . . . uh."

"Box of screws?" Skeg sank into his canoe then backed it away from shore. "Twenty grand."

"I heard you the first time, wiseass."

CHAPTER 28

WHEN THE THREE men moored the *FrigateAboutIt* at Pennekamp State Park there was only one other boat in sight: a crude canoe with a prow carved into the shape of a crocodile head. Johnny and Chewy didn't even acknowledge the stranger as they stripped down then began slipping into skin suits for their first ever foray into the watery world of snorkeling.

Mookie tried not to stare at the canoe. This Skeg character he'd gotten tangled up with was a real wild card. Efficient and stealthy, yes, but also unorthodox and unpredictable.

For instance, what had the freakshow done with Ross's body?

Mookie glanced back to the others, his attention quickly on Chewy, who for some reason had disrobed down to the buff. Not blessed in any regard, his shriveled pecker appeared like the head of a shiitake mushroom projecting from a nap of steel wool.

"Jesus, Chewy. No need to give us a gander at the jewels. At least give the little guy a couple courtesy tugs you gonna whip it out like that in public."

Chewy looked at the other two still in their bathing suits. "Wait a minute. You can put this thing on over the swim trunks?"

Mookie turned away, shaking his head. "You're a regular native."

"Cover yourself up already." Johnny slid his muscular legs into the thin neoprene then tucked his arms into the sleeves and zipped up.

Once suited, the mobsters looked comical in the snug black outfits, Mookie and Chewy's soft and dimpled physiques now presenting as a few too many cannolis and a bit too much tiramisu.

"Boys back home could see us now."

Mookie set down his cigar then picked up one of the three mask and snorkel sets, twisting it around a few times before figuring out on which side of his head to set the snorkel. Despite looking out of place in the Keys, the guys had spared no expense in fitting themselves with the top-shelf equipment. Only the finest masks and snorkels. Only the priciest fins. They'd even geared up with a top-of-the-line Cressi Geronimo speargun in case they decided to run to the Bahamas, where spearing lobsters was legal.

Mookie handled the speargun.

It was roughly three feet in length with a Hawaiian-style barb at the tip of the elongated shaft. The handle, composed of African blood wood, provided a sturdy noncorrosive grip, and a double-braided shock cord gave the gun an effective shooting range of fourteen feet. He set it against his shoulder like a rifle.

"You boys best watch out for seal poachers all slicked up in them suits."

"Let me see that thing." Johnny yanked the speargun from Mookie. "Been a long time since I did me some killing. I'm going to give this bad boy a go."

"Yeah?" Chewy suctioned his mask over his eyes and nose then spoke with a muffled tone. "Snushi for lunch?"

Mookie eyed toward the canoe. "Maybe you want to do that another day. Fish and Game catches us they can confiscate the sportfisher."

Johnny laughed. "Yeah right, Mook. You and I both know who Fish and Game works for around here."

Mookie hadn't thought of that. "I'm just saying. Wrong guy sees you sticking fish on a protected reef, might rub him the wrong way."

Johnny panned the waters. "Who's going to say something?"

Mookie gulped deep. "Suit yourself. But the sales guy said them things can be tricky underwater. You shoot your prick off, don't come crying to this guy."

"Trust me. I know how to discharge me a weapon." Johnny slipped his fins over his feet then duck walked through the gate and onto the swim platform. "You two coming in or what?"

Mookie waved him on. "Go ahead. Be in a minute. Me and Chewy got a thing to discuss."

With a single lunging stride, Johnny plunged into the water feet-first with the speargun clamped tightly to his chest.

*　*　*

From his position underwater two-hundred feet away, Skeg witnessed the skin diver enter the ocean, a spume of bubbles forming around the dense mass in the crystalline tides. As the bubbles dissipated, the diver buoyed to the surface then nosed over and began kicking toward a cluster of crunchy coral heads cropping up from the sandy bottom.

Skeg, who'd been underwater for over a minute, burped up an air bubble to reduce his buoyancy. He sank down behind a hunk of brain coral then pinched his nose and forced air into his eardrums to stabilize the atmospheric pressure.

Once steadied, he reached around and felt the back of his head. Tucked into his nap of dreadlocks was the poison-tipped spine of a purple sea urchin. He slid the thing from the locks then gripped it like a jail-yard shiv.

He waited and watched. This was going to be easy. Too easy. Like shooting shitbirds in a barrel.

As the overhead splashing grew closer, Skeg kicked a leg, rising through the water column until he sighted his target.

To his surprise, Johnny was gripping a speargun.

He belched an air bubble. Perhaps this task might prove more interesting than he'd anticipated.

He sank back down below the coral and began a deep-water swim around the wide perimeter of the reef. Once downstream from the target, he positioned behind a blind of sea fans and polyps and waited. But as he waited, Johnny kept diving down, prodding the gun tip into various features along the reef then bobbing back to the top with the spear still locked and loaded. Two or three more minutes passed before Skeg felt the cool burn of oxygen depletion pulsating in his lungs.

With no other option, he kicked toward a nearby mooring anchor and ascended upward along the cable, breaking the surface and gasping for breath. He was exposed now. If Johnny looked this way, his cover was blown. Skeg inhaled deeply three times, inflating his lungs all the way to his ribcage, then sank under again, quickly diving down to the coral blind.

This time, as he reestablished his position, he realized he was not alone.

Cruising up from the darker waters beyond the reef was a shadowy figure far too disproportionately large to be real. Despite its titanic size it moved gracefully through the ocean, each fan of its tail causing its own alternating current. As it closed toward Skeg, the mottled markings became detectable in the dim filtered light then grew ever-increasingly more detailed as the beast trolled closer between two fingers of the reef.

At ten feet out, the goliath grouper pivoted a quarter turn then cruised directly up to Skeg, pausing, fluttering its pectoral fins and hovering in the mid-waters a mere three feet from his nose.

Skeg estimated the beast to be north of five hundred pounds and a shade over six feet long. A section of fishing line streamed out of the corner of his mouth from a previous tangle with man.

After a few moments in mesmerizing awe, a horrible thing occurred to Skeg. He reached out and, waving his hands in front of the creature, attempted to shoo it away. But the gullible grouper did not heed the warning. With a slow wavering of its tail, it drifted off through the abyss toward the next thing of notable curiosity in the ocean: a skin diver.

As the fish approached, Johnny sank underwater at the precise time the massive creature passed underneath his feet. An inquisitive and fearless species, the grouper circled back in a broad loping way and gave Johnny another pass.

For a city slicker, Johnny was quick with the speargun.

He raised the device to his shoulder and took aim. A moment later the spear ripped a cord of bubbles through the water then sank into the soft flank just forward of the fish's left dorsal fin.

Bile climbed up Skeg's throat.

Johnny instinctively wrapped the shock cord around his arm and began tugging on the cable. In a frantic fit, the goliath grouper flipped his tail and dove, drawing the cord taut as a tightrope. Johnny, who'd wound the shock cord around his forearm for leverage, now found himself tethered to the fish and unable to shake his arm free.

As the fish dove deeper, Johnny too began to sink away, streaming out behind the beast like a king crabber ensnared in the line of a sinking pot.

Skeg dove down after the duo, making the proper pressurization adjustments as he descended. As a proficient deepwater diver, he understood the tremendous forces at play. But, at Johnny's rapid rate of descent, he could not adjust quickly enough to the atmospheric changes.

Skeg followed slowly behind as Johnny began to writhe against the tethered cord, his oxygen reserves compressing to dangerously narrow levels. Thirty feet down, Johnny's free arm began to flap wildly at his side. At around forty feet, his jaw fell open, and he inhaled a lungful of seawater then immediately vomited leaving a chum trail in his wake. Around fifty-five feet, he seemed to begin to lose consciousness, no longer struggling against the force.

Finally, around seventy feet, the goliath grouper plateaued and darted toward a rocky bulkhead with Johnny still streaming out behind him. When the fish reached a jagged outcropping, it began deliberately swimming in circles, entangling the shock cord to the rocks.

Skeg arrived at the scene with his machete brandished.

Johnny's eyes rolled completely white before exploding red with busted vessels. Then Skeg slashed the blade through the cobalt waters.

As the sharpened edge connected, the two sections of shock cord recoiled in opposing directions. The grouper, confused momentarily by his newly discovered freedom, stalled just long enough for Skeg to reach out and leverage the carbide spear, releasing the tension on the barb. A few clever wriggles of the grouper's broad tailfin dislodged the barb from the flank, then the fish swam off into the distance with only an incidental impalement.

Skeg turned back.

Johnny was not so fortunate. His body was still tethered to the rock, and his eyes bulged like poached eggs. In some last desperate reflex, his legs thrashed against the craggy abutment then went limp, the currents sweeping his feet outward so that his body mass drifted in the water column parallel to the ocean floor.

For good measure, Skeg pierced the sea urchin spine into the prominent vein bulging below Johnny's left ear. The diver's lips parted one final time, belching an air bubble that wobbled slowly toward the surface. Skeg watched it rise through the ocean, like a jellyfish in an upwelling, imagining it released the words *fucking A* as it reached the surface and popped into the afternoon air.

CHAPTER 29

RAY WORKED THE wheel, cruising the Mako at thirty-three knots through the shallow waters on the fringe of Cotton Key Basin. Viktor Jimenez poised near the bow showcasing a flaming red bikini with a long linen shirt unbuttoned and hanging loosely around his shoulders. His mustache tips chattered the wind.

"Raeford, you know anything about some photos?"

Ray felt his cheeks flush with heat, his fingers curl around the wheel. "Pictures? Going to need to be a little more specific than that, commissioner."

"Night of the Dixen gala. Didn't I see you out there working security? Not your usual detail, is it?"

Ray shook his head. "No cameras allowed out there, from what I understood."

The commissioner glanced forward of the boat, sighed then glanced back seeming to think the better of the line of questioning. "You been playing nice with my new friends from Jersey since our last chat?"

Ray nodded. "Solid people. Salt of the earth."

"Good to hear. I'd hate to see you lose that pension you've worked so hard to earn." Viktor tilted his face toward the sun. "I want you to treat them like British royalty from now on. They need something, you oblige. Got it?"

Ray half-shrugged.

"This is not a negotiation."

Ray nodded. "So why are we headed out to Coconut Key anyways?"

* * *

Out at the Coconut Key construction site, a crewman from Big Swinging Richard's entourage boated up to the Viking in his dinghy.

"Richard wanted me to let you know he's sorry to hear the tragic news about your business partner, and he's sorry he can't be here to pass along his condolences in person."

"What?"

"He won't be making the meeting."

"He say why?"

"Things came up's all he said."

"He too big-time to ring a guy in advance?"

The crewman shrugged. "You should try working for the prick."

"I'd rather sew buttons in a Vietnamese sweatshop." Mookie puffed his cigar. "Doesn't that showboat know I got an important somebody coming by here any minute for a little meet-and-greet?"

"Look man, I'm just the messenger here." The crewman cleared his throat. "Anything you want me to relay to the showboat before the big event?"

"Yeah. Tell that prick he'd better play every note we're paying him to play. He cuts it short by one refrain, it'll be reflected in his paycheck."

The crewman nodded. "You guys don't have any gaffer tape, do you?"

"We're more of a duct tape kind of crew."

The crewman nodded then buzzed his boat back toward a group of workers taking a coffee break as Mookie spun toward the artificial island.

The engineering marvel had achieved its first visible acre of raw land, forming the kidney-shaped sandbar that would provide enough square footage to hold the inaugural Big Swinging Richard concert. The rainbowing operation had been suspended for a few days giving way to the concert crew who now buzzed about erecting the stage, connecting generators and unfurling microphone cords and other sound equipment.

"These chuckleheads is Union boys." Mookie looked at Chewy. "I got a feeling they ain't going to get things handled in a timely manner without some serious micromanagement."

"You want I should look after this stuff, boss?"

"I'll take care of it. Why don't you put in a call to Chopper? See if things are on schedule."

Mookie waddled into the cockpit, fingered a Cohiba from the humidor then sauntered back on deck. "There he is."

"Who?"

Mookie pointed the cigar as Sheriff Livingston eased his center console through the break in the turbidity barrier and angled their way. As he approached, Commissioner Jimenez moved toward the bow.

"Afternoon, commissioner." Mookie stepped down to the transom platform. As the Mako neared, he caught the bow rail while Ray cut the wheel and reversed, drawing the stern alongside the Viking.

Mookie hitched a line to the forward cleat then glanced at the commissioner. "I see you brought your bitch along with you today, commissioner. I'd known, I'd have stocked-up on some puppy treats."

Jimenez belted out a hearty laugh. "He's a good little mutt most of the time. Does exactly as he's told as long as I keep him fed and watered. Isn't that right, Raeford?"

Ray gritted his teeth. "Loyal as a lapdog."

Mookie took the commissioner's outstretched hand and helped him onto the platform. "Glad you finally made it out." Mookie pointed at the swimsuit. "What's that? One of them European things?"

"Brazilian actually. What do you think?"

"Not my speed, but for some reason, you pull it off. Must be the tight physique."

The commissioner glanced around, his forehead wrinkling up. "Am I early?"

"All apologies, Viktor. Apparently this Richard character got a case of the sniffles. Nodules and whatnot are inflamed or something. He's resting up. Wants to make sure the pipes are in shape for the big event."

"Well, that's certainly a disappointment."

"Don't fret. Things work out, you two can hang out backstage before the show."

The commissioner nodded then stepped to the rail, planting his arms akimbo and glancing toward the island. "Well, to hear about this is one thing, but to actually see it in person . . ."

"Sight to behold, ain't it?"

Jimenez nodded then turned back to Mookie. "You understand I wanted to check this out in person before committing to anything. You know, being in the public eye and all." The commissioner surveyed the crew bustling about the new sandbar. "This is quite the production."

"I can promise you, we Saluccis don't do nothing half-assed." Mookie pointed toward the main stage. "That's where you'll be emcee-ing, should you decide to do us the honor. Emceeing for Big Swinging Richard, nonetheless. That's something for the résumé, especially down here in the Sunshine State."

Jimenez twisted at his mustache then pointed toward the main stage. "I'd be right there."

"Front and center. It'll be your voice booming through them giant JBLs."

"Good sound quality?"

"Better than good. Solid gold. Forty-eight thousand watts rattling the bikinis right off the gals dancing in the crowd."

The commissioner snapped his elastic waistband. "I think you're right. This is better than any smear campaign my PR department can cook up against the competition. The exposure from this thing will be priceless."

"So then it's a deal?" Mookie pushed an open hand toward the commissioner, and they sealed the moment with a hearty shake.

Mookie reclaimed his hand then glanced back to the construction, discretely wiping a handkerchief over his fingers. "It'll be our privilege and honor. I like to take care of those who take care of us."

"Good to know you understand how things work down here."

"I'll put my people in touch with your people first thing tomorrow morning and have them iron out the details."

Jimenez eyed across the deck toward the salon. "Mind if I duck into the bathroom for a second?"

"Not at all." Mookie put a hand into the commissioner's back, urging him toward the door. "Down the steps, first door on the left. Just remember to pump the tanks, you drop a deuce in there."

As Jimenez disappeared into the cabin, Mookie stepped back toward the stern and nodded at Ray. "See, lapdog. I told you we was good people. Nothing to worry about."

Ray shifted on the leaning post. "So I hear another one of you guys went missing. What was this one's name? Johnny Bagels?"

"Can you believe the luck? Fella goes for a snorkel and never comes back."

"Another accident, you think?"

"Tough to say, officer. No body. No evidence. But what else could it be? Wasn't no one else around."

"Maybe somebody set him up. You want me to sweep your boat for foreign DNA?"

"Wouldn't do any good. We gave her a scrub down just yesterday. We wanted to cleanse ourselves of the whole rotten incident with Johnny. You know, it's therapeutic to do these kinds of things after a tragic incident."

"Maybe you'd be willing to part with a DNA sample of your own."

"Funny you should say that, officer. I gave one to my gal just last night."

"Joke all you like. But seems to me as if somebody around here's got a thing for making you guys disappear."

"Just a string of bad luck is all."

"You want me to keep an eye on you two? Make sure one of you doesn't go missing next?"

Mookie scoffed. "I'm a big boy, officer. I can take care of my own."

The sheriff laughed and folded his arms over his chest. "A big boy, Mookie? Don't kid yourself. You're downright obese."

CHAPTER 30

FIVE O'CLOCK ARRIVED. Five o'clock in the summer Keys was hot, damp, exhaustingly thick. Time to crack another beer, turn off the inside noise then head out into the warm wind and keep suckling booze into the happier hours.

This afternoon, however, was all about sitting idle, trying to be patient, refraining drink, as Jack awaited his five o'clock engagement with Summer. But as five bled into five-thirty then drifted on toward six, he sat on the Moppie, beer-less, tapping his foot uncontrollably on the deck.

Summer was fashionably late on occasion but never this late. Had she had second thoughts and decided to cancel? If so, there'd be no way for her to call.

Jack waited, ears perked, listening for the thump of footfalls, the zing of a moped, even the shrill of a personal watercraft.

But nothing.

Only the road traffic out on the Overseas Highway carried his way. Big lawn-maintenance vehicles, linen couriers and ice trucks headed home for the day. And beater cars shuttling half-sexy, half-sad women listening to sappy ballads croon over cracked speakers on their way to wait tables and tend bar. Somewhere deep in their handbags hid packs of menthols, inked-on cocktail napkins, last night's unmentionables balled up and tucked deep. Somehow, someway, they'd drifted down from the Middle Forty-seven in search of someplace wet and warm. But their preconceptions of a tropical paradise were far too lofty to ever be achieved. Islamorada, like most places south of the peninsula, was a crooked little Village of Islands in both contour and disposition. Its shores were deceptively inviting, luring green dreamers toward its shallows with the cunning prowess of a false lighthouse. Upon arrival they were given a quick education into the harsh economic realities of living on a small island chain that catered primarily to tourism. Menial jobs, like dishwashing and oil changing, were abundant if you were willing to work for scarcely enough to pay rent on a single room in a doublewide.

Now, as they commuted in for the dinner shift, their eyes darted back and forth, wrestling their lingering hangovers as they came down from the shots, the whiskies on rocks, the lines snorted off toilet tanks the night before. In their post-high haze they dreamt in sepia tones of long ago Topeka and French Lick and changing seasons, always anxious for that first drink of the day.

But the seasons rarely changed in the Florida Keys. The rich stayed rich. The bourgeois stayed high. The tourists stayed long enough to get laid and stomp a few coral heads before jetting back to the Ozarks to deny some poor schmuck's insurance claim on a small-print loophole in his health care policy . . .

Jack checked the clock again. Seven sharp. Two hours late. Now what? Did he risk stopping by Summer's bungalow? What if her dinner plans from the previous night had evolved into breakfast and so forth today?

Unable to sit still any longer, he snatched the pole brush from the cabin then squeezed a stream of boat soap into a five-gallon bucket. Cracking open the spigot, he fanned water into the container. Once a snowy foam mushroomed over the lip, he began churning the brush head up and down in the suds. Next, he worked the coarse bristles over the textured decking drawing semi-clean stripes of white in the dingy fiberglass.

The clock read 7:15. Still no Summer. Where was she?

Jack stabbed the bristly brush into the bucket, slopping a brownish sudsy liquid over the rim, then mopped it around the deck again. He worked the gunwales then the bulkhead then flung open the fish boxes and scrubbed the interiors.

Abandoning the brush, he dialed open the hose nozzle, angling the water, forcing the soapy muck toward the transom. Adjusting the spray, he focused a tighter water stream then sluiced the muck across the soapy deck until a murky brownish runoff gathered in the corners then slowly spiraled out the scuppers.

When the water finally drained away, he cut off the spigot then glanced around. Nothing appeared cleaner. It seemed he'd only shifted the dirt from one area to the next. He tossed the hose onto the dock then checked the clock again: 8:19.

The sun bled out like orange marmalade, waxing toward darkness. He couldn't stay put any longer.

The Volkswagen seat was damp from an afternoon burst. He wiped the water away then sank into the crunchy vinyl. When he reached Summer's bungalow, everything was quiet.

He'd been hoping for music rising from the backyard. Hoping she'd simply had one too many and forgotten about their meeting. Hoping she was passed out from a recreational day of drinking or napping away on an afternoon dose of Percocet. Even hoping she was simply there but not alone . . .

He knocked. Nothing.

He slipped the key into the lock, eased open the door then called out. Nothing.

He moved through the bungalow then glanced into the backyard. Nothing.

His stomach began to rise like a rollercoaster clicking up the tracks toward the apex. What had Summer gotten herself into? Who had she been meeting for dinner?

He ducked into the galley kitchen then flickered on the light. A bluish patina warbled about the room. Shiny tile counters glowed along their pillow-top edges. Coffee stains darkened the once-white grout joints.

A window cutout gave way to a bar-height counter littered with paperwork. Jack moved around to the bar. A legal pad filled with frantic notes was stacked atop newspaper articles regarding Coconut Key. He rifled through the articles. Words like benthic fauna, turbidity readings and riparian rights were highlighted throughout the thin pages.

A glance at the legal pad revealed a name: Salvador Keane Gosling, 8:00 Tuesday evening. That was yesterday. That would've been her dinner date.

A phonebook was open and a particular place of business circled in red ink: Salty Johnson's Waterbike Rentals.

Jack dialed the number, and Salty answered on the first ring. Jack hung up, locked the door behind him then cranked up the Acapulco.

* * *

Jack parked then wandered around a warehouse and down to the docks. It was the first time he'd seen Salty's operation up close.

It was horrible, as expected.

In front of the small metal building, a row of lifejackets sagged over a laundry line stretched between two poles mounted into concrete-filled radials. Nearby, a poorly constructed tiki bar thatched in dead palm fronds sported two horizontal canisters that tumbled slowly, one mixing a frozen red concoction, the other tumbling something green.

A small wooden sign tacked up behind the bar stated a discount for cash purchases, a little something Salty could tuck straight into his jean shorts without having to cull out thirty percent for Uncle Sam.

Islamorada was largely an under-the-table society.

Too jumpy to sit still, Jack barked out a few *hellos* then paced back and forth along the seawall until a man finally appeared puttering toward the water lugging one five-gallon gas can in each grip. The glint of his faux diamond earrings twinkled in the dusk providing a complimentary flash to the surplus of golden nuggets swinging in the scooped neck of his *Briny Life* tank top.

"You Salty?"

The man nodded and huffed, as though forlorn by that fact, then passed by Jack, panting so heavily each breath whistled though his deviated septum. Salty reached the service dock then set down the weighty canisters next to a WaveRunner. Oddly, each of his middle fingers was swaddled in gauze and medical tape.

Jack lurched up beside him. "I'm looking for a woman."

"Ain't we all, pal."

Jack shook his head. The dude had the air of an ex-carwash manager who'd once specialized in peddling weed. "Listen up, Salty. This is serious shit. The woman I'm talking about rented one of these crotch rockets from you yesterday. Her name's Summer."

Salty unscrewed the gas cap on the watercraft then hoisted one canister with both arms, sinking the corrugated spout into the tank. "Yeah. Right. That bizzo was supposed to bring that watercraft back yesterday. I'm fueling up to go looking for her now."

"You haven't seen her since yesterday?"

Salty hefted the gas can farther upright then the contents gurgled more audibly into the tank. "No, I haven't."

"And you're just now going looking?"

"What's it to you, pal?"

"Do you have VHF radios on these things?"

Salty shook his head. "Everybody takes their cell phones. Plenty of service. As long as you don't stray outside the designated riding area."

"No phone calls from her either?"

Again, Salty shook his head. "Goddamn tourists." As the gas continued to transfer from the can, the burden of the weight seemed to bleed from Salty's shoulders. He stood more upright, now balancing the can with a single hand. "Every now and again one of these idiots gets lost in the backcountry even with the GPS. Once you get turned around out there, everything looks the same."

"Did Summer mention anything about where she was going?"

Salty shook his head. "She rented the thing for the entire day. That's unusual."

"You allow them to go out to Coconut Key?"

A line of concern formed across Salty's forehead as he *tonked* the empty gas can onto the dock. "Who are you, anyway?"

Jack cinched a firm grip around one of Salty's biceps then jerked upward. "Are you keeping something from me?"

Salty winced. "I'm sure she's fine."

"What are you talking about?"

Salty incidentally shot Jack a bird with each middle finger as he flaunted the bandages. "That skunk ape dude. From the papers."

"What about him?"

"The sicko paid me a visit last night. Clamped live oysters to my fingertips. I thought I was going to have to get the things amputated."

Jack let go of Salty's arm then drew a hand over his dampening mustache. "What did he want with you?"

"Told me to close up shop, or he'd be back to close it up for me."

"What did he look like?"

"Crazy looking dude with dreadlocks. He's huge too. Basketball-player tall."

Jack set his hands on his hips. "What else?"

"The guy's a freak. He started preaching to me about renting out kayaks instead of water bikes. Called me a fossil fuelhead or something like that. Then he promised to disembowel me if he had to come back."

"Did you report it to the police?"

Salty wriggled a musty lifejacket over his shoulders. "I got enough problems without getting tangled up with no cops."

"What else did he say?"

"Nothing really. Except—"

"Except what?"

Salty hiked a leg then sank down onto the foam seat and straddled the floating watercraft. "He got all kinds of sideways when he noticed a brochure of Coconut Key in my shop."

Salty snugged the kill-switch lanyard around his wrist. "After that he stormed out, and I had to steam those oysters just to get them off my fingers." He thumbed the electric start button. "I was afraid to go looking for that gal last night. But now—"

The engine fired, and a safety telltale fountain of water streamed skyward from the rear of the craft. A wave of blue oil smoke drifted up

Jack's nostrils. Worse, a piston kept misfiring, causing the engine to bray like a sick donkey.

Jack spoke over the raucous. "Why don't you shut that thing off, and let's take a walk up to your office?"

"What about the bizzo?"

Jack yanked the kill switch lanyard returning a nice calm quiet to the marina. "Come with me, Salty. I need to borrow your phone to put a call in to Sheriff Livingston."

"What's going on here? Am I in some kind of trouble?"

* * *

The Mako came off plane then crawled toward Salty's watercraft operation. The sheriff flipped a series of inflated fenders to the outside of the hull then bumped up to the dock.

"So you haven't seen her since yesterday?"

Jack hooked a crunchy dock line around the forward cleat. "It was about nine in the morning, and she was heading out on a scavenger hunt. See what she could dig up about Coconut Key. Then she was meeting up with somebody later yesterday for dinner."

"Any idea who?"

"Maybe." Jack raked his fingers through his mustache. "I assume you heard about that recent WaveRunner attack out at Crane Key."

The sheriff nodded then popped a toothpick into his mouth. "Same MO as the last time. Syrup in the tanks and all. Looks like our guy is back in town."

"This Salty. He the first one to open up a rental place in Islamorada since the last rash of attacks?"

"Sure is. Why?"

"The last go-around you guys thought it was just a drifter passing through. Some sicko with a healthy distaste for personal watercraft. But what if this guy's a local. Maybe he never left. Maybe he's just protecting his own turf. You have anything on file from that case?"

"Hang on." Ray situated behind the helm and flickered on his onboard computer. A few keystrokes later, he dialed down the squawk on his VHF and began to speak. "There was one guy questioned in the incident when the attacks first started happening. Released though. No hard evidence to hold him on anything."

"Any priors?"

"One sec." A few keystrokes later, the screen changed. "Says here there's no prior arrests, but he does have an infraction back in the seventh grade." The sheriff swapped the toothpick from one side of his mouth to the other. "Apparently he stabbed some poor kid in the scrotum with a sea urchin spine."

"Jesus." Jack cupped his hands in front of his crotch. "What for?"

"Retaliation against a bully."

Jack's face flushed. "Wait a minute. We've got three dead developers. One gets gigged with a stingray, one gets stung to death by a jellyfish and the third goes missing while snorkeling a reef. Not to mention my little wound." Jack rolled his hand, examining the healing blisters. "Sounds exactly how this kid all grown up might react when provoked."

Ray pointed the damp end of his toothpick at the computer screen. "There's something else. A few Fish and Game violations for illegal harvesting of some pretty exotic species."

"Harmful ones?"

Ray nodded. "Some actually deadly."

"This is our guy, Ray. It's got to be. The WaveRunner attack. The developers. He's protecting his turf."

"Like some kind of deranged animal?"

"More like an animal being threatened. Like an animal being pushed out of its habitat."

"Don't go making excuses for this guy, Cubera."

Jack jumped onto the Mako and positioned behind Ray. "What's this guy's name?"

"Salvador Keane Gosling."

Jack's fingers sank into Ray's right shoulder. "That's who Summer was going to see."

"It gets worse." Ray turned to Jack. "His one known alias is Skeg."

The blood drained from Jack's face. "I'm going to string that sonofa-bitch up by his ankles." He leaned over Ray's shoulder. "Do we know what this bastard looks like?"

Ray flipped the screen to the next page, and a mug-shot appeared. The subject was younger and the hair darker, but the long dreadlocks were tough to forget. No doubt, it was the pervert who'd been loitering in the canoe at Summer's place. And, most likely the one who'd broken in and rummaged through the SunState documents. Not good. Had this Skeg character targeted Summer because of her involvement in the Co-conut Key permitting? And, armed with that information, what un-speakable things was he capable of? "I know how they connected."

Ray pushed up from the leaning post. "More importantly, do you have any idea where they met for dinner?"

"Not a clue." Jack eyed across the watery expanse through the warm nightfall settled over the backcountry. Then he slipped the pistol from his shoulder holster and tucked it into his waistband.

"That's a good way to shoot your dick off."

"I've got a permit to carry this thing."

"A *concealed* weapon permit."

Jack stuffed the gun deep into his shorts pocket. "Better?"

"Don't start going vigilante on me. We both know that can be a slip-pery slope for you."

"Fine then. Then let's get out there and do what we can to find her."

"We've got to follow certain procedures, Jack. You know that."

"Don't expect me to act rational here, Ray."

"There's protocol, and if we follow it, we can probably have a team assembled and out on the water first thing in the morning."

"Fuck protocol, Ray."

"We all get humbled at some point, Cubera." The sheriff cranked his outboards. "I'm serious, Jack. Let me get to work on this using the proper channels. In the meantime, no Wild West shit out of you."

"We're talking about Summer here, Ray."

"Go home, Jack. Kiss the twelve apostles. I'll be in touch as soon as I've got a team assembled and ready to roll."

CHAPTER 31

AS THE NIGHT dragged on, the stadium lights from Tipsy's kept the marina as light as an Alaskan summer. Every time Jack thought about ducking into the cabin for sleep, his heart palpitated, his mind reeled, he couldn't think straight.

Where was Summer? Was she okay? Had this guy done something with her? Worse yet, to her?

He wanted to be out there, searching. But where?

He settled into the fighting chair and tried to think rationally. But nothing made sense. His thoughts were muddled, out of place and out of context, blurred with uncertainty. As he sat waiting, wrestling his inability to find order in the disarray, thundering footfalls drew him forward in his chair. He leaned forward as the kid, arms pumping like a track star, raced down the dock and leaped onto the boat. He landed with the prowess of a young athlete then swiveled to a stop and flipped the hair from his face.

"It's all over the news, Jack. That body we found. They found the guy's boat. His Boston Whaler. It was drifting off the coast of Jupiter. He just now got reported missing. They think there's a serial killer loose in Islamorada."

"Calm down, kid. Right now I've got bigger issues to deal with. A girl's gone missing. A very important girl, and—"

"Your girlfriend?"

Jack slumped in the fighting chair. "Go back to your boat, kid. Lock your doors and stay inside."

"Don't just tell me to go home. We found that body."

"I'm all out of sorts, kid. I can't get my head right."

"Suck it up, old man."

"Look here, you little shit." Jack jumped up from the fighting chair, gathered the kid's shirt in his fist then shoved him against the cabin bulkhead. As Jack lifted the kid off the deck, the kid's eyes bugged out, and his lips moved for some time before the ringing in Jack's ears quieted enough for the words to register.

"Get off your ass and do something."

"What do you expect me to do?"

"You're the adult here. Figure it out."

Jack considered the words, slowly sliding the kid down until his feet toed the ground. Jack released his fistful of shirt then patted the kid on the head like a faithful mutt and turned away. The kid was right. Enough sitting idle. To hell with Ray and his proper protocol. The time had come for decisive action.

What did he really know about this Skeg character anyway? What had he learned since taking on this case?

As his wheels began to grind forward, the anxiety eased enough so that his thoughts began to coalesce. The truth was he'd gathered a healthy chunk of intelligence about Skeg in recent days that might help dial in his whereabouts. For instance, the man was accustomed to roughing it. Sleeping outdoors. Growing his own food. Living in minimalist conditions. No doubt the guy had the ability to self-sustain in the harshest of environments.

Jack paced along the rail. Of course. It made complete sense. Most people weren't foolish enough to endure the harsh, buggy environment of the Islamorada backcountry, but this guy was different. After he'd been exiled from Shady Acres, he could easily have paddled away and established camp on one of the hundreds of scrub islets that pepper the backwaters of the Florida Bay. Despite being a Florida State Park, many areas were rarely, if ever, visited due to their extreme shallows and remote locales. They were perfect waters for shallow-draft boats like handcrafted canoes. Theoretically, a man with Skeg's skillsets could live out there for decades, unfettered, unseen, and undisturbed by the machinations of the scandalous modern world known as Islamorada.

Of course, one would need fire to survive in the backcountry, if for nothing more than the companionship. That would explain why the recluse often reeked like smoke.

In truth, the backcountry offered the perfect cover for a man like Skeg. From there he could come and go, taking out developers one at a time, in relative anonymity. It wasn't much to go on, but it was better than sitting still. "What are you doing for the next hour or so, kid?"

The kid shrugged.

"I need you to help me prepare for a hunt."

Midnight came and went as the two prepped the skiff for an expedition into the backcountry. Jack shuttled two extra gas cans aboard as the kid ducked into the Moppie cabin and rounded up a flare gun, a case of water, a handheld GPS and the waterproof chart in case Jack's electronics crapped out. Finally, Jack strapped his leather shoulder holster into place then sank into the skiff. The kid tried to climb aboard.

"Stay here. If I'm not back by this time tomorrow, get in touch with Sheriff Livingston."

"Come on, old man."

"That old man shit's not going to work this time. This is serious business."

Reluctantly, the kid shoved the boat away from the dock, and Jack motored out into the night. As he cornered from the marina, he scanned his provisions one last time. When going on a hunting trip, knowing your quarry before setting out was imperative to preparing accordingly. Suddenly, he wished he'd packed slightly heftier gear, like a speargun or a whaling harpoon.

CHAPTER 32

THE CROCODILE PROW rasped against the shores of mainland Islamorada. Skeg dragged the wooden boat onto a sandy patch tucked between two neon manes of purple bougainvillea then covered it with tufts
of loose sawgrass.

Moving like a gymnast, he stepped along a fallen foxtail palm then
sprawled on a public park bench set amongst a ceiling of banyan trees.
The placard on a granite pedestal deemed the postage stamp of land a
community park dedicated to Virgil Riesling, a now-deceased sugarcane
baron who most certainly donated the parcel in exchange for political
favor.

The park was so irrelevant and ill-placed the only reason to ever visit
it would've been to conduct research on the West Nile virus or, perhaps,
to peddle weed.

Skeg draped his arms over the bench back then sprawled his legs
outward, the smattering of sunlight trickling through the canopy and
twinkling his silver chest hair like tinsel on a Douglas fir. He dozed off
for a midday snooze in that reclined position then awoke shortly thereafter to a vision of a sassy cat woman shrouded in a haze of cigarette
smoke.

Skeg straightened his slumped posture then worked the heels of his
palms into his eye sockets. When he moved them away, his porky little
Italian friend, Mookie, had materialized next to the woman's elbow.

"This is Blanch." Mookie rolled his eyes. "She insisted on coming along. Wanted to meet you in person. Didn't believe me when I told her about you."

Skeg stood and tugged at the hem of his alligator skin vest. Blanch shuffled a half-step backward.

"Oh, my. How tall are you?"

"Christ almighty. You too?"

She nodded.

"Five-nineteen."

"Five-nineteen?"

Skeg snapped the vest tight to his shoulders as her kitten brows furrowed then seemed to register something.

"Oh, I get it. What's that, like six foot seven?"

"You're pretty good with the math, pussycat."

Blanch settled her eyes just below Skeg's waistline. "I'm surprised I haven't seen you around before."

"Zip it, cupcake." Mookie took Blanch by the elbow, spun her a quarter-turn then. "How about you give me and the Skeg here a few moments alone?"

"Sounds intimate." She slid a damp cigarette filter from her lips.

"That's right, babycakes. We're going to get into some heavy groping so go wait for me in the Navigator."

Blanch exhaled a cloud of white exhaust into Mookie's face then slunk away like a dejected call girl, down the pathway and out of sight.

Mookie turned back, working a lighter over his cigar nub, bringing it back to life. He kept his eyes crossed, his attention on the cigar tip, as he spoke through muffled lips. "So how's the swamp life treating you?"

"I didn't come to chitchat."

Mookie tucked the lighter back into his pocket then withdrew an envelope of cash from his silk shorts. He tossed it over.

Skeg snatched it mid-air and checked the weight. "Feels a little light."

"It's ten Gs. Like we originally agreed."

"You forget about our renegotiation?"

"Didn't seem right, you changing the price on me like that halfway through the thing."

For Skeg, it was about principle. "You're going to want to come up with the other half."

"Or what?"

Skeg shrugged. "I don't know. Maybe you get some bad air in your tank on a scuba dive. Maybe the generator on your boat leaks carbon monoxide into the cabin while you're asleep. There's a litany of options, but I promise I'll find a good one."

Mookie plucked the cigar from his mouth then huffed. "I knew I should've flown in my own muscle from Jersey for this gig." He flipped the butt into a mucky puddle between two banyan roots causing a hissing sound as the cherry snuffed out.

Skeg's good eyed winked wide open. Freaking litterbug. He didn't have time for this joker's nonsense. Not anymore.

With a closed fist, Skeg lunged forward and cracked the bridge of Mookie's nose. A deft explosion of blood shot downward, spattering his silky ensemble. Mookie's eyes pinched shut as he cupped a hand over his nose and mouth, his groans echoing in the cesta-like curve.

When he finally spoke, his voice was warbled and nasally. "Wha you do dat for?"

"Ten more grand. Tonight. Meet me out at the construction site. And throw that flipping cigar butt in a proper waste receptacle before I shove it up your rectum."

CHAPTER 33

SKEG TETHERED HIS canoe to a construction barge then crawled from the waterline, up the side of the boat and onto the deck. A bait bucket swung from his belt. Inside the container a peculiar species, the size and weight of a Brandywine tomato, wriggled and pulsated.

Skeg clambered onto the deck, stretched upright then unhitched the bait bucket. Mookie stood on the deck alone, back turned, puffing away on a cigar. Skeg maneuvered around a series of hydraulic pumps then snuck in behind him with the bucket swinging in his fingertips.

"Evening, shitbird."

"Jesus H." The portly man spun around. "Big freakshow like you shouldn't be sneaking up on a guy." His nose was swollen like a rotten eggplant and both eyes were ringed with blue and yellow bruises like a surprised coati. He lifted the tail of his silk guayabera, revealing the butt of a Glock. With his free hand, he pointed the damp end of his cigar at Skeg. "No more funny business outa you."

Skeg grinned, his white teeth ablaze in the moonshine. "I felt bad for busting your nose like that so I got you a little something to say I'm sorry."

"You did what?"

Mookie waddled over with his hand on the pistol as Skeg set the bait bucket on the deck then pried open the lid.

Mookie glanced inside. "What in God's creation is that gooey nonsense?"

"An aphrodisiac. For you and your lady friend. The pussycat. Cook it up right, and it'll give you a rock-hard boner that'll last for a week."

"What are you trying to say?"

"It's a blue-ringed octopus."

Mookie scoffed then stuffed the cigar back into his mouth. "What the frig I want with an octopus?"

Skeg plucked the slimy creature out of the hold by the top of his mushy oblong head, careful not to get his fingers anywhere near the mouth. The leggy creature thrashed around looking for purchase then began to pulsate in bright yellows and rings of iridescent blue.

Skeg pushed the thing toward Mookie. "Hold out your hand."

"I'm not touching that slimy thing." Mookie shook his head. "I appreciate the gesture and all, but I don't need no help popping a stiffy. Maybe think about a box of Cubans or something next time you want to extend an apology."

Mookie waved Skeg off then turned back toward the newly formed sandbar and the concert scaffolding rising along its shoreline. "Can you believe this place? This is going to be the most luxurious neighborhood south of Star Island."

"You sure about that?"

"Friggin' unbelievable is what it's going to be."

Skeg stepped swiftly toward him then pressed the underbelly of the octopus against the man's hairy nape. He held it there for a two count before Mookie spun around in protest, slapping at the air then pawing for his gun.

"What do you think you're doing?"

"A little kiss from my friend." Skeg retreated a few paces then returned the octopus to the bait bucket.

"You're lucky I don't put a slug in you on general principle." Mookie slipped a handkerchief from his pocket then pawed it across his neck.

"You got the rest of my money?"

Mookie tossed the envelope onto the boat deck at Skeg's feet. "Ten grand. Now that's the last of it. You and me, we're done doing business."

"There's something I've been meaning to ask you."

"I'm done conversating."

"Just one question."

"What?"

"Why would anyone in their right mind build an island in the middle of an archipelago?"

"Wouldn't you like to know?"

"Doesn't make any sense."

"Maybe not to a swamp man."

"Don't worry. I'll get the answer out of you one way or another."

Mookie hooked his cigar with an index finger. "Look here, wiseass. You need to tone down the creepy factor. Now take that money and paddle back to the swamp where you belong."

"What about the last guy? You don't want me to ace him too?"

"Chewy's gone. He got freaked on account of the other fellas going tits-up. He's on the road right now headed back to Jersey. So you and me, we're done. Our little business arrangement has been put to the proverbial bed."

"To be honest, I wasn't quite finished."

Mookie grabbed at his neck where the octopus had bitten him, his eyes swimming in their sockets. "What now? You want me to pay for Chewy even though you didn't do the deed?"

"Not at all. This next one's on the house." Skeg sneered. "You feeling anything yet?"

"Yeah. Feeling like I oughta throw you off this friggin' boat." Mookie massaged his fingers into his neck and glanced around the boat deck like a man looking for a cool place to lie down. "Man is it hot out tonight or what?"

"I think it feels nice. Maybe you're coming down with something."

"Not a chance. I got an immune system that could fight off the plague."

"You sure? You don't look so good."

Mookie daubed the handkerchief at the sweat beads cropping up across his face. "Just a little overheated is all."

"Maybe you got some bad seafood."

Mookie's head wobbled as his eyes flashed toward the bait bucket then back to Skeg. "What the frig was that thing you put on my neck?" His head bobbled again, then he stumbled toward a hydraulic pump and braced himself against the housing.

Skeg lunged forward, snatched the Glock from Mookie's waistband then tossed it over the boat rail.

"Wha's the matter with you?"

"I imagine your lips are starting to tingle a little bit now. You may even be feeling a bit lightheaded already. Don't worry. That's normal. That's a symptom known as paresthesia."

Mookie drew a swollen white tongue over his dried lips. "Symptom? Symptom of what? What did you do to me?"

"It's funny. You don't even feel the critter sink his little beak into you, do you?"

Mookie's shirt dampened around the nipples. He wrestled it open, flinging buttons into the air. His areolas lactated, secreting a creamy substance the consistency of drawn butter.

"Can you feel your body starting to seize up?"

Mookie sank to his knees. "Fug you freagshow."

Skeg stepped closer and loomed over him. "That's the tetrotodoxine. Ten-thousand times more poisonous than cyanide."

Mookie toppled from his kneeling position onto his side, now struggling to open and close his fingers. His legs pedaled at the air as though riding a bicycle underwater.

"What you're feeling now is your kidneys and liver shutting down."

"Why you doin' this?"

"You really don't know?"

Mookie's ribcage heaved as he began to asphyxiate under the weight of his own chest. His muscle control bled out as his trembling body slowed toward complete torpor.

Skeg hunched over the body, his dreadlocks cascading around his face, his nose a foot from Mookie's. "In a minute you'll experience complete muscular paralysis. You'll be trapped inside your own body aware of everything that's going on as you slowly suffocate."

With a grunt and a gurgle, Mookie ceased writhing, his eyes wide open and his body as stiff and contorted as a rigor rat.

"Of course. I could reverse the effects if I wanted to, but I'm going to need a few things in return before I agree to that."

CHAPTER 34

JUST BEFORE DAWN a bone fisherman cutting through Toilet Seat Pass spotted a scuttled WaveRunner bobbing nose-up off the southern tip of Plantation Key.

The call came in over channel 16 on Jack's handheld VHF. He plugged in the location on his GPS then swung about and raced into a warm August headwind hoping to be the first responder to the scene.

Ten minutes later, he closed in on the waypoint. No other boats were in sight.

The flats fisherman who'd called in the scuttled vessel, obviously not interested in missing the morning bite, had zip-tied a glow stick to the nose of the craft then sped away. Jack detected the neon-green glow fifty yards out then angled his skiff alongside the craft and cut his running lights. Using a fillet knife, he sliced the glow stick loose and tucked it into his gear bag, out of sight.

The water returned to its usual darkness, although somewhere toward shore a boat buzzed along at a quick clip. He surveyed the space between his position and the coastline, finding a telltale anchor light that appeared to fly like a cosmic orb across the horizon. It was still too dark to see the outline of the vessel, but he feared it was Ossie.

For the past ten minutes, the officer had been chattering over the radio with the bone fisherman about the exact whereabouts of the scuttled craft. Jack wanted no part of Ossie.

Not today.

Suddenly, the vessel cut Jack's way, its red and green bow lights rapidly growing brighter as the craft approached.

Jack slipped out of his shirt, unsheathed and stowed his gun then sank into the water. Leveraging against the WaveRunner rub rail, he attempted to right the craft, but its cavity was filled with water and too heavy to roll.

He dove under and worked his fingers around the console, locating the dry storage compartment. He twisted the latch, wriggled his hand inside and came out with a contraption.

He bobbed to the surface, tossed the thing into the skiff then pulled himself back onto the boat. As he sank onto the steel bench, the approaching craft clicked on a spotlight, the beam sweeping side-to-side in a manner used by prison guards searching for escapees at night.

Jack fired his outboard then twisted the throttle. He stayed low in the boat to prevent his silhouette from being noticeable against the purple dawn which now bled upward from the horizon. Twice the light beam swept directly over his position, but each time he turned back the distance between him and the other vessel had increased. Ten minutes later, he slipped into a mooring yard and hid in the shadow of a forty-foot ketch.

When he looked up again, the sky appeared to have come awake in an instant, the dark purples giving way to the soft pastel blues of a fresh day.

He hauled the confiscated GPS out of the bilge and thumbed the *on* button.

The thing flickered then the screen streaked with a bizarre pattern of colors before dissolving back to black.

Despite being water-resistant, the saltwater had rendered the machine useless. He'd been hoping to retrieve the breadcrumb trail left behind by Summer. A geographical telltale of where she'd gone on the WaveRunner would've greatly narrowed the scope of the search area, and, perhaps, even led him straight to her position. On a last-ditch effort, he unscrewed the waterproof backing and opened the device. A microSD memory card, no larger than a pinky toenail, was wedged into its port.

He slid the card out then tried it in the similar slot on his own GPS. Perfect fit. He flicked on the unit then scrolled through the presets until the recent history—in the form of a breadcrumb trail—began to take shape across his LED display.

According to the readout, Summer had run her watercraft out to Cotton Key Basin then to Crane Key. Those two stops would've been to visit the Coconut Key construction site then to visit the scene of the tourist attack, like she'd suggested.

From there, however, the path took a less-discernible course. A spaghetti-like trail meandered through the backwaters, twisting and turning, zigging and zagging, ultimately resolving at something that, judging by an onscreen digital icon, designated an anchorage on the leeward side of a nameless islet.

As the sun broke away from the horizon, Jack set the Costa Del Mars over his eyes then raced the skiff across a light chop until he reached the sheltered bight of the waypoint. Anchored amid the waters was a spanking white catamaran, main down and furled, the tail of the jib popping in the crosswind.

The anchor was out but had obviously been set at a different tide and wind current. The vessel had swung down current, forcing the left pontoon into shallower waters. The boat now sat aslant, one keel sunken into the sandy bottom, the other not, so that the vessel listed to starboard.

Jack eased over then boarded the boat. "Anybody home?"

Along the topside were apparent signs of recent activity. A couple of champagne glasses rolled about the deck like fallen bowling pins. A few food plates had slid from the table and now resided upside down on the bench cushion, their edible contents oozing oils and spices into the foam.

A quick duck into the cabin offered little in the way of direction. But Summer had been on this vessel, or at least at this anchorage. The GPS trail proved that. But then what had happened? Where was she now?

There were no signs of struggle. Quite the contrary. Everything Jack saw pointed toward a dinner engagement. A quiet interlude of champagne and shellfish.

Had this Skeg character carted her off to places unknown to do unmentionable things against her will? Or could she have gone willingly?

No. The scuttled WaveRunner discounted any theory that she'd gone willingly.

So where exactly had he taken her?

Jack eyed the distant mainland then spun back toward the expansive backcountry. The horizon was peppered with islets, layer upon layer, each one receding further into the backdrop, the succession of lines dithering against the pastel sky.

For a moment, Jack considered hailing Ray, but decided the better of it. Now was not the time to be doing things by-the-book.

He guided the skiff out of the bight, banked left along a tidal rip then cornered a secondary stippling of islets heading north. Here the vast expanse of the backcountry changed in immeasurable ways. No more telltale markings of condos rose in the distance. No more radio towers cluttered the landscape.

He lowered his sunglasses against the watery glare and began searching the seascape for clues. The wealth of the morning was wasted combing a cluster of mangrove islands north of Crane Key. The afternoon proved just as disappointing exploring a section of bay farther northwest. As the day waned he began to question his tactics. In twelve hours he'd seen little more than a few sharks, a couple dozen loggerheads and six manatees.

Around dusk, he came across a bone fisherman hung up on a flat.

"Need a hand?"

"Like you wouldn't believe."

Jack sloshed through the shallows then, hitching twin bowlines over their shoulders like yoked oxen, they hauled the lodged boat until it tipped freely in the tides.

Jack dropped the line and let it sink into the water. "Seen anyone else out here today?"

"Nothing but me and the spoonbills."

"How about the bite?"

"Electric. Big tarpon dragged me over these shallows. That's how I got hung up."

"You know your way back to Islamorada?"

The man shook his head. "I came out of Flamingo."

"Am I that far north?"

The man nodded. "Just around the next break."

Jack preened his mustache. He'd come much farther north and west than he'd anticipated. Maybe he'd goofed. Maybe he'd ventured too far from Islamorada. Had he overlooked some remote area closer to the mainland?

Of course.

There was one particularly shoal-ridden tract about two miles offshore, not too terribly far from where he'd first discovered Ross's body. The waters were notoriously skinny, even for seasoned anglers. To get caught on one of the flats on a vanishing tide spelled certain disaster. Only a boat with the shallowest of drafts could navigate the area. A hand-crafted canoe, for instance, would bode quite well in such an environment.

Jack glanced back to the fisherman. "You need anything else?"

"All good. Thanks for the help." The fisherman thumbed an electric start button, then his four stroke began to purr. "I'd better get back while I still got a little light. You headed in?"

Jack shook his head. "Just getting going."

"Night fishing?"

"Hunting."

The man's brows furrowed.

"Big game."

The fisherman clicked his engine into gear then maneuvered into a blue tongue of deeper water and put his craft on plane.

* * *

Dark descended slowly against a rising full moon so that it never really felt dark out. The orange light of day simply gave way to the bluish hue of night. The cicadas erupted. The occasional firefly winked in the darkness.

Jack killed his outboard then transferred the last five-gallon canister of gas into the fuel tank. With nightfall arriving, firelight would be easier to spot against the backdrop.

He cranked the engine and started south. A quarter-mile later, he wrapped a lobsterpot line around his propeller and spent the next three hours untangling the mess. By the time he got back up and running and reached the search area, it was nearing midnight.

Despite the skinny waters, the flooding tide allowed enough depth to accommodate the shallow draft of his skiff. He killed his engine and drifted with the currents, his eyes working over a cluster of islets for imperfections, his ears working the wind for unnatural noise. Fifteen minutes later, his vision began playing tricks.

He sat quiet, narrowing his sights at a wraith slipping across the horizon, the thing merely a shade of darker darkness set against the night.

When it finally broke into the brighter sky between two islets, it materialized into the full silhouette of a canoe occupied by a man of large stature.

Jack handled his paddle and propelled the skiff one quiet stroke at a time in the general direction. As he studied the boater, a cloud swept over the moon, and he lost the visual. When the cloud moved on, the thing had evaporated in the haze of darkness. For thirty minutes, Jack studied the waters to no avail. He was about to fire up his spotlight at the risk of revealing his position when the faint cry of something unfamiliar drew his attention toward a nondescript islet off to his east. He steadied his eyes in the direction as the noise wavered in and out of audibility in the undulating breeze.

He stroked toward the island. A faint light became visible in the distance, a single cell of orange that fell just east of a slick of wet white moonlight running off toward the edge of the world.

He tilted the outboard from the water then locked it in the upright position, letting his craft drift slowly closer to the island on the flooding tide. As the orange light assumed the flickering ways of a fire, the bits of noise grew louder then began to string together.

What was it? A conversation? A radio? A musical instrument?

Yes.

Something stringed and hollow-bodied. But not a guitar.

The tinny broken notes were too delicate, too pitchy, carrying across the wind like tinsel butterflies. Less than a quarter mile out, the strumming grew louder, the actual chords now discernible even in the shifting breeze. Was it Tahitian? Samoan? Even Micronesian? Certainly South Pacific.

As Jack dipped his paddle and angled toward a small relief in the thick foliage, the island's atoll configuration began to emerge. A wreath of mangroves surrounded a sandy beach, encircling a small tidal pool. Here and there a splash of firelight etched through the branches lending Jack flashes of unnatural color, glinting objects, manmade things.

Unfortunately, what he'd thought was a break in the foliage wasn't much of a relief at all. While an area of mangrove branches appeared to have been pruned upward to some degree, passage under their low-slung limbs was achievable only if negotiated in a boat in a nearly prone position.

As he searched the atoll for another entry point, he got his first peek at the man called Skeg. It wasn't much of a look, just a glimpse of tanned hide and wild hair. The recluse squatted on a cypress stump, his broad shoulders hunched over and a fist cinched around a ukulele neck, the thing toy-like in his massive hands. Jack touched the hard pistol butt under his shirt, but as he did the strumming ceased and Skeg disappeared.

The cicadas returned.

Seconds later, Jack's natural drift offered a full view of camp. The scene proved unsettling, almost abstract set against the remote backdrop. As his mind worked to process what he was seeing, his thoughts quickly reverted to an odd warming sensation creeping down his left arm.

He glanced down at the arm. A black dart of some sort with a pink feathered flight dangled from his left biceps. Were those roseate spoonbill feathers? Was that shaft crafted from a sea urchin spine? As he yanked the dart free, his head was suddenly engrossed by vertigo.

His mind warbled on a wave of confusion as he glanced around, his eyes catching on the peculiar primeval image of a crocodile swimming his way.

"Well, hello there, shitbird. I'm guessing you're here for the girl."

CHAPTER 35

THE SCREAM OF swarming mosquitoes engrossed Jack's ears as his brain slowly fought to regain consciousness. Mental flashes flickered as he scrabbled for reality.

What was real?

The darkness. And the gritty textures against his cheek. The sand that crunched between his molars.

His body felt riddled with lactic acid. His legs were seized up, cramping. Nothing felt familiar, not even the tongue in his mouth, swollen and rolling slowly behind his teeth hunting for hydration.

An eye struggled open, a single eye that worked around the socket in a slow spiraling way until registering that its body was splayed out in the prone position along some foreign beach.

But where?

As the eye began to ping information to the brain, Jack's arms were forced into the small of his back, then the whiskers of a rope gathered around his wrists. Next, a loop of rope slipped over his feet, around his ankles and drew taut.

A series of grunts and snorts lifted Jack's legs against the rope tension. The noose around his ankles grew tighter as his body plowed through the sand one heave at a time until he was afloat, upside-down, dangling from the bough of a banyan limb.

Night had elapsed, and in a dawning light Skeg's steel blue irises reflected the rising fire ashes before they smoldered in the thick air with wafts of acrid smoke.

Skeg gathered his dreadlocks into a fist then pinned them behind his head with a pair of slender bones. "It's Jack, right?"

Jack flinched, grunted, his body twisting like a piñata in a mild breeze. "Jack Cubera."

His throat was dry as parchment, his thoughts flagging, as he fought to discern his whereabouts. But the blood pooling in his skull made clarity difficult. His wrists and ankles began to swell. The slow rotation of his upside-down body offered up reality only in small bits, convex and distorted as though shot through a wide-angle lens. Six or seven rotations passed before things began to coalesce into some semi-rational calculation of where he was detained.

It was a camp of sorts situated around a fire pit. A pair of cypress stumps were placed fireside for sitting. A hammock stretched between two hearty boles flanked one side. A pair of burlap slacks hung from a laundry line alongside a tuft of unknown herbs pinned up to dry. Approximately ten feet away, one of the Jersey mobsters, Mookie, dangled upside down on a neighboring banyan branch, one of his forearms striated with the same whipping blisters Jack had seen on Ross's face. Mookie was unconscious, his chest rising and falling in labored breaths. Jack's skiff was beached just fifty feet out.

Skeg lumbered to the fire then hunched and tended to a tea kettle dangling over the fire. "You ever had 'shroom juice before?"

Jack's gut instantly soured. "Not since my Dylan days."

"Dylan, eh? I was always more of a JJ Cale man myself."

Skeg exhausted a hearty laugh then crashed off into the understory, the crunching of dead leaves underfoot tapering off toward silence.

"Jack."

The hoarse whisper arrived as Jack rotated away from the fire. When he returned, the whisper came again from the fringe of camp. He searched the perimeter, through the thickets and palmetto patches, through the dawning light, discovering Summer tucked under a lush spread in a seated position with her back against a princess palm and her arms bound around the trunk.

"Are you okay?"

She offered a brief nod then her head lolled, her chin coming to rest on her chest, her body falling forward and pulling up against the bindings.

Jack rotated away again and lost sight of her. When he spun back, Skeg was back in camp. Although an older specimen, he flaunted a solid six-and-a-half feet of gangle and mahogany muscle. One of those powerful physiques disguised by great stature that come at you quicker and from a longer range than you ever anticipate. He moved in and hovered over a makeshift workstation—a Haitian tap-tap hood spanning two stumps. Scattered about the brightly painted steel panel were various feathers and bones, barbs and spines, some already fashioned into darts for a blowgun. It appeared this Skeg character had a predilection for homemade weaponry.

Jack nuzzled his chin against his shoulder. His leather holster remained in place, but the Ruger was gone. It appeared his escape would need to take place without the aid of a firearm.

But with what? And how?

Jack eyed the cornicello winking up from Mookie's chest fur. Was it big enough to be used as a weapon? Could Jack wedge it between his fingers then drive into Skeg's neck like a nail? Would that be sufficient to stall the man long enough for him and Summer to escape in the skiff?

Jack wiggled his wrists against the bindings. There was enough slack to get them working back and forth against the rope. The first few pumps of the wrist worked as a telltale. Quality of rope. Amount of flex. Precision of knot. Within thirty seconds, he'd created enough dwell around his wrists that the numbness in his fingertips evaporated under the painful but welcome burn of blood flow.

As he continued to work the bindings, he glimpsed at his ankles and saw his chance. It was a longshot but something to work toward. Skeg's mistake had been the noose-style knot.

As long as tension remained on the line, the knot was inescapable. But ease that tension, and it would slip right off.

Jack looked back to Skeg who was bent down, administering some sort of liquid into Summer's mouth with the aid of a dropper.

"What are you doing to her?"

Skeg wheeled his head around, his upside-down orientation offering up a scowl where a grin should've been. "Helping her detox."

"*Helping* her?"

"This is passionflower extract. To ease the withdrawals."

Skeg pointed toward an herb garden tucked along the fringes of camp. A series of fifty-five-gallon drums were clustered under an intricate network of banana leaves to catch rainwater for irrigating a crop, ranging from blackberries to kale to natural herbs. "The poor thing's got more meds running through her blood than the fat Elvis Presley."

Skeg stepped back to the fire, hauled the kettle from the flames then strained a milky concoction through a swatch of cheese cloth drawn taut over a hollowed gourd. The murky contents filtered through the fabric slowly leaving a funky residue of soggy mushroom caps and stems in their wake. He set down the kettle then rifled through a medicine bag, withdrawing some sort of handcrafted utensil that immediately spelled trouble.

Skeg stepped toward Mookie, twirling the contraption between two fingers. "It's a hypodermic, shitbird. Made from a catfish barb and sea sponge plunger. Pretty ingenious for a scallywag, don't you think?"

The comatose Mookie did not respond as a soft wind drifted in, spinning Jack away from the fire again. When he returned, Skeg had pierced the tip of the hypodermic into Mookie's radial artery and now sank his thumb against the plunger, pushing a dosage of the murky liquid in the bloodstream. Once finished, he took Mookie by the jaw, studying the man's eyes until they began to flutter open then close, each open interval a little longer than the preceding. "Top of the morning to you, Mookie. Let's see if that little shot of psilocybin will do anything to help loosen your tongue." Skeg released Mookie's jaw and glanced over his shoulder. "How about you, Jack? Care for a trip down Memory Lane?"

"Maybe just a sip of water instead."

"Sorry. This is the only soup du jour." Skeg tossed the hypodermic onto the tap-tap hood then began a slow lap around the morning fire as a moan seeped from Mookie's lips. Skeg lumbered back over and, with a thumb and forefinger, pried the lid open on Mookie's left eye. "You feeling anything yet?"

"Fug you."

"That's the idea. Let the anger out and the love rush in."

Skeg snatched Mookie by the shoulder then spun the body in a clockwise fashion, the branch above groaning under the strain. With each building rotation, Skeg lashed out and slapped the body, whipping it faster until Mookie's eyes sprang wide open, his frizzled hair spinning out like cotton candy from the centrifugal force.

"Slow me down. Please slow me down."

"Not until I get some answers."

"I'll answer your questions. Please just stop the spinning and let me down."

Skeg gave the body another twirl. "First things first. Why are you paying me to ace your buddies?"

Jack shook his head, blinked away the confusion. Had he just heard that right? Was Mookie responsible for initiating the killings?

"Out with it, shitbird."

"Them dirty dicks have been banging my Blanch. Every one of them."

"Hmm. All this killing over the pussycat?"

"And less partners means better proceeds. That's it, Skeg. I promise. Come on, now. Slow me down."

"Brotherly love, eh?" Like a hand to a fan blade, Skeg slowed the spinning body until it stalled into a gentle side-to-side sway. "So that begs the question, Mookie. Better proceeds from what sort of revenue stream?"

"The island, Skeg. The real estate dealings."

"Sorry. That just doesn't pass the sniff test." Skeg whipped the body into another spin.

"Lot sales. Lease options. You name it. The thing's going to be a cash cow."

"So why build an island from scratch where so many others already exist?"

"No such thing as too much waterfront real estate."

"Two billion, Mookie. That's what the build is expected to cost."

"Got to spend it to make it."

"That thing's got about as much chance at turning a profit as a government venture."

"Slow me down and give me a second to help you understand the numbers."

Skeg stepped over to the banyan tree then unhitched the rope holding Mookie aloft. Leaning back against the weight, he slowly lowered the body toward the ground, driving Mookie's head into the sand like a billiard stick into chalk. The frizzy head spun to a halt, then the body flopped over. The portly mass looked like a beached beluga.

As Mookie rolled around, Jack pressed his palms together and forced his fingers against one another until he felt a large strand of the rope break free, allowing enough slack for his nails to start slice along the fibers like dull blades.

Mookie rolled onto his side, his heavy breath creating a drift in the grains of sand. "Dear Jesus. Many thanks for letting me down. My head feels like I got water on the brain."

"I wouldn't thank me just yet." Skeg snatched him by the ankles and dragged his body over to the banyan tree.

"What now, Skeg?"

"I don't want to spoil the surprise."

Skeg propped Mookie against the bole and lashed his arms together behind it. Then he stepped to the workstation, wriggled the long digits of his left hand into a thick rubber glove and returned with a slopping bucket of live Apalachicolas. "Did you know that oysters are a natural aphrodisiac?"

"What's with you and the stiffy remedies?"

"You get to be my age, priorities change."

Skeg, with his gloved hand, began tracing an index finger around Mookie's right areola. Once the nipple started to perk, he tweaked it a few times with his thumb and forefinger and brought it fully erect.

"Hey, hey, freakshow. What do you think you're doing?"

"Getting you all hot and bothered with a little foreplay."

"I ain't into the kinky stuff."

"Don't worry. This is more masochistic than kinky."

Skeg fished an oyster out of the bucket then held it like a hockey puck. Working the thick blade of the shucking knife, he parted the shell-halves a quarter-inch. "A real estate venture, you say?"

"You got it, Skeg. Timeshares. Long-term rentals. Not to mention the retail space."

"That's some pretty deep shit you're shoveling, Mookie." Skeg planted a forearm against Mookie's neck then slid the bivalve over the erect nipple. "Care to indulge me on what's really going down?"

Mookie's eyes sprang wide. "You wouldn't dare."

"Have it your way." Skeg released the shucking blade, and the oyster snapped shut like a rattrap.

For a second Mookie fell eerily silent then a curdling howl escaped his lips causing a great white heron to take flight, its wings thumping as it lifted away. Jack sped up his efforts, several more strands of cord popping apart as Mookie slobbered and cooed for several minutes before Skeg reclaimed him by the chin.

"What's your real game, Mookie? Any fool knows this isn't a straight real estate deal."

"What . . . do you . . . care about some . . . dev . . . development?"

Skeg slapped Mookie across the jaw. "Why not in Miami? Or Daytona Beach? Anywhere but here."

Mookie glanced at the oyster dangling from his nipple then back up to Skeg. "You don't understand."

Skeg hoisted another oyster from the bait bucket, this one the size of a hamburger bun. "Then speak to me like I'm a small child."

As Skeg worked the shucking blade into the second oyster, Mookie began to whimper.

"Come on, Skeg. Me and you. We got a history."

"First it's the nipples, then it's the tip of your little prick."

"I got cash, Skeg. Lots of it. Let's talk numbers."

"You know that's not my motivation."

Mookie's chest heaved up and down. "Don't you see what's going on here?"

"You really want to push me, I know a nice family of resident hammerheads who've recently acquired a taste for Italian."

"How much do you want? Just give me a number. You gotta have a number."

"You know what I want."

"It's imports, Skeg. All right? It's imports. We're setting up a pipeline for an import business."

"Imports, eh?" Skeg tipped Mookie's head up by the chin. "Then tell me when they're coming and how they're coming in."

"First shipment's day of the big Coconut Key concert." Mookie's eyes turned glassy. "Skeg, why are you doing this to me?"

"The fact that you don't know pisses me off even more. Now, who's bringing the stuff in?"

"I can't, Skeg. I just can't. They'll castrate me."

"Who's gonna touch those grungy nuts?"

As Skeg slid the open bivalve over the other erect nipple, another rope strand popped, and Jack's hands broke free, the section of cord slipping off his wrist so quickly it hooked momentarily on the tip of his index finger then flipped off and gathered in the sand below.

"Last chance, shitbird."

"But wait, Skeg! I just—"

Skeg released the blade, and the second oyster clapped down, cartwheeling an eraser-sized hunk of brown nipple through the air before it landed, with a hot sizzle, in the glowing embers of the campfire. Mookie, whose eyes had instantly rolled white, gasped a small breath then slumped forward against his bindings.

Skeg scratched his chin then rapped his toes into the ribcage of the semiconscious lump. "Hey, shitbird. You still with me? Shitbird?"

CHAPTER 36

"SO, JACK, I'M still trying to figure out how you fit into all of this."

Jack kept his eyes intentionally fast and true on Skeg, not glancing toward the fallen rope on the ground. "Just an innocent bystander who got dragged into the fray."

"Sounds a little suspect. I mean, first you try to steal my dead body and now you're here to get my girl."

"*Your* girl?"

"Word is you two parted ways." Skeg glanced toward the sedated female. "Now I'm hoping to win her over with a persistent leer and my irresistible charm."

"No offense, Skeg, but Summer thinks my lifestyle is a bit on the rustic side. I'm not sure she's equipped for this standard of living."

"Honestly, this island's starting to get a little too crowded for my tastes, anyways."

"You sound like me."

"Don't flatter yourself, city slicker."

"Seriously, Skeg. You and I aren't so different."

"Save your breath, Jack Cubera. You're going to need it."

"These developers are about to take away my home too. They're planning to tear down the Soggy Dollar to make room for a ferry dock for Coconut Key."

Skeg settled an empty gourd into the sand between his feet and transferred the tea into it. "Replacing old concrete with new concrete. What a travesty that would be."

Skeg submerged the tip of his crude hypodermic needle into the broth, drew back on the plunger then, tapped the syringe and shot a thin line of tea into the air. "I assume you've seen a rendition of the monstrosity these shitbirds are planning to build."

"It's disgusting."

"All of that concrete and glass in the middle of my bay." Skeg stepped toward Jack, the hypodermic upturned. "It's disgusting. Mortifying. Irresponsible. And immoral."

"Not to mention illegal."

Jack watched Skeg approach, then widened his eyes and flashed them toward the fallen rope then back to Skeg. "I didn't mean to—"

For a brief flash, Skeg glanced down to investigate. As he did, the twin barbs pinning back his hair came into full view.

Jack swung his hand around, latched onto a barb, and withdrew it as Skeg's head reared. With an uppercut motion, Jack drove the bone just behind Skeg's chin in the soft meat between the bite of the jawbone. It sank fast and quick through the flesh and lower palate until halting at the hilt that was Jack's clenched hand.

Skeg doddered backward, the bone protruding under his chin, his jaw dropping, his teeth baring, his mouth distorting and howling like a black bear struck by an eighteen-wheeler. Each time his mouth changed shaped the white line of the bone shown through the cavity behind his parted lips, skewered through the lower pallet, pinning his tongue to the roof of his mouth and exiting up and through the hood of his left nostril.

Jack got his body swinging then whipped his torso upward, snagged the line and relieved the tension on the ankle noose. He pointed his toes, slipped the noose free of his ankles then dropped down, collapsing as his blood-dead feet hit the sand.

He was aware of radiating pain but unable to understand it. He spun on the numb appendages then collapsed and slithered toward Summer, working his elbows in army crawl, his feet pushing, his toes digging into the cooler sand under the surface.

Ten feet out, a hand clamped around one of his ankles and was quickly noosed into a rope. As Jack glanced back, a jerking motion brought the noose tight and his leg straight, nearly popping his knee from its socket. Then his body began to drag backward, face-down, across the sand. He tried to dig his free foot into the ground to halt the progression, but Skeg's broad shoulders and thick thighs did not falter.

Ten yards later, the sand now rasping the skin from Jack's chest, they swept by a tree that split into two trunks near the base. There, nestled in that Y propped the ukulele. Jack snagged it by the neck as they whisked by, the hollow body booming against the trunk and causing Skeg to momentarily stall his progress and the rope to slacken.

Jack rolled onto his knees gripping the ukulele with all ten fingers like a tennis backhand. As his body rose and spun toward Skeg, he swung the instrument up and around, as though to put top spin on a tennis ball, contacting Skeg with the hard abalone-inlaid edge of the body.

As Jack followed through, the ukulele crunched under the impact, the neck cracking away from the body. The nylon strings lost their usual tension, bouncing around like spaghetti and braying out like some dying animal as the whole contraption wobbled and collapsed and dropped to the sand.

The shot had connected squarely, catching the beast along the tender cheekbone just forward of his right earlobe. Skeg slumped on his heels, eyes half-rolling in their sockets, a steady thread of blood running down his neck. He fell to his buttocks, the white stingray barb still protruding through his open mouth and nostril although snapped off just below his chin.

He would not be down for long.

Jack scrambled quickly toward Summer, dropped to his knees and gnawed against the salty strands of her binding with his incisors until finally the first hitch began to unfurl. Once the first loop broke free, he unbound the next, about to make a clean escape. He took Summer by the hand, tried to shake her awake, but she was limp, her head slumped backward, her eyes swimmy and despondent, glazed over with a glossy sheen.

He looked back to where Skeg had been, but only a blood trail leading into the scrub suggested a direction of escape.

Jack hauled Summer onto his shoulder like a sack of feed then stumbled in the direction of his beached skiff. As he neared the boat, something sharp and warm sank into the dense muscle of his solar plexus. He glanced down. A pink dart dangled just below his left rack of ribs.

As he staggered forward, Summer's weight became overbearing. His bare feet slogged through the sand. His legs begged to buckle.

A moment later, he collapsed forward, tumbling Summer from his shoulder and thumping her onto the beach with a concussive thud. She moaned then rolled face-side up, her lower lip and teeth red with blood and caked with a cinnamon-coating of sand.

He took her by the forearm, latched his fingers tight then began to crawl on his three available appendages, inching her toward the awaiting skiff. His progress came to an abrupt halt as something with a greater strength tugged her in the opposite direction.

He glanced back. Skeg's enormous mitts now clamped around each of Summer's ankles. The beast began to back away, grunting and snarling like a rabid wart hog. Jack's grip faltered, and his vision began to waver as her body slipped away from him, her feet leaving parallel grooves in the sand as they receded.

Moving solely on instinct, Jack rose up, staggered forward then dove toward the wild man, grabbing a fistful of dreadlocks in each hand as his weight crashed the two of them to the ground with a sickening impact.

An elbow drove into Jack's abdomen, and his wind compressed. A desperate diaphragm spasm followed. As he begged for breath through shallow gasps, Skeg maneuvered behind him and wrapped an arm around his throat, the biceps applying a suffocating pressure to his Adam's apple.

Jack's face lost blood, his arms began to slow, kicking helplessly, his arms flailing back, his hands trying to gouge eyes, rip nostrils, rake flesh as his oxygen tapered toward zero.

Finally, his fingers penetrated the open mouth of the beast and cinched around the skewered barb. As Skeg's teeth clamped down over his digits, Jack yanked on the bone, snapping it into two sections, his fingers escaping the mouth as Skeg howled from the pain.

Skeg rose upward, arms swinging, and struck a blinding elbow into Jack's cheek, connecting with the crisp sound of snapping bone.

Jack toppled backward into the shallows, struggled onto an elbow and watched helplessly as Summer's body was dragged into the underbrush and out of sight. Something primal told him to claw after her, but something practical told him it would be his last move. Go out like a savage beast or hope for another chance. Against all emotion, he turned back toward the skiff, crawled to it then gripped the cool metal bow. The world slowed. Every action took hard, concentrated thought. His mind made decisions but his body could not react. Somehow, he got his chest half-leaning, half-resting against the bow of the boat.

Luckily, his weight at this exaggerated angle proved force enough to get the skiff sliding down the easy grade of the beach and leveling out in the shallows as it began to float.

Everything was instinct now. There were no more decisions.

His hands and legs worked independently of his brain as he nosed over the bow, crashing into the boat, his face slamming into something blunt and his ribs striking hard against the metal bench seat.

That searing white pain ignited him. He pulled himself onto the bench, nearly upright, and yanked at the pull cord.

The engine turned but did not fire. Once again he yanked, but nothing.

A third jerk of the cord barked the engine to life.

He tried to discern a hopeful escape route, but his chin bobbed off his chest, and when he brought his eyes back up, his vision began to fade toward black. Somewhere around him, another dart plinked off the gunwale then rattled onto the metal deck. He throttled the engine then retreated in the general direction of the mangrove break, snapping limbs against his body. The next moments played out as tangles and whipping branches and ever-increasing intervals of black. Then something warm sank into his head. He fumbled his fingers along and found a third dart pierced through his upper right ear so deep it had pinned the flap to his scalp.

He left it there. His fingers were too weak to pull it loose from the cartilage as he worked the tiller, breaking free of the strangling branches then aiming for the deep cut that seemed like it might be the right direction.

For the second time, his chin sank against his chest. The initial dart still protruded from his midsection, its vibrant tail feathers now curiously amusing to his swimmy and delirious demeanor. A brilliant line of blood trickled downward from the entry point and spread across his waistline.

The dampness of the blood felt cool against the boat breeze.

He reared his leaden head once again, his slow involuntary blinking keeping time with his decelerating heartbeat. Somehow he'd forded the shallows and broken into the open waters of Cotton Key Basin. As his lids sank one more time, his hand slipped from the throttle grip then his body keeled forward, cracking his skull against the metal bench and planting his cheek into a puddle of salty muck that sloshed about the bilge.

* * *

Jack awoke face down in the skiff with his legs entangled above and behind him, feet ensnared in the straps of a lifejacket. His body shivered against a chill, despite the insidious heat. His skin felt ablaze with a chemical burn. The sun on the metal decking blistered his skin as he planted a forearm then craned his neck to figure out his location.

The tiller, having been knocked off course, had forced the captainless craft into the tight counterclockwise circumgyration that disoriented Jack. He had no idea how long he'd been in orbit. He squinted against the blinding sunshine, hoping to find some telltale sign on the nearby shore, but the bow of another boat arrived, crunching into his, its angular deadrise riffling over the low freeboard of his skiff as the two hulls ground together.

His outboard silenced.

Then his arm buckled, crashing his face back onto the metal decking and turning the world black again, as hollow and forgotten as the womb.

261

CHAPTER 37

JACK'S HEAD FELT like a railroad spike had impaled his medulla and been left there to rust. His brain seemed drained of fluids, sagging around his spinal stem like a rotten cantaloupe. His vision blurred from eyes encrusted with dried gunk, and his skull billowed with the constant hum of a tuning fork.

His hearing was also awry. He dragged his fingertips over his cheek toward the side of his head, discovering the ragged fibers of a raw gauze pad encapsulating his ear and muffling his sense of sound.

Only then did his eyes began to focus. On the whitewashed wall to his left, a rack of electronic devices beeped at regular intervals. He was tethered to an IV drip bag by a plastic tube that sank through a vein in the interior bend of his left elbow.

Twice in his life he'd been hospitalized.

At birth.

And now.

Uneducated in the protocol of being bedridden, he did what came naturally. Jolting upright, he yanked free the leash binding him to the drip bag. A seething pain coursed through his extremities, manifesting in his joints like a rasp abraded over a severed spinal column. He inhaled, sucking air through his teeth, as his feet flopped over the bed edge toward the floor. His joints seemed to swell with a noxious fluid the consistency of liquid mercury.

He rested for a moment, his chest rising and falling with heavy breaths, before peeling away two heart monitors stuck onto circular patches shaven in the sparse chest hair above each nipple.

As the monitors fell away, a few sporadic beeps pinged on the EKG then an alarm began to sound.

A female nurse into rushed the room. "There's a reason we stuck that IV in your arm."

She was a stern gal, a Harley Davidson sort, who wouldn't be offended by the term *riding bitch*. She flashed Jack a look of disapproval then demanded he get back into the hospital bed.

Jack sighted her name tag: Zoe. "The lovely Ms. Zoe."

"Mrs."

"Of course." Jack moved as stiff-jointed as a zombie across the room. "What can you give me for the pain?" His skull throbbed with each enunciated syllable.

"You need to get back in the bed."

"If you can't prescribe something, maybe my nurse down at the local liquor store will be able to help."

"You're not being a very good patient."

"Don't worry." Jack yanked open the bathroom door. "I'm not a patient anymore." He stepped into the room then clicked the door shut.

The nurse's words now arrived slightly muffled through the metal slab. "You're pretty funny for a guy that almost died a few hours ago."

Died? Jack cranked on the faucet then dragged a few handfuls of water over his cheeks. The water felt acidic across his skin as though he'd contracted a low-grade fever. What exactly had happened? He tried to recount the events leading up to his current hospital stay, but his short-term memory was crippled by the pain radiating through every muscle and nerve in his body. He peeled away the hospital gown then stepped into his shorts, slowly hauling them on. He slipped his arms into his shirt then dragged his fingers over his cheekbone. The area was tender, an under-the-surface stone bruise sensation indicative of a stress fracture. His chest skin appeared sand-burned. Next, he peeled back the gauze covering his wounded ear. The upper flap swelled with a red infection around a darker purple center—an apparent entry wound to something sharp.

Ah, yes. The feathered dart.

He tossed the gauze into a stainless waste bin then stepped back into the room with the nurse.

"Good to see you back among the upright," a familiar voice broke from behind him.

Jack craned around.

Ray stood in the doorway. Out of some forgotten cordiality, he removed his SHERIFF cap then stepped into the room and spoke in a concerned tone. "Jesus, Jack. You're shaking like a detox patient."

"There may be more truth to that than I care to admit."

"You need to listen to the nurse. Stay here and get some rest."

"I'm fresh as a daisy."

Ray rolled his eyes, his head slowly shaking. "When we found you your pulse was just over forty beats per minute. They say if you'd dropped below thirty-five you'd be on the wrong side of the sod right now."

"Found me?"

"You were out cold in your skiff near the Cotton Key Basin. Damn thing was running in circles. She's a little dented up from us ramming into her, but she still floats."

"I'll be sure to send the department a repair bill."

Ray shook his head. "We pulled a dart out of your ear. Made from a sea urchin. It was a good look for you."

Jack mustered a laugh. "Very tribal."

"You should consider a bone through your nose to accessorize."

"Enough, gentlemen."

The nurse took Jack's arm in a firm grip, pulled his shirt off his right shoulder then peeled back a bandage covering several lacerations that glistened with an antibiotic jelly. Jack studied the wounds in the mirror, a faint memory emerging of ripping through mangrove branches in a hasty retreat.

The nurse said, "You should feel damn lucky that dart was hanging out of your head when they found you, or we might not have been able to diagnose what was wrong in time to give you the antidote."

"I feel like a ninety-year-old man."

"That's the remaining toxin in your bloodstream. It'll work itself out of your system."

"The kid told us you took off in the middle of the night. Not a smart move, Jack." The sheriff tugged his hat back over his head. "Do you remember anything that happened out there?"

Out where? Jack combed the cobwebbed corners of his brain, finally lighting upon a vision of Summer, fading, receding, drifting beyond Jack's reach. "Where's Summer?"

"What about her?" Ray asked. "Did you see her? Was she . . . okay?"

A wave of panic rushed in as the events began to return. "I had her, Ray. I had her in my arms." Jack planted both hands on the bedrail and slumped his weight forward. "I was carrying her on my shoulder. We were almost to the boat. Then all of a sudden I couldn't move. My body seized up. It was like I was running in wet cement."

The nurse nodded. "That was probably the neurotoxin."

"I fell, and she spilled onto the ground. Then he was there dragging her away from me, and I wanted to go after her. But I couldn't. I couldn't find the—" The bedrail began to rattle under Jack's grip. "I let her go, Ray. How could I have ever let her go?"

Ray shifted his holster. "We've got some pretty good resources out looking for her right now."

Jack shoved away from the bed. "Jesus, Ray. What's *pretty good?*"

"Four sheriff vessels, a Coastguard Ribby, a single-engine Cessna operated by a sea turtle rescue group out of Big Pine, and three Grumman Widgeon pilots who donated their own time and fuel."

"Anything?"

"We used your GPS to locate Skeg's island. By the time we got there, the place had been vacated. Nothing left out there but a hobo camp."

"What went on out there, Jack?"

"Mookie did a little more talking than he was hoping to do."

265

"Mookie was there?"

Jack nodded.

"What did he cough up?"

"When's that Big Swinging Richard concert?"

"Tomorrow. Why?"

"Turns out Coconut Key is just a front for an import business. Some big shipment's coming in tomorrow."

"Drugs?"

"No idea."

Ray slipped his cap back onto his head. "Drugs might explain the Venezuela connection a little better than a plastic surgery racket."

"It does neighbor Colombia. In fact, that northern border region between the two is some of the most fertile and productive land for growing coca."

"The hailing port on Valenciano's Baglietto was Maracaibo. That ring a bell?"

"It's right there."

"You sure know a lot about that area, Jack."

"I wasn't always a PI." Jack began buttoning his shirt.

Ray shook his head. "The good news is Summer's still alive."

Jack slipped his feet into his flip-flops. "At least she was last night."

"That wasn't last night, Jack. That was two nights ago."

CHAPTER 38

MIDNIGHT HAD CRESTED by the time Skeg first made out the name *Bogart* on the stern of the enormous craft. He kept his paddling steady, a fine cadence of dip, pull, release, repeat as he cut across the water through the designated mooring yard for Coconut Key construction vessels. His rustic canoe rode low with two in the boat, Skeg at the stern and Summer bound at the ankles and wrists on the floor near the bow.

As they neared the mooring yard, Summer, who'd been teetering in semi-consciousness, came to with a certain clarity Skeg had not seen since the abduction. "Welcome back, sunshine."

Summer gave him a sideways glance then wormed her body into a sitting position, the small of her back against the gunwale.

"Here." Skeg tossed his bota into her lap. "It's water. Drink some. You need to rehydrate after that detox."

Summer, with her bound hands, held the bota away from her mouth and shot a stream over her tongue then swallowed hard. Her voice rattled awake. "Can I ask you a question?"

Skeg grunted. "Five nineteen. That's six-foot seven."

"What?"

"My height. Isn't that what you wanted to know?"

She took another swallow of water. "I want to know why you're doing all of this."

Skeg stalled the paddle and let the boat glide. "Truth is I'm tired of people treating this beautiful place like a playground. They jet in, stomp on some coral heads, pump our pristine waters full of fossil fuels then jet on back to Middle America to sell pharmaceuticals to our obese, anxiety-ridden population. As far as I'm concerned, mainland Islamorada is already too infested and too far gone to worry about anymore. But my bay. My backwaters. With the right intervention, they still have a solid chance at survival."

Using the paddle like a rudder, Skeg slipped the canoe alongside the access ladder running up the portside of the dredger.

"What are we doing here?"

"I finally got Mookie to come around. Turns out he's a real chatterbox when he's buried to his chin in the sand at the start of a rising tide."

Summer tossed the bota into the bilge. "Where is he now?"

"Feeding the hungry."

Summer's eyes trembled. "What are you planning to do with me?"

Skeg sighed then leered at the veiled outline of Summer's flesh contoured against the thin fabric. All that sultry temptation. All young flesh and sweet skin. All smooth and supple to turn a sedate old hermit into a lusty horndog.

And those tits. Gracious. "That depends. We've got a few hours to kill before things really get exciting. You up for making an old scallywag's dreams come true?"

* * *

Jack and Ray leaned on opposing gunwales of the Moppie as it bumped back and forth against its stern lines, the portside of the bow occasionally kissing against a piling. Ray was talking, but Jack wasn't listening. His mind was transfixed on the rhythmic *thonking* of riggings against aluminum masts and an image of Summer radiating in his mind. Finally, he broke the trance. "Boats, Ray. I think it's got to be boats."

"Jesus, Cubera. Are you even listening to me?"

Jack shook away the confusion. "What?"

"That's exactly what I've been trying to tell you. It's got to be boats. How else would you smuggle drugs into Florida?"

Jack kicked open his cooler lid, thought the better of it and flipped it shut. "Hang on a second." He ducked into the cabin then returned and unfurled his Upper Keys nautical chart across the lobsterpot. As he studied the markings, Ray moved in and hovered over his shoulder sucking on the toothpick.

"What are we looking for, Jack?"

Jack pulled a piece of paper from his pocket and handed it to Ray.

"Read me those numbers."

"What is this?"

"The numbers I pulled from the Disenchanted Clam."

Ray recited the longitudinal and latitudinal coordinates as Jack located the digits on the map then traced his fingers until they intersected.

"Right here." Jack tapped a finger on a dark blue area on the map.

"Looks like the middle of nowhere."

"It is the middle of nowhere."

"What am I missing here?"

"Let me ask you something, Ray. Why would anyone waste money adding buoyancy to a Hinckley?"

Ray shrugged.

"Exactly. It's completely absurd. That's a pure showpiece boat right off the production line. You'd be foolish to change it in any way. Unless . . . what if the Hinckley's going to be used as the mule boat? What if the hull reinforcement was installed to help haul a big shipment? To keep her from running low in the water and drawing undue attention? That would also explain why Blanch gutted the cabin and never had it redone."

"More room for cargo."

Jack nodded. "And a high-dollar boat like that, nobody would suspect a thing." Jack stroked his mustache. "That's one possibility."

"And the other?"

"Gus Callahan owns a boat too. Either way, I think some international drug runner gets the stuff close then passes it off to the Stateside mule."

"What about that Chopper guy and his plane?" Ray rolled the toothpick between his lips. "Maybe he's bringing the stuff in up from South America then passing it off a couple miles out at sea."

Jack tapped the spot on the chart. "A GPS waypoint in the middle of nowhere sure would be the perfect rendezvous spot for this sort of deal to go down whether it's coming up by boat or plane."

"So would the Honey Hole."

Jack nodded. "Mookie's plan could be to make the exchange off-shore then bring the stuff into the construction zone. With all the traffic in and out of that place, he could pass it off to dozens of distribution boats without anyone ever knowing."

Ray nodded. "That would certainly explain the heightened security they've got working out there."

"The only problem with Mookie's plan is it's not going to happen."

"It's not?"

"Not if that Callahan clan has anything to do with it. They've got something cooking to pull a fast one on the Jersey crew. My guess is they're going to hijack the shipment."

Jack raked his fingers through his mustache. "We need to tail *Bogart* and the Hinckley tomorrow morning and see where they wind up."

Ray slid the toothpick from his lips. "We'll have to split up."

"I know."

"Which one do you want to follow?"

"Blanch knows my face. You head out to the Hinckley, and I'll keep an eye on *Bogart*."

"We need to watch for drop planes too."

Jack nodded. "One thing, Ray. Be careful out there at the Hinckley."

"You think the woman is dangerous?"

"For you and your dry spell."

"What are you talking about?"

"Just go into it with your guard up. Don't let your judgment get skewed by her peculiar tactics."

"Stop beating around the bush here, Jack. What are you saying?"

"I'm saying the woman shakes hands with her vagina so you may want to watch how you return the gesture."

CHAPTER 39

GUS AWOKE BEFORE dawn. Ossie made sure of it. He'd been up, prodding his old man off the couch at four a.m. and urging him to get moving. Gus, who'd dozed off sans skivvies, stepped into a pair of yellowing briefs, slipped on some cut-off denims then slid on a pearl-snap cowboy shirt.

"You got the coordinates?"

"Yup." Gus tapped his temple. "Right here."

"Okay then."

"Money says this broad is late."

"Certainly not for this."

"How much you want to wager?"

"Get going, pops. Don't you be late. You don't want to get tied up in that concert traffic."

Gus drove down to the docks, ferried out to his mooring near the construction site then fired up *Bogart*. By first light he steamed through the pass and angled toward the Honey Hole at thirteen knots. As he breached the marginal cut on the southwest side of the Alligator Reef Lighthouse, he paid special attention to his depth and heading. A beached boat or bent propeller today was unacceptable. He patted the dashboard and prayed all the pumps would run true. There'd be only one chance to pull this off cleanly. Any hiccups at all could have far-reaching repercussions involving things like cell mates, sodomy and so forth. This did not jive with his vision of retirement.

271

Once beyond the reef line, the full orb of the sun broke the horizon. It glowed warm and soothing on his skin. Four more miles of open ocean to go.

Twenty minutes later, Gus brought *Bogart* over the Honey Hole then sank his giant anchor into the ocean floor and waited until the hook took hold. As the aft end swung down current, he dialed up the brightness on his dredging monitor then propped his feet on the dashboard and watched and waited.

A few moments passed with Gus idle, nearly drifting into a morning nap, before an indistinguishable bumping sound resonated through the starboard side of his hull. He poked his head out the window to see if he'd hit someone or something, but all remained clear. When he looked back, there was a quick series of footfalls up the staircase then the inspector, Jack Crevalle, sauntered into the wheelhouse swinging his NOAA badge.

"Well, hello there inspector. I certainly wasn't expecting you today."

"I suppose that means you didn't pack me any cold beer again either."

* * *

Ray approached the Hinckley from the west. Just as suspected, it was anchored at the remote GPS coordinates discovered at the Disenchanted Clam.

A hundred yards out, he bled off the throttles then edged the Mako closer until the name *Exit Strategy* became legible. Music, perhaps *Slippery When Wet*, piped over the wind. Blanch lounged astern in a metallic silver bikini, her skin a shade of mocha difficult to reconcile with a natural suntan.

At twenty feet out, he dropped the throttles to an idle and held position by intermittently bumping the engines in and out of gear.

Blanch pushed up from her lounging position then saluted a hand over her eyes to buffer the ocean glare. "Well, hello there, officer. Something I can do for you on this beautiful morning?"

Ray rafted up. "Interesting place to drop anchor."

272

"Just a lonely gal working on her tan."

"Well then." Ray slipped his sunglasses over his eyes and studied the woman. Her breasts rode high in the tightly bound bikini, so high as to reveal the under-cup incisions winking pink in the morning light. He narrowed his sights on them. Was there some connection between the development and those implants after all? "Mind if I come aboard for a routine inspection?"

"Is that a metaphor?"

Ray grinned then planted his hands on the Hinckley gunwale and swung his legs over as though dismounting a pommel horse. He boomed onto the Hinckley, his black boot heels leaving twin scuff marks on the decking where he landed. "My bad."

After a quick visual sweep and finding nothing suspect, he stepped toward the cabin door and thumbed the latch.

Blanch swung her legs over the edge of her lounger and sat upright. "It's locked."

"So unlock it."

Blanch smiled, a kittenish sort of thing, then reached back and unbound her bikini top. As the fabric and string fell away, her boobs jiggled around for a moment before coming to rest. Ray tried to forget his lengthy drought. Tried to remain professional. Tried to remain focused. On her eyes. "Where's the key?"

"I must have misplaced it."

"During the retrofit?"

Blanch stood and slunk over to Ray, her boobs grazing his shoulder as she leaned in. "Come now, officer. Let me mix you up a drink."

Ray took each of her biceps in a firm grip and forced her back a half-step. "You can either go back to your lounger or I can handcuff you to the wheel."

"Oh, my. Handcuffs."

Ray grabbed her left arm and spun her a half-turn, forcing her wrist into the small of her back.

"Get your hands off me, you cocksucker. You've got no right to detain me."

"The way you throw those tits around. Let's call it lewd and lascivious battery." Ray clicked one cuff over her left wrist, snapped the other cuff around the wheel then tossed her a towel.

He glanced back at the door. "Either come up with a key, or I'm going to kick it in."

"Are you threatening me, officer?"

Ray brought a leg up then thrust his boot out, cracking the heel directly against the metalwork latch. The helm shuttered, but the door stayed put. A second kick sent the door swinging so hard and fast it nearly bounced back into its latched position.

"You can't just break in there."

Ray withdrew the flashlight from his utility belt. "Like I said. Routine inspection."

"I'm calling the cops."

"Hail the Coastguard while you're at it. They tend to get a little pissy if they miss out on a good drug bust."

Ray clicked on his flashlight, handled his Glock then ducked down the steps into the dark space. He passed the beam along the walls. As Jack had suggested, the fiberglass patchwork was clearly visible in a raw and unfinished state. As he swept the beam toward the fore of the cabin, something shifted in the darkness. He adjusted his gun angle and redirected the beam, discovering a pile of suitcases and a duffel bag. And there, half-hidden amid the luggage, crouched Oscar Callahan, dressed in denim shorts and a Big Swinging Richard T-shirt ringed at the armpits, his eyes beady and yellow in the beam of light.

"Oscar Callahan."

Ossie shifted the luggage aside then pushed up from his crouch, his eyes darting between the exit and Ray. He held the duffel bag in one hand, his second hand hidden behind it. "Sheriff."

Ray trained his weapon at Ossie's chest. "Your mommy make you sit in the corner?"

"I was getting sunburned on deck so I ducked inside to cool off."

"It's got to be a hundred degrees in here."

"But it's shady."

"It's shady all right." Ray eyed the luggage. "You guys taking a trip somewhere?"

"Plan was to shoot over to the Bahamas for a long weekend."

"Bahamas? I guess they pay you FWC guys better than us lowly stiffs at the Sheriff's Office." Ray leaned in. The name Gus Callahan was inked on the ID badge of the duffel bag in Ossie's grip. "I see the old man's joining you."

"Soon as he gets done working."

"Nice to see family coming together like this."

Keeping the gun sighted on Ossie, Ray plucked a nautical chart from an outside pocket of the duffel bag and flipped it open. A course was charted up the Intracoastal nearly the entire Eastern Seaboard, stopping at a discreet port of call just off the New England coast. "Block Island?"

"That was our plan B. In case the Stream was too big to cross."

"Lovely up that way this time of year."

"Nice break from this awful heat."

"Sweating like that, you might need a doctor more than a vacation." Ray put a boot tip into one of the bags. "Lot of luggage for a long weekend."

"Blanch isn't exactly a light traveler."

"I suspect this whole boat was planning on departing the Florida waterways a little on the heavy side."

"You're making a mistake, Ray." The hand that Ossie had been hiding behind the duffel bag began to drift upward with a pistol in its grip.

"Put that thing down before I plug one into your shoulder."

Ossie brought the duffel bag up and around in a wheelhouse motion, whipping it so close to Ray's face it knocked the toothpick sideways in his lips. As it fanned by, Ossie released his grip, the bag booming into the hull, then he scampered by Ray toward the exit. As he scrambled up the steps, Ray got a fistful of waistband and yanked him down, his tailbone making a cracking sound like a broken bat as it connected with the hard fiberglass deck. The gun went skidding off in the darkness.

Ossie tried to clamor back onto his feet, but Ray slammed the Glock butt into his shoulder and settled him back down. "Don't push me, Ossie.

I'm right on the cusp of calling the Salucci family and leaving you two out here to fend for yourselves."

* * *

Jack leaned against the *Bogart* helm, eyeing the horizon for suspect air and boat traffic, when something struck him as oddly different. The boat was quiet. No internal rumblings or vibrations. The sucking pumps did not appear to be cranked up and running at all. A quick check of the onboard computer monitor revealed a desolate ocean bottom with no suction hopper in action.

Jack had assumed that if Gus was involved in a drug play, he'd at least have the pumps going and the suction boom out and operating to make everything look on the up-and-up.

He glanced over as Gus slipped a pill into his mouth and struggled to swallow it down.

"So Gus. You not sucking sand today?"

Gus's eyes sprang open. "What's that?"

"Not running the pumps today?"

"Not just yet. The whole system got a bit overheated on the run out, so I'm giving the old gal a chance to cool down."

Jack dragged his finger along a dark seam visible across the screen. "That's the good sand, right? The angular stuff?"

Gus nodded then reached up and clicked off the screen. "No point burning up electricity."

"Right."

"If she doesn't cool off in another few minutes, I'm just going to weigh anchor and take her into the shop. Chalk this up as a maintenance day."

"You certainly burned a lot of fuel getting out here just to turn around and head back." Jack glanced at the temperature gauges. Everything appeared to be running normal. "Be a wasted trip for me and you both if you have to take her in."

"Sorry, inspector. Good thing for you, it's just the taxpayers' dollars. Me, I've got to foot the bill for my own stupidity." He rattled out a plastic laugh then hooked a finger into his shirt collar and began tugging it away from his neck.

Jack glanced out the window and studied the skies, spotting only the occasional commercial airliner bombing over to Jamaica or the Caymans or the Yucatan Peninsula. There was no sign of any floatplanes or smaller personal watercraft fit for muling weighty loads.

"Hate to say it, inspector, but I should probably haul up and haul ass."

"I may not know dredge boats, Gus, but I know engines. Give her a few minutes and see if she doesn't come around."

Gus slumped against the captain chair. "I really think I should get going."

"Like I said, give it another minute."

After thirty more minutes of searching the skies and thwarting Gus's attempts to head back to shore, Jack began to doubt his instincts. Maybe his intuition was off. Jack gave Gus another once-over. The armpits of the man's snap-button shirt showed dark rings, and his forehead now gleamed with a glossy perspiration.

"You have radar on this thing?" Jack asked.

Gus gulped and nodded. "Like I keep saying. I should probably get this ole gal over to the shop so I don't have any more downtime." He flashed a crooked smile. "Can't pay the bills with downtime."

"Won't take a second."

"Not sure the radar's even working right."

Jack reached across Gus and clicked on the device. The sweep began to circulate around the screen marking little more than a small patch of rain about a mile and a half out. As he watched, a second mark appeared on the outer perimeter of the image. Could it be his floatplane? Jack studied it for a few moments then determined it wasn't moving fast enough for an aircraft. Maybe they were bringing the stuff in by boat after all.

Gus dragged his sleeve over his forehead. "So, inspector. What are you looking for now?"

"Just curious if I'm going to get hit by any rain or foul weather on the trek back to the mainland. I'm in the little boat today. You know how it is when a squall kicks up in these parts."

Gus eyed the radar. "Looks to me like you've got nothing but clear sailing. Probably best you get going before the afternoon heat hits and starts turning things south."

Jack eyed the radar as the onscreen spot closed toward their position. With a shaky arm, Gus reached over and clicked it off. "Seriously, I got to go. Hate to do this to you, but—"

"Just one more second, Gus."

Jack snagged a pair of binoculars off the helm then slid open the side window and steadied the things against his eyes. As he dialed in the resolution, a blue-hulled sportfisher with a tuna tower came into focus. "Damnit." He recognized the vessel as a local charter boat, a reputable outfit out of Key Largo with no possible ties to the case.

He dropped the binoculars from his eyes and gave a last visual sweep of the horizon for curious boats, planes or anything out of the ordinary. But nothing. He was about to duck back inside and hail Ray on the VHF when the water about twenty yards off the starboard side began to swirl and rip in a way that suggested something large and ominous moved just below the surface.

As he watched on, the curious currents and boils closed in on the dredge boat's position, then, five yards out, the forward progress halted and an irregular pattern of bubbles began popping at the surface.

"Holy shit." Jack ducked back inside to find Gus, wide-eyed and frozen, his forehead beginning to rain down large rivulets into the collar of his shirt.

Jack shoved him aside and clicked on the computer monitor bringing the underwater camera back to life. As he did the vague outline of a large torpedo-shaped object began to take shape. He dialed the brightness down on the monitor, and a submarine, no less than a hundred feet in length, came into full view.

Jack turned to Gus, now digging around his pocket for another pill. "You expecting someone?"

Gus chomped down on a blue tablet and gulped, seemingly unable to form enough spit to swallow the medicine. "I don't know what that is."

"Well, I may have a pretty good idea."

The two turned back to the monitor as the submarine pivoted a quarter turn then began to discharge bubbles from an indeterminate spot on the underbelly of its hull. A moment later, the bubbles dissipated and, in the clear waters below the vessel, small round packages began to appear, trickling out and settling to the ocean floor like eggs from a spawning salmon.

Jack leaned into the screen and studied the discharging payload. He considered the samples he'd found in the bait cage and the corresponding data sheet in Ossie's boathouse. Elastomeric and waterproof. Not prone to rupturing or leakage. An ability to endure impact, fluctuating atmospheric pressures and ocean temperatures. Of course. This is what Ray had seen a sample of on the Viking. A specially reinforced breast-implant shell designed specifically to handle high-performance situations, like modern-day drug trafficking in the Keys. It was the perfect packaging.

Jack turned and eyed the captain, who seemed to be drifting off to a lonely place. "Anything you want to tell me, Gus?"

"I don't know nothing about nothing."

"Fire up the suction hopper and suck a few of those things up."

Gus said nothing.

"You realize I'm with NOAA. That makes this Federal."

Gus didn't move so Jack wrenched his arm behind his back and reclaimed the captain's full attention. "Time to get to work."

Gus reluctantly flicked a switch and cranked the pumps. Toggling a joystick, he maneuvered his underwater camera, highlighting the thousands of bricks littered about the ocean floor. He zoomed in and, on-screen, the space-aged silicone packages appeared like little more than an opaque jellyfish the size and shape of healthy Double-Ds.

Gus pushed the joystick forward and to the left then guided the nose of the suction device toward a few samples in the cluster of packages that continued to spill from the submarine. As the first package disappeared into the tube, Gus wormed the suction hose along the ocean bottom with masterful precision. One more brick. Then the next. Then another again. Like a video game, one-by-one, the implants disappeared into the hopper until he'd whittled the pile down to a few strays that had rolled off into the perimeters.

"Nice work, captain."

Gus shrugged then swept the camera along the ocean floor one last time looking for stragglers. As the camera panned, Jack studied the screen until an odd reflection in the glare of the computer monitor caused his heart to skip.

He took a deep breath then rotated slowly around toward the thing responsible for that reflection: Skeg—all six-feet seven-inches of the towering beast. In his right hand, the lost Ruger casually pointed at Jack's vulnerable midsection. From Skeg's other hand, a lacy brassiere dangled by the tip of his index finger.

"Summer lovin', Jack. Happens so fast."

"What did you do to her?"

Skeg half-laughed as Gus fumbled a couple pills from his pocket onto the helm.

"Hold on just a minute, captain." Skeg waggled the gun Gus's direction. "How about the reader's digest version on how to operate this dredger before you get completely blitzed?"

* * *

Around noontime on event day, Commissioner Jimenez and Swinging Richard climbed into Richard's private helicopter then lifted off and headed out toward Coconut Key. The pilot flew low to the deck, following the line of road traffic and explaining the news over the headsets while Viktor kept his nose pressed to the window.

Turns out, news of the free Big Swinging Richard concert had swept across Florida via social media and transformed the event into a full-blown Charlie Foxtrot. By sunup that morning, the Overseas Highway was already logjammed with beachniks who'd been drinking and driving all night to make the inaugural show. With traffic at a standstill, many partygoers had abandoned their vehicles to complete their migrations on foot, pausing only occasionally to whiz into the shoulder sawgrass and stretch their road-weary legs. Average civilians most of the time, the blend of sea and drink devolved them all into bumbling *woo* people, their incessant whooping and hooting rising like Tourette's outbursts each time the pilot swooped down and buzzed the crowd.

"Woooo!"

In honor of the event, the commissioner wore a Hawaiian shirt, a foam headpiece shaped like a square grouper and pupils engorged the size of buffalo nickels from a healthy cut of cocaine from Richard's personal stash. As the helicopter settled onto a makeshift landing pad at the Coconut Key site, Viktor's thoughts drifted elsewhere. What was going on with the delivery? Was everything unfolding as planned? Why had he not heard back from Mookie? He dragged a handkerchief over his sweaty cheeks. The last thing he wanted was to disappoint Uncle Val. No telling where that might lead.

"You feeling all right, commissioner?"

"Just a little jumpy is all."

The two disembarked from the helicopter then were escorted into a backstage area with a view of the crowd.

"Don't you get anxious before a gig like this?"

"Honestly, they're just paydays." Richard unscrewed a vial of cocaine and tapped a bit onto the skin between his thumb and forefinger.

"I don't know. This is really something special going on out here today. I've never seen so many Dickheads in all my life."

Richard snorted the bump. "You certainly dressed the part."

"I plan on mixing it up with the constituents once this master of ceremonies thing is done."

"You're really just an announcer."

"Master of ceremonies has such a nicer ring to it."

"Either way, try not to do anymore of that blow before you get onstage. You're already looking pretty geeked-up. You at least need to maintain a modicum of composure."

"Don't you worry about me."

Soon over five hundred pontoon boats, dual consoles and personal watercrafts had swarmed the perimeter of the construction site, nosing up to the silt fence and tying off to its surface flotation. By one in the afternoon, a daisy chain of crafts stretched all the way from shore to the silt fence providing everyday landlubbers access to the watery mayhem. In addition, an ambitious outfit off Duval Street had trucked in a fleet of thirty-six Sea-Doos, each now shuttling two people at a time to the site for ten bucks a head as fast as they could make the roundtrip. Meanwhile, pontoon boats hawking twelve-dollar tallboys and eight-dollar cups of smoked mullet dip idled around the crowd, thousands of which now bobbed in the surf on cheap inflatable rafts in a rainbow of colors.

Viktor stepped toward a secluded corner of the wing and dialed Mookie for the third time in the past two hours. It rang six times then dumped into voicemail. He left a message. "Enough with the silent treatment, Salucci. Call me as soon as you get this. I need to know if the package has been safely delivered."

He snapped the phone shut then moved into the mainstage wing, eyeing around the curtain and into the crowd as though he might find the Jersey crew amid the madness. A stagehand in a headset approached him at a fast clip. "You about ready, commissioner?"

Viktor checked his cellphone again to no avail, then nodded at the stagehand. "How long?"

"Richard's on in five. You come in on cue."

Fifteen minutes later, Big Swinging Richard sauntered onto the stage, cleared his throat into the microphone then opened with a pitchy rendition of *One Drunk Night on Coconut Key*.

The intoxicated crowd went ballistic, losing their inhibitions and bathing suits with the deft prowess of Stiffy's dancers. In what had become a tradition, the women then lobbed their bikini tops toward stage at the lead singer, one glittery affair catching on the neck of his Takamine six string and a second star-spangled piece hooking around his ear. As Jimenez awaited his cue, he rang Mookie once again with the same result. Then he slipped the phone back into his pocket and considered his options. Maybe things had not gone down as planned. Maybe it was best to suspend further communication at this point.

Six songs into the first set, Richard reduced the strumming tempo to a simple baseline then raised a single hand to the sky and brought the crowd to a hush.

A small cry rang out from a distant Dickhead. "*Wooo!*"

"How are all you doing out there today?" The crowd erupted as Richard thrummed a gritty G-chord. "I am proud to bring to you our master of ceremonies, the man who paved the way to make this island known as Coconut Key a possibility, Monroe County's own Commissioner Viktor Jimenez."

Under a diminishing din of applause, the commissioner jogged onto stage, his Hawaiian shirt unbuttoned and flapping in the crosswind, his square grouper hat bouncing about his head. He smiled, nodded at Richard then pressed his newly waxed mustache to the microphone. "Ladies and Gentlemen. The moment you've all been waiting for has finally arrived. Let's get ready to start your engines."

As a symphony of woos rang out, Jimenez began to gyrate his hips and grind on the microphone stand as Richard strummed another gritty G-chord bringing a sea of gas-powered blenders grumbling to life. The drummer, who'd been snapping his hihat and bumping his bass, began popping his snare as the band climbed into their most notorious number one single, *Splendor in a Blender*.

Jimenez, still poised at the microphone, waved his arms at the crowd to the left of the stage and an eruption of gas-powered drink makers barked into full-frappé mode. As his arms swayed toward the right side, the left blenders died down giving way to a second eruption of a two-stroke combustion from the other side. Then back to the left, then to the right, and back again, the cultish crowd oscillating like a floor fan.

Finally, Jimenez shoved both arms directly toward the heavens, spirit fingers wiggling, and brought all the gas-powered mixers to a screaming howl at once. And there it remained, in that high-octave hysteria, as more boats poured in and the crowd continued to swell.

CHAPTER 40

WHILE RAY WAS busy relaying location information to the Coastguard, Oscar Callahan somehow managed to gnaw through his zip-tie binding and escape over the edge of the Hinckley. All Ray saw when he looked back was a wild flailing of arms and ankles, the sort of hysterical improvised freestyle stroke one uses when attempting to flee an aggressive shark.

Ray knew that feeling first hand. No way he was going in after Ossie. Not out here offshore where the hammerheads and tiger sharks grew to the size of school buses.

He slipped his Glock from its holster and trained the weapon on the fleeing target. Then he glanced over and caught Blanch eyeing him with the look of a woman into blackmail.

"Shoot him," she said. "I promise not to tell a soul."

Ray let the barrel fall away from the target. "If I wasn't so close to retirement, I might just roll the dice." He glanced back to the water at Ossie and planted his arms akimbo. How in the hell was he going to wrangle that little rat back in the boat without getting wet?

* * *

Jack's eyes drifted from the snub-nosed Ruger to Skeg's face. The hood of Skeg's left nostril was scabbed over and swollen with infection. The underside of his chin fared better. Only a pencil-sized ring of redness shown through a wino-length salt-and-pepper scruff. Jack guessed the

284

interior mouth wounds were far worse, the bacteria buildup in the oral cavity on par with a Florida Turnpike urinal.

"Looks like somebody whipped you pretty good."

"Do I really look like I'm up for a chitchat?" Skeg's words arrived thick and slightly slurred, most likely his tongue swollen at the core from having been skewered by the barb.

Skeg escorted Jack and Gus down the staircase. As Jack shouldered through the heavy metal door, the sun broke around a cloud, bringing to life all the shiny fittings and stainless screw heads generally hidden amid the otherwise utilitarian gunmetal and rust of the commercial vessel.

Out on the deck, Jack paused, glanced back, the August heat rising off the steel in a wavering mirage. He guessed Skeg had stowed away on *Bogart* early in the morning before it had left the mooring yard. His plan had probably been to uncover the remaining players in the drug deal and hand-deliver them the same fate as the Jersey crew.

Jack showing up had thrown a wrench in the works.

Jack also suspected that a man so recently displaced from his homestead would've had very little time locating a safehouse for precious possessions, particularly those possessions who, when conscious, bit and fought and screamed for help. Jack glanced around. Most boats over a hundred feet have a secure room. A special place with padded walls, thick doors and heavy locks, in case a crewman decides to test the captain's authority. In a pinch, that room usually doubles as a morgue.

Jack shuffled a step. "Where's Summer?"

"Being held for collateral." Skeg's eyes reflexively flashed toward a small porthole window amidships, and Jack wondered if he'd just tipped his hand.

"Try and get cute, and she'll pay for your mistakes." Skeg waggled the gun. "Now both of you. To the dinghy."

Jack glanced the direction insinuated by the gun barrel then started toward a buttermilk-colored dory, oversized, built to handle about ten or twelve passengers and a four-foot chop. The watercraft suspended just above the rail by twin davits and thick nylon lines, the bow and stern fastened with guywires and turnbuckles to the railing at opposing eyelets to prevent the thing from swinging while *Bogart* was underway.

As they neared, Skeg told Jack to sit still then eyed Gus. "Captain. Reach into the dinghy and grab the Danforth. And make sure to get the anchor chain and line too."

"What's going on?" Gus asked.

"Jack's going for a swim."

Jack's eyes flashed wide.

"Come on now, city slicker. What would you expect from an old scallywag like me?"

Gus reached a hand into the dory, clanked and jangled things around a bit then hauled out the galvanized device and trailing terminal gear. Due to the weight on his single hand, he swung it down by his side with a quick falling motion then set one hand on each side of the cylindrical stock and curled it chest high for Skeg's approval.

"Great. Now move toward the tail. Both of you."

Gus fumbled with the coil of anchor line and chain, working the collection of loops over his arm and down into the bend of his elbow before settling into a slow, wobbly walk. Jack followed behind with the somber shuffle of a man being led to the gallows, each movement of the foot raspier than the one before, each blink of an eye like some clock ticking toward finality. There were a few possibilities. Maybe Skeg would use the anchor to sink him—tie him to the tag end of the line then heave the anchor overboard and let the force rip his ankles or wrists out of their sockets before yanking him over the rail. Or maybe Skeg would just put a slug into that soft intersection of spinal column and brain stem—one of those quick, cold shot that leaves no room for guesswork—then lash the anchor to the body and roll it over the side.

"This thing is done, Skeg. We busted up the deal. Let's get the sheriff out here to handle things in a proper manner."

"The sheriff works for the county, Jack. Monroe County. Hell, the county commissioner's one of the main reasons we're in this mess to begin with."

"They've got no choice but to handle it at this point. This thing is way too big to cover up."

"Aren't you a little too old to be so goddamn gullible?"

When they reached the stern, Jack spun a half-turn then leaned backward against the railing, checking its height. The top metal bar, round and alligatored with several layers of marine paint, fell just across the small of his back, about six inches above the fulcrum of his body weight.

Skeg popped the gun butt into Gus's shoulder and said to tie Jack up. "Wrists first then ankles. And no funny business. Leave one of the knots loose, and you'll be the next one down there feeding the fishes."

Gus eyed Jack, his pupils diffused and addled, no doubt, from the medley of terror and pharmaceuticals. He seemed apologetic as he eased toward Jack. Then, for a split second, Gus stalled, the Danforth held tight by the stock, chest high, as though wondering where to set it down to free his hands for the knot work.

"Let me help you with that." Jack reached out and death-gripped a single anchor fluke in each hand, as though to unburden the weight from Gus. As he did, Gus released his grip, and, in a single fluent motion, Jack brought the weighty piece to his chest then hitched onto his tiptoes, bringing the fulcrum of his weight above the railing, and pitched his body backward, feet over head, over the side of the boat.

The momentum of Jack's legs carried him through a full flip, the broadside of the massive boat coming into focus as he freefell. As his body continued to rotate, his vision caught the trailing anchor line spooling out in small loops that straightened as he fell away.

He sucked a deep breath and clutched the anchor tight to his chest as his body knifed into the water, elbows tight, toes pointed. He rode the weight of the anchor into the cool bluewater, away from crackling gunshot rounds now stippling the surface, the bullets changing angles like diving birds on a bait ball before fizzling out.

Finally, Jack released the anchor and kicked for safety under the massive hull. With his oxygen diminishing, he came up against the underside of the boat just forward the massive propeller then propelled himself on the barnacles and chines, hugging the upward bend of the hull until he popped up through the surface, inhaled then went back down.

Now, with oxygen to work with, eyes salt-stung, he oriented himself, maneuvering under the boat along the portside, coming up quick where he'd left his skiff. With a fast burst, he flopped onto the skiff gunwale, balancing on his waistline. He worked quickly, buckling a lifejacket around his Hawaiian sling then spearing a lobsterpot marker over the barbed shaft. Next, he draped an old boat shirt around the lifejacket and propped the thing into a reasonable likeness of human figure working the tiller on the craft.

Then he untied the skiff from the dredger, dialed in the choke and wedged a fish hook into the throttle grip, pinning it open at full speed. Two yanks on the cord later, the engine blew a cloud of oil smoke as Jack fell backward, shoving the thing and sending it careening in the direction of the shoreline.

As the skiff sped away, a few more gunshots cracked off from the main deck in its general direction. Perfect. Skeg had taken the bait. Nobody would suspect the prey to circle back for the predator, particularly when the prey was unarmed. Jack had abandoned Summer once. He wasn't doing it again.

He sank low and swam in a quiet sidestroke, tucked tight to the hull, eyes level with the waterline. As he reached the access ladder near the stern, the water around began to swirl and the hollow hull began to vibrate with engine noise.

Jack kicked his feet, buoying his body as far above the waterline as he could, his fingers just able to hook around the bottom rung on the ladder as *Bogart* started to move.

The rung was rusty. Metal bits flaked under his grip.

Using only his arms, he pulled his body to the second rung then the third. His legs kicked wildly at the air, his body twisting and slapping against the iron hull.

He went up for the fourth rung, got a hand around it then the other then lost the first. His body spun out, bounced backward against the hull, his biceps burning as the boat began to gather speed. A subtle sway to starboard threw him back into a forward orientation, a foot kicking at the wind, trying to grip the side, finally finding purchase against the lowest ladder rung. He set his weight on the step, secured his other grip then began scaling up the vessel, hand-over-hand.

CHAPTER 41

RAY SCRAMBLED ONTO the Mako, cranked the engines then whipped it around in a semicircle, pattering over the chop, gliding the boat directly in Ossie's escape path. As he stalled the vessel, Ossie reared his head up from the water like a startled nutria then dropped his legs into a doggy paddle and surveyed the distant shoreline.

"Give it up, Ossie." Ray moved to the rail and rapped the sharp tip of his gaff against the gunwale. "Backup should be here any minute to give you a dry ride back to shore."

Ossie took a deep breath, nosed over then disappeared underwater, resurfacing fifteen seconds later in a full forward stroke on the opposite side of the Mako. Ray tied a dock line to the gaff handle then idled over and threaded the hook through the waistband of Ossie's denim cutoffs.

With a quick hitch of the line to an aft cleat, he spun the boat around and plowed toward the Hinckley, his catch rolling and flailing, hacking and half-drowning in the wake like a poorly skirted ballyhoo bait.

By the time he rafted up to the Hinckley, all but the waistband of Ossie's denim shorts had shorn away. Ray hauled Ossie onto the Picnic Boat then released the tension on the gaff, and the band of denim dropped to the deck like an unattended hula hoop. Ossie, who'd apparently opted to go san-skivvies for the day, balanced half-naked, Porky Pigging in his Big Swinging Richard T-shirt that, to Ray's dismay, not only stopped short of his waistline but also proved to be an egregious case of false advertising.

Oddly, the impropriety of a mother and son in the same state of nudity appeared lost on the two accomplices as Ray linked them together with the cuffs and forced them to the floor.

Ray narrowed his eyes at Blanch. "Why'd you hire Jack to find Ross when you knew he was already dead?"

She shrugged. "If I tell you, what's that going to get me?"

"Depends on if you're the one who killed him or not."

"I would never have killed that fat bastard. I almost loved him. But I knew nobody would suspect me being responsible for his disappearance if I was paying someone to track him down."

Ray started to reply but the two VHF radios in the immediate vicinity began to squawk and squelch with an excited voice.

"*Mayday. Mayday. Mayday. Vessel Bogart out of control. Vessel Bogart out of control.*"

Ray jumped off the Hinckley and lunged for the VHF radio mounted on his helm. "*Bogart. Bogart.* This is Sheriff Livingston. Come back."

A long quiet silence elapsed then a different voice, this one throaty and gruff, broke over the channel. "Afternoon there, Sheriff. Sorry. Just a false alarm. Nothing to worry about here. Nothing at all."

* * *

Jack rapped his knuckles on the hurricane-proof porthole, and Summer's head snapped up, face drawn and gaunt for a moment then fleshing out and coming to life as she registered who peered back. She popped up from her stoop and moved to the window, her short stature offering the visual of only her upper lip, nose and eyes from Jack's vantage.

"Are you okay?"

Her voice arrived muffled and disconcerting as Jack could not see the lower lip moving as words poured out. Jack told her to calm down and stand back. He hunted around for a moment then unstrapped a fire extinguisher from a nearby wall and began crashing the butt end against the door knob, the *tonking* like a metal bridge pile being driven into bedrock.

But nothing gave. The entire entryway had been engineered to thwart such aggressions. The task required something more heavy duty.

Jack started across the open deck, hunting for a fire axe, a crowbar, a more substantial safe-cracking tool, but the giant vessel pitched wildly to the portside then rolled back to starboard. Keeping his stance wide and low, he hustled toward the rail as the dredger slalomed through the last channel markers of Snake Creek, gathered speed then redirected its course, the bow aimed directly at the mayhem unfolding out at Coconut Key.

CHAPTER 42

ONLY THE SOUNDING foghorn of an approaching dredger stifled the concert crowd for a brief but memorable moment. To Richard, the massive bow of the ship appeared like a steel tidal wave rolling toward the floating entourage of fans as those drifting on rafts paddled desperately for safety. As the vessel steamed toward the island without regard for anyone or anything in its path, boats blocking the break in the silt fence zoomed away seconds before being crunched to bits by the hull.

At the helm, Richard noticed a curious man sporting a head full of silver dreadlocks and sneer from ear-to-ear.

By the look of things, he was a rabid Swinging Richard's fan, just like the rest of the mob. He gave the captain an overzealous wave, assuming the boat was something staged by Mookie and the gang for theatrical effect.

When the boat finally breached the silt fence, it appeared to throttle up and pivot slightly, bulling directly toward center stage. As the water grew shallower, the bow plowed into the newly formed shoreline cascading a wave of sludge out either side. The massive propellers roiled the water at the stern as the metal ribs of the hull groaned and snapped under the strain of dry land.

The beached Dickheads scattered like roaches in a newly lit room.

As the vessel dug harder into the beach, the drive shafts ground and seized inside their housings. A few seconds later, a pair of concussive explosions bellowed from the boat hold before trickles of blue oil smoke began to seep from every newly formed fault in the metal sheathing.

293

Richard craned his neck upward in awe at the bow that now loomed thirty feet over and just twenty feet shy of his position on the stage.

When a sheriff boat swept around the stern with its lights flashing and bullhorn sounding, Richard finally suspected something was awry. Falling back on some primitive *the show must go on* instinct, Richard began plucking his Takamine, orchestrating the Jibs into a cheery rendition of *When Paradise was Twice as Nice* while somewhere in the sea of fans a series of *wooos* rang out.

* * *

Skeg leered down from the broad windshield of the *Bogart* bridge at the thousands of misfits who'd trickled in to get smashed on rumrunners and dress themselves up like redneck peacocks.

The majority of attendees conducted themselves like junior high delinquents on the last day of the school year. They, too, harbored a serious predilection for wet denim, both the men and women, the majority of whom wore it cropped so high up the thigh the white tails of their pockets fell below the frayed hems. Scrunched up cowboy hats and bucket lids abounded, as did men wearing women's brassieres strapped over their heads and around their chins like leather pilot helmets—a Big Swinging Richard classic.

Games specially designed for the crowd, like toss the toilet seat and fling the G-string, played out on the virgin fringes of Coconut Key. Vessels were equipped with less skill-oriented games, one which utilized a Boobometer—a cardboard slab cut into a series of increasingly larger holes in which women would insert their tits to check the size.

Skeg shook his head. It was shitbird season in full swing.

He tripped a series of dashboard switches then manually shifted a lever, swinging the dredger's giant dispersing boom around like a tank muzzle.

The audience from both water and beach gazed up in amazement, perhaps sensing the giant offloading tube was an oversized T-shirt cannon loaded with tank tops commemorating the historical event.

The boom settled into position, then Skeg sank a thumb into the pump button, listening to the starter turn over and grinning like a possum sucking on a lemon.

* * *

The abrupt impact into Coconut Key had flung Jack forward, the right side of his head making decisive contact with an iron bollard rising from the deck.

He'd gone down fast and hard, dropped nearly unconscious from the contact, his ear searing with pain, having been crushed between the two hard and unforgiving features of his skull and the bollard.

As he wobbled to his feet, the deck beneath him shuddered and vibrated then fell quiet then shuddered and vibrated again. An accompanying noise played out as cyclical and rolling, the turn of an engine, the spin of a starter, the attempted firing of a pump.

Jack reclaimed the fire extinguisher, crept through the door leading up to the bridge then hurried up the steps on his tiptoes. Once at the top, he ducked below the half-wall separating the staircase from the wheelhouse and poked his head around the corner.

Gus was out cold, slumped in a corner, while Skeg manned the helm, his hands working a series of levers and buttons as somewhere below deck the pump starter continued to roll over.

Jack eased the safety pin from the extinguisher handle, then dragged a few deep breaths through his teeth and came around the corner ready to fire. But, before he could sight the nozzle, a broad fist cracked across the bridge of his nose. Instantly, his world went black then blurred to yellow then went black again. He lost his balance, stumbling back, then his right heel missed the floor, fell prey to the first staircase step. His weight shifted, and he began falling backwards, tumbling, his backside bouncing off the treads, his feet flipping over his head until he crashed onto the landing a flight below.

As his vision stabilized, he pushed on to all fours, shaking away the initial sting. He grabbed the fire extinguisher off the floor then came up quick, bounding up the stairs.

This time he didn't hesitate. He whipped around the corner and onto the bridge with the extinguisher nozzle compressed, valve opened and screaming, a hard powder blast ripping across the room. The initial stream hit Skeg between the shoulder blades and mushroomed out. As Skeg spun a half-turn, the Ruger in his right hand, tucked close to his waist, Jack redirected the stream into Skeg's mouth and eyes before the entire room became engulfed by a rolling whiteout.

Jack ducked back behind the half-wall, Skeg hacking and spitting, the floor of the wheelhouse beginning to vibrate again for a moment before smoothing into a gentle, consistent rumble.

The rainbowing pump had fired.

Somewhere amid the fog, up near the helm, Skeg let out a sick laugh then blasted the vessel air horn a few solid ear-bending belts. Outside the vessel, the music fell silent, the Jibs pausing the melodic tempo they'd been holding since the boat's arrival.

"Let it go, Skeg. Whatever it is you're about to do. This thing is finished."

"Come on, Jack. Don't be such a buzz kill. Don't you want to see it snow in the Keys?"

Jack came around the corner again this time with the fire extinguisher raised. He caught the faint outline of Skeg and the dark silhouette of the snub-nose then struck down with the metal tank, cracking the knuckles on Skeg's shooting hand and skidding the gun across the deck to some indeterminate point amidst the haze. As Jack rewound for a second blow, an enormous hand lashed forward through the cloud, cinched around his left wrist then wrenched it back so far the tank slipped and bounced across the floor.

Jack sank his teeth into the goon's backhand, grinding down on tendon and bone. A wild yelp broke the air as the hand recoiled into the fog. Jack rifled his leg upward and made a lucky strike, punting his foot square into the low hanging fruit between Skeg's legs.

A low groan followed, then a snort, then a thud.

Jack dropped down on all fours and scrabbled about on his hands and knees for the Ruger. From out of nowhere, a swinging foot appeared, catching him on the exposed ribcage with a snapping sensation. A bone cracked, perhaps two or three. A second kick came down like a pile driver impacting him at the base of his neck. His arms buckled then his cheek slammed into the steel decking.

Jack rolled and, with another lucky kick, caught his foot on one of Skeg's ankles. Skeg went crashing down to some unknown location as Jack scrambled onto his feet, a broken rib seeming to lacerate the soft tissue of his left lung.

A voice called out from nowhere. "Cubera. You in here?"

It was Livingston.

"He's somewhere up near the wheel, Ray. And he may have my gun."

A second later, the boat shuddered as somewhere deep in the belly of *Bogart* the massive pump engaged. Jack put his head down ready to bull into the mist, blindly wielding haymakers until he connected with something warm and fleshy. But three loud booms collapsed the air into an orchestra of shattering glass.

Jack's hearing began to warble as a hot breeze whipped into the cabin then sucked away the foggy haze. As he regained his bearings, he rushed the helm. Where the massive windshield had once been now gave way to a table-sized hole ringed with ragged glassy shards, one nasty edge garnished with a hunk of mahogany flesh.

Beyond the windshield, the dispersing boom was aimed like a tank muzzle over the throbbing crowd, a pristine stream of pure cocaine streaking out like a jet-engine contrail, pluming into the thermals then sinking like an illicit London fog.

Jack leaned out the window, glancing down in time to see Skeg release his grip on a bulwark ledge and crash down to the metal decking twelve feet below.

He hit hard, his left leg buckling outward then his entire six-and-a half-foot frame splaying out like a boneless ragdoll. Jack reeled back toward the staircase, seeing his Ruger on the floor, snagging it along his way. When he came up, Ray was already ahead, halfway down the stairs, his gun drawn, his steps fast and loose. Jack hit the steps hard, slipping down the first series then catching his heels and taking them two at a time until his feet planted onto the landing.

Ray kicked open the metal door, and they shielded their eyes from the mist of cocaine. A trail of blood from the wounded goon suggested a side-to-side staggering pattern of escape. It led halfway across the deck then disappeared behind a mechanical housing.

They moved out slowly, guns drawn by their ears, completely exposed on the open deck. Ten feet out, Skeg's head appeared above the housing, a blow gun set against his lips. Jack and Ray dove away in opposite directions as a dart went zinging between them, imbedding itself in the tweedy braids of a hawser.

Jack scuttled for safety as the first marine patrol officer came over the rail, eyes wild with adrenaline, ready to kill something. Jack looked back toward the housing as the wounded Skeg rose up and took off, half-galloping across the long open deck toward the portside rail. Jack sighted his weapon, trained it true to the small of Skeg's back then let the gun drop away. Skeg took two more lunging strides then leaped out like a swimmer off the blocks and disappeared beyond the rim of the vessel.

* * *

A cool burning sensation filled Jack's lungs as he hustled over to the rail then scoured the waters below.

The sea teemed with bobbing heads and half-deflated rafts, empty beer cans and spent fireworks, all lending the place the look of a watery landfill. But Skeg was nowhere to be seen, probably down deep, riding the undercurrents, moving along like jetsam, his eyes alert for somewhere dark and shadowy to reemerge.

Jack glanced over to the dispersing boom as the cocaine continued to stream out then rain down like a fine dusting of snow. As matter of legal protocol, a team of officers and a flotilla of police operatives were soon deployed to hunt for the perpetrator. To avoid incidental cocaine ingestion, the police wore full-face respirators as they conducted their search. Most of the concert fans, however, seemed unconcerned and unaffected, carrying on in the cocaine fog as though the fleet of vessels and a beached three-hundred-foot dredger were all just props staged in the basin for their amusement.

Ray pulled up alongside Jack at the rail. "The bridge is clear. Any sign of Skeg?"

Jack shook his head.

"Summer's safe. They're taking her to see the medics now."

"I should've been more careful, Ray. I shouldn't have been so—" Jack clamped a hand around his ribs then released a long deep breath. "It could've gotten ugly, Ray. Real ugly."

Ray nodded toward two uniformed men escorting Summer across the beach toward a medical boat nosing up to the shoreline. "She's fine. They're just checking her out. It's all just routine stuff. Then you can tell her whatever it is you can't tell me."

"Did you hear if—?"

"What?"

"Did that creep do anything to her?"

"I don't know." Ray glanced away. "But don't worry about what you can't change. Trust me. Nothing good can come of it."

Jack reached out, squeezed Ray's shoulder then let his hand slide away as a pair of officers hustled Gus across the dredger deck in cuffs.

Ray shook his head. "Expensive little snow storm blowing around out here."

Jack glanced toward the dispersing boom as the cocaine stream sputtered then coughed out its final grams. "Looked to be around ten tons."

Ray slid a toothpick between his lips, his face stoic and deliberate. "Extravagant front to mule some cocaine into the country."

"Not really." Jack pressed his fingertips against his tender ribcage. "How so?"

"This island build-out was just the beginning. Once the construction was done, they would've had a front for their drug pipeline until the end of time."

"Been a long day for an old goat like me, Cubera. Can't say I'm following you."

"A drug sub comes up from South America, dumps the payload at the Honey Hole and the dredger sucks it up all under the guise of the ongoing beach renourishment needed to maintain the Coconut Key coastline. It all takes place underwater. Nobody ever sees a thing."

"And with all that they still turn a profit?"

"This first load alone had a street value north of three-hundred million."

Ray nearly inhaled his toothpick. "I knew I should've gone into the private sector."

"Maybe we should think about it, Ray. Me and you starting up our own little operation. My experience and connections. Your work ethic. Could be fun."

"Maybe in my younger days. But not now. I'm too close to the end."

Jack coughed, his lungs burning against the effort. "How much more time do you have left to serve, anyway?"

Ray checked his watch and mumbled under his breath for a moment. "Two years and thirty-one more days if my math is correct."

"You'll be fine, Ray. You've faked marriages longer than that."

"Don't remind me."

The two watched on as a thumping sound emerged and a helicopter appeared, half-veiled in the fog, then traced along the crowd. Jack assumed it was either a medevac or a police aircraft, but as it closed toward their position that notion quickly passed. The private helicopter swept in without regard for anyone or anything that might get windswept, then hovered directly over Coconut Key and lowered a rescue line.

Big Swinging Richard swooped in to catch the loose end. He hitched the safety lanyard around his waist, made a swirling motion with an index finger then ascended upward, disappearing into the belly of the craft. By the time Commissioner Jimenez rushed out to the pickup site, the helicopter was already long gone, clearing the airspace for three new ones that rushed in from television outfits out of South Florida.

"Maybe it's time I get the Moppie back in to shipshape. Polish the brightwork. Flush the tanks. Tune up the diesels."

Ray rasped his fingers through a tightly cropped sideburn. "You coming down with something?"

"I just need to find my way back to that simple place. Somewhere quiet. Out of the way. Someplace with a certain sense of distance."

"Nothing but cold beer and tight lines?"

Jack nodded. "Sounds pretty damn good, doesn't it?"

* * *

Sheriff Livingston crossed the beach toward Commissioner Jimenez, who'd been mugging for several television cameras and doing his best to spin the unfortunate news event for political gain.

When Viktor saw Ray approaching, he cut his interview with one crew short and strode toward Ray with an air of confidence and swagger. "Livingston. I need a word with you."

Ray stepped up toe-to-toe with the commissioner. "Not until I have my word first."

Jimenez sagged on his heels.

"Your uncle. This Valenciano character."

"What about him?"

"They say he's a billionaire. Just the kind of guy who could finance a drug ring like this."

"You best tread lightly here, Raeford."

"You seen him lately?"

Viktor grinned. "Can't say I remember exactly the last time."

"On his Baglietto a few days ago. That sound about right?" Ray let the information settle in, knowing Viktor would be putting the question together with the racy pics Jack had confronted him with at the gun club.

"No crime in seeing family."

"Your Uncle Val is a felon. The guy's not even allowed in this country anymore."

"Where are you going with this, Livingston?"

"Your little meeting was inside US waters. That's aiding and abetting. Info like that sure could put a dent in a political career." Ray shifted. "How about you stay out of my hair until my retirement, and I'll stay out of yours?"

"Not much hair left over there to stay out of."

"Then you shouldn't have any problems making that happen."

Viktor slipped the wax tin from his front pocket, swabbed a finger over the paste then twisted his mustache. "I misjudged you, Livingston. You're not the dumb hillbilly I figured you for."

"Funny you say that, commissioner. You're exactly the asshole I pegged you to be."

* * *

Ten minutes later, Jack made his way off the dredge boat and waited while Summer signed a few documents then was released by the medical attendee. As he stepped across the sand toward her, she half-smiled, half-teared-up, her fingers shaking as he took her outstretched hands.

"Are you okay?" he asked.

"I don't know what I am."

Jack reached out to cup his hands against her cheeks and draw her in, but her legs buckled, and he caught her under the arms and hoisted her back to her feet. He assumed she was exhausted, overcome, the unmitigated realties of the ordeal finally settling in.

He steadied her by the shoulders and asked again if she was all right. She trembled a little under his touch then let out a long sob.

"Let's get you home, Summer. Get some sleep. Give yourself some time."

"Time to what?"

Jack brought her forehead into his chest then locked both arms around her, fearful he might damage her but more fearful she might slip away forever.

EPILOGUE

BY DAY'S END, *Bogart* was stripped down like an El Dorado abandoned in a ghetto. The concert goers had scaled the side of the dredger then stormed the bridge, their eyes wild with booze and cocaine psychosis as they barked and scowled like pirates overcoming an enemy ship.

Anything with value was pilfered. Electronics were pried from the dashboard. Lifejackets were stolen. One resourceful Dickhead even tapped into the gas tank then peddled the diesel for half the price of the onshore marinas. By nightfall, over four hundred people had been hospitalized from the cocaine-dust exposure. The silt perimeter fence established around the project had been mauled by errant boat propellers, the once continuous two-mile square now severed through-and-through in seventy-three places. Throughout the night the individual flaps broke free of their underwater holds and drifted toward the ocean on an outgoing tide.

By the following day, only a few committed tourists remained. Jack and the sheriff conducted an intensive sweep of all area vessels, finding one couple sunburned the color of boiled crabs, boffing on the crunchy synthetic turf lining their pontoon boat floor.

They let the couple finish then told them to leave the Keys for good. Told them they were no longer welcome in the archipelago. Make that the entire state of Florida. Except Disney World. You can still visit there as long as you don't stray into downtown Orlando.

The sheriff escorted them back to the boat ramp and waited until their vessel was on the trailer and heading east. "Can you believe these people?"

"For the record, Ray, Florida is the lowest state."

By week's end, the last stretch of the tattered silt fence broke free and drifted away, wrapping around a bridge piling before the current went slack and it sank to the ocean floor. News of the deceased developers proved enough to scare away those who'd relocated to Islamorada to participate in the construction project. The prospect of getting paid on any outstanding invoices looked grim. Jack and Ray continued to closely monitor the situation as the bulldozers were craned off the island then shuttled away on industrial barges. The ferry boats ceased operation. The other vessels associated with the undertaking weighed anchor and sailed north to Florida's Big Bend where government dredging contracts were being divvied up amongst anyone with the proper skin color and sexual genitalia.

As August bled into September, Coconut Key eroded down to the point it was no longer visible above the waterline. The constant erosion from the currents and tides degraded the unnatural efforts grain-by-grain. When the first gust of cooler autumn air swept over the archipelago, Cotton Key Basin had fully returned to its original state. Above sea level the site appeared merely as a tract of open water in an otherwise watery expanse. The silt had settled. The once turbid water returned to its crystalline and oxygen-rich state. The habitat-specific species that had fled during the construction period slowly crawled and flipped and wriggled and skittered their way back into newly sprouting forests of turtle grass.

For a time, in one small portion of the Sunshine State, the natural world prevailed, somehow reclaiming a little bit of its old self.

Life in Islamorada returned to normal, whatever that meant, as normalcy in the subtropics was something only occasionally anticipated, rarely expected and damn-near never achieved.

One evening not long thereafter, Ray stopped by the Soggy Dollar and boarded the *Subtropical Highlife.*

"Damn, Jack. Boat looks good."

Jack nodded. "Polished the brightwork, waxed the gelcoat, flushed the tanks. Even changed the plugs and tuned up the diesels."

"You coming down with something?"

"Just getting ready to go gridless."

"You get any farther off the grid, your interior lights might cut out for good." Ray stepped toward the lobsterpot and flipped through a stack of nautical charts. "So you're really going through with this?"

"Time for a change of scenery."

"Maybe I'll resign and tag along."

Jack winked. "I appreciate the offer, but I've already got a boat mate."

Ray grinned. "So where are you two headed, Romeo?"

Jack shrugged. "Saint Johns. Saint Kitts. Saint Vincent. I don't know for sure. Just wanderlush around the Caribbean. There's got to be a Saint Somewhere out there for me."

"Not so sure I'd bank on that one."

Ray twisted off a beer cap then tossed it into a five-gallon bucket as Jack sank into the fighting chair then reached into his cooler and withdrew the first of the twelve apostles. He twisted the cap then rocked back, the night's sky alit in a starry wash like Jack had not seen in some time. Late the night prior, somebody had borrowed his .38 and squeezed off seventeen rounds, silencing every new sodium light in Tipsy's parking lot and returning a soft darkness to the marina. "Nice and dark out here tonight, don't you think?"

"Speaking of that." Ray took a swig and exhaled. "I got a complaint last night that somebody was out here discharging a weapon. You wouldn't happen to know anything about that, would you?"

"Vandals would be my guess. You know as well as I do this whole little Village of Islands is going to shit."

Ray pulled up a chair next to Jack, and the two gazed up at a meteor shower streaking to life. "Getting a little grumpy in your old age, aren't you, Cubera?"

"You're one to talk."

"It gets old getting old once you get to be my age."

"Better to burn out than to rust, Ray."

Jack preened a few dewy beer drops into his mustache and watched a meteor streak toward the horizon then die away.

"Don't kid yourself, Cubera. Most of us rust from the outside in. But you started rusting from the inside out a long time ago."

As the two polished off their third beer each, Summer approached down the long stretch of dock, appearing and dissolving in the staggered lights. She strode with a certain confidence, her legs running upward a quarter mile before disappearing into denim short shorts, a suitcase in her left hand.

Ray stood, tossed his empty bottle in the bucket then turned to Jack. "That'd be my cue."

"I'll be in touch, Ray. Just as soon as the time is right."

"I'll watch the horizon for smoke signals." Ray clamped a hand around Jack's left shoulder. "I don't suppose you're leaving a float plan."

Jack laughed.

"Safe travels, Cubera." Ray released his grip then started down the dock.

Jack watched as Summer and Ray greeted one another, exchanged a hug and a few brief words then continued in their diverging directions. When Summer reached his slip, Jack took her suitcase then helped her aboard and asked if she wanted a drink.

"Maybe just a beer. I'm laying off the heavy stuff for a while. Going to try and clear my head."

Jack twisted open a bottle of beer then handed it her way. "You all packed and ready to roll?"

Summer nodded. "I'm a little nervous."

Jack smiled and pulled her close. "Weather's perfect right now for a crossing. We'll hit the cut tomorrow morning right at daybreak then head east/northeast through about eighty nautical miles of open water before we reach the Bank. From there it's only another hundred or so miles to the Berry Islands."

"Did you say daybreak?"

"Straight into the sunrise."

"Two weeks, Jack?"

He shrugged. "Two weeks. Two months. Two years. You have anywhere you need to be?"

She shook her head. "Just back to simple."

"Agreed. How about we just get going and see if the tides can take us there?"

In loving memory of Ross J. Biggins. The biggest Dickhead the world has ever known.

Thank you for reading *Portside Screw*. If you'd like to be added to my list of loyal readers, please email me at gregdew@hotmail.com or go to my website at www.gregorysdew.com. Also, if you enjoyed *Portside Screw*, a positive review on Amazon would be greatly appreciated. It's easy and will only take a minute. Just go to https://amzn.to/2G73PNK, select a star rating, then write a 20+ word blurb on why you liked the book, who should read it, etc. Thanks for taking the time!

Gregory S. Dew currently resides with his wife in Ponce Inlet, Florida where he spends his days fishing the backwaters, watching sunsets and moonrises, and indulging in a variety of chilly beverages, whether it's five o'clock somewhere or not. He can be contacted via this website at www.gregorysdew.com.